What reviewers are sayi
Wolf Mates

An American Werewolf in Hoboken
"This light-hearted romp is sexy and fun -- vintage Dakota Cassidy. A fast, fun read -- a perfect beach book (though the people in the next lounge chair over will wonder why you keep laughing so hard)."
-- Gillian Fitzgerald for Sensual Romance

What's New Pussycat?
"Ms. Cassidy's trademark sexy humor shines. With plenty of laughs and sexual encounters guaranteed to knock your socks off, What's New Pussycat? will have you laughing loud enough to get those 'she's gone crazy' looks from your family."
-- Jodi, Romance Junkies

Moon Over Manhasset
"A wonderfully funny and touching werewolf tale... with interesting secondary characters and a crash course of emotions for two unsuspecting people."
-- Jessica, Fallen Angel Reviews

Ruff & Ready
"5 Angels! The chemistry between Emerson and Lassiter is off the charts but is balanced by the honest emotion and friendship that binds them."
-- Tewanda, Fallen Angel Reviews

www.ChangelingPress.com

Wolf Mates

Dakota Cassidy

ISBN (10) 1-59596-346-4
ISBN (13) 978-1-59596-346-8

Publisher:
Changeling Press LLC
PO Box 1046
Martinsburg, WV 25402-1046
www.ChangelingPress.com

Printed in the U.S.A.
Lightning Source, Inc.
1246 Heil Quaker Blvd
La Vergne TN 37086
www.lightningsource.com

Anthology Editor: Sheri Ross Fogarty
Cover Artist: Sahara Kelly
Cover Design: Bryan Keller

The individual stories in this anthology have been previously released in E-Book format.

Wolf Mates: An American Werewolf in Hoboken

Dakota Cassidy

Prologue

He ran as though the hounds of hell chased him, pounding the pavement with swift, measured strides. The click of his nails echoed in the rain soaked, empty streets. Flashes of buildings passed in a blur as his eyes sought frantically to find food. His long tongue slipped out of the side of his mouth, draping down over the thick hair that covered his chin -- er, muzzle.

Panting, he eyed each alleyway from his peripheral vision, searching...

The smells of the city assaulted his ultra sensitive nose. He sniffed the air, picking up the scent of broiled steak, pork chops with thick brown gravy, veal medallions in a creamy white sauce with sliced onion, and a sprig of parsley for garnish. Scalloped potatoes... no wait, they were au gratin.

Oh, hell he was hungry.

Shit, he really *loved* veal too... Wee little succulent morsels of calf that he couldn't have right now because he was too damn busy playing this stupid game of "here, doggy, doggy." Which he wouldn't be doing if it weren't for this *vision*.

A sharp whistle stopped him in his tracks and again his ears pricked to the tune of, "Here, doggy, doggy!"

Address me as I should be addressed. It's Mr. Werewolf to you...

If he could sigh he would. Instead he flared his nostrils and huffed.

Did it get any worse than this? I mean, c'mon... *who* was this vision anyway? This soulmate who was supposed to rock his world? And where was it written that he had to play Mission Impossible just to get laid? This was above and beyond the call of duty for a little horizontal mambo.

He hated all of this mumbo-jumbo folklore crap he'd been taught since he was a child. He really just wanted to hang out and play Nintendo 64. But the call of a good lay beckoned... or that's what he heard it was going to be anyway. A good lay... good as opposed to *none*. He sure as hell hoped his soulmate appreciated this, cuz it was a crappy way to hook-up in his estimation.

The Prophecy has spoken, Eva'd said...

Prophecy? Hah! What kind of prophecy had you running around a town called Hoboken, with the butt crack squad hot on your heels? What kind of prophecy was found in a bowl of chicken noodle soup? But his family members claimed Eva knew all. How one could "know all" from processed chicken in a can was beyond him.

Although, legend had it that if he didn't follow his stupid path of destiny, he was shit for shineola. He'd have to face the mojo of all mojos. So, rather than risk the possibility that this destiny of his was flat-out stupid and it wasn't worth a really freaky curse, he ran.

Fast.

Because he couldn't afford to be caught and miss this prophecy thing.

Racing down a deserted, dimly lit street, he spied a chain link fence that might be his ticket outta this.

Except he had four paws and not a pair of legs to climb said fence.

Well, *shit*.

The thunder of feet diminished behind him. Maybe they'd given up. His ears pricked to the tune of the clink of the fence as the men climbed it.

A bright light cornered him as he swept past a dumpster, only to find a dead end.

Fucking ducky...

"Hey look, he's friggin' huge," one of the men commented.

Ahh, the animal catching engineer... isn't that what they called them now? Bright indeed, very bright. Damn right he was huge and he was going to take a bite out of his engineer ass if he came any closer.

"Wait," one of the bright twins said, "I've got something for him." He began to dig around in his pocket and pulled out a plastic bag.

He watched skeptically from the corner he was backed into and sniffed the air.

"Look, puppy... look what I have..." Wiggling the meat in air, the *animal catching engineer* shook it at him. Obviously this was meant to entice him.

He sniffed liberally the air that surrounded the meat. Oh, fuck that. It was going to take a helluva lot more than some cheap round steak to get him to bite. He was a filet mignon kind of guy...

His stomach growled in protest, meaning, round steak was better than no steak.

Well, okay, he'd bite. He could easily knock this guy out as he snatched the meat from him. Snarling, he came closer, moving in on Einstein's hand, exposing his teeth.

Teeth... it was all about showing them the teeth. Freaked everybody out.

He leapt in an arc Bruce Jenner would be envious of, snatching the meat and gobbling it halfway down his throat when he felt the sting of the dart.

If he could, he would have sighed at how predictable that had been. Well, fuck, he thought as he fell to the ground with a hard thud and the world began to spin... looked like he was going to the pound.

Chapter One

"Jesus Christ in a mini-skirt, he's ugly, huh?" JC Jensen stood in front of the large metal cage, skeptically eyeing the unkempt beast who stared with defiance right back at her. She estimated he must stand at least six foot when he was on his hind legs. JC wrinkled her nose. He smelled, too. The whole damn place smelled.

Yuk.

"Well, yeah, lady, he sure ain't of the cute and cuddly, 'C'mere snookums, come sit on my lap' variety. And none too friendly either." The nice man at the pound should never try his hand at selling cars, she mused.

The overgrown, odd-looking beast sent out a low, menacing growl, as if to validate the attendant's accusation. His teeth, or maybe a better word was *fangs*, were kind of yellow. Oral hygiene obviously wasn't his forte, or his prior owners'.

JC couldn't put her finger on what drew her to this mangy mutt. There were dozens of cute, cuddly balls of fluff in the joint, all barking for her attention.

Damn she hated this -- she wanted every last frickin' one. But noooo, she homed in on the meanest of the lot, knowing full well his chances for adoption were like zilch.

He was a filthy mess and downright mean looking, but when she let her fingers curl into the small openings of the cage he'd sniffed the air with interest. Then he'd come closer, pressing his cold, wet nose against her finger. Oddly, she felt no fear, though she probably should, but she didn't. Rather, she felt her heart lurch and a strange sense of tranquility.

"How'd he get here?" she wondered aloud, running a slow finger under the monster's chin.

"He's a stray. No wonder. Look at him for Christ sake. He's mean *and* ugly. Found him cornered in an alley. Animal control came and got him. I heard that was some fight trying to get him into the van even after the dart gun. They say he might be part wolf. I say he's part ornery. He's overstayed his welcome now. He's officially on his last day of 'death row'."

JC's stomach did a nosedive. Euthanasia? Put him to sleep, nip the old ticker in the bud. Lights out... For good?

They were going to *kill* him.

Crap.

She didn't need a dog. Her life was so busy she was never home. But, when she *was* home, she came home to nothing. It was becoming lonelier by the year.

She should walk away *now* and find a nice kitten. They took care of themselves and didn't need a whole lot of maintenance. They amused themselves with thread or something. An even bigger plus, they cleaned *themselves*. They sat in your lap and snuggled with you.

JC couldn't fathom this monster sitting in her lap.

Something about this mutt's eyes, dark and earnest, made her think twice about the feline persuasion. He nudged her hand lightly and she cupped his chin through the cage, scratching the underside of his jaw. His gray fur was matted and probably had a village of fleas starting up their own "boy band" in it.

"You are one mighty fine mess." JC cocked her head at the piercing gaze he pinned her with. Her heart sped up when he licked at the palm of her hand. Shit, he was as ugly as the day was long. Bigger than a Clydesdale and in desperate need of some doggy deodorant...

He's also destined to die, JC.

Oh, all right already. She examined him one last time.

Jeez Louise, he was butt ugly. But she couldn't bear the idea that he was due for "Old Sparky."

It *must* be love.

"I've never seen him act like this," the attendant noted, cutting into her thoughts. "He's usually snarling and growling at anything that moves. You must have that animal magnetism or something. Half the time we can't even get near him." As the attendant moved closer to the cage, she felt the low vibration of tough guy's growl beneath her fingertips.

She tapped his nose with the palm of her hand. "Stop that right now. If you want a home, you're going to have to chill out, buddy. Quit with the junkyard dog act and behave." She sighed with resignation. Her mind was made up.

"Tell me, oh gnarly one, are you housetrained?"

* * *

Good gravy, she was such a sucker for a good case of hard-up. The practicality of bringing this beast back to her very small apartment was flat out nuts. Yet she found herself out in the reception area, signing the papers to 'adopt' him. These days that entailed giving away your first-born and paying the obligatory fifty bucks to 'help out' the shelter. Grabbing her purse and the leash they'd provided her with, she hooked it to his collar and gave him a tug. He planted his big ass firmly on the floor and refused to budge. Talk about looking a gift horse in the mouth.

"Aw c'mon, you brute, I'm gonna take you home and feed you. What more could you want?"

Solemn brown eyes gazed back at her, unblinking.

JC knelt beside him. God, he was huge and so friggin' hairy. "Look, Cujo, I saved your life for crap's sake. Now don't make an ass outta me. Let's get the hell out of here." She tugged on the leash again, this time with a bit more force.

Nothin'.

The pretty blond receptionist held up a bag of dog cookies from behind her perch at the desk. "Looks like you could use one of these. He's been known to be difficult."

"Hey look, Lassie, doggie treats." JC sniffed the interior of the bag. Gawd, they smelled like an elephant's butt. She pasted a smile on her face and pulled one out. Wiggling it under his nose, she tried to entice him. He staunchly refused, defiantly turning his head away.

JC dropped the leash and whispered in his pointy ear. His position shifted almost as though he were really listening to her.

"Hookay, bud, I could just leave you here, ya know. I mean we could skip the warm fuzzy part. You know that part where I take you home, bathe you, feed you and let you sleep next to me on the floor beside my bed? Sorta like Timmy and Lassie, together at last. We can totally skip that and shoot right to the part where they *put you to sleep!*" She hissed her last words for emphasis.

The mutt's massive backside miraculously lifted. His long snout nuzzled her hand before he walked toward the glass doors with a slow shuffle. Turning, he looked at her as if to say, "What are you waiting for?"

JC followed him, chucking him under the chin. " 'Bout damn time. Now come on, you beast. We need to get you home and get you a bath, but first we need to think of a name for you. How do you feel about 'Pain in the Ass'?"

* * *

"Okay, champ, it's bath time and don't even think about yanking my crank over this. You smell like death and there is no way you're sleeping in my bedroom smelling like that. So let's get all the shitty stuff outta the way now and then I'll give you a nice bowl of that kibble we bought." She turned on the taps and added some of the flea dip that came so highly recommended for good measure.

He arrogantly sniffed at her crotch, wedging his big snout between her thighs.

"Stop that! I can't begin to imagine where those people at the pound got the notion you were unfriendly. I can't keep you off of me."

She'd taken him to the local pet store where all the 'in dogs' went to get the necessary *must haves* in life. He'd been unpleasant to say the least, baring his teeth at every man that passed them. The cute guy with the poodle didn't stand a snowball's chance in hell of getting past Cujo. Thankfully, he'd maintained himself long enough to get a dog bowl and some dog food. She'd grabbed a cute doggie toothbrush as well, to clean up those teeth.

He'd sat rather stoically in the backseat of the car on the way home. Occasionally he sniffed her ear, making her giggle. He seemed content to take in his surroundings, watching the scenery fly by the car window.

When they'd reached her apartment she'd let him go, fully expecting he'd want to check out his new surroundings. As long as he didn't discover her new carpet with his leg in the air she was good with it.

However, he didn't explore much. In fact, he didn't leave her side at all. Now in her tiny blue and yellow bathroom he was literally going to have to be surgically removed from her ass. His massive gray body pensively sat on the bath mat filling up the small, tiled space.

"Man, Cujo, you really smell. Okay, lover, in you go." JC wrapped her arms around his bulky torso and yanked him into the tub. He didn't fight her, but he certainly wasn't helping matters. He sat stiff and unblinking as she sprayed him thoroughly with the showerhead, running her hands through the thick coat of hair.

Nothin' like wet dog to get those nasal passages open.

JC yammered at him, speaking in soothing tones to keep him calm and still. "Oh, look at you, sweetums, you're such a good boy. Here comes the smelly stuff. I have to let it sit on you for fifteen minutes according to the bottle. Whaddya say we get to know each other while we wait?" She began working up a soapy lather, scrubbing at his thick hair to cover all flea-riddled areas. Satisfied, she sat back on the toilet seat and scratched behind his ears to keep him occupied. He tilted his head, allowing her the best advantage to his happy spot.

"You know what I want to know, don't you? Where did you come from? I mean did someone own you at one time, or were you just hatched? Was someone cruel and abusive to you?" Her stomach churned at that. Leaning forward she bracketed his muzzle between her hands, searching his warm, brown eyes. "That would *really* piss me off. I don't care how mean you are. You don't deserve to be abused over it."

His big, pink tongue swiped her nose. She made a face at him. "That breath is a tough deal, Cujo. Good thing we got that toothbrush, huh?" He reared his head back and turned away from her.

"Oh don't go getting all defensive, silly. That dog food is supposed to help with the bad breath thing too. Look, it's already time to rinse, are you ready?"

Twelve bath towels later, he was like a brand new dog. She worked diligently to loosen the mats in his hair and dug around under the bathroom sink for her blow dryer.

"Now don't get all freaked out on me, but I need to dry you so you won't catch a cold. Sit, okay?" That was probably the wrong way to address him, but the big beast seemed to listen best if she took the more friendly approach. Again, he didn't budge, patiently waiting while she plugged in the dryer and got the new dog brush from her bag of purchases. While she attacked the task of drying him, JC did the high pitched voice thing all those dog trainers said worked to ease a dog's fears. Not that he seemed to care much. He was pretty unimpressed by her efforts.

Clean and dry he was quite impressive. His dark gray fur lightened considerably with a good cleaning. Softer threads of black were now visible down the length of his back. The fur around his face was full and fluffy -- if only she could get her own hair to do that -- and he smelled a hundred times better than he had an hour ago. Her beautician's hands primped and scrunched.

"Between you and me, kiddo, you have the most fabulous hair. And believe me when I tell you that compliment doesn't come easy from the best beautician in Hoboken. You are one big ball of fluff..."

Fluffy...

"I've got it! How do you feel about the name Fluffy? Never mind, you don't care, do you? Well, I love it and it suits you I think, with all of this hair you have. I hope you don't shed, Fluffy..." JC threw her arms around his thick neck and gave him a squeeze, ignoring the odd rumble he made low in his throat.

Chapter Two

Fluffy? F-L-U-F-F-Y? He ticked the letters off mentally. This was the single most humiliating encounter he'd ever endured.

Fluffy?

Christ, was she out of her mind? Who named a "dog" of his size and stature Fluffy? A poodle made complete sense, even a Chihuahua... He was not fucking fluffy!

Full, with a thick coat, Y-E-S. Fluffy, N-O. She'd made him look like an overgrown chia-pet. Was it not enough that he'd had dog treats shoved under his nose and a *leash* slapped on his neck? To degrade him this way by giving him a name better suited to a bunny rabbit was almost more than he could bear. All the other doggies in the neighborhood would secretly laugh at him...

Damn woman, if she wasn't so friggin' good lookin'. If her scent wasn't driving him out of his ever lovin' mind, he'd pick up and go the hell home. However, his prophecy must be fulfilled and she was apparently it. She sure as hell smelled like it. She looked like it too. She had the most gorgeous ass he'd ever seen. Her firm, round breasts were nothing to scoff at either. And her hair... Hair a man could wrap around his fist as he came. Just touching her shoulders, it fell in raven ringlets around her heart-shaped face. It would make a beautiful coat...

Fluffy... Like hell. He was... he was... he was a freakin' man in what she thought was a dog's body, was what he was. How long could a guy keep this up?

Oh, and that 'sweetums' crap was gonna stop.

Dog? If he could spit right now, he would. Instead, he opted to give himself a good scratch. There were some finer aspects to this particular form. He could lick his own balls. He scratched again behind his ears.

How the hell had he gotten fleas? In the damn pound that's how.

His ears, finely tuned, pricked to the sound of her voice. Did she say dinner? Shit, he was *not* eating that dog kibble bullshit.

Yes, he was, for now anyway. Until he could make himself known, unleash the man in him... Jesus, he sounded like a commercial for Viagra.

With resignation, he shuffled down the hall to the kitchen to eat his "dinner" and answer to the most ludicrous name in all of Hoboken... *Fluffy.*

* * *

JC was scooping kibble into a bowl and working on cooking up a steak for her dinner when Fluffy squeezed himself between her and the table.

"Hey handsome, hungry?"

He sniffed her ass in response.

"Quit, would you? You don't need to sniff my ass. You already know who I am. I'm the girl responsible for that beautiful new hairdo you're sporting. Now, be a good boy and eat your dinner, and I'll eat mine." She smiled at him, rubbing the top of his head with the heel of her hand. "Dinner for two, isn't it romantic? Pretty soon we'll be picking out a china pattern together." As she set a place for herself, he stood beside the bowl sniffing the rim.

This was god-awful. What'd she call it? Some cheesy-liver crap. He didn't care how many tender, bite size nuggets they included. It sure as hell did not smell like real *anything.*

The aroma of the steak under the broiler was breaking him. His stomach growled with discontent over his bowlful of kibble. He nudged a piece or two with his nose.

"See? It's good, isn't it?" His eyes followed the steak as she pulled it out of the oven and set it on the counter.

Yahooo! Real meat. His taste buds did the happy dance.

The doorbell rang just as she was putting the finishing touches on her plate. Wiping her hands on a towel she gave him the 'don't screw with me' look. "Now, listen up, Fluff, don't go getting all territorial on me here. It's probably just one of my friends. Believe me when I tell you men have not been beating down the door to my sexuality as of late. So chill out and eat your dinner. Got it?" She scratched his ears and went to answer the door.

Thank God. Now all he had to do was resist the temptation to stand on his hind legs and firmly sink his teeth into that tender steak. Hell, it smelled so good. Maybe if he just smelled it.

Paws firmly planted on either side of the flowered plate, he took a whiff. *Holy T-bone!* He needed this bad.

He could just lick it. She'd never know. He raked his tongue over the salted surface.

Hell. His instinctive nature to devour it was threatening to overwhelm him. *If I just take a bite…* well of course, she'd know he did. She'd scold him and they could go on about their business. So he wouldn't get one of those doggy treats that tasted like shit on a shingle.

Big deal -- hit me where it hurts.

One bite and no more.

He clamped down on the meat, holding it with one paw, tearing just a small bite off the edge. Savoring the texture on his tongue, his stomach rejoiced.

He was certain he heard angels sing 'hallelujah' in the distance. It had been so long since he'd had a decent meal. It was a little overcooked for his liking, but who cared at this point?

Dropping down off the counter he attempted to fend off the temptation to gorge. He sniffed the bowl of kibble. No freakin' way was he eating that.

Her feelings would be hurt. She'd gone to so much trouble to pick just the right variety out. Reading the ingredients on the package, vitamins and protein, everything a good pet might want in an owner.

He would *not* eat dog food and he was *nobody's* pet. Now if she wanted to pet him…

He grabbed the bowl between his teeth and tipped it over behind the fridge, pushing it to the back with his paw. It was the best he could do for now. His stomach rumbled noisily again. That steak was calling his name. Well, it wasn't calling this new, utterly ridiculous *dog* name she'd given him… but calling him nonetheless.

He could resist. He would just walk away…

Shit, no he couldn't.

Half, that's all he'd eat. Just half -- it was too big for her anyway, he reasoned.

Finding a comfortable spot, he rested his lower body against the cabinets and dug in. *Half, only half,* he reminded his overactive stomach.

A screech laced with horror invaded his love-affair with the steak.

"Fluuuffy! What are you doing?" She stomped toward him, clearly not pleased.

"His name is Fluffy?" a male voice guffawed loudly. "He's friggin' huge, JC."

Shit. Foiled, screwed, it was the doghouse for him. He slid guiltily from the counter, turning to identify the new *male* voice who'd entered the kitchen. His ears stood up attentively.

Why, thank you. He preened over the intruder's words.

"Yeah, he's huge all right, and in a *whole* lot of trouble. He ate my steak!"

Well, not the WHOLE steak, and who the hell is this anyway? His eyes landed on the dweeb who'd interrupted a perfectly good meal. Definitely not a member of the tall, dark, and handsome club. He had that beefed-up look about him that meant he cared more about making his payment to the place he pumped iron in than he did about his girlfriend. His eyes were deeply set under a hawk-like forehead. Kinda beady if you asked him. Course, no one would ask him. He was the *DOG.*

He sat back on his haunches and narrowed his eyes at the interloper, waiting.

Grabbing JC by the arm, the man pulled her close to him. "Listen. Forget the dog. Let's go out. I'll buy you dinner."

She squirmed free of muscle man and rubbed her arms, moving closer to Fluffy. "I appreciate it, Jess, but no thanks. I have a lot to do tonight."

"Like what? Hang out with this mutt?" He hovered closer to JC, his thick body pushing Fluffy out of the way.

Mutt? I'm sorry, did I hear that correctly? Wanna see my big MUTT teeth, asshole? He placed his bulk between them again and gave Jess a warning growl.

"Go lay down or something would you?" Jess nudged Fluffy, hard with his knee and reached again for JC. Fluffy barked sharply in warning. This guy just didn't get the picture.

Don't make me bring out the "big gun," bud.

"Look, Jess, I'm tired. It's been a long day. I already made dinner and I don't want to go out." JC let her hand rest on Fluffy's back. He nuzzled it, staying close to her.

"I just don't get you, JC. We had a good thing goin' and now you want to throw it all away." Jess ran his finger down JC's cheek but she shrugged him off.

"Yeah, we had a good thing going until you decided to stick your Mr. Happy where it didn't belong. Go home, Jess."

"It was only once, JC, and you know I was drunk..."

Ah, of course you were -- that explains everything.

"It doesn't matter anymore, Jess. We broke up. It's over. Now go home." JC turned her back to him, looking over her plate. Apparently, she was concentrating on what she might salvage of her half-eaten steak.

Jess was obviously not accustomed to the word *NO*. "C'mon, JC, let's try to work this out. I'll take you to your favorite restaurant and we can talk." He persisted in sliding his arms around her waist from behind as his hand grazed her breast.

That's it, nobody grabs my woman's boob! Time for you to go. Fluffy growled just before he jumped on Jess' back. Standing as tall as Jess, he used his full weight to knock him forward.

Jess reacted quickly by shoving Fluffy hard, knocking him to the ground. "Get the fuck off me, you damn mutt!" he snarled at him.

It was over faster than it began. With one swift motion, Fluffy backed up against Jess, lifted his back leg and let go.

A large yellow puddle formed on the tile of the kitchen.

JC's eyes widened as she bit her lip to smother a giggle while Jess hopped around from foot to foot.

"He peed on me! I'll fucking kill him..." Jess yanked the dishtowel from the rack and dabbed at his sodden jeans. His big, ugly face wrinkled with disgust.

JC began to laugh, the husky rumble making it all worthwhile for Fluffy. "I *really* think you should go now, Jess. Fluffy doesn't like you much, do you, Fluff?" He answered her by brushing up against her thighs protectively.

Jess beat a hasty retreat, shooting a fierce look over his shoulder at Fluffy. "Okay, JC, but you'll miss me when I'm gone."

As if he hadn't threatened that a time or two.

"Well, don't worry. If I find myself overwrought with loneliness, I'm sure I'll be compelled to pick up the phone and call your cheating ass," JC called after him as the door slammed in her face.

Looking down at Fluffy, she tugged his ear gently. "You ate *my* steak."

And saved your ass. Your very pretty ass.

"But I'll forgive you, because you did get rid of Jess and he's not easy to get rid of. So I guess I'm not eating steak for dinner, am I? Well, hero, I think it's soup for me."

Fluffy nuzzled her hand to show his remorse. His ears stood at attention, waiting for forgiveness.

"You beast. Listen here, sweetums, whatever I put in your bowl is *yours*. If it's on a plate, you can be pretty sure it's *mine*, unless the plate is on the floor. Got it?"

Well, he couldn't in all good conscience consent to that, now could he? He avoided her eyes and nuzzled her hand again instead.

She smiled down at him, her blue, almond shaped eyes crinkled at the corners. "I'm going to take that as a yes, Fluff. God, if only you were a man, you'd be perfect."

* * *

He was sprawled out on the bed, his large paws tucked under her pillows. The blankets were a rumpled mess after he'd given himself a good back scratch. They smelled of her sweet scent, sunshine and cinnamon.

"Hey." JC patted his belly. Just a little lower and she was *so* there. No -- she wasn't ready for that yet. He fought his lustful thoughts and slowly opened his eyes with a yawn.

"This," she tapped the bed, "is mine, cookie. That," she pointed to the mat on the floor, "is yours."

He lifted his head to see her more clearly. She had a towel wrapped around her head and one wrapped around her body.

Naked... she was naked beneath the blue towel.

The gentle swell of her hip brushed up against his legs as she sat down next to him. Pouring lotion into her hands, JC smoothed it over her calves, working her way up to thighs he just knew were silky-soft.

He sniffed the air. Cucumber-melon for sure. Her small hands made circular motions, rubbing in the cream higher and higher. Lowering the towel, she let it rest at her waist as she dabbed some of the lotion on her shoulders. Her breasts thrust upward, her taut nipples beading from the cool air.

"And what are you looking at?" she chuckled.

He turned his head guiltily. "I told you to get on the floor, handsome." JC stood and pointed again to his "bed." Fluffy slunk off the bed, sliding to the floor and curling his big body on the mat.

Letting the towel fall to the floor, JC found her nightgown at the end of the bed and slid it over her creamy skin, the glow of the lamp shading her soft contours.

His groin tightened and he tensed at the familiar call of his body to *shift*. He willed his muscles to relax and obey, focusing on remaining in his wolf form. Because that could be bad... *Hey, JC. I'm da man. Your man. I just look extra furry right now. Don't worry, I clean up real nice.*

It was all he could do not to shift and show her he was no *dog*. Patience was required here. He didn't quite understand much more than JC was his prophesized mate. He felt her inside of him. He knew her soul. Now he had to find a way to get to know the rest of her without scaring the bejesus out of her. It wasn't going to be easy. *"Hey, JC, glad you adopted me at the pound. Thanks for rescuing me from 'death row.' By the way, did I mention I'm not just any wolf? I'm YOUR wolf, baby. Wanna mate?"*

He really wanted to mate, and mate they would, if he had anything to say about it.

Soon.

Turning off the bedside lamp, JC scratched his muzzle before climbing over him and getting into bed. Her hand hung down over the edge of the mattress. He licked her palm, savoring the soft texture of her skin on his tongue.

"Night, Fluffy," she whispered to him, her sultry voice slicing through the velvety darkness.

Goodnight.

Chapter Three

Moonlight streamed in from the window, soft, white shafts of light illuminating the sleeping form on the bed. He stood patiently, watching the slow rise and fall of her firm, rounded breasts. Covered in sheer white cotton, the shadow of her nipples scraped the fabric with each breath she took. Beaded and tight they thrust upward. Her nightgown skimmed the top of one thigh, the creamy expanse of skin leading to the soft folds of her sex. His mouth watered with anticipation as he imagined the velvet slide his tongue would experience in the moist lips of her cunt. His nostrils flared at her scent, smelling the musk of her need mingled with the night air softly blowing through the window.

He lifted a strand of her long hair from the pillow, inhaling the fresh scent of her fruity shampoo. The silky, soft wisp curled around his finger, glistening in the darkness of night. His heart sped as she stirred and whispered his name, low in her throat. "Max…"

She stretched her arms upward exposing the outline of her lithe form. His cock swelled and lengthened with yearning. Soft hands tugged him forward so he knelt on the bed beside her. Lifting the sheer material, he tugged at the nightgown until she was naked. Her slender thighs spread in welcome.

He heard his own low moan in his ears when she grazed the thick patch of hair above his shaft. Her nails scraped the tender skin, gliding over his belly to caress the ridges and planes of his abdomen.

He sucked in a breath when she firmly grasped him in her palm. He thrust forward in the soft tunnel, as his head fell back on his shoulders and he circled her wrist to guide her. His hips rotated slowly, letting her caress him to pulsing madness.

Gritting his teeth, he stilled her hand, bringing it to his mouth and kissing her palm. His tongue began a heated path along her arm. Slowly, he found his way to her shoulder in long strokes of tongue and lips. He hovered closer to her breasts, dragging his tongue between the two creamy swells. She raised her arms to cradle his head, clutching at his hair and tugging him closer to her nipple.

He captured the tight peak between his lips as her hips arched upward off the bed and she moaned softly. He allowed the pebbled surface to linger on his tongue before he suckled. Her hands tightened in his hair when he drifted toward the apex between her thighs. His hands massaged the supple skin of her leg, feeling her muscles tense as he slowly ran his fingertips over the outer lips of her pussy.

With forefinger and thumb, he spread the soft flesh, making her gasp.

He smiled against her breast, loving her sharp intake of breath when he grazed the swollen nub of her clit. She pulled him from her breast to her lips. Gazing down at her, he watched the tip of her pink tongue lick at his mouth. The soft sweep of her lashes fluttered when she felt his cock flex in response. Bracketing his face, she swept her silken tongue over his lower lip. His muscles tightened and his heart hammered in his ears as she explored him with her tongue.

He couldn't hold back any longer, he devoured her mouth, tangling his tongue with hers, sliding it in and out of the hot recess. Pressing her into the bed, he ground his throbbing cock into her thigh as his fingers continued to fondle her creamy folds. He let one drift to her wet passage and inserted a finger in slow increments.

Small hands dug into his back as she kissed him feverishly, spreading her thighs wider. He tore himself from her mouth, and strung a trail of kisses along her ribs, over her hips and across the flat plane of her belly.

She rolled toward him, lifting her leg and pressing her soft body to his. He felt the outline of her ribs against his abdomen. His cock was inches from her mouth as she clamped his head between her silken thighs. He felt her fingers circle his rock hard shaft, then the moist warmth of her mouth as she enveloped him. His body shook while she held him between her lips and ran small circles over the sensitive flesh. He lay with his head pressed to her thigh, inhaling the musky scent of her pussy. Moving quickly, he removed his finger and straddled her body.

His knees bracketed her head and his cock was deep in her mouth as she drove him to madness. Leaning forward, he slid his tongue between the lips of her cunt. He fought to maintain control when her hips bucked and she hissed against his cock. He pressed his tongue flat against the inner folds and dragged it over the soaking wet flesh. Burying his face in her sweetness, he laved her clit, swirling his tongue in and out, as he slid his hands under her ass and kneaded the firm flesh.

Cupping his balls, she fondled the tight sacs as she rose up on her heels, pressing his tongue to her. His hips jerked toward the warmth of her mouth, and he found himself rhythmically circling her head, dipping his cock in and out of her lips. She wrapped her arms around his torso, dragging him to her so they lay tightly together.

Skin against skin, he felt every inch of her silken form flush against his rougher one. Her beaded nipples scraped against his stomach, her hips crashed against his face. His cock throbbed against her tongue, his balls grazing her nose. Her nails tore at the flesh of his ass, his gripped her calves tightly.

Tongues suckled and licked, the wet suction pounding in his ears as he devoured her pussy. She tensed beneath him when his teeth grazed her clit. He felt her mouth slacken around his cock as she rocked against his tongue, clinging to him and crying out as she came. He smoothed his hands over her thighs, gentling the small remaining shudders.

His cock burned now, with the need to imbed himself in her tight warmth. Shifting position, he turned her on her stomach. Still above her, he leaned back on his haunches to admire the curve of her ass. Her head rested between his thighs, cradled in her arms. Her long hair streamed around her shoulders, the dark silk a stark contrast to the white of the sheets. Her back rose and fell with short gasps for breath. Her eyes rose to meet his, waiting, searching. He tangled his hands in the long black tresses, caressing her cheeks. He let his hands roam over her skin, stopping at the taper of her waist, lingering. Kissing a path along her spine, he nipped at her skin lightly, allowing him time to rein in his desire.

Slowly, he would make her his slowly. Her flesh pebbled as the cool breeze rustled the curtains and swept over her skin. He positioned himself behind her, and she lifted her hips without any encouragement. He saw the lips of her sex glisten, smelled the desire he'd created with his tongue. His shaft throbbed, hot and harder than he could ever remember.

Grasping his cock, he knelt behind her and slid it through her smooth cunt, teasing her clit with the head. Her hand reached between them and rested on his, gripping his wrist. He rolled his hips, moving in and out of her wetness, slowly. She groaned when he moved closer to her passage. He took a deep breath, steadying his need to slice through her. Bracing his hands on her ass, he pressed the head of his cock into her. She reared up, arching her back, and impaled him with one swift movement of her hips. His hands tightened on her ass, as he fell forward and sank himself in her tight walls. Her inner walls clenched his cock in response, welcoming him, pulling him inward.

Possessive hands grasped her hips, holding her still, settling deep inside her, letting his cock swell with the sensation. Impatiently she writhed, jamming her hips against him, her body pleading with him to fulfill her. He stroked her long and deep, she in turn milked his throbbing cock as they melted into a rhythm.

The slick slide of friction and her creamy depths roared through his veins in waves of heat. Clenching her hips tighter, he slammed into her, holding on until he heard her scream with release.

Her head came up off the bed as her orgasm ripped through her. Twisting the sheets in her hands, she held him tightly inside of her. His breathing became shallow as a surge of white-hot electricity jolted his cock and tore through him. Thick-hot spurts of come poured out of his shaft leaving him gasping to fill his lungs with air.

He draped his body over hers as they fell to the bed in a tangle of heaving, sweat soaked bodies.

A voice rudely intruded upon the sexual cloud he floated on.

"Hey, Fluffy!" The words sliced through his brain like a knife. He moaned, refusing to open his eyes as someone nudged him.

"Hey, buddy, open your eyes. I think you're having a doggy-wet-dream."

Oh, *GOD*.

* * *

"I've got to get to work, Fluffy. Now listen up," JC said as she put her coffee cup in the sink and turned to pet him on his big head. "I want you to eat your breakfast like a good boy and stay OFF the furniture. One hair on my couch and it's curtains for you. Oh, and if you pee in the house? You die. Hear me?"

Fluffy sat quietly listening to her speak. His head tilted to the side as his tail thumped a staccato rhythm on the kitchen floor, but his eyes held hers.

She grinned at him. "I'm beginning to wonder if you actually understand me." Checking to be sure his water bowl was full and he had all of his new doggy toys, she grabbed her purse and threw it over her shoulder. One last glance and she reluctantly shut the door.

The thought that Fluffy would be there to greet her at the end of the day kept her motivated to move swiftly. She was feeling rather proud of herself for finally making the move and adopting a pet. Lord knew, it had to be smarter choice than getting another boyfriend.

After a series of so-so relationships, she'd given up on finding 'Mister Perfect.' She couldn't even find 'Mister Happy-Medium.' Jess was the final deciding factor in giving up completely and just letting whatever happened, happen. Her heart was still intact after him so why tempt fate? She could be perfectly happy going home to Fluffy every night. She had her friends, and a decent job. She'd never become rich working as a hairdresser, but she didn't fight to make ends meet either. JC smiled. Life was good in many small ways. It didn't have to include a boyfriend in her estimation.

Maybe it could include a vibrator, though. She laughed to herself as she swept up the last bits of hair and rushed off to head home to Fluffy.

* * *

A huge moving van was parked in her spot when she pulled up in front of her apartment building.

JC double-parked and flew out of the car, ready to give someone hell, when the most amazing pair of buns she'd ever seen bent over in front of her. Buns encased in a faded pair of blue jeans that had a hole at the waistband and one smack dab in the middle of his left, very round cheek. She could see his underwear…

They were red.

Boxers or briefs?

Good gravy.

Those buns were pulling boxes from the back of the truck. JC folded her arms across her chest.

"Um, excuse me, but you're in *my* parking space." Mister Booty dropped the box, the muscles in his forearms flexing. A fine sprinkling of dark hair led to hands that had long, tapered fingers. He turned around slowly and her breath caught in her throat.

Holy heavenly... she bit her lower lip. Her anger over losing her parking space dissipated into sharp pangs of lust.

He was utterly breathtaking in a rough, sort of unpolished, way. The sharp, angular planes of his face were accentuated by his light tan. High cheekbones gave way to deep grooves on either side of his luscious lips. Brown eyes flecked with amber and lined with a thick fringe of lashes gleamed. The sun, just beginning to fade, flashed one more smile of brilliance on his thick black hair.

His yummilicious lips curved into a warm grin. He stuck out his big hand, making the thin white T-shirt he wore pull tightly against his thick biceps. As the chilly fall breeze whistled, it blew his light cologne under her nose, spicy and fresh. Awareness fizzled up and down her spine.

"I'm Max Adams. I guess we'll be neighbors if I'm in your parking spot."

Max... She took his offered hand, relishing the way it enveloped hers. A warm tingle of pleasure threaded through her fingers and shot up her arm. Her mouth was hanging open -- she just knew it. JC squared her shoulders and pried her tongue off the roof of her mouth.

"Nice to meet you, Max Adams. I'm JC, and yes, this is my parking spot. But it's okay. I can see you're busy. I'll just take Mr. Clements' spot. He doesn't usually get home until around eight or so. Do you think that will give you enough time to finish?" She peeked over his shoulder to see what he had left in the truck.

"I'm almost done. If you'll grab that box and take it inside with you, I'll have one of the guys move the truck and I'll put your car right where it belongs." Max grinned again and her knees jiggled like tapioca.

JC found herself digging around in her purse to hand him her car keys and take the box.

"Which apartment is it?" she asked as she climbed the steps.

"I think I'm right across from you, Two-C." He winked at her.

Oh, hell. She pondered the ramifications of stud-o-licious moving in next door to her. He probably had too many girlfriends to count and a revolving door to match. She dropped the box on the floor by the door and surveyed the large living room.

His sectional couch was covered in boxes but she could make out the rich, masculine colors of red and gold. A bookcase lined one wall, filled with an assortment of books.

A hunk who actually reads books, real books not involving pictures of naked women. Novel concept indeed.

She heard his heavy feet coming up the steps and approaching the door. Max's body brushed hers as he inched past her. His muscled chest pressed up against hers for a brief moment, and her nipples seemed to think that was A-okay.

Pathetic.

JC sucked in a breath of air and let it back out discreetly. The space between them pulsed with something she couldn't identify but definitely existed. JC watched his nostrils flare and found the small scar just above his lip fascinated her.

Looking up at him she commented, "You've got quite a collection of... of books there." *Very bright observation indeed, JC. Way-to-go. Dazzle him with your above average IQ.* That couldn't have been her voice that came out all husky and seductive-like, could it?

His shoulder just touched the top of her head as he leaned into her. Lord, he was fantastic. He smiled that oral hygienist's wet dream of a smile. "Yeah, I love to read. Nothing too heavy, mind you, but I love a good story. Do you read?" He tilted his head to the left and cocked one eyebrow with apparent interest.

"Sure, when I have the time. Not the stuff you read though."

His eyes twinkled with interest. "Romance novels, right?"

He made it sound like Tolstoy.

How had their lips gotten this close? She could see right past those pearly whites to his fillings. His toothpaste-fresh breath fanned her face. JC ran her tongue over her lips nervously. "Yeah, romance novels." She sagged back against the door.

Affirmative, he was frosting her wheaties.

Hookay, time to go.

"How about a beer?"

Or, she could stay.

No, Fluffy was waiting.

"That would be nice, but it'll have to be another time. I have to go feed my dog." God, Fluffy was the most perfect excuse in the universe not to throw this man down on the floor and have unbridled sex with him. *Thank you, Fluffy!*

"Ya mean the big gray, good looking beast I saw in the alleyway?"

"You couldn't have seen him, he's inside." Panic began to settle in the pit of her belly.

"Well, I'm pretty sure it was him. Your neighbor from upstairs told me you had a new dog that looked like a hound from hell. He was in the alleyway when I went to the dumpster to ditch some of these boxes."

Oh shit. "Are you sure?" She squeezed out the door, past his big frame, and went across the hall to her apartment.

Max followed closely behind her and jingled her keys under her nose. "You forgot something."

Grabbing them from him, she thrust the key into the lock and flung open the door.

"Fluffy! Fluuuffyyyy. C'mere boy, c'mon snookums, don't hide on me. I'm home. Don't you want to eat?" Max was right behind her when she crossed the hall into her bedroom.

"Look, the window is open. That's how he got out." The cool night air rustled the curtains confirming Max's statement.

"Oh no! I have to go find him. Why would he run away?" Her heart sank in her chest. Tears burned the back of her eyelids. She swiped angrily at them. She'd only had him for a day but she'd become attached to the idea of having him here when she came home. Maybe he just wasn't meant to be inside. The guy at the ASPCA said they thought he was part wolf. Wolves liked to roam free, didn't they? Howl at the moon?

JC leaned out the window and called his name. Max's strong hands grabbed her waist and pulled her back inside, turning her to face him.

"You might fall," he scolded. "Look, maybe he's just the kind of dog who likes to be outside. I bet he comes back. I would if I were him." His grip lay loosely on her hips as his amber flecked eyes searched hers. "He'll come back," he assured her again. "In the meantime why don't you come back to my place and we'll have that beer. I might even throw in a pizza if you help me unpack." His thumb made a lazy pattern across the small of her back and her spine arched into the digit willingly. Her nipples tightened sharply and heat was rapidly building in her nether regions.

JC couldn't help but smile as she backed out of his reach. It wouldn't do to have an orgasm here in front of her nice new neighbor... "Only a *man* could think of food and alcohol when in a time of crisis."

"So what do you like on your pizza?"

"I get a choice?"

"Only if you help me unpack."

"I'm afraid to leave. What if Fluffy comes back?"

"Fluffy? You named a dog as handsome as that Fluffy?"

"Well, in case you didn't notice, he is pretty fluffy. And nobody seems to think he's all that good-looking but you -- and of course, me."

"Really? Well, there's no accounting for taste. I happen to think he's magnificent."

JC's heart fluttered in her chest. Why should she care if he liked her dog? "So do I. Do you really think he'll come back?"

He grinned at her. "I'm betting on it. Some dogs just need to roam. He'll get hungry and he'll come back."

"You're not just saying that because you need help unpacking, are you?"

"Well, yeah. It's part of my devious plan to get you to help me find a place for my paper plates. After that, I'm going to seduce you." His teasing eyes burned in the darkening bedroom.

JC shivered with a chuckle. "Okay, but the pizza's on you." *Hold the seduction, please.*

Chapter Four

JC was busily rearranging his kitchen cabinets when the pizza arrived. Max set plates out for the both of them at his scarred-oak kitchen table and lit a candle.

He pulled a chair out for her and gestured for her to sit with an inviting smile. "C'mon, you've been working hard over there. Sit and relax. I want to get to know my new neighbor."

Could we do that in the biblical sense, please? Jesus, what was wrong with her? Her nipples had taken on a life of their own and the *downstairs* portion of her body felt like it had just gone through the rinse cycle of a washing machine. She was eyeing him up like he was the only heterosexual male at a convention for gays. Her eyes strayed to the tight press of his jeans as he leaned back in his chair. Now, there was a package to behold and not the kind a girl normally got under her Christmas tree.

Whoa, chill out, JC. Chill nothing, he was sexy and she was sure to begin panting any second. An urge to run her tongue over those luscious lips prompted her to sit up straight in her chair and attack her pizza with vigor. Shoving food in her mouth had to be better than forcing herself on this poor, unsuspecting man. Her mouth watered and it wasn't over the pizza.

"Have you lived here long?"

JC shrugged her shoulders as she wiped her mouth. "About five years in this apartment. I moved here when my folks moved to Florida to retire."

"Not a Florida kind of girl, huh? I need the change of seasons personally."

So did she. So when her parents announced they were moving to Florida, JC had kissed them on the cheek and waved goodbye. No thongs for this girl. "I like the change of season too. It just doesn't seem like Christmas if it's eighty degrees and green. Besides, I have the salon I couldn't leave."

He chuckled. "Yeah and I love the mountains. Not too many of those in Florida. You own a salon?"

"Co-own. My partner is my friend from high school. She's married now, so she works much less. Where do you come from, somewhere here in Jersey?"

"Yeah, I come from Columbia."

Columbia? The sticks. "What brings you to this part of Jersey?"

He tipped his head back as he took a swig of beer. "Business."

Business? Who gave a damn about business when you could watch Max drink a beer? His lips worked the bottle like a hooker worked Forty-Second Street, the muscles convulsing as he took a long pull and smiled at her with satisfaction.

JC stuffed more pizza in her mouth. Between bites she asked, "Business? What kind of business?"

"A little bit of this and a little of that. Mostly preservation. Wildlife preservation."

Well, was that vague enough for you? So he was into the environment. What did she care what he did? She just wanted to screw his brains out.

OMIGOD. Did she just think that? Oh yes, indeed she had. What the fuck?

Max leaned across the table and pulled some cheese from her chin, gently pushing it into the corner of her mouth. The tip of her tongue grazed his finger briefly before he slid it over her lower lip. Their eyes locked.

JC gulped, but she couldn't pull her gaze from his. Max's brown, amber flecked eyes mesmerized her, dragging her toward him. Her breathing became short as they stared at one another and so did Max's.

When he spoke it was low and harsh. "Christ, I'm having some pretty risqué thoughts about you right now, JC."

Offended... yep, that's exactly what she should be. However, she wasn't and JC wasn't exactly sure why not. She just wasn't. She was tempted... and if that made her a tramp, then tramp on, girl! "R-risqué?" Squeaking -- she was squeaking.

Leaning into her, he laid his chest over the table, bracing his hands on it, and inched toward her lips. "Definitely."

JC's nipples tightened to sharp points and poked at her sweater. Okay, she was going to walk on the wild side, go out on a limb. "And those risqué thoughts are?"

Max's eyes narrowed, his lips speaking words that didn't offend her. They made her wild with lust. Slowly and precisely he said, "I don't know if you're *ready* to hear them."

Oh, but she was, silly man. Her tongue ran over her bottom lip, and her throat was dry when she said, "Try me."

Max's nostrils flared and his eyes flashed dark and brooding. "I want to spread your legs and bury myself between them…"

Ooooh. Oh… oh… oh. Oh, my.

JC's thoughts exploded as a visual of Max throwing her on top of the table and ripping her jeans off flashed into her mind's eye. She squirmed in her chair, barely able to contain the impulse to rip her clothes off for him. "O-okay…" she said on an intake of air. JC burned, her breasts ached and her pussy throbbed with a need -- that, in her thirty years of life, she'd never before experienced.

Max was abrupt as he stood, knocking his chair over behind him and grabbing her so fast she clutched his bulky arms to steady herself. His hands yanked her roughly to him, pressing her hips flush to his and grinding against her roughly.

Max bent JC back over the table, shoving the pizza to the floor as the bottles of beer fell and the glass shattered on the tile. It was a vague, distant sound in JC's ears, dominated by the pounding of her heart and the ache between her legs. His eyes never left her face as he positioned himself between her legs, sliding her roughly to him.

Max unzipped his jeans with slow ease, pushing them down over his lean hips. His cock, hard and thick, fell forward onto her thigh. JC's hands clenched into tight fists, so strong was the desire to reach between them and clasp it. Max hiked her legs over his hips and put both hands on either side of her body. His eyes devoured her as he rubbed his cock between her legs, still in jeans. It throbbed between them, so hot she could feel it through her clothing, scraping the cleft between her thighs and making her hips rise to meet his thrusts.

JC was nearly frantic to feel her skin against his, but Max didn't remove her jeans. Instead he laid over her and cupped her breasts -- breasts that arched upward for his touch. He shoved her shirt and bra out of the way, stroking them, thumbing her nipples until she gasped. Still Max watched her, intense and penetrating, just before he pressed his hot mouth to her breast and enveloped a nipple.

JC's body reacted violently, her back bowing as she gripped the sides of the table and molten fire licking at her cunt. Max pulled at the tight peak, tugging it away from her body as he rolled his tongue over it. She clenched her eyes shut and fought a scream, half-filled with frustration, half with indefinable pleasure. The steel of his flesh rubbing between her legs coupled with his hands on her breast was more than she could bear.

A whimper escaped her lips when Max reached between them and cupped her pussy, dragging his thumb over the cleft. She wanted him to take her clothes off and ram into her, hard and heated. Her breath was raspy as she squirmed beneath him, straining to the feel of his lips and hands. Leaning over her, he let his tongue find her exposed belly, kissing it as he worked his mouth over her lower abdomen and down between her legs. Max nipped at her through her jeans and JC stopped breathing as teeth grazed, her heart throbbing and every nerve on fire with pounding heat.

His big hands tore at the button on her jeans, and dragged her zipper down, tearing them off in a swift motion and taking her panties with them. JC felt the brush of his naked thighs between hers and the slide of his hands as he lifted her hips in them. Max's hot cock slipped between the lips of her pussy, caressing her clit, moving in the wet recesses.

JC gripped his wrists as he cupped her ass, kneading the flesh, massaging it. She wrapped her legs around him, silently pleading with him to enter her. She gyrated her hips, begging to be impaled, thinking of nothing but the stiff length that teased her.

Forceful and hard, Max plunged into her, and JC threw her head back, arching up into him and digging her nails into his wrists. He filled her with searing heat, stretching her until she thought she might explode. Each plunge was slow to begin, picking up speed as he ground against her. JC's muscles clenched around his length, and her legs tightened around his waist. Max pulled her roughly toward him with each thrust as their hips crashed together. His jaw clenched tightly and his throat arched, tensing.

Her nipples turned to tight beads as climax tore at her, screaming for release. Max hissed sharply when he slid nimble fingers between her legs, spreading her flesh. He mumbled something incoherent as he found her clit, swollen and throbbing, caressing it until JC couldn't prolong the need to come.

From somewhere deep within her a howl boiled to the surface, erupting and shattering the silence, tearing from her throat and rocking her whole body.

Her legs clamped his waist as she pushed upward, meeting the slick slide of his cock one last time before feeling the heat of his release, thick and plentiful. Max yelled into the silence along with her, long and loud.

A slow descent from the madness she'd just experienced began as her body calmed. Tears stung her eyes as the room around her came into focus and she slowly drifted back to where she was.

Never. Not in all her sexual experience had she *ever* had an orgasm like that, rich in texture, well defined and so sharply sweet. JC released Max's wrists as she heaved with each breath she took, closing her eyes so she didn't have look at him.

Max's hands soothed her skin, sliding over it with gentle fingers. "Look at me, JC."

Um, no. I think not. She couldn't look at him after that wanton display of lust. Only sluts boinked guys they'd known but mere hours. Jesus, all he'd done was order her pizza and she was buck naked on his table, slapping her legs around his waist, banging him for all she was worth.

JC shook her head. *No*, she would *not* look at him. Eye contact was absolutely out of the question.

Max's hand cupped her chin and dragged her face upward. "Look at me, *now*, JC."

"Mm-mm." She shook her head again.

His sigh was long. "JC, look at me."

"No."

"Well, why the hell not?"

"No."

"You're behaving badly. It's not nice to ignore the man who just made love to you on his kitchen table."

Pass the salt. "No."

"Now, c'mon. You have nothing to be embarrassed about." Max laid over her. Letting his full weight rest on her and using two fingers, he pried one of her eyes open.

As he came into focus, her heart lurched. God, he was so sexy.

His cheeks were ruddy from their lovemaking and his eyes were amused at her refusal to look at him.

"Go away," she said from clenched teeth.

He shook his head. "Nope, and I'm not letting you up until you open your eyes and talk to me."

JC kept her one eye closed and shook her head.

Max shifted his hips, withdrawing from her. "If you don't look at me, I'll make you stay in the wet spot," he threatened jokingly.

And it *was* wet. JC squirmed. "What do you want to talk about?"

"What we just did," he said on a chuckle.

Did he want a blow-by-blow? *JC, here, reporting for "Screw-U," live from my hunky, brand spanking new neighbor Max's kitchen table. Woo, baby, did I ever just do it with a guy I knew all of a couple of hours. Does that put me in the schtupping Hall of Fame? Yup, that's me down here, underneath all this finely sculpted flesh...* "We just had sex..."

He nudged her with his nose. "Yeah, we did... kind of suddenly. Are you freaked out?"

Oh, no... me? Freaked out? HAH! I do this sort of thing all the time. Why just last week when the guy upstairs moved in I tickled his fancy too, except the location was different. We used his friggin' countertops. Jesus Christ in a mini-skirt! "Yes, yes I *am* freaked out," she said with incredible calm, defying her stomach's jumbled mess.

"I don't do this as a rule, JC."

No, no of course not. I mean really, how often does a man *find himself screwing the first female he sees? Next to never, right? That would be so* un-male-like. *Women were more prone to sex with complete strangers...* "I'm sure," she retorted back.

He let go of her eye and bracketed either side of her face. "No, you're not sure, but you will be."

"I think I have to go. I need to see if Fluffy's come back. He'll be hungry," she said flatly.

Max nuzzled her face with his nose, slipping down her cheek to her ear where he nibbled on the silver stud earring she always wore. JC felt the heat rise in her cheeks again as shivers coursed along her spine and her body rose to press to his of its own accord. Max sneezed hard in her ear, jolting his whole body and making her jump.

"Bless you."

He sneezed again and his eyes began to tear. "I'm sorry, are those earrings silver?"

"Um, yeah." JC finally opened her eyes and scanned Max's face as it became red and blotchy. "Are you okay? What's wrong?"

He pushed himself off of her as fast as he could, swiping at his mouth with his arm as a series of sneezes wracked his body.

JC sat up, yanking her sweater down, and asked, "What's wrong?"

Max shook his head as he rubbed his eyes with the bottom of his T-shirt. JC couldn't tear her eyes from the lower half of him. The contours of his well-muscled thighs bulged as he walked back and forth across the floor. "It's okay. I'm --" *ahchoo* -"allergic to silver is all," he said on another watery sneeze. *Ahchoo, ahchoo, ahchoo.*

JC took the opportunity to slip off the table, scoop her pants up and find the bathroom. She located it and cleaned up, throwing her pants on and grabbing some toilet paper for Max for lack of tissues.

Feeling much more secure clothed, JC tapped the gloriously half-naked Max on the shoulder. "Here, I think you need these and I have to go."

Max grabbed her arm with one hand as he wiped his eyes with the other. He threw the tissue on the floor and walked her backwards toward the counter. "You can't leave until you kiss me goodbye." He smirked at her, winking one bloodshot eye.

JC found her body had its own ideas as it molded to his. His cock was again hard and pressing against her thigh. Heat assaulted her in sharp pinpricks and she knew she had to leave before she clung to his thigh like a contestant on Survivor clung to a granola bar. "I have to go," she said firmly.

Max's lips found hers, touching them with a whisper of a caress. "Not before you kiss me goodbye. You don't think you can just love me and leave me, do you?"

JC couldn't stop the giggle that escaped her lips. "Okay, one and then I hit the road, Jack."

"It's Max," he teased, "a name you won't soon forget." And then his lips crushed hers as his tongue slid into her mouth, making her gasp.

They hadn't kissed, not even when they'd made love, but

nothing could have prepared her for the surge of electricity that passed between them. Her tongue dueled with his, meeting him stroke-for-stroke, until she found her arms wrapped securely around his neck, standing on tippey toe to taste as much of him as she could.

The firm slide of his lips and the hot press of his cock made her head spin. Max groaned when she ran her nails over his scalp and moved his hips, pushing against her.

Hookay. Time to go, otherwise she was going to get her jammies and pink fuzzy bunny slippers with the plastic eyes and move the hell in with him.

JC tore her lips from his, their breathing ragged and said, "Thanks for the pizza… er, it's been -- well --" What the hell did you say after a one-night stand? Fun? Nice? The best orgasm in the history of JC orgasms?

Ducking under his arms she called, "Goodnight," over her shoulder and ran to the door, pulling it open and zipping next door. His laughter followed her across the hall as he called back, "Tomorrow. I'll see you tomorrow night."

JC closed the door behind her and leaned up against it, just breathing. Oh, *GOD*! She'd slept with her neighbor… Jesus, he wasn't even in the building more than a few hours and she was all over him like ketchup on fries. Her face flushed and her nipples tightened at the mere thought the visual of him naked evoked.

JC wandered to the bathroom, stripping her clothes off to shower when a thought struck her. She'd just had the most incredible sex of her life… what if he never wanted to have sex with her again? What if she really was just a one-night stand?

It took her breath away. Max may well have used her and she would never get to use him back because she'd behaved like a child. That would mean they'd never get jiggy again.

Well, damn.

JC shook her head as if that would help to clear the muddled mess her brain was in. What was she thinking? Climbing into the shower she let the hard spray pound on her head. Maybe it would knock some sense into her. So he was good in bed… er, table… big deal. Other guys were good in bed, she was sure of it. She'd just never experienced it. So what if he didn't want to have sex with her again. That was just fine.

Yeah, who needed orgasms that rocked the planet and did the earth moving thing?

Not JC Jensen... not a lot anyway.

JC stepped from the shower and toweled off, heading toward her bedroom. Her heart sank -- she'd forgotten about Fluffy and it was freezing in here. Her eyes flew to the window. They'd left it open... shit. Gathering the towel around her she tucked it between her breasts and closed the window.

A cold, wet nose sniffed under the edge of her towel. JC flew around, kneeling down and throwing her arms around Fluffy's neck. "Dammit, Fluff, don't do that to me. I was worried sick about you!"

Fluffy licked her ear, then backed away and fiercely shook his head before he sneezed.

Chapter Five

"Cut it out, Fluff! Stop yanking my crank and c'mon. You're going to the vet like it or not, especially after that little rendezvous last night. Didja get laid?"

Fluffy cocked his head. *Why, yes, yes I did indeed get laid.*

"Because if you did, we could be in big trouble. Can you see the look on Mrs. Edwards' face if I have to explain how her Chihuahua, Phoebe, got knocked up by *you*?" JC shook her head as she tugged harder on the leash, dragging a reluctant Fluffy out the door and down the stairs. She glanced briefly at the apartment across the way, then tugged his collar more firmly, leading him the rest of the way down the stairs and to her car.

Aha… methinks the lady digs me.

That put a skip in Fluffy's stride as he followed behind JC and hopped into the back seat of her car. The vet's office wasn't so bad.

It could be worse… sorta.

When he'd heard her make the appointment on the phone this morning, he had to wonder if a rabies shot would hurt his human form, but then he didn't have a lot of choices short of shifting right before her very eyes. That might freak her, especially in light of last night.

JC kissed the tip of his nose. "You're a good boy, snookums. Now behave when we get to the vet or you'll be in big-doggy-shit." Fluffy licked her nose in response.

Yeah, yeah… Good. He'd be good. Fluffy sat up and rested his head on JC's shoulder from the back seat of her small car, burying his nose in her hair.

Damn, she smelled good. He couldn't wait for the day to be over so he could drag her back to his apartment and bury his nose elsewhere. Last night was equally explosive for him. He'd wanted to rip her clothes off and keep her naked until she screamed for mercy.

Wait until she found out who he was. Then she'd really scream… but she'd adjust, he soothed himself. Finding out your dog was also your lover had to weird a chick out. Of course he wasn't a *dog*, he was a *wolf.*

Somehow, he had to get her to come back home with him to the woods where his pack lived. He'd take it from there. Eva said it would be okay and he'd have to trust that. He also had to admit she was right, even if she did prophesize from a bowl of chicken soup. He'd never felt the supposed bond his pack members spoke of until meeting JC. Now that he'd found his mate, he wasn't letting her go.

As they pulled into the driveway of the vet's office, his stomach rumbled. He'd skipped his morning kibble and now he was paying for it.

JC came around the car and popped the door open. "C'mon, handsome. Now I want a solemn promise you'll behave. This is a public outing. No growling, menacing showing of the teeth or biting. Hear me?" She ruffled his ears and pulled him toward the door of the vet.

Well, that pretty much left all of the good clean fun out of the question. He trotted behind her and refused to acknowledge the leash, averting his eyes.

It was *pink.*

Jesus, how did she get a pink leash? Was there no dignity?

JC went to the reception desk while all of the nice doggies and kitties eyeballed him from the waiting area.

As JC talked with the receptionist, Fluffy sat beside her and squirmed. If the other animals could talk they'd make fun of him. He could sense it.

Was it his hair? He'd caught a glimpse of it today in that full length mirror JC had on the back of her door... it *was* fluffy.

Patrons of the vet in the waiting area scooped up their smaller animals and tucked them safely in their laps with wary looks directed at him.

Good, this was as it should be, he thought. He was, after all, a wolf -- as in the Red Riding Hood variety -- and he'd chomp them all into little pieces if they dared crack wise.

JC led him to an empty chair and grabbed a magazine, keeping the leash held tight in her hand. Fluffy slumped down to the floor and sighed. A rabies shot... of all the indignities...

A French poodle eyed him from the corner of the room. Fluffy eyed him back, staring him down. The toy poodle, in all his curly white, pink bowed splendor, growled a warning. He wore a sweater that said Precious.

Fluffy snorted. *Yeah, okay, c'mon, Precious. Ya wanna piece a this?* Fluffy opened his mouth a bit and gave the delicate poodle with the stupid pink bows a gander at his teeth.

The poodle backed away, cowering under his owner's chair with a yip in weak defense.

That's right, back away from the big, bad wolf slowly, bucko.

A dachshund came trailing in, yipping and jumping beside his owner's feet unleashed. Fluffy buried his head under his paws to silence the sharp bark.

Gawd, they were yappy little beasts, neurotic, nervous balls of hair.

A nose nudged his. Lifting his head he stared into the soft, doe-like eyes of the dachshund. It backed away in a playful stance and barked again, its auburn hair, shiny and long, bounced and behaved quite nicely, he mused. Must be nice to have such a manageable coat.

Christ, could a guy get a break here?

"Wow, he's big, huh?" The owner of the dachshund assessed Fluffy with a whistle.

Fluffy would have smiled cockily if he could have. *Why yes, thank you. Indeed... I am big and if you don't make your wee little friend get the fuck off me, I'm going to indulge in some dachshund delight.*

JC chuckled, "Yes, he is big and he seems to like your dog, which, based on his past performance, is unusual. What a good boy, Fluffy!" JC praised him.

Yes, he was a good dog. Good, good, good.

The little dachshund gnawed on one of Fluffy's ears contentedly. He wondered absently -- as he fought not to chomp on the critter's leg -- if everyone in his pack had suffered this same humiliation on their lifemate quest? He didn't remember *anyone* coming home to the pack and regaling tales of trips to PETsMART or the *vet*.

"What's your dog's name?" JC asked.

The elderly man sat beside her. "Killer."

Killer? *Killer*? What the fuck was that? How did he end up with a name like *Fluffy* when this dog with ADHD had a name like *Killer*?

This was grossly unjust.

"And your dog's name?"

"Fluffy."

The old man coughed, clearing his throat. "Er, Fluffy?"

He felt the whole room go silent and then a twitter rippled through the crowded waiting room. They were mocking him. He could feel it right down to his doggy toes, er, paws.

He felt like a boy named Sue.

He'd show them Fluffy all right. Fluffy sat up, knocking Killer off his back, sending him skittering sideways on the smooth tiled floor and stiffened his spine, like he was lord of the jungle, growling low and threatening.

JC's foot gave him a nudge without breaking a stride in her conversation. It was a warning.

Oh shit. *Good* -- he was supposed to be good. Crap. He slumped back down and Killer went to town on his ear again.

"JC Jenson and Fluffy?" a pretty nurse from behind the reception desk called. She came around and popped her head out the door and her eyes widened when she took in Fluffy.

That's right, girlie. Be afraid, be very afraid.

"C'mon, big guy. Let's go and you *behave*," JC admonished as she rose and tugged his pink leash.

Fluffy strolled past all of the mean puppies who had silently mocked him, holding his head high. The nice nurse backed up against the door as far as she could as they passed her. He looked back at the crowd of she-she-foo-foo dogs with their stupid sweaters and hair bows and smirked as if to say, "See how scary I am? Even the nurse is afraid of me."

Fluffy trotted off behind JC, admiring her ass, as they entered the examining room. He yawned and sat beside her, nuzzling her leg.

When the doctor came in the door, he stopped dead in his tracks and gave Fluffy the once over.

Thaaat's right, Doc. Fluffy stuck his chest out. *I'm mean and ugly and I ain't afraid of you and your needles.*

"Ms. Jensen, I'm Doctor Jacobs. So this is Fluffy... when you said he was unusual, I didn't realize *how* unusual."

JC's laugh tinkled through the sterile air. "The animal shelter said he might be part wolf."

Dr. Jacobs knelt in front of Fluffy and scratched his head. "Hey, big guy." Fluffy eyed him nonchalantly. *Hello, Dr. Jacobs. Nice to meet you. Could we do this thing? I'm hungry and I want to go home.* Damn, he should have hunted last night instead of laying around thinking about JC.

"I think we're going to need help getting him on the scale," Dr. Jacobs commented as Fluffy caught him covertly eyeing JC's breasts.

Well, well... like my woman, do you?

The doctor poked his head out and called for assistance. A big, burly woman with a mean looking face pushed her way in and stood with her arms crossed, waiting to be instructed.

Wait, they were going to pick him up and put him on the scale? Fluffy sucked in his gut. *Shit...* As Florence Nightingale grabbed him around his torso he let his body go slack. Her flat, round face turned red as she huffed and puffed to schlep him over to the scale, plopping him down unceremoniously on the cool metal.

Dr. Jacobs perused the scale, giving sidelong glances to JC's breasts. "Wow, he's one hundred and fifty pounds..."

Of lean, mean, fighting machine, and don't you forget it.

"I think watching what he eats would be a good thing. He's not overweight, but I'd definitely say he's on the husky side and could run toward heavy. He's a big dog. You'll have to watch his hips. I'd ration his food carefully."

"He doesn't seem to like the food I chose for him. He's been dumping it behind the refrigerator, but he sure likes my steak," JC answered.

Guilty, he thought. How the hell can a wolf live on kibble alone? A diet? He didn't need a frickin' diet, but he'd better watch his protein nonetheless. He didn't need hip trouble.

"How's his temperament? Is he difficult, lazy?"

Lazy... please. And difficult? Not a lot... just when asshole doctors are busy checking out my chick or her stupid ex-boyfriend shows up.

JC grimaced as she came to stand by Fluffy. "Well, he is very overprotective and somehow he keeps getting out of the house. I think he likes to roam. It concerns me that he might get a disease."

Dr. Jacobs pried Fluffy's mouth open with two fingers and frowned. "Gingivitis..." he mumbled. "His teeth are pretty yellow. He could use a good cleaning."

He did not either have gingivitis. Fluffy let out a low, resonant growl because it was pissing him off that this guy's fingers were in his mouth, accusing him of bad oral hygiene.

Dr. Jacobs jerked his hand out of Fluffy's mouth and watched him skeptically for signs he might rip his hand off at the wrist.

The thought grew in appeal.

Well, there was just no pleasing this man was there? He was too fat. His teeth were yellow. He should be on a diet. He was grouchy...

"He has fleas," Dr. Jacobs said.

And to top it all off he had fucking fleas... the mere thought made him use his hind leg to scratch furiously at his back.

JC nodded. "I bathed him when I brought him home and did one of those flea dips."

Dr. Jacobs looked up and smiled at JC, his eyes sweeping over her lush body. "You did the right thing by bringing him in. He needs his shots to begin with and we can recommend a healthy diet. As to his roaming, well, that could be cured by neutering him."

His testicles shrank, tucking themselves safely to his body to protect them from the scalpel.

Hookay. No more Dr. Jacobs. There will be no whacking off of the balls, thank you kindly. It was time to go home or the nice doctor was going to get the surprise of the millennium when he shifted into human form and clocked him one right in his doctor-like face.

"I'll have to wait on something like that. It's really expensive and this visit alone is costing a fortune," JC said.

Finally, someone with a measure of sanity.

Dr. Jacobs chuckled. "I understand," he said as he patted Fluffy on his backside. "We'll get you all set up. Vitamins, flea powder, toothbrush, the works. For now, he needs his shots. Gerta, would you help me lift Fluffy to the examining table?"

Gerta scooped him up again and dumped him on the table. JC came to stand in front of him, giving him the opportunity to bury his snout in her breasts. Fluffy sighed contentedly.

Dr. Jacobs grabbed the scruff of his neck. "Hang onto him would you, Gerta?"

Nurse Ratchet placed her arms around his torso and JC held his nose in the palm of her hands. "It'll only hurt for a minute, Cujo. So behave, hear me?"

Behave, behave, behave. If he kept behaving he'd have no nuts, he mused as the sharp sting of the needle penetrated his thick skin.

Fuck it. That hurt. Fluffy let out a howl of discomfort, shrill and piercing.

Dr. Jacobs held his ears.

Good. He hoped they rang for days on end.

Chapter Six

JC took Fluffy home and he collapsed on the floor of her bedroom, snoring softly. She smiled at his big body sprawled out in sleep. Poor thing, one trip to the vet and he was as meek as a kitten. She rubbed the top of his head with affection, then got up. Closing the bedroom door behind her she set out to clean her apartment and forget about Max. He'd niggled at the back of her brain all day long and now it was time to abolish him completely. With like cleansers and stuff.

Her nipples tightened just thinking of him.

Shit. What was she going to do? The man lived next door to her and she'd nailed him in less than two hours. He was going to label her the apartment house slut and move on to his next prey. Talk about easy…

JC found some old sweats and a T-shirt, changed into them and dug under her kitchen sink to find her cleaning products. Like scrubbing the grout on the kitchen tile was going to wash away the memory of last night.

She slammed the bucket full of hot water down on the floor and tied her hair back. No man was going to make her tingle like that. So there… or was that no man had ever made her tingle like that *before*?

Oh, what difference did it make? She'd done something totally out of character and behaved like the apartment house slut in the process. There was no taking that back now.

"Hey, good lookin'. How goes it?" a deep voice rumbled from her doorway.

Damn, she really should remember to lock the friggin' door so lust evokers like Max couldn't get in. JC's heart skipped two beats and her legs wobbled from her position on the floor, which just happened to be ass end up.

Good gravy.

Without looking up, JC mumbled, "Fine, thanks."

Max came to stand over her, his boot clad feet at her eye level.

"JC? Are we still not looking at me?"

He was a real brain surgeon.

Max knelt down in front of her and propped her chin up with his finger. "Answer me."

Her eyes scanned his deep blue ones. Did one-night stands come back to have a two-night stand? "Why do I need to look at you?"

"Because you think I think you're loose."

JC groaned. And what of it? Did they have to discuss it? Maybe do a little therapy as a couple over it? "I'm cleaning my floor. I don't have time to think about whether you think I'm loose." Not really anyway.

His lips moved closer to hers as he grazed them with a whisper of a kiss. JC's stomach did a nosedive and her loins joined it. "I don't think you're loose. I do think you should come have dinner with me and we can get to know one another."

Dinner? Where? In the den of iniquity across the way? Oh, no. She was not going back to Two-C. No way. "Where?" she asked tentatively.

Max grinned and winked. "My apartment."

No, no, no. "What time?"

Max nuzzled her jaw and avoided her ear. "Six."

Sex at six worked. "Should I bring anything?"

Pulling her upward, he fit her body to his. "Nope. Just you."

And my libido? JC gulped. "Okay."

He smiled just before his mouth moved over hers and he slipped his tongue between her lips. JC's body had a will of its own as it molded to Max's and she let the silky slip of tongue taste her own. A sigh escaped her. His kiss was like coming home to something she didn't fully understand and at the moment didn't care to ponder. It was familiar, yet new and unidentifiable. Her arms wrapped around his neck and her breasts strained against his hard chest.

"Ouch!" Max yelped as he tore his lips from hers. His hand went to the back of his neck and he rubbed it.

"What's wrong?"

Max shrugged his shoulders and smiled again. "Just a kink in my neck, which I assure you will be fine by the time you get to my place for dinner and that means I have to go if I'm going to cook."

JC couldn't help but laugh. "Are you going to dial the pizza guy up again?"

He squeezed her one last time around the waist before letting her go. "Hey, I can dial more than just the pizza guy. I have all sorts of take-out menus. You'll see, and I'll see *you* tonight," he said over his shoulder with a wink. Max shut the door behind him and JC sank to a kitchen chair, her knees weak and her thoughts fuzzy.

There was just no resisting him. Max was virile and funny and hotter than molten lava and she'd had the best sex of her life with him. What was a girl to do when he blatantly made his intentions clear?

He wants to make you dinner, tramp. He didn't say anything about more sex.

Well, why not? Was she unattractive? Did he just want to make up for being a cad and ripping her clothes off the night before by making her dinner? Was he a man-tramp with a conscience?

That would suck. She didn't need a kiss-off meal, thank you.

The phone rang -- a sharp shrill intrusion on her thoughts. Diving across the kitchen, JC grabbed it. "Hello."

"It's Max."

Ah, the man-tramp calling to cancel. JC tried to sound casual, like it didn't bother her at all. "What's up?"

"Could you leave the earrings off tonight? My eyes watered for an hour after you left."

If he kept his lips to himself he needn't worry, now need he? But she found herself chuckling instead and said, "Okay, no earrings."

His deep rumble of a laugh came through the receiver. "Cool. I'll see you at six. Bye, JC."

JC hung up breathless and pissed at herself for agreeing to do anything. If this was a kiss-off meal then so be it.

It better be good.

* * *

Yak, yak, yak. Fluffy yawned and eyed the alarm clock on the bedside table. If JC didn't quit talking to him like he was an Oprah episode she'd be late for their dinner date and so would he. Good thing he'd snuck off and pre-ordered everything. His stomach growled, intruding on their little heart-to-heart. Christ, he could devour a stable full of steer.

"I don't know, Fluffy, what do you think? I mean why would he want to make me dinner if he just wanted to make up for last night?" JC sat at the edge of her bed and played with the edge of her red, silky dress.

Damn, she looked hot in it.

"This is nuts, don't you think, Fluff? We hardly know each other and I had sex with him. I never do things like that. I've never had a one-night stand."

Good to know. Now get over it because it's going to happen again and again and again. Tonight, if he could help it.

"But he's so incredibly magnetic. When I see Max, hear his voice, I'm drawn to him and I can't stop myself. I can't explain it."

Fluffy stretched from his place on the floor and cocked his head toward her. *Naturally...* his cock rose to the occasion of sex with JC.

"I will not have sex with him again tonight. And that's a promise --"

What? No sex? Fluffy's ears perked up. *Wait a minute here...*

"-- no matter *how* sexy he is. I'm only asking to be hurt and I don't need that. He lives right across the hall. How will I feel when he dumps me and moves on to the next available woman?"

Oh... *that* was low. JC didn't even know him and she was making assumptions and not very nice ones either.

He was not a player.

But he was in a hurry. According to Eva if he didn't get a fire under his ass and present JC to the pack soon, that bad mojo thing was going to happen. None of it made sense to him, but he wasn't risking any bad karma. God knew the pack didn't need any trouble. They were in deep -- just in misfits alone. Another thing he didn't have time to dwell on. Being the Alpha male of his pack was nothing short of organized chaos.

Flopping back on the bed, JC stared up at the ceiling. If she didn't get her cute butt in gear he wouldn't have enough time to shift, let alone set the table.

Okay, enough of this. JC knew him all of one night and they'd done the wild thing for the better part of it. She was worried about something that she didn't quite understand and he didn't have a lot of time to dwell on how to get her back to the pack while trying to make her understand. So he had to move quickly or he'd be lifemate-less and that was beginning to disturb him far more than he'd anticipated.

Jumping up on the bed with his front paws he licked her cheek, then headed for the door, signaling the need to go "potty" as she called it. JC ruffled the top of his head. "Okay, I'll walk you before I have to go to Max's. Will you be okay alone for a little while?"

Yeah, yeah, let's go already. He pranced on the floor and JC chuckled, snapping his leash onto his collar. When she opened the door to the apartment he bolted, yanking free of her and running as fast as he could down the stairs. JC yelled after him, but he ignored her in favor of his opportunity to fly through the door just as someone else was coming in.

Bad dog, he thought, *no biscuits for you.* He was going to be in a shit load of trouble when JC got home.

Now he just needed to shift, shave and change. Oh, and brush his teeth so they wouldn't be *yellow.* Stupid vet. He couldn't help it that his wolf form had bad teeth. They worked just fine when he was gnawing on meat.

Shaking off his brisk run, Max/Fluffy stopped in the alleyway under his apartment to shift. He clenched his teeth, gritting them.

Nothing.

Well, shit. Must be all the shifting getting to him.

Okay, Max, my boy, *focus.* Think tall, dark and handsome. He willed himself to relax as the tension from his wolf form released in small bursts. The crunch of bone flexing and stretching took over. He busied himself thinking about JC until he stood erect and in human form.

Ahh, that was better. Max cracked his neck and looked down. *Oops.*

Fuck, he was naked and it was more than a little evident he'd been thinking of JC. Despite the cold night air, his little buddy didn't seem to feel the effects.

Sighing, he climbed up the stairwell to his window and slipped into the warm apartment. Seeing the time on the microwave he rushed to throw some plates and silverware on the table, then headed for the shower.

He caught a glimpse of his reflection in the mirror and stopped to inspect his teeth. Pulling his lips back he examined them.

Max snorted. He did not have gingivitis.

Chapter Seven

Damn dog. Maybe having him neutered was exactly what he needed, JC thought as she knocked on Max's door. Max opened it smiling and smelling of a vaguely familiar cologne. His burgundy knit shirt hugged his muscled chest and jeans that fit snugly over every ripple in his thighs made her mouth water.

JC's nipples responded in kind. *Hell's bells. Girls, could you please give me a break? Absolutely no sex. Are we clear? We are celibate -- as in sexless in Hoboken.*

Max's eyes roamed over her body appreciatively before he leaned in to kiss her cheek and murmured, "I like red on you."

Her body leaned against his momentarily before she reminded herself this was a non-sex date.

No sex.

Letting Max lead her into the kitchen, she hung back just enough to keep a distance between them. Pulling out a chair, he offered it to her and she sat down, scooting around his bulky frame to avoid touching him.

"I hope you like steak," he said.

Yes, steak, no sex, please. "I like steak." JC smiled politely.

"Good." Max began to bring covered dishes to the table. Whatever it was it smelled heavenly. "Steak Diane," he commented absently as he served her.

Yeah, I'll bet. Did Diane teach you to make it too? As he placed his serving of steak on his plate, JC grimaced. It jiggled.

Max sat down beside her and chuckled at the face she made. "I love mine rare, but I pegged you for a medium kind of girl."

JC cut into hers and found that it was just right. After she slid a piece in her mouth, she decided Max could cook for her anytime.

Cook, but not boink. No boinking. Nosexnosexnosex.

They talked about a little of everything as they ate and JC found herself warming to his every word, giggling like a stupid girl in high school when he said something clever. Which was nearly every sentence that came out of his mouth.

He was particularly quiet when they talked family, mentioning only that he came from a large brood and they all lived back in Columbia. Then why would he move so far away? The smile on his face told her he obviously loved them. JC decided not to push the issue as she gabbed about her own parents and her salon.

JC helped him clear the dishes. The moment they were washed and dried she said, "Well, Max, this was very nice. Thank you. I don't think I've had a meal that was this good in a long time." JC began to back away toward the kitchen doorway. "So maybe we can do this again sometime, okay?" That was very noncommittal. She congratulated herself.

Max was beside her in a matter of seconds, hovering over her with his big body. "You were going to just eat and run? I feel cheap, used," he teased.

Hah! She could teach him a thing or two about cheap. "Well, Fluffy... he ran away again and I have to go see if he came --" his lips brushed hers -- "back..." Oh, hell he was doing that magnetism thing and it was making her knees like butter. JC's hands went to his chest to push him away, but instead she found they kneaded the flesh beneath them.

"Fluffy came home last night, didn't he?" he asked as he nibbled at her naked earlobe.

"Y-esss," she hissed when his tongue found the rim of her ear.

"Then why don't you stay a little longer," his words enticed her.

"I can't, Max. I just don't do things like..." His large hand cupped her breast through the thin material of her dress.

"Like this?" he asked as he began to move them together, thumbing a tight nipple.

JC arched toward the caress. "Yes, like this."

Max groaned against her neck, "I don't usually either, JC. I don't make a habit out of having sex with someone I don't know, but with you it was different."

Oh, she was going to fall for his bullshit. She could feel it between her legs. What the hell? What was another roll in the sheets of lust between neighbors? It beat giving him a casserole.

The only thing she could do was respond to him. Her will to leave his apartment un-ravished was gone. Max took her silence for acquiescence and scooped her up, carrying her to his bedroom and laying her on his big bed. The sheets were cool on her back and countered her heated skin. Closing her eyes, JC damned her slut theory to hell as her nipples beaded and a rush of white-hot heat slithered between her thighs.

Max pulled his knit shirt over his head, tearing off his jeans. JC was treated to a closer look at the finely sculpted Max. Ripples of muscle led to narrowed hips and long, lean legs. He stole the air from her lungs when her eyes landed on his cock. JC had never spent much time appreciating a man's body, but Max's was something to behold. His erection was thick and firm, jutting forward, and her heart sped up as she anticipated it entering her.

Max slipped her shoes off and ran his tongue over her calf, nipping the skin, lifting her dress as he reached her thighs, and grazing the tender skin inside them.

JC squirmed beneath the sear of his lips. Hot and firm, they swept over her skin. When Max reached her panties he growled, nudging her legs apart and hooking his thumbs under the waistband as he slid them off. His hair brushed against her thighs as he dipped his head to run his tongue over the crease between her thigh and pussy.

Max's hot breath drove her to arch upward, her legs spreading willingly as she held her breath, anticipating the unknown. Max's fingers skimmed the outer lips of her pussy with a light touch, tracing them, separating the curls, hovering over her cunt with his lips. JC's hands went to either side of her, tensing, bracing herself for the slide of his wet tongue.

His exploration was agonizingly slow, whisper light kisses of heat. He spread her flesh with two fingers and shoved a hand under her ass, gripping the flesh. JC fought the impulse to beg for him to put his mouth on her aching flesh. Max's tongue snaked out, taking a quick swipe of her clit. JC bucked, reaching for more. Her hips lifted to meet his tongue and Max complied, making a long pass over her exposed flesh.

JC's fingers tore at the blanket beneath her, clutching it to stop from grabbing Max's head and jamming it against her cunt. Max teased her clit, tugging at the swollen bud, sending sharp jolts of electricity over her flushed skin. His thick finger slipped into her and

Dakota Cassidy: Wolf Mates

her pussy clenched it in desperation. JC rocked against it, rolling her hips as Max licked her.

Max drove his finger into her, now slick with her need. He plunged into her, latching onto her clit and suckling it. JC felt the throb between her legs catch fire. Her legs came up to wrap around Max's thick shoulders and her gut clenched, preparing for orgasm.

With her eyes clenched tightly shut, JC strained against Max's mouth as the first tendril of electricity wound its way upward, tearing through her with the same sharp clarity of last night. She could have never anticipated this kind of rush, this wave so intense she had no choice but to ride it as it pushed her over the edge.

JC came with a scream that erupted from her throat and tore at the silence of the room. Max groaned against her cunt, decreasing the pressure of his mouth as her lower body drifted back to the bed.

Gasping as Max covered her body with his, JC clung to his shoulders, digging her fingers into his flesh. His cock, hot and heavy, rested between them, but JC moved her hands down over the slope of his back to wedge between them, cradling his cock.

Now Max was the one to arch up, his neck stretched back, the bulge of muscle and veins rigid and pulsing. JC pumped him with slow strokes and Max's hips pressed toward her hand. She tugged him upward until he straddled her body, leaning back, jabbing into the warm tunnel of her hands. His balls were heavy in her hand, full and tight. Wetting her lips, JC led him to her mouth, As her tongue tentatively tasted him, Max gripped her head, ran his hand over her jaw.

She took him by slow increments, allowing the thick length to inch between her lips, tightening her mouth around him until she reached the base of his shaft. Max's finger slithered into her mouth too, rubbing against her tongue, slipping under it to caress his own rock hard flesh. Her nipples tightened, scraping against his ass that now sat on her chest, but Max repositioned himself. Remaining in her mouth, he swung his legs over her so he sat behind her, making her tilt her head back, allowing his entire cock better thrust. She tugged at him, moving her head up and down, swirling her tongue over him. Max leaned over her and pushed deeper into her mouth as his hands pulled her dress up over her breasts and cupped them. He gently pinched her nipples, groaning when she wrapped her arms around his waist and sucked at his cock with force, lifting herself up to take all of him over and over.

Max pulled away from her and yanked her dress off, throwing it to the floor impatiently and lying down behind her. Lifting her thigh, he pulled it to drape over his hip and in one forceful plunge, positioned his cock between her legs, driving into the slick passage of her cunt. The thick invasion made JC gasp in surprise -- it was so sudden -- but as Max drove into her, she found she wanted more. Harder, faster...

Reaching up, JC circled his neck, digging her fingers into his scalp, slicing through the silk of his hair, pulling his head to her neck. Her ass lifted against his strokes, her pussy clenched him, milking the steel between her legs. Max splayed his hand over her waist, moving her with him, pressing her firmly against his broad chest.

She felt his cock twitch within her. When his fingers drifted to her clit and his breathing was ragged, JC couldn't stop the rage of climax. It sucked her in as her sole focus became his cock, taking her to a place that was beyond what she'd experienced last night, beyond anything she'd experienced ever.

Max took his last stroke on a howl, a howl that muffled her own as she too responded to the call of her own need to let go. When she did it overwhelmed her, ripped through her, flooded her with searing heat.

JC clung to Max, her breath short whistles of air. Max's chest rose and fell against her back in a rapid rise and fall. His hands caressed her, roaming over her hips, stroking her thighs. "And to think you wanted to eat and run," he chuckled near her ear.

Silly, misguided her.

Chapter Eight

JC began to feel the cool of the air and the drip of the ever infamous wet spot, bringing with it the reality of what she'd done *again*. Her hand went to her eyes, covering them, and she bit her lip.

Max let go of a long sigh. "Now I know what you're thinking, JC. Cut it out," he said firmly. "We made love again and if I have it my way, we'll keep doing it."

Oh, God. This man was delusional. She was never coming back here again.

Suuure. She was, after all, really good at sticking to her guns, or his gun...

Max tilted her chin up, turning her to look at him. "Now don't start. I don't think you're loose, not even a little. I don't think you 'do' anything that moves into this apartment building and I'm not going to let you deny what's between us. So stop all of those thoughts that are racing through that pretty head of yours *now*."

Man, he talked good game.

"And I am not talking good game. Your prickly cynicism troubles me, miss."

Her tongue moved like it was mired in mud. "Max, I don't do this sort of thing. I mean we just met each other and I can't just go screwing men I hardly know and -- and -- oh, my *GOD*," she yelled, sitting up and ignoring the rush of semen from inside of her. "We had unprotected sex, Max!" JC scrambled to the edge of the bed, her stomach tight as panic settled in. "Not once, but twice!" JC jumped off the bed as if it burned her, taking the sheet with her, but Max followed close behind, following her to the bathroom. Oh, Jesus Christ in a mini-skirt! How could she have been so fucking stupid?

Max grabbed her by the shoulders and whipped her around to face him. His face was calm and that only served to infuriate her more. "I've been tested, JC. It's okay. Relax, it's not your cycle..." Suddenly he clamped his mouth shut.

Her answer came out on a high-pitched wheeze. "How the fuck do you know anything about my cycle?" *Her cycle...* he was right. She knew her menstrual cycle like she knew ice cream and potato chips around that time of the month. She'd just finished her period. Relief washed over her and then panic rose again as she realized Max couldn't know anything about her cycle.

"JC!" he commanded loudly, "look at me and stop freaking out. I saw your calendar in the kitchen. I assumed the skull and crossbones sticker on it meant your period just passed."

She began to laugh. That was exactly what it meant. Oh, thank the good Lord. JC leaned against him, sagging in relief. "You're right, but we still shouldn't play with fire," she mumbled against his chest.

His deep chuckle bounced off the walls in the bathroom. "I promise to buy condoms. Now about this tramp theory you have goin' on. Cut it out. I don't do 'this' as you call it, either. That's the God's honest truth. So, let's clean up and I want you to come back to bed with me. Tonight you're sleeping here, so when I wake up we can do 'this' thing you don't do after knowing a guy only a couple of hours, again."

"You are a very pushy man, Max, but I *can't*. Fluffy will be waiting for me."

Max rolled his eyes at her. "Did you leave the window open and some water out for him?"

JC nodded.

"Good because he probably won't come back until morning anyway. Now move that cute ass of yours," he commanded with a smile as he went to the sink and began rinsing a cloth. He handed it to her and turned to leave. "You're not going anywhere, so let's go."

The idea of sleeping near Max all night long held great appeal. The desire to lie pressed closely to him made her shiver. His forceful tone no longer cajoled her and she found herself responding to his demands. Nobody told her what to do, but when Max had it made her feel strangely safe.

JC cleaned up and wrapped the sheet around her, waddling back out to the bed where Max lay sprawled out. He oozed sex appeal as he patted the bed. "C'mere, woman, *now*."

JC had no will left to resist him as shaky, sex weary legs carried her to the bed. Climbing in beside him, JC snuggled closer to his side as Max enveloped her in his strong embrace.

Well, this was A-okay. He was warm and hard and... her

neighbor that she'd known just over a day.

Max shook her gently and chided, "Stop thinking that. By tomorrow it'll be like you've always known me."

Oh, good, she thought as sleep crept in, *that would cut out a lot of time consuming crap the getting to know you process presented.*

Oy.

* * *

JC woke to the sound of Max's harsh, whispered hiss.

"I said okay, Derrick. You know, I honestly don't know what you all would do if something really bad happened. Tell Eva to quit with the hissy fit. I'll be there later today and then do me a favor? Tell her to stop eating so much damn chicken soup, otherwise I won't be able to keep up. I love her, but she's making me nuts with her prophecies."

JC sat up with a bolt of energy. Who was *Eva*? Her eyes narrowed. Max had a woman, didn't he? Well, didn't that just figure? And she was sick because she was OD-ing on chicken soup.

Pig, pantywaist, jerk.

JC was just about to blow his Popsicle stand when Max bounded into the bedroom with a grin on his face and pounced on the bed beside her.

She didn't even realize she'd dropped the sheet from her breasts as she said through clenched teeth, "Who's Eva, Max?"

Max leaned over and enveloped a nipple, teasing it to a tight point with the skill of his tongue. He dragged his tongue over it and JC moaned. "My grandmother," he said after another hot lick. "No, I'm not married. No, I don't have a girlfriend. Now quit being so suspicious and be quiet because if I don't put this," he grabbed her hand and ran it over his cock, hard and pulsing, "between your legs soon, I'll explode." With that he pushed her back to the bed and sat between her legs on his haunches, spreading them wide.

JC felt the heat of his gaze sweep over her naked flesh. Max leaned over her and kissed her, sliding his tongue between her lips just as he drove his cock into her.

JC whimpered, welcoming the hard thrust by wrapping her legs around his waist and stroking his tongue with hers.

Max's sinful groan against her mouth mingled with his carnal words, "Christ, JC... you're tight and so wet," made JC's heart pound and her hips rock against his. It wasn't long before his forceful thrusts brought her to climax, a gentler release than last night. Burying her face in Max's neck, she inhaled the clean, showered scent of him as he tensed within her and came too.

When they both were able to breathe normally, Max's eyes sought hers. "I have to take a ride back home. Wanna come?"

JC's heart thumped in her chest. "Today?"

Max nibbled on her lower lip. "Yep."

"To see your family?"

He grinned. "Yep."

What man asked you to go meet his family after only knowing each other for two days?

"I thought we might spend the rest of the weekend there. Come with me. It'll be fun. You'll love my family."

But he lived in a cabin or something with no microwave or cable television. There were bugs where he lived. Icky bugs and maybe even spiders. JC fought a shudder from under him.

"I take it you're worried about the bugs and gross stuff, right?" He chuckled. "I promise to kiss it and make it all better if you get bitten."

Well, sure that made up for all the other gross stuff in the woods. JC liked the city, she liked Hoboken, and she liked her salon, but she liked Max almost as much. What could a couple of days hurt? But, Fluffy... she couldn't leave him for two days. "I can't leave Fluffy, Max. He needs to be walked and fed. As a matter of fact I have to go home and check on him now." Whew, a narrow escape indeed. JC found she wasn't one hundred percent sure she wanted to escape.

"I took care of him this morning."

"He came home?" Relief overwhelmed her.

Max nodded, his eyes crinkled in a smile. "I told you he would. He came through the window, I guess. He ate and when I left he was sleeping. See? All taken care of."

JC pushed at his shoulders. "He can't keep running away like this. I'm going to have to tie him to something if he doesn't cut it out. The vet said maybe neutering might help his wandering,"

Max snorted as he withdrew from her and headed to the bathroom. "I think that would be cruel. He should breed if you ask me. He's magnificent."

JC's heart swelled again. Max liked her dog and her dog liked Max. Why this mattered to her, she couldn't say. She only knew it was like she'd always had Fluffy and it was important for the man she was involved with to like him too.

Whoa. *NO* involvement with the man-tramp. But a trip to the country would be refreshing if Max was going. How bad could it be to spend time with his family? "Well, you wouldn't have to raise the puppies and find homes for them. I can only have one animal according to my lease," JC reminded him.

JC heard the water running in the bathroom. Max popped his head out and smiled at her. "C'mon, I started the shower for you. You can think about coming with me while you take one."

JC sighed happily. He'd started a shower for her... he was so different from any man she'd ever known. It made her all warm and fuzzy. It couldn't hurt to meet his family and spend the night. It wasn't like they were mating for life, right?

* * *

The ride to Max's family's house was beautiful. As the city grew to a distant dot behind them, JC found she loved the multitude of trees that were now almost bare from the chill of fall. Max held her hand in his lap as he drove and for JC it seemed like a natural extension of this relationship that had happened in two seconds flat. She couldn't put her finger on it, but it was right, at least for the moment. She'd decide for sure when it came to the icky bugs. She'd asked her upstairs neighbor to check for Fluffy. Max convinced her he'd be okay just overnight.

As they pulled into the long driveway of his mother's house, JC began to get nervous. There wasn't much around these parts, was there? Not a Blockbuster for miles. Did the pizza delivery guy even know how to get here? Though beautiful, it was very *rural*.

How did you get coffee in the morning if you didn't have a 7-Eleven? They probably grew their own beans and crushed them in big tubs with their feet like winemakers did.

Max ran a finger down her cheek and leaned over to peck her on the lips. "I know it's very different from Hoboken, but I think you'll like it. C'mon, my mom can't wait to meet you."

Max came around and let her out. JC wiped her sweaty palms

on her jeans. God, you'd think she was meeting Attila the Hun. Breathing the cold, crisp air, she absently watched the spiral of smoke from the chimney on the large house. It was fantastic, just the house JC would want if it could be smack in the middle of *Hoboken*. Then she could sit on the big wrap-around porch with her coffee and pizza just freshly delivered.

The big oak door opened just as Max touched the handle and a woman who looked a great deal like Max threw her arms around his neck. "I've missed you, kiddo. Introduce me to your girlfriend and come inside."

His girlfriend?

"Mom, this is JC. JC, meet Mom."

JC smiled as they entered the big foyer. It smelled of cinnamon and apples. "Hi, Mrs. Adams. It's nice to meet you."

Mrs. Adams enveloped her in an embrace, wrapping her chubby arms around JC's smaller frame. "Just call me Mom."

Max took JC's hand and pulled her away from his mother leading her into the big kitchen. "Mom, I've only just met JC. She might not be comfortable with calling you Mom just yet."

She nodded her raven head, but her blue eyes smiled. "She will be," she said knowingly.

Okay, what was wrong with this picture, JC wondered to herself. Max was hunk-o-licious. He must have brought women home all the time, but Mom sure was in a rush to hook him up. Either he really was a playboy and she was going through the "I want grandchildren" stage, or he had like some mental condition and he wasn't the catch he pretended to be. Wouldn't that just figure? Nearly everything about him was as close to perfect as it could get. He had to have a *glitch*.

JC found herself drawn to the big section of windows by the kitchen table. It had a window seat with cushions and pillows. She could curl up on it and read all day long given the opportunity. Peering out she saw a dog fly past the window. Circling near the edge of the drive he ran back up to the grassy area just under the window. He moved with the speed of lightning.

Jesus, he looked a lot like Fluffy, just a shade or two darker. Max came to stand behind her, circling her waist. "He looks just like Fluffy... you didn't tell me you had dogs."

Max chuckled. "I didn't have much time. We were otherwise engaged. I'm going to go see if I can find my brother. Will you be okay with Mom?"

JC thought about how much Fluffy would like it here. A place to run to his heart's desire. Acres and acres of it. "I'll be fine. She seems very nice. Go ahead and find your brother. I'll help Mom."

* * *

"I told you, Derrick, I haven't told her yet. How would you feel if you were JC?" Max ran a hand through his thick thatch of hair and slumped down in the chair.

Derrick, Max's brother, nodded his understanding. "I'm sure it's going to be hard for her to adjust. If you'd listened to Eva last year, you'd be all done now and have a pup or two. But, no, you put it off and put it off and now look. You have to hurry up and mate so that we can get this pack in gear."

Max hung his head. Granted he didn't want to be tied down last year when Eva'd read this prophecy in her chicken soup. But now that he'd met JC, spent some time with her, he understood the calling the others spoke of. He wanted her and he wanted her forever.

Derrick leaned forward. "Tell me, brother, do you want to have *that*," he pointed out of the back window, "to carry on our legacy?"

Max eyed his cousin Jerry from his chair. Poor Jerry... he just couldn't shift like the rest of them. He got -- well, he got stuck halfway between human and wolf form and nothing helped. So most of the time he wandered around in his human form, but when the moon was full, look out... Jerry was out there howling with the best of them, half man -- half wolf. No matter how hard he struggled, fists clenched and brow dripping with sweat, when he tried to fully shift, he ended up looking like he was constipated. Which in Max's humble opinion was better than poor, neutered Beau. Beau had been captured by the local animal rights activists and "fixed." Max shifted in his seat uncomfortably, but Beau was okay with being neutered, because he was *gay*...

And then there was Hector. Hector hated to hunt. Hunting the small animals of the forest, as he put it, "grossed him out," shudder, shudder. Hector liked the little rabbits. He said they were cute and fluffy, and he had a whole pen full that were off limits to the rest of the family. He *named* them, for Christ sake. Hector was also a vegetarian… what kind of wolf didn't like meat?

Wolves with issues, that's what kind.

Max and Derrick were the last of the pack with any hope of carrying it on. He loved his family, but they weren't your typical wolf pack. Not by any stretch of the imagination. They were a blend of anomalies, misfits to some. All of the other packs mocked them and with good reason Max supposed, but they were *his* pack -- good, bad or indifferent and he'd do what it took to keep the line going.

"Look, Derrick. I know I have to tell her. Imagine her shock when I shift for her. Not to mention the fact that she hates the woods."

Derrick scoffed, his chocolate brown hair shimmering as he shook his head in disgust. "You know, Max? It would figure your lifemate is someone who hates icky bugs! This is the most messed up bunch of wolves I've ever heard of. In all of wolf history, *we* have the only non-meat-eating, homosexual, afraid of small creatures, half-man, half-wolf. We're like the circus freak show. And all I have to say to you is -- you'd better get your ass moving because we need some hope here, Max, and *we're* it."

Derrick's tone was derisive at best. He loved and hated the ill formed pack he belonged to. Derrick wanted to be free to roam and do as he pleased. He didn't believe in lifemates. Unless it was Max's, then he was all for it because it meant he could screw whatever moved without fear of retribution.

They *were* the most normal of the bunch, Max conceded. "What do you want me to do, Derrick? Go out there and shift for her. Tell her her dog Fluffy is me? Jesus, she's going to think we're a bunch of loons."

Derrick got up from his chair and threw open the window. "Hector," he yelled. Hector looked up and smiled, holding out the small bunny to show Derrick. "Would you put that damn thing away?" Derrick snarled at him, but Hector stuck his tongue out at him. Derrick slapped his brother on the back. "Bud, take another look outside. What about *that* doesn't speak loon to you?"

Hector cradled his beloved rabbit, stroking its head and whispering in its big, floppy ear.

Max heaved a heavy sigh. Yep, he needed to tell JC.

Chapter Nine

Max found JC with his sisters in the family room, both with wet heads and towels around their shoulders. "Hey, Max." Avery waved and blew him a kiss. "Long time no see. JC is going to give us a deep, home remedy conditioning. She says we have split ends."

JC was busy digging her way through the thick, rope-like strands of hair on each of Max's sisters' heads. God, they had split ends out the wazoo. No one needed a deep conditioning like the Adams girls. They had wild, unruly hair that needed a great deal of care.

Looking up, she smiled at Max and he winked. JC's heart warmed in her chest and her nipples beaded tightly. He was undeniably sexy in his jeans and T-shirt. Spending the afternoon with Max's family was comfortable and easy. She'd chatted with his mother and drank the best coffee she could ever remember having. Max's mother hugged her often and told her how happy she was that Max had found her.

JC was more convinced than ever that he either had some kind of mental challenge that prevented him from keeping a girlfriend or his mother was just like most mothers. She wanted Max to settle down and have children so she could be a grandmother. What other explanation could there be?

Natalie smiled too, from beneath the curtain of midnight black hair that fell over her face. "Hi, Max. Thank God you found JC. She's a hair goddess."

JC giggled. "I think we can blow dry now. Do you have one?"

Both girls shook their heads. "Are you kidding? The nearest Wal-Mart is like two hours away."

JC cringed. No Wal-Mart. Good gravy. "That's okay. I have one in my bag. Max? Where's my overnight bag?"

Max held his big, lean hand out to her and pointed through the front window. "See that cabin all the way out there?"

JC nodded. "I'm guessing that's where my blow dryer is."

Max nodded again. "Yep. C'mon, it's not far. Ladies," he said to his sisters, "we'll be right back." Max kissed each of them on the cheek and Avery mumbled something in Max's ear that made him frown and shush her. He pulled JC away from his sisters and out the front door.

JC took a deep breath of the fresh air. "It really is beautiful here. Too bad there's no 7-Eleven."

"If you lived here would you miss the 7-Eleven?"

Fuck yeah.

JC breathed again. Max's mother's coffee was better than the 7-Eleven's. "I honestly have to say I was skeptical, but now, I don't know. I like the peaceful surroundings. I love the trees. I grew up in Hoboken, lived there all of my life. This is all new to me and so far, no icky bugs."

Max laughed again, "I told you you'd like it," he said as they followed the cobbled path to the cabin. "This is my cabin."

"You have your own cabin here? Why would you leave it to come to Hoboken?"

Max looked away and pulled her inside. "I told you, I have to do environmental stuff. Sometimes that takes me away from home for a long stretch of time."

JC cocked her head as they entered the warmth of the cabin. The fire was lit and welcoming. "What stuff?"

Max pulled her close to him and nipped her neck. "I help preserve wildlife."

JC's legs went soft and her neck arched to meet his lips. "What *kind* of wildlife?"

Max lifted her hair and nibbled her ear. "Wolves... I help to preserve their packs."

If she could think straight she might have frowned. Instead JC sighed as he worked his way to her mouth. "In Hoboken? There aren't any wolves in Hoboken."

Max began to tug at the button on her jeans and finally gave up. He jammed his hand into them, curving over the soft mound of her belly. He groaned against her lips when he slipped between the lips of her pussy, "How about we talk about this later? Much later."

JC's hips moved to the rhythm of his caress. "But your sisters are waiting..."

Max lifted her shirt and bra, pulling them over her head and kneeled before her. "They've waited this long for a blow dryer; they can wait a little longer because *I* can't wait any longer."

Well, okay… that was good enough for her. Bracing her hands on his shoulders JC dug her fingers into them as he pulled her jeans and panties down. No one had ever said these kinds of things to her. They made her feel desired and naughty all at once. Wrapping his arms around her waist he took her nipple in his mouth and swirled his tongue over it. Her sharp gasp echoed in her ears and her cunt immediately felt the wet sting of heat licking at it. Max rolled his tongue over her belly, licking his way along the soft flesh, and down over the tops of her thighs. His tongue slipped between her legs with ease, delving into her pussy in short precise strokes. JC's hips began to move in a slow circle, letting Max's tongue dip in and out of her aching cunt as his mouth moved against it. He dragged a finger through her wet folds, slipping inside of her, making her buck against his hand. Max pressed her close to his mouth, sucking her clit, taunting it with the rasp of his tongue.

JC came with the feel of his tongue in her pussy and his finger deep within her. Hard, sharp waves of silken heat stabbed at her, coursing through her in rushes of vividly sweet pleasure. Max nibbled until she caught her breath, then kissed his way back up to her mouth. "God, Max…" was all she had to offer. JC wrapped her arms around his neck and let him lift her legs, positioning them over his hips.

"I need to fuck you *now*, JC," he said roughly, his voice thick and hoarse. He unzipped his jeans and pulled his cock free. Without hesitation he gripped her hips and pushed her down onto it, driving hard into her.

JC screamed as he entered her, filling her, stretching her deliciously with his slick cock. Each time they made love, he seemed bigger, thicker, and it excited her that her body did this to his. She clung to his waist, wrapping her legs around and hooking her feet behind him. Her heels rested on his ass, and she pushed against it, encouraging him to thrust harder.

Max's lips found hers, savagely ramming his tongue into her mouth, tangling with hers as they rocked in a tight embrace. He moved them together without missing a thrust, bending his knees to sit on the chair and setting her atop his lap. JC tasted herself on his lips, lips that brought the most carnal of pleasures, lips that moved over hers with finesse.

Max moved his hips upward as he cupped her breasts and thumbed her hard nipples.

JC milked the length of his shaft, tightening her muscles as her clit scraped the top of his jeans, circling his cock with aggressive downward thrusts. She rode him fiercely, her head falling back on her shoulders.

Max came swiftly, howling her name and digging his fingers into her hips. JC came too, with the rise and fall of his cock in her. Slumping forward, JC rested her forehead on his chin and fought for breath. Max buried his hands in her hair and kissed the top of her head, his breath raspy too.

"Woman," he murmured into her hair, "I think you're going to kill me."

JC giggled. "I think in some states we're legally married now."

Max's head popped up and he frowned.

JC ran her hand down his face. "Hey, it was a *joke*." They'd known each other like two and a half days, what kind of booger sugar was he doin', thinking she was serious? Oh, wait a second, here it comes. The old let 'em down easy…

"JC, we have to talk."

JC lifted herself off of Max and tugged a blanket from behind his head with her, wrapping it securely around her waist. "No, we don't have to talk. Just tell me where the bathroom is."

Max pointed down the hall and JC hurriedly scooped up her jeans. "JC, we have to talk."

Yeah, she'd bet they had to talk. I like you a lot, JC. But I don't want anything serious right now. I'm the best lay you've had bar none, but I'm hittin' the highway to other chicks-ville now. Thanks bunches. JC didn't want to talk. She wanted to go home and see Fluffy.

Her heart tightened. Why did this upset her so? What did she expect after whacking a guy she'd known two days? God dammit, God dammit, God dammit. She rinsed off with the washcloth and pulled on her panties and jeans.

Strong hands gripped her shoulders from behind and JC swiped at the tear that formed in the corner of her eye. "We have to talk, JC, *now*."

"No, you redneck Rico Suave, you have to get your horse and buggy and take me the hell home!"

Max growled... like really growled and hoisted her up over his shoulder. "I said we have to talk. Now shut up and come with me."

As if she had a choice. Max flopped her back on the chair in the living room by the fireplace and sat opposite her. Just as she was about to protest, he held up a finger. "Don't. Do not say a word. I have something to tell you."

JC crossed her arms over her chest and sucked in her cheeks. He had to make her listen to him confess he was a player? Jesus.

"Okay," he began, "remember I told you I was into wildlife preservation?"

"Yeah."

"Well, I'm trying right now as we speak to preserve wildlife."

"What do I have to do with wildlife preservation?" The *wild thing* -- maybe -- wildlife -- um, no.

"Look, remember I said it had to do with wolves?"

"Yep." In sheep's clothing...

"I'm a wolf."

"And I'm Little Red Riding Hood."

"No, JC, listen to me. I'm a wolf."

"This is the most original breakup line in the history of breakups."

"JC, look at me."

"Haven't we done this look at me thing before?"

"JC, look at me, really look at me. I'm Fluffy..."

Despite the heaviness in her heart JC began to laugh, then she snorted, followed by howling shrieks of laugh-out-loud belly laughs. Clamping her hand over her mouth she wiped the tears of laughter from her eyes with the other. "Oh -- GOD -- this -- this is -- above and," JC paused to gather her breath, wheezing for air, "beyond the call of duuuuutttyyy," she whistled the last word because it was all she could spit out.

Max grabbed her by her shoulders and looked her in the eye. "Do you remember the trip to the vet with Fluffy?"

JC's brow furrowed. Yeah, it cost a small fortune. She nodded.

"Do you remember how much I weighed? One hundred and fifty pounds."

Oh, big fucking deal, she might have let that slip when her tongue was down his throat.

Max let out an exasperated sigh. "Do you remember Killer?"

JC gulped. Yes, Killer the feisty dachshund. She nodded again, eyeing him warily.

"Do you remember telling Fluffy that you couldn't resist me?"

Um, well, sorta…

"Do you remember me peeing on Jess?"

Hookay. Now it was time to go home. She didn't know what the fuck was going on and she didn't give a shit. He could have found those things out if he'd looked through a window in her apartment.

"But I didn't move in until the next day, *after* the incident with Jess."

JC eased back against the chair and pushed Max's hands away. "Um, look. I don't know what your gig is, but you think you're a *dog*, Max. A dog, ya know woof-woof?"

Max narrowed his eyes. "I am not a dog. I'm a *wolf*."

"And sometimes, in my fantasies, I'm the Little Mermaid, Max. I think you need help. Fluffy is a dog. A *dog* from the pound. *You* are a man who should be in a mental institution." And didn't that just figure? She knew it all along. His Clampett family back at the house was probably just as tweaked as he was.

"JC, I'm going to show you something and it's going to make you freak out. But before I do, I want you to know that these past two days have been the best I've had in my life. I'm falling in love with you."

Oh, good. That's nice. Just fucking ducky. A man who thought he was a canine was falling in love with her. He was every girl's dream come true. Max was just a little too fond of his furry friends, eh? "Yeah, Max, you show me. I'm going home now."

"*NO!*" he roared, scaring the living shit out of JC who cringed against the chair. His face softened again. "I'm sorry. Listen, JC… just watch. I'm going to do something, but I'll try and control it so it isn't a full shift."

Shift? He wasn't working a *full shift*. Oh God, she was going to die in this backwater cabin with a man who thought he was her dog Fluffy.

Max knelt before her and kissed her cheek, soft as a whisper. "I would *never* hurt you, JC," he said fiercely. "I can't stand your fear. Just watch and then you'll understand."

Petrified, horrified, mortified, all the "fied's" rolled into one couldn't describe how frightened JC was, but his reassurances, his kiss, soothed her and that couldn't be right.

Max rose and stood by the fireplace and rolled his neck on his shoulders, cracking his knuckles, he closed his eyes and took deep breaths. JC heard a crunching, a harsh cracking and then it happened... Tufts of gray and black hair sprouted from Max's face, and his nose elongated and grew to a snout. Each muscle in his body rippled, tensing and flexing as he appeared to fight the change in him.

Holy -- fucking -- werewolf...

JC took short choppy breaths. Vaguely she thought of Lamaze breathing techniques, just before she screamed.

Like loud.

So loud and long Max held his hands over his ears and shifted back, rushing to her side.

JC stuffed a fist in her mouth. The press of her cold, clammy hand between her teeth kept her from passing out.

"JC! Talk to me. Say something. Say *anything*."

"Tach me ome," she said around her fist.

Max ran his hands over her now cold arms. "What?"

JC moved her fist a bit, giving her tongue mobility. "I said, take -- me -- home -- *NOW!*"

Chapter Ten

The ride back to Hoboken was filled with a palpable silence, broken only by short sentences of explanation. JC couldn't speak if she wanted to. She wasn't prone to histrionics, but Jesus Christ! Max's jaw clenched and unclenched. His hands remained tightly fastened to the steering wheel.

When they pulled up beside their apartment building and Max came around to let her out, she pushed her way past him, running up the stairs and fumbling for her keys to open the door. JC didn't listen to Max call her name. She slammed the door and fell against it, heaving a sigh of relief.

Fluffy!

She remembered Fluffy and flew to her bedroom. The window was still open and his food bowl filled with the food Max had said he left for him. He would come back, she reassured herself. He would come home tonight just like he always did and it would be okay. JC tore her clothing off and found a T-shirt. It was Max's... she brought it to her nose, inhaling his scent. JC threw it on for lack of anything else to wear and wearily pulled back the covers of her bed. Burrowing under them, she slept with the scent of Max in her nose, blocking out everything else.

* * *

JC woke with a hard knot in her belly to the dark, cool of her bedroom. As her eyes focused on the room around her, the horror of what happened refreshed itself and sank in. Sitting up, she looked to the mat on the floor and then the open window. Fluffy was still gone... and somehow she *knew* he wasn't *ever* coming back.

Tears filled her eyes and anxiety tore at her throat. She would never see Fluffy again... Pieces of Max's words came back to her from their car ride back. He was sorry he had to tell her this way. Yes, he knew most people didn't believe in werewolves, but they really *did* exist. She was his *lifemate*... he knew this because a prophecy told him so in some kind of soup. It was how he was so sure he was falling in love with her, because Eva said so. At first he didn't believe it, he liked his life just fine without a lifemate, until she'd found him in the pound. Now, after only two days, he knew he didn't want to live without her.

He hated kibble…

JC choked back a laugh. *Kibble…*

Yes, if she would consider the possibility of mating with him, she'd have to come and live with him in the sticks of New Jersey. He'd do everything in his power to see to her happiness. No, she didn't have to become a wolf and no, he wouldn't rip her throat open if she refused. No, she didn't have to howl at the moon. Maybe she could open a beauty salon there… He was the Alpha male of the *pack*… it had to be her decision. He would never force her to do something she didn't want to do.

JC buried her face in her pillow. It was too much information. Werewolves and prophecies and lifemates… oh, my.

The next week was a blur for JC. She went to work and tried to focus on anything but what she'd seen, *heard*. But each night she came home and was greeted with the empty silence of her apartment. Fluffy wasn't coming back and neither was Max. When she came home mid-week, his apartment was empty and the next day it was filled with someone new. Another man, who waved and smiled cheerfully at her, saying maybe they could get together sometime.

No, she couldn't do that. No more sex with neighbors. For all she knew he was probably a vampire. How could she know who anyone *really* was anymore?

JC toyed with the soup in her bowl as the clock ticked in her kitchen. She hadn't heard a word from Max and now it was beginning to bug her. Actually, the numb calm she'd experienced was dissipating and replacing itself with a good pissed off. Where the fuck was he? How dare he dump this shit in her lap and then just leave her with her own fucking thoughts?

Oh, my God, what was she thinking? He was a werewolf! A fucking howl at the moon, rare meat eating, allergic to silver, bona fide fucking werewolf!

Rolling her head on her neck, JC paused. And so what? Okay, so he was just a smidge scary… oh, hell, he was a lot scary, but when had anyone in her thirty years made her feel like Max did? If he were a man, a fully *human* man, by now she'd have been picking out friggin' china and asking people to check off chicken or beef for the wedding reception.

She missed him desperately and he'd been a part of her life for a mere two days.

But, she'd have to move to the sticks of Jersey... leave her salon and her apartment... *leave her quiet, lonely existence...* What was the worst that could happen? They would fail at a relationship. He would bring a dead rabbit home to her instead of flowers?

How would she tell her parents?

JC jumped up and paced the floor, making plans in her head that didn't fully form because she couldn't keep a straight thought. The only thing she did know was that she and Max needed to talk, now that she'd had time to let the reality of this sink in. If missing him the way she did was love, if craving his touch was love, this was *really* love, then she couldn't let the opportunity slide because he was a wolf.

A fucking werewolf...

* * *

JC banged on Max's cabin door with a vengeance. God only knew how she'd found her way back to it. She could thank her good sense of direction and her need to talk to Max.

When he opened the door, she closed her eyes, hoping he was in *human* form.

"JC, look at me," he said quietly.

JC popped her eyes open and sighed. God, he was so fabulous... even when he was Fluffy she'd thought he was magnificent. Taking a deep breath she pushed her way through the door and stood in the middle of his living room. "Okay, we have to talk and why the hell haven't you called me? Don't they have phones here in Hooterville?"

He fought a smile. "Yes, they have phones, but you needed time to think. I wanted you to have it."

"Well I'm done thinking now. If I think much more I'll likely end up in a padded cell."

Max chuckled, but his hands remained clenched in fists by his side.

"So, I thought and then I thought some more and once the

shock wore off I thought again. This is how I see it. You are a wolf, a fucking wolf! You let me adopt you at the pound, fall in love with you as a *dog* and then you move in next door and make me think I'm a slut because I jumped your bones within hours of meeting you. What do you have to say for yourself, Max Adams?"

Max shrugged his big shoulders and gave her a sheepish grin. "I told you I didn't think you were a slut. That's just how it is with *lifemates...*"

"Max? This lifemate thing... how long have you known I was your lifemate?"

Max grinned again, the dimples in his face deepened. "Um, about a year."

"A year?" she said astounded. "And what about this situation," she pointed at the both of them, "could have changed if you'd done this prophecy thing a year ago?"

Max frowned. "Um, I could have given you time to adjust? Wooed you even?"

"Good answer, *Fluffy!*"

"So does this mean you're considering this thing between us?"

"Maybe."

"I'm going to have to do stuff, aren't I? Like buy you flowers and shit?" he teased.

JC burst out laughing. "We'll just have to see. I only know that I've missed you and your alter ego Fluffy, and I'm not as attached to Hoboken as I thought I was."

"The salon?"

"I talked to my partner. It's going to take some reworking, but if I do this lifemate thing she said we'll figure it out."

"So you'll stay..."

JC couldn't wait anymore. She closed the distance between them and threw her arms around his neck, kissing him soundly. "I *suppose* that could happen."

Max breathed deeply. "I've missed you too and we'll have to see what I can do to convince you staying is the right thing to do." He wiggled his eyebrows at her before he slipped his tongue between her lips.

JC moaned at the rush of excitement only Max could create. Her body began to settle against his and it was suddenly all right.

Max pulled away from her and cupped her jaw. "Oh and by the way, that cutesy sweetums bullshit sucked. *Sweetums*," he snorted at her, "nobody calls me sweetums."

"Yeah? Well you sure didn't seem to mind me calling you 'sweetums' while I was scrubbing your balls now did ya?"

He narrowed his eyes to keep from chuckling. "Well, that was a mighty fine scrubbing you gave my balls. Didn't you know all *dogs* like to have their balls scrubbed?"

"Oh shut up! What really pisses me off here is you LET me believe you were some mangy mutt. All the humiliation you suffered along the way -- as far as I'm concerned, you deserved it! I mean, I talked to you about *you*. How utterly absurd is that? You didn't play fair, Max, and now I'm considering moving to the woods and living with you and your pack of -- of wolves?"

Max nodded his head. "I know it's a lot to take in, baby. But I am what I am. You don't have to be a wolf too, you know. Though I bet you'd have a beautiful coat."

JC shook her finger at him. "Don't you try to appeal to the hairdresser in me, buddy. How the hell do I explain this to my mother? Hey, Mom, I have a new boyfriend. His name is Max and he lives in the country. Have I mentioned he's a wolf? Yeah, just like the kind you see on National Geographic. Nope, we don't need Halloween costumes here in the sticks, we have Max!"

Max laughed as he scooped her up and carried her off to the bedroom. "We have a lot to talk about, but could it wait? It's been a week since I've seen you and well, you know…"

JC giggled, "Yeah, I think I do know. Take me to your den and ravish me."

Just as they hit the bed, Derrick, the brother she'd heard about but didn't meet, burst through the door to the cabin, yelling Max's name.

"Ya know," he commented to JC as he kissed her, "I'm not sure how I feel about this Alpha thing if it means I have to take care of everything."

Derrick popped his head in the door with his eyes closed. "Can I look?"

JC laughed and Max said, "Yes, Derrick, you can look."

"I've got a big fucking problem, brother! Goddamn Eva and

her prophecies!"

Max jumped up from the bed, concern written all over his face. "What *now*?"

Derrick leaned back out of the door and picked something up. He showed it to JC and Max. "*This* -- this now." He held up a pet carrier.

Max's eyes widened. "What the --"

"-- Fuck?" Derrick yelped. "Yeah, you got it. Eva sends me off to the pound today with some mysterious bullshit about finding the blue container."

Well, JC thought, it *was* blue.

"And?" Max said hesitantly as he eyed the pet carrier.

Derrick narrowed his eyes and held up the carrier with two hands in front of Max. "And this is *my* fucking *lifemate*!"

Max and JC both peered inside the dark interior of the carrier. Something stirred, dark and shadowy...

"Meow..."

Special Thanks to the Lakota Wolf Preserve

The inspiration for this story came from several places, one being my love of wolves that began after a trip to the Lakota Wolf Preserve in Columbia, New Jersey two years ago. Please note, though I make light in my books, I take the plight of *any* animal very seriously. I gathered much of my visual information after my trip to the preservation and I will never forget a gentleman by the name of Dan Bacon, who owns and operates this fine establishment. His dedication, love and tireless efforts to care for these great, mythic animals extend beyond the boundaries of selfless acts. His story and how this preservation came to be isn't something you come across everyday. It remains with me to this day.

If you'd like more information on the Lakota Wolf Preserve, please visit http://lakotawolf.com/index.htm

Wolf Mates: What's New Pussycat

Dakota Cassidy

Chapter One

"Meow."

"Do you see?" Derrick Adams hollered as he held up the cat carrier, thrusting it in his brother Max's face. A black paw, claws unleashed, reached out to swipe at Max's face. Max reached his finger into the carrier's front. "Hey, kitty…" he cooed, making an irritating clicking noise with his tongue.

The paw reached out again, unsheathing its claws once more, and the cat carrier hissed. Max jumped back as the cage rocked in Derrick's hands.

Tell me, foolish one, what makes humans believe that we kitties enjoy a finger shoved in our faces? Bring it here, boy-toy. Lemme show you what pretty teeth I have…

Mortals were so unbelievably stupid, especially *male* mortals. Even if they were good looking, Martine Brooks thought. She felt the hair on her back lift in irritation as the silly human tried again to soothe her with a finger that might result in a bloody stump if he didn't back off.

He stuck his handsome face in the opening of the cage and purred at her. Martine yawned.

If only you knew how desperately stupid you look. Max, is it?

However, in order to keep from blowing her cover, Martine had to play the game. She'd yet to figure out what she was undercover for, but *whatever*. She only knew she shouldn't shift and she sensed that, even if she didn't know the reasons why. It did, however, mean *something* was preventing her. Be it intuition or premonition, she just knew her best bet was to remain in her cat form. At least for now until she could figure out what in all of creation she was doing here. Martine prepared for a good howl, thus indicating that the pretty boys should go away and leave her the hell alone while she waited to be set free and get some wide open space to shift in.

This time she got closer to the cage opening and howled for all she was worth into Max's face. As pitifully as her vocal cords would allow, just like she'd seen other cats do on Animal Planet.

"Maybe you should take her to your place and let her out of the cage, Derrick?" the pretty dark-haired girl said as she winced.

Well, duh. Very astute. A good stretch was just what she needed. She'd suffered as much indignity as one girl could handle in a lifetime.

The man named Derrick shook her cage. "Be quiet, would you! God," he complained, "she could wake the dead. So, Max, what do you intend to do about this?"

Max shook his head and slapped Derrick on the back. "Nothin' I can do, Derrick. Your prophecy is your prophecy. You know Eva's chicken soup."

Yes, it was good for the soul, wasn't it? What prophecy? Martine wondered.

Derrick held up the cage again. She really wished he'd stop rocking the damn thing. A hairball was bound to hurl from her throat at warp speed if he kept this up.

"This -- *this* -- is my prophecy?" Martine heard Derrick yell, disbelief lacing his tone. "How in all of the animal kingdom can *this* be my prophecy?"

Max shrugged his shoulders and the pretty dark-haired woman spoke again. "I didn't believe it either, Derrick, but who can say when you'll find love -- or with whom?"

Love? Um, no, no.

What was this, Mutual of Omaha? No love. Martine needed to get the hell out of this damn cage and shift so she could get the frig away from these people and their wing-nut prophecies. She believed in spells and stuff. No prophecies.

"Well, Derrick," Max said. "Guess what? She's all yours. Eva hasn't been wrong so far. Now go away. I have pups to make." The dark-haired woman giggled, rather flirty and stupid if you asked Martine.

But NO ONE was asking the cat.

"My lifemate is not a goddamn *cat!*"

Whoa... stop right there, hot stuff. Lifemate? Did these people dig into the catnip or what? She didn't have a lifemate. Martine belonged to a warlock and had for many years now, cursed to spend the rest of her life at his beck and call. Oh, Escobar was just gonna love this. She was Escobar's familiar and he wasn't going to be too pleased about this little turn of events.

"Wolves do not mate with *cats!*" Derrick roared and shook the cage again for emphasis. Martine's stomach lurched.

Wolves? Like woof-woof? Full moons and carnivores?

That was it. Martine couldn't stop the roll of her stomach. She heaved a long moment and then coughed, opening her mouth wide.

"And now, it's gonna puke," Derrick said sarcastically.

Ick. Martine gagged and finally relieved her throat of the ball lodged in it since this lunatic had stuffed her into this cage.

How's that for ya? A round hairball lay at her feet.

Whew, that was better.

Unattractive, but better.

* * *

Hookay, this was nothing like her kitty condo.

Martine scanned the rustic looking cabin Derrick brought her to. He came back down the short hallway carrying a towel.

HAH! No way in the universe was that as comfy as her pillow. She had a special one designed just for her. It was frilly and lacy and downright girlie, stuffed with feathers. No K-Mart blue light special was going to be her bed.

And that was that.

Derrick came toward the cage and hesitantly touched the latch. "Listen up, cat. If you scratch me, I'll make Chinese food out of you, hear me?"

Oh, the indignity of it all. Sweet and sour Martine...

Martine sighed and eyed the burgundy terry cloth towel as Derrick set it down by the fireplace. At least she'd be warm until she could get the frig away from this loon.

"Look, see this?" Derrick held up the towel as if she were a simpleton. "This is your nice bed. Go lay on it until I can figure out what the hell I'm supposed to do with you."

Do? There was absolutely nothing to *do* with her and she wasn't sleeping on of all things a *towel*.

No can do.

How had this happened? Where was Escobar? Martine couldn't remember a damn thing since she'd gone to take a nap yesterday afternoon. Next thing she knew she was peeking out of the wrong side of a cage and being dragged around like so much luggage. Intuitively, she knew she should remain quiet and so she had.

Until now.

Now she was fed up.

Derrick unlatched the cage and moved to the side quickly as though she'd rush him like a saber-toothed tiger. She was a house cat in her shifted form for heaven's sake. A domestic, if you will.

Sissy...

Martine decided to play nice as she gracefully hopped from the cage and stretched from neck to toe. Ahhhh, that was good. She approached Derrick swiftly, wrapping her tail around his calves as she rubbed up against him.

Martine experienced a small ripple of something she couldn't quite place. Hmmm, he felt oddly *good*. She arched her back and slid up against his legs again.

Oh... Well, now what the heck was this about? No one sent a shiver of nuthin' up her spine, let alone some werewolf, dammit! Twirling her black tail around his calf, Martine purred, hoping he'd stroke her back. Why she wasn't sure, but it never hurt to be friendly.

Derrick clomped his big, boot clad feet over to the small kitchen and began digging around in his cabinets instead. He produced a can of something and held it up to show her as she sat on the braided carpet by the fireplace.

"This is for you. I don't have much so don't get too excited."

What, no caviar? Fine, just fine...

As the electric can opener whirred Martine perused her surroundings. Derrick could certainly learn a thing or two about home décor. This place was about as stark as it got. Very manly, very boring. Thank God he didn't have deer heads mounted on the wall... but then if he was a wolf, he wouldn't hang one on his wall would he? He'd flambé it or something.

Martine's experience with other shapeshifters was limited to say the least. Escobar -- her warlock -- discouraged her from them. In fact, he discouraged her from much of anything but *him*. Escobar had taken her in after her parents' death -- cursed and all, but he frowned upon her socializing, especially with others of her kind. In order to stay with Escobar she had to remain in his circle of power where she was safe. So she didn't question it, but this -- this had to be some huge mistake.

Martine scratched her ear and forgot the niggling feeling that something was desperately wrong with this picture. Escobar would come to get her and all would be well.

Derrick strode over to her place beside the fire and dropped a can in front of her. "Here, I figured I'd better feed you."

How kind... Martine sniffed the can and turned her nose up.

Derrick bent down and looked her in the eye. "What's the matter? It's got bacon..."

He said it defensively as if it were caviar. Beans? Baked beans? She sniffed again... with *bacon*. That made the world undoubtedly all right again.

Martine swiped at his handsome face playfully, because well, he *was* handsome. Thick shoulder length hair the color of a black hole grazed his chin as he leaned forward to eye her dissatisfaction.

Whew! Nice lips, baby. Firm and not too full as to be botoxy. He had stubble, stubble she wanted to run her tongue over.

Um, hmmm.

This *couldn't* be something she should be thinking. She certainly hadn't before. Men came and went -- she had her playtime and then she made them disappear.

Literally.

Poof. Off to the land of the eternally quiet. No fuss, no muss -- absolutely no carpools and mortgages for this kitty cat -- *ever*.

"So what do you need to keep you quiet while I go hunt down Eva? A ball of yarn? Catnip?" Derrick asked as his green-blue eyes assessed her.

Martine turned, pointing her ass in his direction and swishing her tail. Yarn? *I should think not. Not unless you'd like to be tied up with it.* Now that held possibilities. Martine shivered.

"Okay, look, I'm going to go find Eva and her chicken soup. You stay here."

As if she had anywhere else to go. Martine stuck her nose up in the air and wandered off down the hallway.

"Hey!" Derrick called after her. "Don't even think about using the facilities until I've gotten you some cat litter. You hear me?"

With the scoop away formula if you will, please. Martine would have snorted if she could. Cat litter -- *indeed.*

Chapter Two

Martine spent the afternoon wandering Derrick's home. As she hopped onto his bed, she lay down on the pillow where he must rest his head every night, because it smelled *tres fantastique*. Just like he did.

Crimeny, how utterly sentimental and stupid.

As she scratched her back on the obviously cheap cotton sheets, she pondered this situation. Okay, so far, she'd heard about lifemates and prophecies, werewolves and some broad named Eva.

She had an innate premonition that shifting was not a good idea and Escobar was nowhere to be found. She couldn't even get a vibe from him.

So, essentially the math told her she was in deep kitty litter.

What to do, what to do?

Martine decided to take a peek outside and see what was what. As she jumped to the windowsill she got her first glimpse of her surroundings.

Trees, many trees. Snow covered hilltops and not a frickin' thing else.

A penthouse suite it ain't.

A man off to the left had a large cage filled with rabbits. He was feeding them, pulling each one out and cuddling them in his big hands.

Was he a werewolf like Derrick and Max? He must be if he lived here and he certainly looked comfortable in his surroundings. What kind of wolf played with bunnies?

The nice wolfie needed some carnivore therapy.

Martine let her head rest against the window pane and tried to remember how she'd gotten here. Having never left Escobar, she was at a loss for what was next. Did she have to live here forever with the cranky knuckle dragger? Martine shivered. Derrick was cute, but not cute enough to replace her kitty condo or her caviar. He was a *werewolf* for goodness sake. He couldn't keep her. It wasn't allowed. As far as Martine knew she could never leave her warlock and *that* was Escobar. She was cursed. If she didn't stay with Escobar bad things would happen. She didn't know what, but *bad* was the word Escobar always used when she asked.

Martine jumped down and meandered out to the kitchen again, eyeing the worn couch as she went.

Maybe she'd scratch it all to hell or something...

* * *

Derrick stormed into the main house where his mother greeted him with excitement. She clapped her hands and hugged him hard. "I'm so happy for you, honey! When are we going to meet your lifemate?"

Derrick narrowed his eyes at his mother and removed her clinging arms from his neck, holding her at arm's length. "Well, I suppose if you have any mice I might be able to entice her to come play for awhile."

Coreen Adams frowned and her hand flew to her throat. "Um, what?"

"Yes, Mother. My lifemate is a cat."

Coreen began to chuckle. "Really? I hope she's not Siamese. They can be snippy, you know. Is she one of those calico cats? Oh, they're so pretty, Derrick, but then again if she's a Persian, well they have spectacular coats. I mean --"

"Mother!" Derrick roared. "I have a cat for a lifemate, for Christ's sake. This can't be right."

Coreen clucked. "You know Eva. She's always right. Look at Max! He got the woman of his dreams."

"Mother, JC's *human*. That's just a bit less like the antichrist to a werewolf. We are canine, Mother. Canine as in we don't dig the little kitties, ya know? We're supposed to chase them, not mate with them!"

Coreen shook her finger at Derrick. "You know, you have a cousin who had a parakeet as his lifemate --"

"Mom! Stop, please. I can't take any more of our kooky family, okay? Just tell me where Eva is and I'll get this straightened out." Derrick headed toward his grandmother's portion of the house.

"She's not here, honey. She's in Africa. On some sort of Peace Corps mission I think."

The fucking Peace Corps? How the hell was he supposed to find out what was going on if Grandma was saving the world one bowl of chicken soup at a time?

Derrick shook his head. This was insane. How did he end up the Beta of this pack of whack-jobs? What other wolf pack anywhere had lifemates that were anything other than wolves? No wonder they were ridiculed far and wide.

Coreen came up behind Derrick and gave him a squeeze. "I know we embarrass you. I'm sorry..."

Yes, Derrick Adams, you are a first class asshole. Derrick gripped his mother's arm with affection. "No, Mom, don't be sorry. It's me. I do love you, you know that, right?"

"Of course I do. Don't worry, this will all work out and before you know it, you'll fall in love with -- with -- er, the cat."

Derrick closed his eyes and took a deep breath. No fucking way was he going to hook up for life with a cat or anything for that matter. He liked single and an *occasional* mingle.

Coreen turned Derrick to face her. "Now, how about a can of tuna for your sweetie? I bet she's hungry."

Derrick groaned.

* * *

Martine sat contentedly on the back of Derrick's couch when he arrived back home two hours later, carrying a brown paper bag.

Ahh, Neanderthal man had shopped. How quaint.

Martine continued to pump the back of the sofa with her claws -- a silent revolt against her current predicament.

Derrick began to unload cans by the dozen and stack them on the counter. Canned cat food? Martine narrowed her eyes. No canned food. None. Nada. A big fat no-no. No one was reducing her to eating processed gunk.

It was caviar or nothing and if he didn't produce it soon she'd hock up another hairball smack in the middle of his ugly, brown couch. If she could just shift she could go get her own caviar somewhere here in Clampetville. The really good kind and she couldn't remember the spell for it anyway. It was usually just *there*. In large quantities. But she didn't want to shift yet. Derrick was in for a big surprise if she did. It was better to toy with men -- they were simple creatures, after all.

Derrick came to stand in front of her with his hands on his slim, jean clad hips. "Look, I brought you some food and this." He reached over to the counter and bobbed a feather on a long pole in front of her. "See? This is what you claw to death. *Not* my furniture." Derrick shook the feather at her and ran it under her nose.

Martine backed away and cocked her head at him, letting her tail swat the air. A feather…

As if…

He grabbed another toy off the counter and placed in front of her paws. "It's a stuffed mouse," he stated. As though he'd given her the Hope Diamond and she was supposed to be like grateful or something. "Something to keep you busy while I figure this out."

Martine sniffed it, and then sniffed again. Oh, what was in *that*? She took another long whiff, nudging it with her nose.

It was simply *intoxicating*.

Martine picked it up with her teeth and dropped it down on the sofa, hurling herself on top of it. Scooping it back up with her mouth, she savored the rush of adrenaline it provided as she rolled around on the couch, thus falling to the floor in an ungraceful heap. Exceptionally unladylike.

But who gave a fuck? This was glorious! Almost better than champagne, Martine thought as she flew over the living room floor and skidded into the front door, smacking into it like it was home base and she'd just made the winning homerun.

Derrick chuckled. "Nothing like a little catnip to make everything seem better, huh?"

Martine heard the word catnip, but chose to ignore it in favor of the incredible adrenaline rush she was having. Grabbing at the mouse again, she set off running down the hallway and into the bedroom, where she planned to suck every last ounce of catnip out of her mouse.

Leaping for the bed, she must have misjudged her mark because she smacked into the foot of it and crashed to the floor.

As she lay stunned, Martine eyed the curtains that hung to the floor.

Now those would be very cool to climb…

* * *

Martine was exhausted. She needed a twelve-step program for catnip. Jesus, what a hangover. She lay sprawled on the cool oak of the armoire in Derrick's room, too tired to do much else but remain immobile.

When the door opened and Derrick entered, he eyed her, coming to stand over her all big and hunky like. His head just looking over the top of the dresser to peer at her.

Wow, he was dreamy... all brash and rough looking. Martine rolled on her back and wiggled seductively, then just as quickly rolled over and sat on her haunches. She shook her head. Obviously she was still residually affected by the catnip -- because her behavior was just a smidge shy of slutty.

"So catnip is the way to your heart. I see you had a good time." Derrick noted the shredded curtains and his bed all askew.

Martine purred with satisfaction that he'd noted her rebellion. *Take that for stuffing me in a cage and being audacious enough to consider canned cat food worthy of me!*

For the first time since they'd arrived Derrick took a finger and ran it under her jaw, scratching it. A shiver coursed down her spine. "Are you a shapeshifter or what? This makes no sense. How can my lifemate be a cat that I can't even talk to?"

Martine leaned into Derrick's solid hand. *Ask me if I give a crap about talking right now, Derrick.* Right now, *using* the boy-toy was all Martine had in mind. Why couldn't she shift now -- of all the times to fucking utilize a good skill?

Derrick gave her one last scratch and left, heading toward the bathroom.

Noooo. Come back... I have another itch.

Martine heard the water running and hopped down off the dresser. Oompf. She stretched her legs and shook off the lethargy. No more catnip.

Peering around the corner of the door to the bathroom Martine had her first glimpse of a naked Derrick. Her wee kitty heart sped up.

Oh-my-hell... As Derrick prepared to get into the shower he stretched, reaching upward in a long sweep of naked arms and bare torso. His skin was lightly bronzed, glistening planes of lickable ridges and valleys.

Yeah, baby… Martine's eyes strayed to his narrow waist and well, his *not so narrow* nether parts.

Holy shapeshifter!

Oh, he was perfection! Like nothing she'd conjured up in a spell before. Long and muscled, but not overly so, tall and as sleek as one of her own kind. His chest was broad and firm, a perfect place to hide when one needed shelter and he had thighs like redwood trees.

Martine panted and leaned against the door. She was weak with lust and she was going to have him. Even if it was in a roundabout way.

As Derrick soaped up Martine used every brain cell she had left after her catnip overload and tried to remember a spell she might use to have her wicked way with Derrick without him realizing. Martine was determined to show him she was more than just a cat.

She wasn't *always* a cat, only when the need arose and it had *arisen…* Under normal circumstances she was a woman who played hard and wasn't ashamed to feed her sexuality. Tonight would be one of those nights she indulged in the buffet of sexual activity -- and the hell with her premonition. She would shift and screw his brains out, then return to her cat form afterward. She could keep him in a semi twilight state. A state that made him aware enough to respond and was long enough for her to ride him to glorious victory and when he awakened, he'd think it was all a dream.

Chapter Three

Her long, supple body slithered over his firmly muscled one in the bed. Naked and on fire Martine crept over Derrick's sleeping form.

Okay, so it wasn't *totally* him offering acquiescence -- she was kind of invading his dreams, but whatever, Martine thought as she focused on her task at hand. Doing Derrick...

He stirred beneath her, the lower half of his body arching upward slightly as she straddled his abdomen, leaning over him and letting her long, black hair caress his chest. Her tongue snaked out, slipping along the firm line of his lips. She lingered on the soft surface, lightly licking.

Derrick moaned, his chest vibrating beneath her. Martine rubbed her pussy against him as she lay, her mouth over his, straddling his head with her elbows. The crisp hair at his belly grazed her clit, sending jolts of fire to her already anxious nerve endings.

Martine took his mouth in a slow possession, pressing her lips to his and slipping her tongue in to glide over Derrick's in a forceful stroke. His large hands found her ass, kneading it, gripping it as he enveloped her in his strength. Martine clutched his hair, raking her fingers into the thickness and pulling him deeper into their kiss. Derrick took command by suckling her tongue, sliding his own deeper into her mouth.

Martine pulled away, gazing down at the man who set her senses on fire like no other boy-toy in her recent boy-toy conjuring. His eyes were closed, but his hands roamed freely, moving to cup her breasts. Martine gripped his wrists as he gently pinched her nipples, turning them into tight, hard points. She lowered them to his mouth, gasping at the hot cavern surrounding them as Derrick cupped them together and laved them in wet, heated strokes.

Martine squirmed against his chest, rolling her hips as she pressed her breasts deeper into Derrick's mouth. He nipped at the tight buds, and sizzling sharp pangs of white lightning settled in her cunt. Martine pulled away roughly and lifted herself toward his mouth. His arms circled her, cupping her ass and pulling her to his lips. Lips that seared her as he pressed them flush to her aching pussy.

Derrick hovered for a moment until Martine grabbed a handful of hair at the back of his head and rammed her hips in the direction of the tongue that she sought with a frantic, fiery need.

His tongue slipped inside her, slick and hot, jolting her, making her groan with need. Her breath caught in her throat, lodging there as she bit her lip to keep from crying out. The dizzy effect of Derrick's tongue sent sharp pangs of white, hot heat to her pussy. As his lips explored her, Martine rocked against them, savored the slick rasp. Circling her clit, Derrick suckled it, keeping the swollen bud aching with desire. Strong hands reached up to cup her breasts. Twisting her nipples gently, bringing them to stiff peaks.

Martine's stomach clenched as the easy rhythm increased, creating friction, delightful pangs of electrifying need. Her back arched into the moist heat of his mouth as her orgasm drew near. Her thighs trembled and Derrick's hands reached for her waist, spanning her flesh, pressing her to his greedy mouth.

She came with the speed of light, hard and heavy, letting the heat rip through her body as she cried out. It left her panting and gasping for air that had become rife with sexuality -- thick with the tangible smell of need for release.

Martine slid back over Derrick's body, down over the rippled plane of his abdomen as he shifted his hips beneath her, jutting them upward against the pressure of her weight. Martine was dizzy with expectation as she neared the hard shaft that lay between thickly muscled thighs. Her night vision was superb -- even in human form -- and as she gazed upon Derrick's cock, it was all over but the crying.

Martine's chest tightened as she licked her lips, anticipating the slick, hot glide of tongue over flesh. Her heart sped up, racing in time with the electricity sparking through her veins with hot jolts.

Martine let her hair graze his cock, draping it over the rigid flesh, enjoying the sharp intake of breath Derrick took as she lingered, letting her hot breath caress him.

A long, slow swipe of tongue made his hips rise, bolting upward, and his hands found her hair, gripping at the long strands, threading his fingers through it as he pulled her to him.

Closer, Martine took her time, circling the head of his cock, licking it swiftly, lightly. Her hands cupped the heavy sacs of his balls as she teased him with her tongue. His skin was hot and sweet. She lapped at it, savoring the moans she heard from above her.

In a motion of catlike grace and desperate need, Martine enveloped Derrick's cock and he bucked, clutching her head tighter, her slow descent making the muscles in his thighs tense and bulge.

Gripping each thigh she kneaded them as she sat between them and allowed Derrick to glide between her lips. She tasted the surge of hard flesh between her lips and sensed his impending climax.

Derrick pulled out of the hot cavern of her mouth, leaving Martine disappointed. She'd hoped to taste him, the essence of him, but he dragged her upward with arms of steel and rolled her over, his hard length pushing her into the bed, his heavy weight delicious and thickly muscled against her own.

Martine arched upward, wrapping her long thighs around his waist as Derrick took control and thrust into her powerfully, as Martine gasped for breath.

His cock was steel in her tight depths, plunging with no mercy into the wet depths of her. Martine's pussy clenched around him, matching his thrusts as his arms scooped her up and crushed her to him.

Derrick moaned low in her ear, sending shivers up her spine and another wave of climax to her cunt, now on fire with a multitude of sensations Martine had never before experienced.

Martine frantically drove her hips toward the cock that filled her, stretched her, made her blood pound in her ears. Derrick hissed a breath in her ear and her hands found the muscled flesh of his ass, digging her nails into it as he swelled within her and found his release.

Martine rode the wave with him, as hips crashed together and a fine sheen of sweat slickened their bodies, gluing them together. Her nipples tightened sharply, scraping against his bare chest as she let go and came with a fierce yell.

Derrick's lips found hers in their final thrusts and he mumbled incoherent words she neither could understand nor wanted to.

She only wanted this man to stay inside of her forever -- or until she was done using him purely for the incredible lay he was. She couldn't have conjured up a lay this good if Escobar himself taught her the ultimate screwing spell.

As Derrick settled against her, his large frame sagging in release and soon, a sound sleep, Martine allowed herself the simple indulgence of a last roam of hands over his hard back.

Sighing deeply, she realized she had to shift back to her cat form. For now, anyway. Until she knew what in all of the animal kingdom this was about.

* * *

When Derrick awoke, Martine was perched happily upon the chest that had just last night pressed to hers with an urgent heat.

His eyes opened wide and Martine peered happily into them. Man, he was dreamy. It was time to say good morning to her newly acquired boy-toy.

"Meow," she offered as she eyeballed him, sort of husky and low.

Derrick wrinkled his nose and sneezed so hard it knocked Martine off his chest and onto the bed.

Derrick swiped at his tongue with his fingers. "Dammit, feline, I have cat hair all over me!"

Martine purred contentedly.

If you only knew, wolf man...

Chapter Four

Martine decided it was time to take matters into her own hands. Derrick didn't want a kitty for a lifemate and she sure as hell didn't want Derrick for life. Just for a couple of earth shattering, screaming orgasms... or ten. He had no clue what he was denying himself, and Martine was about to show him.

Martine style.

Hopping off the unmade bed, Martine crept toward the bathroom. Screw not shifting. She may as well reveal herself. After last night, she wanted Derrick to drool over her. Froth at the mouth so to speak.

She had a feeling Escobar would frown upon her shifting to her human form in front of anyone. According to him she wasn't allowed to do that because he was giving her respite from whatever curse she was doomed by. Escobar claimed he'd kept her hidden and safe. Martine had never asked why -- she simply did as she was told because Escobar said so. He was all she'd had since almost as far back as she could remember. Her memories of her parents were vague at best, riddled here and there with a hauntingly familiar scent and faint traces of a childhood now but a blur.

Escobar allowed her to indulge in her pleasures as long as she kept them quiet and, more importantly, private. Which she did. She conjured up many, many pleasures with the simple spells she'd learned from Escobar.

Okay, so sometimes the hotties she whipped up had trouble with King's English, but so what? Who needed a man to talk if he fucked like a house on fire? Mute was a good attribute in most men.

Martine suffered in the spell department more often than not, but it didn't matter. She didn't want to keep the men she conjured up -- just play with them and then they could go back to wherever she'd taken them from. The taken from part was a little fuzzy for her. Martine had no clue where they came from... When she learned to create a man, she quickly realized a real witch she'd never be. Her spells were weak and small compared to Escobar's, but they sufficed when in a pinch.

Derrick, however, was a whole new ball of wax. Sexually speaking he beat the crap out of even some of her best creations. Even the guy she'd managed to conjure up who looked just like Brad Pitt. He was hot all right, but he had this twitch that became irritating after a while.

Ah, well. Now Derrick was her mission. She planned to have him and have him again for good measure, then get the frig out of this strange place where there was no cable TV and jumping over a broom at sundown seemed to be everyone's favorite form of entertainment.

Unacceptable.

Martine peeked around the corner of Derrick's bedroom door and saw his coat was missing from the rack in the small living room.

Good. She needed quiet when she shifted. Total body concentration, and Derrick's presence didn't allow for that. Scampering off to the bathroom, Martine focused on her human form.

Which was going to blow farm boy's socks off.

The slight crunch of bone and flesh mingled with a long moan vibrated off the tiles in the bathroom. Martine rolled her neck on her shoulders and stretched her arms.

She took a quick peek at her nails and smiled. Thank God, she hadn't ruined her manicure with all of this nonsense. She'd bet it would be hard to find a good manicurist in this neck of bumfuck woods.

She took a good long look at herself in the mirror. Her almond-shaped green eyes held the anticipation of a sexual conquest who was actually a living, breathing specimen of the opposite sex. A first for her.

How cool was that?

* * *

Derrick popped open the door to his cabin and stopped dead in his tracks.

Holy hotter than Tyra Banks…

Green eyes met his from across the room, sizing him up with a bold stare and a brazen tilt to her head. Thick tresses of shiny hair the color of a moonless night hung in long strands over the breasts of a woman clad in his old flannel shirt. Perky breasts too, he thought briefly while he tried to remove his tongue from the roof of his mouth.

A raven eyebrow cocked over those green eyes, and her curiously silent lips, full and pouty, remained tipped in a knowing smile. Long legs swung over the small breakfast bar as she hopped up and over and seated herself at the edge of the counter. Her dainty feet hung loosely, swinging as she tucked his shirt around her creamy thighs.

A bead of sweat broke out on Derrick's forehead as he shifted his stance.

Jesus Christ.

"Meow, Derrick." A breathy, throaty voice filled his ears with a hint of a mocking tone.

Meow indeed.

Wait a friggin' second? Meow? This was the *cat*? *His* cat?

Aw, c'mon. No way. No freakin' way.

"What's the matter, Derrick? Did you forget to bring a new toy for the kitty to play with?" she challenged with a chuckle.

He swallowed hard. Speaking would be the obviously manly thing to do. He cleared his throat. "You are?"

"Here, kitty, kitty…" She smiled seductively, her glossy lips slipping into a pout.

"You're the cat?" he asked in disbelief. He knew his question was kind of squeaky and girlie on the way out. But for Christ's sake. Who knew that hairball would turn into *this*.

"That's me. The cat. The *goddamned* cat, as I recall you saying. I should be hurt, but I find myself willing to overlook that in favor of other, more important traits you have."

"Traits?" He was bewildered. By her scent, which, p.s. was making him fucking nuts, by her husky voice, by her finally shifting, by *her*.

"Yes, your traits, characteristics, you know? Like your ability to fuck."

Whoa, okay. His cock shot to the heavens as the verb fuck slipped over her tongue. The word had a whole new meaning said by lips like that. He still was unable to speak and that might be a good thing, seeing as he wasn't thinking clearly. "Fuck?" Oh, that was brilliant. Truly astounding construction of a sentence, Derrick.

She hopped off the counter and strode toward him with a graceful speed that was precise and deliberate. Her hair swung to her waist in cascades of brilliant black. His cock reached for the stars as she slithered nearer.

She came to stand before him and his nostrils flared with the scent of her hunger, thick and tangible. "Yes, Derrick, fuck. You are quite adept." Smiling she moved closer still. She was long and tall, her head just reaching the top of his chin.

Derrick looked down into the green eyes that mocked him, but he still struggled for words as he fought to comprehend what she was saying. How could she know he was adept... Holy shit! She was from his dream last night?

A cat? The cat? "Explain," he choked out in as much manly fashion as he could muster.

Her tongue ran lightly over her lips. "I said you are adept at fucking. You know, sex? I want to have more. Sex, that is. So I'll go get naked while you fumble for more than one word every sixty seconds, and then we'll fuck." Her words came out with a purr to them. She pivoted gracefully and headed down his short hallway as he stood rooted to the spot.

Hellloooo up there! Did you hear that? The kitty wants to fuck! Um, cock to brain -- you are on sensory overload. Snap the fuck out of it and go get 'em, tiger, er werewolf!

His *cat* looked like that?

Cat -- dog -- freakin' armadillo, buddy, she wants you. So take off your clothes and go get her. Like now, before I explode.

Okay... okay. He could do this. If the kitty wanted to play, he was all for it. How could he not be all for it? The sway of her hips alone could make a guy come. He wanted to know what made her decide to shift and why. But he wanted to devour her more.

The scent of her in his nose and the taste of her on his lips this morning when he'd awakened was something that had haunted him all day long. Smart man that he was, he'd never made the connection to the friggin' cat.

He'd thought it was just a wet dream.

And now he knew it wasn't.

He tore off his shirt with haste and went to stalk his prey, stake his claim, beat his chest in total Neanderthal fashion.

But not before he took off his shoes, he thought as he bent to unlace them, half hopping half tripping to the bedroom. He stopped at the door leading to his small room and inhaled sharply.

His *cat* lay on the bed with nothing but a smile on. His cock pressed painfully against his jeans.

Again, he was speechless and well, speechless. She was sinfully, decadently, fucking fabulous. Every creamy, sinuous, long, graceful inch of her. Her legs stretched for miles, lightly muscled and lean. Her feet were dainty and arched as she wriggled them under the comforter at the bottom of the bed.

Her name -- it might be good to know the name of the person/cat whose pert, round breasts he was ogling. Now if his brain could just send a signal to his good grammar skills… "What's your name?" Aha! He speaks.

Stretching her arms above her head in a sweeping arc that was both fluid and sensuous, she smiled at him. "Martine."

Martine… Hookay, good, now that the meaningless introductions were over he could really stare at her breasts and her nipples that were tight and flushed with color.

Martine smiled again and wiggled a finger at him. "C'mon, let's stop pussyfooting around so to speak." She patted the bed beside her and giggled, throaty and low. "Take off your clothes, Derrick, and come here."

Psssst, Derrick. Do what the nice lady tells you and let-me-out! As if mesmerized, Derrick tore at his jeans and threw them in the corner.

He approached the bed with less speed. It wouldn't look good if he behaved like an anxious kid in high school. Besides, no one else took control in the bedroom. He held the reins or it didn't happen.

"Derrick." Her tone held a warning.

Okay, maybe she could hold them for a little while, but then it was all about being a manly man. Derrick wasted no time as he lunged for her, straddling her long, lithe body with his bigger one.

She smiled again, that "cat that swallowed the canary" smile and reached up to place her small hands on his chest, kneading the muscled flesh.

His cock throbbed, burned, could beat a brick to death it was so hard. Derrick leaned forward to taste her lips, soft and full, sweet and tangy. He ran his tongue over them, let the soft plane of them seep into his light caress as she threaded her hands through his hair and pulled him deeper into their kiss.

Martine found his cock and held it firmly, gripping it in a gentle squeeze of soft hands and teasing fingers. He bucked over her, driving into the tunnel she'd created as his mouth devoured hers. She pulled him upward by his rock-hard shaft and tilted her head to lock eyes with him before she licked her lips and took him into her mouth with an agonizingly slow, deliberate slide of her tongue.

He clenched his teeth to keep the roar in his throat from erupting as she bathed him with her wet, warm tongue. Martine's hands found his balls, tight with need, and cupped them, rolled them gently in her hand as she rode his cock with her mouth. His legs tensed and his hips thrust to meet the bob of her head as she took him deeper and deeper. Derrick drove into her mouth as his cock burned and he reeled with his yet untapped desire, thick and hot, fighting not to come.

Derrick pulled from her mouth and winced at the cool air on his wet shaft. He could have stayed in her mouth forever, but she had places he wanted to explore with his lips and tongue and he couldn't hold out much longer with the kind of skill she possessed. It was mind blowing...

She whimpered as he pulled away, sliding down her body with his lips, over the slope of her shoulder and down to just the tip of her full breast, avoiding the tight nipple. Derrick let his tongue savor the underside of it as he teased her soft skin and she writhed beneath him, supple and firm when he began to plant hot kisses along each curve. Martine's hands wound in his hair, clutching him to her as he captured a nipple and tugged at it with firm pulls, running his tongue over the tip, laving it with long strokes.

Her long legs wound around him, urging upward toward the cock he wanted to ram into her, but he wasn't ready to succumb to her tight depths just yet. He needed to taste the slick cunt he knew waited for him. Her breathing was ragged as he cupped each breast, bringing them together and bathing each nipple alternately.

Martine bucked beneath him, mewling small, breathy sounds of delight when he let go and paved a path of tongue and lips over her firm belly, caressing her ribcage beneath his hands as he went.

Her scent, spicy and musky, filled his nostrils making his head spin and his tongue burn to lap at her wet flesh. Settling between her thighs, Derrick lifted her legs high and wide, exposing Martine's flesh to his gaze. He closed his eyes as the sight of her, the sheer power of his lust, made his gut clench and his body quake with need. He gripped her knees before running his hands over the silken expanse of her thighs, tracing a pattern of heated caresses. Derrick let his hands swoop down over her and rest between her legs, savoring the heat of her smoothly shaven pussy.

Martine's impatience became evident as she gripped his wrists, her hands small in comparison to his own, her skin a stark contrast of ivory against his own olive complexion. Lifting her hips she offered herself to him with a sigh. Derrick leaned forward and inhaled, devouring her hunger mingled with his own as he dipped an urgent tongue between the slick lips of her cunt.

Derrick heard Martine hiss and exhale sharply, her belly caving beneath his hands as he delved deeper, lapping the essence of her cunt. Finding her clit, he circled it with slow deliberation, wrapping his lips around the swollen nub.

Martine's hips rotated beneath his lips, lunging forward when his finger slid into her, gripping it as she clenched her muscles around him. Her depths were hot and slick and the taste of her juices sent a bolt of electricity from his mouth to his cock.

Impatient hands yanked at his shoulders, digging into the flesh as Martine drew him away and up to her again. As he hovered over her she opened her eyes and snaked her tongue out across his lips, obviously savoring her own taste on them. She purred, wrapping her arms around his neck and clinging to him, letting her nipples scrape his chest.

Derrick slid a hand under her back and rolled Martine to her stomach. She immediately lifted her perfect ass in the air, ready to accept him as she slithered the upper half of her body to lay low on the bed.

Derrick fought not to tear into her, his cock raging, pulsing with need. His hands found the smooth globes of flesh, round and firm. He squeezed them and Martine responded with a low, husky moan, so he kneaded harder, reveling in her taste once again as he feathered kisses over her ass.

Derrick positioned himself between Martine's thighs and swallowed hard. It wouldn't do to take her with the abandon he struggled to contain until he heard her whisper, "Fuck me, Derrick, hard. *Now*."

That was it -- he couldn't stop now if he wanted to. His cock poised at her opening only for a moment before he drove into her, hard and hot. She was slick and wet, tight and heated with the first stroke. She gasped from the force of his thrust, but when he hesitated, she hissed again, "Derrick, don't stop. It's okay, fuck me. I *need* you to fuck me!"

And he did.

Lights flashed behind his closed eyes as he clenched his teeth and rode her relentlessly, pushing into the silk that clenched his swollen shaft with a frantic rhythm. Each stroke he took she matched, driving back into him with a strength he'd never guess she possessed for one so small, but she took each thrust with pleasure, tightening her small hands into fists beside her head when he reached around her and fondled her clit.

Derrick's climax roared through him. From the base of his cock it shot upward, tearing through him with white-hot heat.

Martine shuddered beneath him, the slap of their flesh echoing in his ears as she came too. Derrick heard his own yell echo off the walls of his small bedroom as he growled his release, pumping into Martine until he knew she was spent too.

Her legs collapsed beneath her and he fell forward on her, her small body heaving against his larger one.

Jesus fucking Christ! he thought fleetingly as she nestled against him. Derrick remained as speechless as he had been since he'd first walked through the door. It was the most incredible lovemaking he'd ever encountered, bar none.

Better not to think of what that meant and focus on the fact that he'd just done a cat. Wasn't there like a law of nature that this was defying?

But, hell, cut a guy some friggin' slack already. Maybe this lifemate thing could be a cool gig for a week or so...

Chapter Five

Wow, wow, wow! Martine's head still spun from the magic that was Derrick. All six foot four *human* feet of him. Living, breathing and well hung too, she might add.

Nothing had ever compared to that -- not any man she'd made up, not even any two men she might have made up. He was a *GOD* and Martine couldn't wait to do him again and again and again... and then go home -- to her kitty penthouse with Escobar and never see Derrick again... Her heart tightened a bit at that.

Well, of course it did! It wasn't sentimental at all, it was *seximental*. Sorta like wishing for the sex you once enjoyed in your youth, but couldn't any longer because you just didn't have the stamina. Who wanted to give *that* up willingly? It had little to do with her heart and a whole lot more to do with her libido. Giving up sex like that would be heart wrenching.

Painful even.

She knew she didn't have a choice but to give it up and that was okay, kind of... not a lot, but kind of... this would have to end when Escobar found her and find her he would, but until then she wasn't going to waste anymore time pussyfootin' around.

Martine giggled at that -- stupid and girlie, just like she'd heard that silly woman of Max's do.

Nudging Derrick, she moved to leave the bed and clean herself, but he held her tighter and her heart skipped a beat.

This feeling -- this new and curious tug of emotion beat the hell out of her catnip OD yesterday. It was euphoric and empowering, leaving her vulnerable.

Um, no -- not vulnerable. Couldn't be a good sign. Cats were aloof and bristly, not vulnerable. "I have to clean myself," she said, "or would you prefer that your manliness leak all over the bed? I don't do sheets." Just in case he was wondering.

Derrick's chuckle skittered up her spine. "Wanna talk about this?"

Yes, this was definitely where the mute aspect of her "created men" came in handy. "Talk." She sat up and cocked an eyebrow at him. "About?"

Derrick let a big hand roam over her back in a smooth circular motion and she found herself leaning into it, enjoying it even. "We did just share something intimate," he reminded her -- as if she needed reminding.

"And?"

"And it deserves discussion."

"Do you talk to all of your little wolf chicks after boffing them?"

"Nope."

"So what makes me a warm fuzzy?"

"You are a *cat*."

Who just ate the canary, baby... "Yeah, meow..."

"How did you come to be? Where the hell do you come from?"

"This is important, why?"

"It's important because I'm supposed to be your lifemate."

Martine finally swung around to face him. His chiseled features were solemn, but his eyes teased hers. "Care to explain that theory to me? I mean, I'm a cat. How can a cat be your lifemate? You're a dog... What is a lifemate supposed to do other than the obvious I've gathered from the title?"

"I'm not a dog, I'm a *werewolf*. It's kind of a long story -- the explanation for why you're my lifemate, but a lifemate is just what the word implies. We are bonded by sources unknown to us for life."

"Really? And what source tells you this? Do I get a say in it? I mean, I don't remember anyone saying, 'Hey, Martine, want a lifemate today with your tender vittles'?"

Derrick laughed again, and his whole face changed as he did. Gone was the hard plane of his jaw, replaced by a grin and flash of white -- and she figured -- some very sharp teeth. "What do you eat?"

"Caviar, naturally."

"Caviar? You're kidding."

Martine snorted. "Well, it beats the hell out of poor Bambi."

Derrick slid his long, thick legs off the bed and rose, naked and unashamed, to go to the bathroom. "Speaking of Bambi, I'm starving. You?"

"Not for rabbit I'm not."

He laughed again and Martine's ears burned. "I was thinking more along the lines of stew."

Oh, whew. "Does stew have caviar?"

He poked his handsome face around the doorway, giving her stomach a small jolt. "That would be a negative. It has carrots and potatoes and venison."

Bambi... Martine shrugged her shoulders and grabbed his shirt from the chair beside the bed. "It'll have to do, won't it? It's not like I have a choice, now do I?"

Derrick swatted her on the ass as he passed her and headed toward the kitchen. "C'mon, lifemate. I'll teach you what the great outdoors is all about."

"It better not include hunting down my cuisine. Do you hear me, Derrick?" she yelled after him. Martine shuddered in distaste. Totally not going to happen. She didn't even hunt mice.

Derrick's laughter rang in her ears as she followed him out to the kitchen to eat stew. She shuddered one more time for good measure.

* * *

Okay, so stew was quite pleasant. It wasn't escargot, but it was pleasing enough in a rather simple way.

Oh, hell, who was she kidding? It was fantastic! She smiled as she slathered more butter on her fluffy dinner roll.

"Not bad, huh?" Derrick asked as he watched her lick her fingers.

"It's adequate."

Derrick offered her more. "Want some more adequate?"

She held her hand up just as a small burp escaped her lips. "No, thank you. I think I've had enough."

He smiled that cocky grin. "Yeah, sounds like it."

Martine pushed away from the small table and went to stand by the fire in the living room. She was warm and full -- it was naptime. Sitting on the floor, she stretched and then curled into a ball, luxuriating in this new, if not simple pleasure of total body satiation.

Sex *and* stew. Did it get any better? she mused as she drifted into a contented sleep.

She felt, rather than saw, Derrick's large presence as instinct told her he was near, his solid frame somehow reassuring in the madness that this adventure was. Warmth crept over her, comfort lent to a peaceful security she couldn't ever remember experiencing in all the time she'd been with Escobar.

Derrick's hand toyed with her long strands of hair, brushing them from her face as he knelt near her. "We need to talk, Martine."

"Shhh, I'm sleeping."

"Where do you come from?"

"Not here, that's for sure."

"I kind of assumed that. No one who lives here eats caviar."

"Then they are as Bohemian as I first guessed."

Leaning over her, Derrick cupped her chin. "Where do you come from, Martine."

A little information couldn't hurt, right? "New York. A better question is how did I get here, farm boy?"

"I picked you up. Eva's prophecy told me to pick you up off the Jersey turnpike. You were at a rest area in a carrier."

Jersey? Of all the utterly foul places to be dumped! Jersey? Wasn't that the land of the Sopranos and polluted oceans? "Jersey? How did I get to Jersey?"

"I was hoping you could tell me that, feline."

Sitting up she crossed her legs and looked Derrick in the eye. "I don't know. The last thing I remember I was in my penthouse. I have no clue how I'd get to Jersey!" Panic began to settle deep in her gut. How could Escobar have let this happen? He was her warlock, for crap's sake! It was he who said she couldn't ever leave him. "Okay, this makes no sense at all. Tell me about this prophecy nonsense. What does it mean, anyway?"

Derrick sighed, his big shoulders heaving. "According to my grandmother Eva, you are my lifemate. She reads prophecies in her chicken soup. She read Max's and he found JC who isn't a shapeshifter like you at all. I was next in line, I guess. I'm the Beta of my pack -- it stood to reason I was the next sucker."

Martine's eyes narrowed. "Sucker? My being your lifemate makes you feel *suckered*?"

"Well, it is a little beyond the realm of believability, don't you think? A cat and a werewolf?"

"What's the matter with cats?"

He winked at her. "Well, nothing... *now...*"

Oh, sure, now that he realized his kitty could fuck like a bunny... "Look, there has to be some kind of mistake, so until we can figure it out we'll just -- just -- oh, I don't know what we'll do! We'll just wait it out until something happens. Like this prophecy comes to an end." Or Escobar showed his cowardly face and whammied Derrick with a spell or two. "And what is a Beta anyhow?"

"Second in line to the Alpha -- the Alpha being Max."

The idiot who couldn't keep his finger out of her face? "Forgive me if I don't get this pack crap. I'm just a mindless ball of fluff. Explain the pack thing."

Derrick leaned back on his haunches. "We're not that much different than a family, I guess. You come from a litter, I come from a pack. Granted we're not the most normal in a long line of packs, but we are family. We stick together. My duties as Beta are to carry on the line of my pack, just like Max's are."

Groovy. Well he wasn't carrying it on with her. "Okay. Thanks for the explanation. Maybe you could just give me a ride back to Manhattan? Tell Eva or whatever her name is this is some big mistake. Maybe she was reading Dim Sum at the time and got confused. I'm not your mate -- life or otherwise."

Derrick shook his head firmly, his thick, black hair falling around his face. "Eva is never wrong and I can't bring you back. It would be going against the prophecy and legend says that's a no-no."

Legend? What fucking legend said a cat and a werewolf should mate for life? Whoever wrote that was smokin' wacky weed. "So you won't take me back to New York?"

"Nope. I don't tempt fate. It's you and me, cat woman."

Life? Cats had nine of 'em... Oh, God. "I'm not your lifemate, Derrick. It just doesn't make sense. It's impossible. I'm a shapeshifter, yes, but I shift into a kitty, not a werewolf. Can you imagine what our children would look like? We'd be a circus sideshow. No, this will never do. I want to go home, tonight."

Derrick's hard jaw tightened. "Look, I'm just as freaked out by this as you are. I like single. I like it a lot and I sure as hell don't want a *cat* for a lifemate!"

Oh, nice way to talk to your lifemate. Way to woo a girl. Wait a minute. Why should she care if he didn't want her for a lifemate? "So, if we're in agreement about the lifemate thing, why wouldn't you want to risk this legend in order to save your single-ness?"

"Um, no. I may not agree with Eva on this, but I don't fuck with fate. Let fate change its mind all on its own. Until then, I'm going to keep doing what I do and hope Eva comes back from Africa soon."

Her prophecy sayer was in friggin' Africa? Didn't they have like a number she could be reached at? "This is ludicrous. I don't want a lifemate. Tell that to fate!" she yelled angrily.

"That makes two of us, Garfield!" he yelled back. Except he was louder and Martine didn't like that. Not one bit.

Martine jumped up and stomped off to Derrick's bedroom, slamming the door behind her and hurling herself on the bed. Garfield indeed! She was much more like the pretty Fancy Feast kitty...

* * *

Strong hands cupped Martine's breasts and she purred, arching into them as a solid chest warmed her from behind.

Derrick... his hands were delicious even if he *wasn't* her lifemate. They could be fuck buddies until it was time to go back to New York.

Her arms wound around his neck as he lifted her shirt and caressed her ribs. His cock prodded her, thick and stiff against her spine.

It did things to her insides that probably shouldn't be happening between fuck buddies, but who gave a shit right now?

Derrick's hand, broad and hard, slid between her thighs, dipping into her already wet cunt. A ripple of pleasure shuddered over her sensitive skin, on fire with his touch. His lips found her ear, nibbling it, rimming the shell of it with his tongue. "I have an idea," he whispered, making her shiver with his low, husky tone. "Seeing as I'm so *adept* and, well, you don't seem to mind telling me so, what say we play this by ear?"

"And what do you mean, 'play it by ear'?" Did this mean they could be fuck buddies? Oh, yippee skippee!

His thumb found her clit and began to roll it gently to a swollen nub. "I mean, why not enjoy each other's company until Eva shows up and explains this -- or whatever is supposed to happen, happens."

Martine felt the curve of his hip nestle hers as he raised her thigh over it. Like she could say no when that luscious cock was poking at her from behind. "So I just stay here and be your plaything until fate takes its course? The prophecy is fulfilled?"

Her hands found his hair and she clenched it, gripping the thick locks as he spread her wet flesh and hovered at her passage. "I'll be your plaything too..." he offered back, letting his words trail off as he slid into her.

"Ooooh, good, be -- be-because -- Iiiiiii -- onlywanttodoyou... oooohhh," Martine cooed, because words were becoming impossible as his thick cock stretched her deliciously. It was right and wrong and right... and all of the things it had never been before with anyone else. Of course all of her "anyone else's" had been men she'd conjured up -- so she had no other comparisons to go on. Maybe all real, live, human men were like this. Maybe they were better.

Derrick cupped her ass as he took her with slow, precise thrusts of his hips. "So shut up and do me," he chuckled in her ear.

Hookay. She could do that. Focusing on nothing but his cock, Martine thrust her hips back at him and shuddered at the sensuous slide of heat against heat. The friction was carnal and sweet, and her pussy ached with a pulsing need for release.

Derrick's hands roamed over her thighs gently. Gone was the urgency of the night before and left was something more tender and as yet undefined in Martine's sheltered world.

She gripped his head to her shoulder as she came. A simmer that turned to a burn erupted in her, wending its way from her toes to her ears. Blood rushed to her ears and made her head swim as Derrick came too, moaning his release in her ear. He wrapped his arms around her waist, tightening his grip on her as he spasmed inside of her, his thick cock jerking as his thrusts slowed.

Martine's chest rose and fell rapidly while Derrick lavished kisses over her shoulders. "Well, boy-toy. I guess you'll do in a pinch," she teased.

"Yeah? Well, you're not so bad yourself, for a cat."

Martine rolled her eyes. "I'm a finicky one too, so you should consider yourself lucky."

Derrick pinched her ass as he withdrew from her. "Well, get your finicky ass in gear. Mom wants to meet you."

Martine's hackles rose. "Oh, no. That wasn't part of the deal. We are fuck buddies -- not betrothed."

"Okay, but if they come beating down the door and decide to camp here in the bedroom I can't be held responsible."

Good gravy... "I can't meet your mother. I have no clothes."

"JC sent some over. She's rounder than you and shorter, but they'll do," he replied as he strode to the bathroom all hard and muscled.

How charming. "Fine. Let's meet mom. I can tell her what I think about this lifemate business and she can call grandma and tell her this ain't happenin'."

Derrick threw a wad of clothes at Martine. "You can tell her whatever you like. Mom has deaf ears. Eva's word is gospel."

Oh, good. Great, peachy keen.

Where in all of hell was Escobar? she wondered as she held up the knit sweater, running her fingers over the K-Mart special.

It wasn't cashmere, that's for sure.

* * *

"Oh! Derrick! She's lovely," a short round woman exclaimed as they entered the big house that was rather warm and inviting, despite its rustic qualities. Derrick hugged the woman Martine assumed was his mother. "Mom, meet Martine, Martine, Mom."

Martine was enveloped in a warm hug that she couldn't have avoided if she tried, yet somehow didn't mind. Martine often wondered if her own mother was anything like the moms she saw on television. "It's nice to meet you too, Mrs..." Her words trailed off as she realized she had no clue what Derrick's last name was.

Derrick bent down and whispered, "Adams. Coreen Adams."

Martine's creamy skin flushed and her pert nose twitched. "Er, Mrs. Adams."

Coreen Adams took her hand and smiled. "You can call me Mom. Now come in and sit down and tell me all about yourself. What kind of cat are you anyway? Persian? I was telling Derrick that I thought you might be, but seeing you now, I'm not sure." She cocked her head as she assessed Martine, her chubby hand gripping Martine's lightly.

Martine's heart tugged a bit. She wasn't even bothered by the prying questions when under normal circumstances her sharp tongue would have sounded off by now. Martine laughed. "I'm a domestic, actually. It's a long story best left for a quiet moment to explain."

Yeah, like how did you tell the mother of the man of your horizontal wet dreams come true you had no intention of explaining anything. You just wanted to fuck and run… best not to reveal, Martine thought.

Coreen Adams patted her hand reassuringly. "Of course, how silly of me. There'll be plenty of time to talk now that you're finally here."

Derrick gave his mom a kiss on the cheek and smiled at her. "Yeah, Mom. Give Martine a break, let her adjust. Heard anything from Eva?"

Yeah, Mom. How is Eva? And why was Derrick in such an all fired rush to hear from her? Humph. Fine, just fine… he wanted out as much as she did.

Good. Very good.

Coreen waved Derrick off. "How should I know? You know Eva. She doesn't call, she doesn't write, she just does as she pleases and shows up when a prophecy floats into her chicken soup."

This prophecy shit was way big with this bunch, huh? Helllooo… Although, she supposed it was as important to the Adamses as Escobar's chants and spells were to him.

Derrick hugged his mother's shoulders. "Okay, Mom. Why don't you get to know Martine and I'm going to go hunt down Max."

Coreen winked. "I think he's in the study. He and JC *finally* came up for air. We'll have new pups soon. Count on it."

Derrick chuckled. "Good, Mom. I'm glad you're so happy."

Pups? Was that like a litter? Good thing Derrick didn't want a lifemate as much as she didn't want one. No frickin' way was she having anything that might ruin her figure. Especially a dog… er, werewolf, er -- wait, what the hell would they have if they had offspring?

It'd be like a bad episode of that cartoon *Catdog*…

Derrick nudged Martine. "Look, JC's outside with Hector. Maybe you could get to know her a little. I think you'll like her."

Did fuck buddies make friends with their intended schtupp's in-laws? Martine let herself be led into the fold that was known as Adams, each reluctant step less hindered by the gentle persuasion of Derrick's mother, who coaxed her with the promise of a bowl of cream…

Somehow that gave Martine a pleasant glow that while unexpected, was just a tiny bit welcome.

Chapter Six

Derrick made a hasty beeline for the study where Max was supposed to be. He was totally freaking out over this whole Martine thing and he needed to figure it out. Max would help. He would help or Derrick would give him the ultimate in noogies.

"Well, well, look who's surfaced for some air," Max mocked as he looked up from the football game he was watching.

Derrick snorted. "Like you should talk, boink-master."

Max gave him a cocky smile and nodded. "Yep, that I am. So how's it going with the little woman? Have you given in to your prophecy yet?"

Derrick sank into the chair beside the couch and shook his head. "This is pretty fucked up, Max. I mean how can a cat be my lifemate? We have the most screwed up pack in the universe."

Max cocked an inky black eyebrow at him. "Ya know what, Derrick? I used to feel the same way you do. I inherited this bunch. It's my job to see to it we reproduce -- as if that weren't a big enough friggin' feat -- it's also up to me to keep this crazy crew in line. It's not easy, you know. But to top things off I have to watch your ass too when your position in this pack is to help me. Not hinder me. All you do is bitch and moan about *you*. What about the rest of us? Why is everything about you? I know we aren't like other packs -- we have some pack members that are a little left of center, but so what? Does it mean we're any less loyal, or for that matter strong?" Max shrugged his shoulders. "It's all about appearances for you, Derrick. It always has been, but for me, now anyway, it's about solidarity and leadership. I love my family, regardless of their 'issues' and I love JC. If I hadn't listened to Eva I wouldn't have found JC and *that*, I wouldn't have missed if you gave me a normal pack with fucking whipped cream on it."

Derrick sighed. His brother was head over the proverbial nookie and someone had to knock some pack sense into him. "Max, JC is *human*. It's a bit different than a cat."

Max leaned forward and eyed Derrick. "On the contrary, know-it-all. She's very different. She doesn't shift at all. She doesn't hunt with me and she sure as hell isn't baying at the moon once a month. Your kitty --"

"-- Martine," Derrick cut in. It pissed him off that Max referred to her as anything but. Then it pissed him off that he gave a flippin' shit.

Max flipped Derrick the bird. "Martine. It's a pretty name. I've heard she's as pretty as her name."

Pretty? She was drop-dead, heart attack inducing fantastic. Pretty seemed less than appropriate when describing Martine. "She's okay."

"Well, whatever she is, she shares a common bond with you that JC and I don't share. She can shift. JC can't."

Derrick ran a hand through his hair. "But JC could if she wanted to. She could become one of the pack if you took it upon yourself to do it."

Max clucked his tongue at him. "See, all you do is think about yourself. JC has to *want* to and if she does, we'll explore that. If not, I'm okay with it. I don't want her to do anything she doesn't want to."

Wasn't that very free love like?

"Where does Martine come from anyway? Has she talked to you about it? Does she have family she left behind?"

"I dunno…" Goddamn, that sounded shallow. It *was* shallow.

"Did you ask?" Max prodded.

"Sort of."

"Sort of? Are you starting to understand what I mean about you, Derrick? In my personal opinion you don't deserve a lifemate. You're too wrapped up in all that is Derrick."

Derrick clenched his jaw. "Look, I asked, but she didn't tell me much and all I know is I picked her up in a rest area out of fear for this legend crap. She doesn't want to hook up for life either, you know."

"So how about you pry? Coax, wheedle. You can do it if you really want to. If you don't, I can't help you."

Derrick had to admit he was curious. But not a lot -- well maybe just a step up from a little. "I'm not asking for help, Max."

Max cocked his dark head at Derrick. "No? Well, I am, bud. I want our line to go on forever and I want to do it with the help of my family. In order to do that I have to reproduce and so do you. You once said to me that it was just you and me. You were right."

Derrick looked away from Max's hard glare. If only that was the problem. He wanted to complete the act that led to reproduction with Martine. Over and over until he banged her right out of his system. When he was buried inside of her he felt something he'd never felt before meeting Martine.

And he wasn't liking it. It was free falling and he wanted his feet on the ground. "You could reproduce enough pups to carry on the line, Max. You don't need that from me," he offered lamely.

Max nodded, his face hard and unyielding. "Yep, you're right. So go on back to Derrick's world and I'm going to go find my woman." Max rose and strode to the door. "Oh, and when you're done with Martine," he said over his shoulder, "do us all a favor and be nice to her. Let her down easy. And make sure you duck. No telling what a broken prophecy will do to a guy…" Max waltzed out the door on a chuckle that rang in Derrick's ears.

He was a selfish putz, but it wasn't like Martine was game for this lifemate thing either.

She wasn't… she said so… she did… he'd heard her.

And now, that very fact was sitting in his stomach like an anchor.

Fine, if she didn't want him, he didn't want her either.

Not much…

* * *

Martine smiled at JC. She was really very nice. It was kind of fun to sit and talk about girl things. Martine had never had a gal-pal.

Just Escobar.

She was beginning to wonder why she never questioned the curse thing. Why it meant she couldn't ever have friends or *real* lovers.

JC came from a city too. Hoboken -- Jersey. Jersey didn't seem so low class to Martine anymore. JC was nice and she was *human*. A rather peculiar experience for Martine. Humans weren't that much different than she was.

Dakota Cassidy: Wolf Mates

Martine found herself smiling as Max came up behind JC and hugged her from behind. "You must be Martine," he said over JC's dark curls. "I'm Max. Sorry about the finger in your face on our first meeting."

Martine giggled. "It's okay. It happens, I guess. Yes, I'm Martine. It's nice to meet you on equal footing."

Max chuckled. "Derrick treating you okay?"

He was treating her to the sexual escapade of a lifetime, thank you. Martine smiled again, slower and with hesitance. "Yes, I'm fine, thanks. Derrick has been very nice." In a *canned* cat food kind of way.

Max nodded. "Good," he said firmly. "If you need anything at all, you just let me know. I'll be happy to help out."

This was her opportunity to ask for a ride back to New York, but Martine found it didn't seem as important as it had yesterday, or even this morning. Her stomach fluttered. "Thank you, Max."

Max smiled again, a smile that reflected his brother's, except it wasn't quite as yummy. "If you don't mind I'm going to whisk JC off for a nap. You tired, honey?"

JC tilted her head up to look at Max and laughed at him. "Yeah, wolfman, I'm beat. C'mon, let's go *rest*." JC's cheeks flushed with color. She looked at Martine and grinned. "It was really nice meeting you, Martine. Come down to the house tomorrow and we'll talk some more, okay?"

Martine smiled back, just because the idea of spending more time with another woman was something that appealed to her. "I will. You two go *rest* up. Bye." She wiggled her fingers at them as she began to make her way back to the big house that held Coreen who was loving and smelled like apple pie.

Derrick caught her on her way up the steps. "Wanna take a walk?"

Martine's heart did a flip that would rival a Romanian gymnast. Good heavens, what was this about? Instead of analyzing it, she acquiesced. "Okay, sure."

Derrick held out a big hand to her and she placed her smaller one in it, ignoring the sizzle of heat that screamed up her arm and went straight to her breasts. Her nipples tightened painfully.

Damn! All of this sex stuff was going to chop off, at the very least, two of her nine lives. Martine scanned the cloudless blue sky and inhaled. It wasn't so bad here. It was quiet. No police sirens or ambulances screeching through her cat naps.

"It's pretty here," she commented lightly.

Derrick nodded. "Yeah, I love it. Do you miss the big city?"

Well, truthfully, what was there to miss? She never left Escobar's apartment. She didn't need to. What she knew of the city was what she'd gleaned from watching the Travel Channel. "I won't lie and say I don't miss caviar, that's for sure, but no, not too much."

Derrick stopped her along their path to his cabin and pulled her to sit beside him on a fallen tree. Martine's nose twitched at the new scents that surrounded her. Fresh and crisp was how she would best describe it.

"Tell me about where you come from, Martine. You didn't just happen."

Did fuck buddies get to know one another? Martine sighed. What was the point of not telling him? If Escobar wanted her to keep her yap shut, he should have rescued her by now. It wasn't like Derrick wouldn't understand. He was well versed in the sublime. "I belong to a warlock. I'm a familiar."

There. Now it was out in the open. *Have at it, farm boy.*

Derrick's eyes narrowed. "A warlock? Like a witch?"

Martine twirled a strand of her long hair. "Yep. A witch, well he's male so he's a warlock."

His eyes grew narrower. "Male?"

Martine was growing impatient under the Gestapo's flashlight. "Yes, Derrick. He's a man. A nice man, who's like a father to me. He saved me from a curse. Took me in when my parents died."

Derrick's face softened. "I'm sorry. What kind of curse?"

This was where everything became a blur for Martine. "I don't know a lot about it. Escobar forbids me to speak of it. I've been with him for as far back as I can remember."

"Escobar being the warlock."

"Yes."

"Explain the word *familiar* to me."

"It means I am a source of energy to a warlock or witch. I sort of lend my energy to his spells."

Derrick brushed her hair from her face as the chill wind picked up and she automatically leaned her cheek into the caress, then pulled away because this was so not okay. "So you can cast spells?"

Martine shook her head and decided to be honest. "Not very good ones. I've learned a thing or two from Escobar, but I never produce the entire package, so to speak." Or someone with a package like Derrick's.

"Where is this Escobar?"

Good fucking question. "I don't know. You'd think by now he'd have tipped the witch world on its axis trying to find me, but nothing."

Derrick's gaze pierced hers. "So how did you end up in a rest area on the turnpike?"

Okay, now he was irritating her. If she had the answer to that she'd be the Amazing Kreskin. Jesus Christ with all the questions. "I don't know. Don't you think I'd tell you if I did?"

His eyes became dark. "Well, I don't know. You seem awfully secretive. You've been here almost a week and the better part of it was spent as a cat. Could be you're hiding something."

Yeah, she was hiding something? Please. If only she could own something as mysterious as that. Martine was beginning to think staying in her cat form had its perks. "You know what, farm boy? I didn't make you come and get me. I don't even know how I got where I ended up. So gimme a break. I didn't ask to come to the hills here and share your outhouse!"

Derrick's shoulders began to shake as he laughed. "Okay, okay. So you don't know anything about how you got here. Chill out. C'mon, let's go back to the cabin. You'll catch cold."

Martine thought that was a fine idea. She stalked off up the path that led to Derrick's "Martha Stewart's answer to a decorator's dream" cabin with quick strides. Like she'd ever ask to end up in a place like *this*.

Jerk.

Stupidhead.

Bunny killer…

* * *

Martine was in the kitchen when he got back to the cabin. He'd admired the graceful sway of her fired up ass from behind as she stomped off in a fit over his questioning her existence.

She'd tied her hair up in a knot at the top of her head and silky strands kept falling around her face, escaping it. The fading light from the kitchen window gave her an ethereal glow that twisted Derrick's stomach into a knot.

Well, hell. It didn't hurt to admire the fact that she was beautiful, exotic, sensual, now did it? No. It was perfectly okay. He'd admired other women for their beauty...

Yeah! He had, so Martine was nothing special.

She was plainly ignoring him as she poured herself a glass of milk and averted her eyes to look out the window.

And this bugged the shit out of him, why?

Squaring his shoulders, he set off to placate the nice kitty. Whoever had said cats were moody must have had one as a lifemate. After all, it made sense to keep the peace between them. It meant more nookie.

"Martine? Look at me and stop behaving like a two-year-old," he demanded.

She slapped her glass of milk on the counter and put a hand on her hip. Hips he liked to hold when he drove into her. His cock stiffened and pressed against his jeans. "Oh, you mean me? The cat? Look, my furry friend, I have no clue how I ended up where I did and your insinuation that I did is really tweaking me! If I knew how to get back to where I came from do you think I'd choose to stay with you? Hah!"

Ooooh, she *was* tweaked. And he liked it. Her pheromones were flying around the room like flies on a hot July day. He sauntered over to her, not that he could help but head in her direction. His shaft was like a homing device. Her anger was pretty sexy and the blood was pumping on an all points bulletin through every available vein in his body.

He hovered over her and looked down into her green eyes, dark with anger. "Yeah? Well, I would take you back if I knew where 'back' was. I can't just dump you at the rest area."

Martine folded her arms over her chest. "And why not? You've taunted me with catnip and cheap canned cat food. What's a rest area dumping in the scheme of things?"

Derrick folded his hand around the back of her head and tilted it backward, gripping her hair in a firm, but tight clench. Their lips were but a breath apart. Her pert breasts just touched his chest and they were heaving. She was pissed. He widened his stance to encompass her legs, giving off a signal that was loud and clear, and fighting its way out of his jeans. "I don't do drive-bys." Their breathing was harsh in the silence of the kitchen, rasping in short, choppy beats.

Her tongue slipped over her lips. "Let go of me."

"Nope."

"If you don't…"

"You'll *what*?"

"Put a spell on you."

"Oooh, big, bad familiar that you are."

Her hands began to push at his chest and then changed course and gripped it. "That's right. Don't you forget it."

"So go ahead. I *dare* you."

"I wouldn't if I were you."

"Well, I just did. C'mon, kitty. Whammy me."

"I don't feel like it."

"Chicken."

"Cat, thank you."

"Whassamatter. Afraid?"

"Of a dog? Fat chance."

"Werewolf, thank you."

"Same difference."

"Big difference."

"Says you, furry one."

"Look who's talking."

"I'm not a long-haired cat. Furry implies long hair."

"Nope, you're not."

"Do you like long-haired cats better than short?"

"Only in their *human* form."

"I *do* have good hair, don't I?"

"You wanna talk product or fuck?"

"Do I have a choice?"

"Always."

"Fuck."

And that was all it took for initiative. Derrick dove for her lips and Martine didn't stop him. She devoured him back, suckling his tongue, dancing with it as her arms that had been pressed to his chest wound up around his neck.

Her body melted into his, fusing them together. His hands tore at her clothes, ripping the buttons on the sweater JC had loaned her so they scattered to the floor. He cupped her breasts as she drove her own small hands into the waistband of his jeans and stroked his harder-than-hard length.

Derrick heard his moan as she milked his heated shaft, vaguely aware of the fact that he didn't moan a lot in his illustrious career as a Casanova.

Tearing his lips from her, he allowed raw hunger to consume him as he pulled her head back to expose her neck. He seared a path of tongue and lips over the long column of it and ended at her nipple. Derrick let his hot breath linger over it, watching it tighten before placing his mouth over and inhaling.

Martine collapsed into him, pressing her breast further into his mouth. He took long licks of each nipple as he let go of her head and jammed her pants down around her ankles, leaving her naked and exposed, but for the shirt that was left hanging around her shoulders. Martine ripped at the button on his jeans and unzipped him with trembling fingers, releasing his cock and gripping it with a fevered caress.

His nostrils flared with the sweet scent of her cunt, he smelled the musky wetness, and his fingers burned to touch her. Derrick lifted her as he felt her jeans fall away, stepping over them as she wrapped her legs around his waist and gyrated against him, lifting herself high against his body.

He gripped her ass, kneading it, grinding her to him as he carried her to the counter, blindly reaching for the edge with one hand outstretched. Derrick set her on the cold tile and Martine bucked against the shock as she settled, scooting the lower half of her body toward him and leaning back on her elbows.

Her green eyes were glazed, shiny with anticipation as she matched his gaze. "I need to lick you, Martine." His body tightened harshly as he heard his words. Saying them, having the freedom to say them without her shying away made his cock scream for her and his head muddled with nothing but thoughts of consuming her, possessing every last inch of her, owning her...

Martine lifted her legs to place an ankle around each of his shoulders and arched her slender spine upward, offering herself to him. "Then lick me, Derrick."

He pulled her forward roughly and slipped his hands beneath her ass, holding her to his mouth. Her legs clenched around his neck as his tongue took its first taste of her. His senses exploded when he took the first long stroke of her flesh. Wet and hot, it glided over his needy tongue with a rush that left his taste buds on overload.

Derrick fought to slow himself. He would scare the shit out of her if he let himself be carried away by this fire that was burning him from the inside out, but Martine pulled his head to her, pressing her cunt flush to his tongue. She trembled beneath his tongue, arched into it, ground against it as he laid it flat over her clit, then swirled it over the swollen nub.

Dragging a finger between the cheeks of her ass, he found her slick passage and inserted a finger, pushing and pulling away in forceful strokes. Her pussy clenched him as her hands clutched at his head and she rode his tongue.

Derrick tasted her release, reveled in it as Martine yelled his name and her legs tightened around his neck, her heels digging into his back.

Derrick let her catch her breath, ragged and harsh, before removing his mouth from her and standing up. He needed to catch his too. He might hurt her and it troubled him to consider it. He stood between her creamy, long thighs and caressed her skin, letting his hands roam over her ribcage, cupping her small breasts, thumbing her nipples, fighting his hunger as it washed over him like high tide. He trailed a finger back to her cunt, slipping into the wet warmth, then back over her belly, along her throat in slow increments until he reached her mouth. He leaned over her, pressing his still jean clad cock to her as she wrapped her legs around his waist. Opening her eyes, she licked his finger, taking in Derrick's heated gaze as she suckled him.

He kissed Martine then, with hungry need, outlining her lips with his tongue, and she clung to him, digging her hands into his hair. Reaching between them he yanked his jeans and underwear off and she let go of his neck to run her hands along his back, molding him to her.

She was sleek and hot beneath him as she rose to meet his hips, letting his cock spread her flesh, tease her clit.

Derrick entered her with more force than he wished, grunting as she jolted from under him and he stilled himself, but she held his face in her hands and locked eyes with him. "I like to *feel* you in me, Derrick. I'm not ashamed to tell you I want to be taken, hard. You won't hurt me. I share your same desires. So *take* me, Derrick." Her breathy insistence made Derrick's cock swell within her.

Derrick bracketed her head with his arms on the cool counter as he pulled back and drove into her satiny heat. He gritted his teeth. "Christ, Martine. I don't want to hurt you."

Martine kissed his cheek, his forehead, and coaxed him by saying, "You won't hurt me, Derrick. I promise." She raised her hips again, moving away and rolling them back up to meet his.

He couldn't stop now if he wanted to and so he ignored his fear and pressed into her once more, hard and slick. Martine's eyes slid closed and her neck arched as she took the harsh thrusts with a long, throaty moan. She encouraged him and Derrick lost himself in the sweet oblivion that was Martine.

Her abandon as she met him stroke for stroke made him dizzy with lust, brimming with heat as it raced to his cock. Martine's small hands stroked his back, clutched his ass, driving him deeper into her, and she whispered his name in his ear as she panted. Taking her lips again Derrick felt his muscles ripple, tense and scream as he held on by a thread. "Come with me, Martine," he said against her lips as he felt her pussy clench his cock, milk his length with her strong muscles.

Martine whimpered and tightened her grip on his shoulders, bowing her back and screaming out her pleasure. Derrick exploded inside her. His seed poured, hot and thick from his cock as he threw his head back and howled.

Jesus Christ was his only thought as he tried to catch his breath. This woman... she was like no other sexual partner on the planet.

Every curve of her meshed with his in completion. Her sexual appetite matched his own carnal hunger.

Christ... this woman...

"Hey, farm boy. Help the poor kitty, would you? You weigh a ton and the tile is cold on my back."

Derrick didn't want to withdraw from her body yet, so he slipped his arms under her and cushioned her spine. "Better?"

Martine smiled that seductive little half-smile that made his gut clench. "Much, thank you," she said as she squirmed beneath him.

"Done with the hissy fit?"

She cocked an eyebrow at him. "I guess."

Derrick chuckled as he lifted her to a sitting position. "You like me, admit it."

"I won't. I like your *cock*."

"Yeah, but you like *me* just a little and you know it. You just can't admit it, *feline*." Derrick scooped her up and off the counter, carrying her to the bathroom as she draped her arms over his shoulders and shook her head.

"I do not."

Kissing the top of her head he realized it was suddenly important for her to *like* him, not just lust for him. Which was fucked up, but as he brought her to the bathroom and warmed a cloth with water to clean her, he also realized he'd never stuck around long enough with anyone after sex to care if they liked him. He'd never wanted to and even though they had been drawn into this by Eva's wacky prophecies -- Derrick still wanted to spend more time with her. His past lovers meant little to him. They were for the moment -- he didn't worry past pleasing them in the heat of passion and then he went along his merry, single way.

Shit.

After cleaning them both, Derrick took Martine back into his arms and carried her to the bed, pulling back the covers. He laid her down and crawled in beside her, pulling her close to his side. Martine sighed softly, burrowing next to him and slinging a leg over his thigh. He found himself possessively giving her a goodnight kiss on the tip of her perfect nose and tucking the covers around her. Warmth, sweet and slow, suffused every pore in his body, creeping toward his chest where it settled in like a bear in hibernation.

Oh, hell.

He was *fucked.*

Chapter Seven

Martine woke with the hard press of Derrick's back to hers and smiled with pleasure.

Then frowned.

This was so not good. Not at *all*. His touch was becoming familiar and his presence, gulp... welcome.

This was *not* the fuck buddy she'd planned on.

Derrick was a player too -- he didn't want her any more than she wanted him -- not forever anyway and certainly not in a way that had anything to do with the mundane -- like watching television. So it wouldn't be good if she ended up wanting -- wanting anything more than a good lay. Best she'd ever had in fact -- or whipped up in a pinch.

Stretching, Martine crawled out of bed and grabbed Derrick's shirt, pressing it to her nose before she threw it over her head. He smelled of the outdoors and some cologne she'd always identify with him if she ever smelled it again.

Shit. This was the girlie, stupid, he's all that and a bag of chips thing she'd seen on afternoon soap operas. Minus the fact that he probably wasn't her uncle's brother's cousin. Silly women, swooning over some tall dark hunk who was destined to break their hearts in an episode down the road.

Derrick was a werewolf.

She was a cat.

Here, kitty, kitty...

Martine squared her shoulders and went to find something to eat. She was ravenous after their night of lovemaking and all screwed up in her head about it.

She had to go back to New York.

Soon.

Her heart clenched at the thought of leaving here and it tweaked her. Dammit!

Fuck buddies didn't have any qualms about waving goodbye over their shoulders and avoiding the door that might hit them in the ass on the way out.

Sex.

This was just about the sex.

Martine sniffed Derrick's shirt again and shivered. Okay, so it wasn't *all* about the sex. There was more. She wasn't sure what *more* was, but it was *there*. In the pit of her belly, in her clogged throat, in her heart that was clenching painfully at the thought of going back to Escobar and her life of kitty condos, caviar and badly produced men.

Derrick was a full body tingle. A roller coaster ride. A rush of adrenaline. A soft place to fall...

A dangerous mixture of emotions Martine was unable to define seeped into every pore of her body nonetheless.

And she wanted *more*. More of Derrick in any way she could get him. She wanted to experience every last emotion -- painful or otherwise with him. Even if it meant when Escobar came calling she had to go back to something that seemed less like a life and more like a prison.

Martine made up her mind right then and there.

Full steam ahead.

Derrick or bust.

* * *

Derrick woke with a smile on his face and instinctively reached out to find the warmth of Martine's slender body, but came up empty and that left *him* feeling empty.

Shit.

The emotions he'd experienced last night holding Martine in his arms flooded him, leaving him overwhelmed. Protective, possessive and pissed that he was all of those things -- were high on his list of priorities at this point. Derrick set that aside in favor of finding Martine.

His body tensed as he realized maybe she'd left. Would she go back to New York alone? Jesus Christ, would she do that? Just take off in her cat form and risk possibly being killed by something along the way?

Derrick bolted upright in the bed and reached for his jeans on the floor, throwing them on and zipping them haphazardly as he stormed out of the bedroom door. He stomped down the hall and blew into the kitchen to stop abruptly, catching sight of Martine at the kitchen table.

She took his fucking breath away, with the sunlight streaming in, glancing over her black curtain of hair. She sat at the edge of the chair, gazing out the window with a faraway look in those amazing green eyes.

Was she lonely for New York and her penthouse? Her caviar and cushy lifestyle? Escobar?

This Escobar dude was pissing him off. Who the fuck did he think he was anyway? And how did one go about finding a damn warlock?

Derrick took a deep breath and wandered leisurely over to the kitchen table, savoring her lithe form, composing himself.

Yeah, like that was possible to do around Martine.

He reached around her and tilted her head up to look at him. "Thinking about me?" he asked because he needed to hear her say it.

Martine's eyes crinkled at the corners and she snorted. "You'd like that wouldn't you, egomaniac?"

Derrick laughed, deep and low in his throat, running his finger down the tip of her pert nose. "Maybe," he admitted.

"Yeah, well don't get your suspenders in a knot over it, farm boy. Quit smoking the crack that is *you*. I like your sexual prowess. That's it," she stated, wrinkling her cute nose, but her almond green eyes flashed something Derrick couldn't ignore. It was more than desire, more than... whatever it was, it wasn't the look of lust she'd given him up till now.

Derrick pulled out the chair next to Martine's and smiled. "Tell me about your life with Escobar."

Martine shrugged and moved the curtain of her hair out of her face, cupping her chin. "What do you care about my life with Escobar?"

"Don't be difficult, cat. I'm curious. Were you raised with others? Do you have friends, siblings? Did you go to school?"

Martine exhaled. "No, I didn't go to school like all of the other children. I've seen it on TV, though. Looked like fun. I'm sorry I missed back to school night and naptime and getting the crap beat out of me on the playground. But I did earn a degree in Speech

Communication on the Internet. I don't have any siblings and I don't have any friends."

Martine said it so matter-of-factly that Derrick couldn't decide if she was disappointed that her life had been so sheltered or if that was just the way it was. "You missed a lot growing up with this Escobar, huh?"

She shrugged, crossing her long, graceful legs. "I guess. I learned other things, things the kids who went to the prom never will. Six of one, half a dozen of the other."

Something occurred to Derrick then. "You're not a virgin," he blurted out.

"Even if I was, I wouldn't be anymore," she said as her full lips curved into a sardonic smile.

Derrick reached out and twisted a strand of her black hair between his fingers. "You know what I mean, Martine. If you've never had any friends and you haven't been exposed to life as most of us know it, how did you become so -- so sexually --"

"A good fuck, Derrick?" Her chuckle was throaty and it mocked him.

"Martine…" he warned.

She rolled her green eyes. "I told you, I can cast spells. Not very good ones, but spells nonetheless. When I want a man, I whip one up."

Ahhh. So she could have whatever she wanted, whenever she wanted it. "So sex is just an easy convenience for you. You wiggle your nose and there it is."

"And it's not *easy* for you? It would seem you don't lack sexual partners, wolf man. You just have to work harder than I do. Just because I don't have to stalk my prey doesn't make it any less valid."

Derrick chuckled. She had a point. "So you create men to have sex with?" Had she created many hunks in her man frenzy? That sent a frisson of irritation along Derrick's spine. She didn't need him, she didn't even have to go to the local bar and scope a guy. She didn't even have to bat those pretty eyes. She just had to say poof or snap her fingers, or whatever familiars did when they were horny.

Martine squirmed a bit in her chair. "Yeah, kinda…"

"What are these men like?"

Martine's sigh was rife with exasperation. "Men. Just regular old men. If I see someone on TV that appeals to me, I try to recreate him for myself. It's not a big deal." She shrugged her slim shoulders and looked back out of the window.

"So they're just like any old guy would be. All working *parts*." He emphasized parts because he had a sick desire to really shoot himself in the foot with some fake guy's twelve inches.

"Oh, I see. This is like a pissing contest, right? Who has the biggest sausage or something? Well, look, sometimes the men I create have -- well, issues, but I assure you that they function rather well, thank you. Now this discussion is over!" She got up and stomped off down the hall in a flurry of long limbs and hair that swung around her shoulders.

Derrick smirked. Martine's irritation told him that he'd hit a nerve. He must have *something* these other men didn't and he liked it that way.

* * *

Martine decided she'd like to get to know Derrick's family better and she was going to do just that. Screw Derrick and his questions about her life, sheltered as it was. Yes, she'd spent a lot of time alone. Yes, her life had been small thus far, but it wasn't so bad. Yes, she'd often wondered what "normal" people did in their daily lives, but she'd brushed that aside in favor of security in the kitty condo of life.

Martine had no complaints. She liked her fake men, caviar and the Animal Planet. They didn't get the Animal Planet here in Timbuktu unless someone went up on the roof and held the friggin' antenna in their teeth while standing on one leg, facing north, when the moon was high.

New York had the Animal Planet *and* the Soap Channel...

Martine zipped up her jeans and moved soundlessly down the hall. Peeking around the corner she looked around, trying to locate Derrick. Well, humph. He was nowhere to be found.

Martine scooted out the door and hurried down the path toward Coreen's house. From afar it looked warm and inviting. A curl of smoke wove its way into the cloud-riddled sky. Martine took a deep breath and smiled, then caught herself and frowned.

What was all this country living doing to her? The great outdoors...

She was turning into a redneck.

Oh, God.

As she wandered toward the back of the house she caught sight of the man she'd seen earlier in her stay. He was taking the bunnies out of the big cage and stroking them fondly. He was great looking, Martine remembered, even if his penchant for small creatures was exceptionally odd for a werewolf. Maybe he was really a parakeet or something. God knew this Adams bunch was one helluva pack of weirdos. An eclectic compilation of various animal species.

"Hey," he said without turning around. "I'm Hector. You're Martine, right?"

"Yeah. Nice to meet you, Hector."

He grinned at her over his shoulder, his smile reminiscent of Max's and Derrick's. "You think I'm weird, don't you?"

Martine coughed. "Weird? Um, no, why would you think that?"

"I saw you watching me out of Derrick's window the other day and the vibe I got was definitely whack job stuff."

Martine shoved her hands in her pockets and gave him a sheepish look. "I --"

Hector stroked a bunny against his cheek. "It's okay. Everyone thinks I'm weird because I don't like to hunt when the moon is full, but they love me anyway. That's what makes this pack special. We don't fit into a neat box, but we're a pack and we love each other."

Martine smiled because they *were* whack jobs, especially if they thought she was Derrick's lifemate. A cat and a wolf... "You know what, Hector? I don't think you're weird at all. I think you all love each other in your own way and no one could ask for more."

Hector ran his hand down the back of a fluffy white rabbit, cooing to it. "So does that mean you'll stay?"

Martine couldn't quite explain why, but leaving didn't seem nearly as appealing as staying did. She didn't want to go back to New York and be alone, even if these people were nuts. She liked nuts. She used to only like them in her truffles, but she could adjust.

Martine shrugged. "We'll see, Hector."

"Derrick really likes you. I can tell. He gets mad and stomps all over the place about you. He doesn't want to, but he does. He's never done that when he's been around other women."

Other women? Martine didn't want to know about the "other" women. Surely that was a bad sign. The old green-eyed monster.

"I think you should give us a chance, Martine. You just might find that this is where you belong."

Martine cocked her head at Hector and smiled. "Thanks, Hector. I'll give it some thought. Catch you later, okay?"

Hector nodded and went back to his bunnies as Martine made her way toward the house.

She was hesitant to just walk in, so she knocked.

JC answered, her long dark hair in a ponytail and a piece of thin paper sticking out of her mouth. She pulled the paper out and smiled. "Hey, Martine! Sorry," she said as she held up the paper. "I was giving Max's sisters a perm. C'mon in and I'll introduce you." JC grabbed her by the hand and pulled her into the kitchen where two women sat with curlers in their hair and magazines in their laps. "Avery and Natalie, this is Derrick's lifemate, Martine."

Martine shifted from foot to foot. This lifemate thing was really a kind of big deal with these people. She felt like she had a label stamped on her forehead. Martine raised a shy hand and waved at them.

"Damn…" Avery said. "You're a cat? How cool is that? Nice to meet you."

They accepted her shifted form as if she were simply declaring she was from another country. Martine wondered vaguely what they'd think if she were, say, an armadillo.

Natalie waved and smiled at Martine. "Man, Derrick got lucky, huh, girls? You should see some of the women he comes ho --"

"Natalie!" JC interrupted sharply. "Martine is *the* woman. No more talk of anything else."

Natalie blushed. "I'm sorry, Martine. I didn't mean… Well, it doesn't matter. You *are* the one and we're so glad you're here."

Martine didn't know how to define the warm curl of happiness she was experiencing, so she tried to ignore it even if it did make her chest tight. "It's all right," she assured Natalie. "I like being here too."

JC nodded her consent. "Does this mean that you and Derrick have decided to make nice? I know it's hard for you, Martine. I really never imagined myself living way out here, but I love it now and I love Max."

"How did you *know* you loved Max?" Martine really wanted a simple answer to that.

JC stopped rolling Avery's hair and smiled. "I freaked out at first, when I found out he was a wolf. That was some scary shit, I'll tell you, and then, I went home and Max came back here and all of a sudden none of it mattered. Not that he was a werewolf, not that I was human, none of it. I didn't want to stay in Hoboken without Max. It just all came together and I knew I didn't want to be without him. I couldn't imagine never talking to him again, being near him again, the -- you know, doing the good stuff again. So here I am." She smiled at Martine, comforting and sweet.

Martine was overwhelmed. If these were signs of love she was in deep kitty litter. Her heart thrashed in her chest and her fingers shook.

JC cocked her head at Martine. "You, okay? You look a little pale."

No, she was not fucking okay. She needed to think.

A lot.

"I'm fine, JC, and thanks. I think I just need to catch my breath here. I'm going to take a walk. I thought I might come hang out for a bit, but now I find that I really need some alone time."

JC smiled and came to hug Martine. "It's all about the acceptance. Acknowledging it is the first step," she assured her.

Yeah, Martine thought as she headed back out the door, *it was like a damn twelve step program with this bunch.*

Chapter Eight

Martine ran, sprinting over the winter-deadened grass and stretching her feline legs as she went. She needed to think and in her cat form she was free to escape to places no one would look for her.

Crossing a field, Martine skipped through a pasture of horses, avoiding the puckey.

Oh, yuck. Who could live in a place like this? It stunk! This was nothing like her penthouse. Nothing like it, yet as she came upon a tree and circled it, the idea of napping on a limb high above the world below appealed to her.

Reaching her claws upward, she dug them into the bark and scratched for all she was worth.

Love.

What the hell was that about? If Derrick was her lifemate, certainly they could have been properly introduced long before this.

Martine climbed the tree in three long strides, carefully choosing a branch that was thick enough to curl up on.

Think. She needed to think. About Derrick and this country living and being a part of a family she rather liked. She needed to figure out where the hell Escobar fit into this and what would happen to her if whomever had cursed her found out she'd left her warlock.

A chill skittered up her spine. This curse thing... what was it all about anyway? No harm had come to her so far. What was the big deal?

The big deal was Escobar and the fear he'd instilled in her to never stray from him. So she didn't. Not until now and this freedom was a little empowering. Which brought her full circle to Derrick and this gnawing feeling that he meant more to her than just a good lay.

Martine yawned and curled into a ball. No more Derrick, no more lifemates, no more wacky chicken soup theories.

She needed a nap. Some caviar would be peachy, but a nap would have to do.

* * *

"Where the hell is my cat?" Derrick yelled as he stormed into the Adams house and stopped in front of Max at the kitchen table.

Max looked up from the table and frowned. "Now she's *your* cat? How nice. What's with the sudden change of heart? You starting to like the scoop away, multiple formula cat litter all of a sudden?"

"Shut up, Max. I haven't been able to find her anywhere and she's been gone for hours." Derrick's stomach was in a knot and he couldn't figure out why. He just needed to find Martine. Jesus, she was a pain in the ass.

"She was just here a few hours ago, Derrick. We had a nice chat," JC said as she came from the family room and went to sit with Max at the kitchen table, smiling that secret smile at him only the two could share.

"Hours ago? *Hours?*" Derrick yelped.

JC nodded. "She said she needed to catch her breath -- who wouldn't with you for a lifemate -- and then she left."

"Well she's not at the cabin so where the hell is she?" Derrick erupted, pacing the length of the kitchen.

Max caressed JC's hand and asked, "What time was she here, honey?" He shot an angry look at Derrick. "Quit yelling. She's probably just out wandering somewhere to get away from you."

"It was probably four hours ago, Derrick, and she just said she needed to think. Maybe that might be a good thing for *you* to do too."

"Four hours? Jesus Christ! She's a pampered feline. She's never left her cushy penthouse and she's what? Off hoeing the land now? No, something's wrong," Derrick insisted.

JC snickered. "Why would you care anyway, Derrick? Weren't *you* the one who was just complaining about a cat being your lifemate?"

Max pushed himself out of his seat and slapped Derrick on the shoulder. "C'mon, Derrick, let's go find your kitty." He kissed JC on the lips and grabbed a jacket.

Derrick followed close behind Max as they went out the door and headed down the wide front porch steps. "Shit, Max, she could be hurt."

"Um, yeah, Derrick, she could be, you dipshit. Why didn't you come find her sooner?"

Derrick sighed his exasperation. "Because she was pissed off and I figured I'd better let her have a chance to chill out."

"Good, really good job, Derrick," Max said sarcastically. "Okay, look, can you smell her?"

Derrick flared his nostrils as the wind picked up. "No. Shit. I can't smell a thing!"

Max looked at Derrick pointedly. "If we shift we can cover more ground. Let's do it."

"Max, you don't think she tried to get back to New York, do you?"

"No, I don't think she tried to do that," a voice, soft as a whisper, low and melodic, said from behind Derrick.

Both Max and Derrick turned to find a tall, slender man walking out of the darkness just to the corner of the steps. He wore a tunic and his blond hair was scraped back from his face in a ponytail. His skin literally glowed in the dark of the night, iridescent and pale, and his eyes glinted in the moonlight.

Derrick's nostrils flared and his muscles flexed. "Who the fuck are you?"

The tall man held up his hand in a calm, slow fashion and said, "I'm Escobar, her warlock."

Derrick charged Escobar, snorting like a bull, but Max grabbed him and shoved him hard. "Stop it, Derrick! For Christ's sake, calm down. Maybe he can help us find Martine!"

Derrick shoved Max back. "He's the one who got us into this in the first place!" Derrick yelled over the increasing wind. The night grew colder, a brisk wind picking up and forcing Derrick to pull the collar of his jacket over his throat. Jesus, Martine wasn't used to this kind of weather. She'd freeze to death. He had to find her.

And that's when he knew he wanted Martine forever.

At the very second when he thought he might never see her again. Beautiful, long, graceful, smart-mouthed damned cat.

Derrick knew because the thought of her hurt out there somewhere made his stomach heave and his heart so heavy in his chest he'd rather rip it out than feel like this.

He stalked over to Escobar and jammed his face in his. "How do you know she wouldn't go back to New York, warlock?"

Escobar's face remained as serene and calm as if Derrick had just asked if he liked vanilla or chocolate ice cream. "I know my Martine. She won't venture far, but she's not used to the wilds of the great outdoors either." His statement was a warning.

Derrick placed his face inches from Escobar's and said through clenched teeth, "Then can't you put out the mojo on her or something? Like smell her out with that magic of yours? And why the hell are you showing up now?"

Escobar took a step back and gave Derrick a knowing look. "No, Derrick, I can't just summon her. Martine does as she pleases and obviously she's chosen to go off on her own, which doesn't surprise me, young man. You are a little hot under the collar."

Max yanked on Derrick's coat. "Derrick, stop it. We have to find Martine and we'll deal with this -- this --"

"Warlock," Escobar offered with a gentle tone that Derrick detected held a bit of condescension.

"Don't go anywhere, Escobar," Derrick warned. "When I get back we have some things to talk about, got that?"

Escobar rocked back on his heels and cocked an eyebrow at Derrick. "Oh, indeed."

Derrick gave him one last angry frown and turned to head toward the field with Max following closely behind.

"Escobar, are they gone?"

Escobar chuckled at the sound of his beloved's voice. "Yes, darling, they're off to find my wayward familiar."

A short round woman sidled up to Escobar and he wrapped an arm around her shoulders. She peeked up at him with adoring eyes. "So how long do you think it'll be before they get back here with her? It's been a long day, sweetheart. I'm tired."

Escobar kissed the top of her head with affection. "Patience, my Eva, patience..."

* * *

You know, life in the backwoods of New Jersey just plain sucks, Martine mused as she considered her latest predicament. Sighing, she attempted to untangle her hair from the branches and shivered. God, it was cold in Clampetville!

What had she been thinking when she'd shifted to human form? Clearly she hadn't been thinking. Actually, truth be told, she'd been dreaming about farm boy. Nice, very nice. Way to top all of this really good backwater shit off.

Sex, sex, sex. Her fuck buddy was going to be the death of her.

Okay, so she got a little excited and shifted in her sleep, now she was caught on the tree from hell and freezing her ass off, because of course when she'd shifted, she'd ditched her clothes.

Of all the indignities...

Martine struggled to turn her head to get a better look at exactly how badly she was caught, but she couldn't move her head more than an inch or two.

Tears stung her eyes and she swiped at them furiously. Shit, shit, shit! If she were back in her penthouse at home none of this would have happened!

Inching backward, she attempted to loosen the grip of the limbs, or at the very least alleviate the yanking on her scalp. Her back was up against the thick base of the tree, but her head was pulling to the left.

A low growl from below made her freeze. It rumbled in her ears and vibrated through her chest.

Uh-oh.

Maybe it was Derrick in werewolf form? Martine cleared her throat and squeaked out, "Derrick?"

Another low rumble sounded, fierce and deep.

Hookay, maybe not Derrick. Why would he growl at her?

A relative?

Here doggy, doggy...

"Um, hello? Are you related to Derrick Adams? You know, big, hunky dark-haired guy? Kinda cranky? Because if you are, I'm his lifemate. So if you were thinking of --"

"Grrrrrrrrrrrrrrrrrr!"

"-- of well, of eating me, you might want to reconsider because you'd be in big trouble and then they'd come hunt you down and it could be baaaad, very bad if they got a hold of you. I'm only trying to save you the --"

"Grrrrrrrrrrrrrrrrrrrrrrrrrrrrrrrrrrrrr!"

"Troouuubbblle of being eeeeaatteeennnnn alive," Martine managed to fairly screech with terror in her voice.

Scratching. It was scratching at the base of the tree. Oh, shit! She could slit her wrists for not taking a higher limb, but she'd never climbed a tree before so she wanted to stay close to the ground. Oh, gooooood!

She was going to die. Yep. Right here in a freakin' tree with no clothes on and her damn hair tangled up in a limb, she thought hysterically.

Good.

Fine.

Whatever.

The scratching became louder. Martine heard the bark being torn and the low, hungry continual growl of whatever the fuck was down there.

She could shift! Shift into her cat form and climb higher into the tree! Oh, sometimes it was good to be a shapeshifter. Not that she'd had much success so far. If she had she could have done it much sooner, but Martine couldn't shift if she was stressed and having her hair all caught up in a tree was stressful.

She did, after all, have nice hair that was literally being yanked out by its roots.

Martine closed her eyes and tried to focus on her body, but Old Yeller was down there tearing up the tree for all it was worth and she couldn't feel the vibe of her body.

Oh, shifting don't fail me now!

And suddenly there was silence.

Oh, blessed relief, now maybe she could get some peace. She scrunched her eyes shut.

"Grrrrrrrrrrrrrrrrrrrrrrrrrr!"

Martine popped an eye open and stared into the eyes of the scariest damn dog she'd ever seen in her life. He'd climbed the short distance from the ground and was looking to make her his meal.

Oooh, those were some big teeth he had, dripping with saliva and giving her that "oh what nice gams you have" look. His demonic red eyes narrowed as he lifted his jowls and growled again. His head was tremendous, solid and bulging. He was a golden color, Martine saw in her moment of panic, thinking it was rather pretty in the moonlight.

Death...

Well, okay, so she was going to die. Not a problem, but she would have liked to tell Derrick goodbye just one more time and thank his family for being so kind to her.

Her heart ached as she thought about never seeing him again. Of course, she wouldn't know that, would she? They'd bury her out in the hills somewhere and have fried chicken and potato salad or something afterward.

Martine held herself still and refused to budge. If her throat was going to be ripped out, then so be it. But she'd be fucked and feathered if she'd die a coward.

"Grrrrrrrrrrrrrrrrrrrrrrrrrrrrrrrr."

Yeah, grrrrrrrrr, she thought. *Do it already*, was her last thought before a streak of dark shadow tore across her vision in a graceful arc.

And then Cujo was gone.

Just like that.

Martine was hanging onto consciousness by the skin of her teeth, but when she felt the soft fur of whatever had just saved her from a very undignified death, she fought to keep her state of awareness.

A cold nose nudged her hand and from her limited vision, she tried to look down without moving her head.

Blue-gray eyes lifted to meet hers and Martine caught her breath.

Oh, hell, please let this be Derrick. She really couldn't take another fucked up werewolf tonight. "Derrick?" A definite squeak coming from her dry throat.

He laid his furry head at her shoulder and nuzzled her ear.

Martine blew out a breath she must have been holding forever. Peace stole over her and she closed her eyes. It *was* Derrick...

Good doggie was her last thought before she passed out.

Chapter Nine

"Baby, wake up. C'mon, feline, it's time for you to open those pretty eyes."

Martine fought to fend off the fog that enveloped her head as she pricked her ears to the sound of Derrick's voice.

A hand brushed across her forehead, solid, warm, slightly callused. "C'mon, Martine. Wake up, baby."

Baby? Was this Derrick of ye old grumpy exterior? Calling her *baby* no less. This was definitely reason to open her eyes.

Lips, firm and heated, whispered over her cheek, nuzzling her.

Martine opened her eyes in increments. "What happened?" she asked groggily.

"You were almost eaten alive by a big, bad dog because you didn't stay where you belonged. What were you thinking, going off into the woods by yourself, Ms. Park Avenue?" he whispered into her ear.

Martine struggled to sit, but Derrick held her in place with a firm hand to her shoulder. "I was thinking, is what I was doing and I got all caught up on a limb and then... well, then..." She tapered off because it got ugly from there on out.

"Yes, that's exactly what you did and a dog, rabid mind you, came along and decided to make you a midnight snack. Don't ever do that again, Martine. Understand me?" Derrick said, urgent and hissing each word in her ear.

So did this mean like she would *have* the chance to "never do something like that again"?

He moved to lie over her torso, his eyes finding hers, filled with things Martine didn't understand.

"I'm sorry. I couldn't shift and then... you came to get me..." Martine's throat clogged with emotion and she wasn't quite sure why.

Derrick ran a thumb down her cheek, cupping her jaw. "Just like I'll *always* come to get you, familiar."

Always? Her confusion must have shown on her face because Derrick said, "Always, Martine. We're lifemates, cat. Adjust."

Martine's heart warmed. "You were pretty impressive there, farm boy," she teased as Derrick slid his arms beneath her and pulled her close.

Derrick chuckled. "Yeah, rednecks and all, ya know?"

Martine giggled and then said with all seriousness. "Thank you, Derrick. I'm sorry I caused so much trouble."

"Well, don't you worry your pretty little head, a head that has a whole lot less hair now too."

Martine's hand flew to her hair. A chunk of it was missing. Of all the goddamned things to lose. "My hair," she wailed into his neck.

"I could have left you there, you know, naked, vulnerable, *with* hair."

"Product," she mumbled.

"Huh?"

"Product. I won't need as much now."

Derrick chuckled again and kissed the top of her half-haired head and laid her back down on the bed. "It'll grow back, lifemate. Now you rest and we'll talk in the morning, okay?"

Who was this man? Tender and gentle, caring for her as if she were as fragile as china?

Who gave a crap? Derrick wasn't grumpy. Things were looking up!

* * *

"Is she awake?" Eva asked.

Escobar smiled. "Yes, and I'm sure once she hears what we've done we're in for some mouthing off."

Eva chuckled. "Who cares as long as they're together?" she said jauntily.

Derrick came around the corner of his living room after making sure Martine was comfortably situated in the shower and stopped short. His face changed from content to a mask of fury. "You!" he shouted at Escobar. "What are you doing here? And what are you doing with my grandmother?"

Eva went to Derrick and hugged him hard to keep him from Escobar. "Don't be a shit, Derrick. Escobar is a good man as you'll soon find out."

Derrick hugged his grandmother back and then held her at arm's length. "So read any chicken soup lately, Gram? What the hell is going on here?"

Eva looked guiltily up at Derrick, her blue eyes hesitant. "Well, honey bunch, that's what Escobar and I are here to talk about."

"Escobar!" Martine had showered and was now in the middle of the living room, wearing one of Derrick's T-shirts and not looking too happy. She ran to Escobar, first hugging him, then swatting his shoulder. "Where have you been? I've been so worried and how the hell did I get here? What is going on?" Martine shot Eva a confused look.

Eva stepped forward and took Martine's hand, pulling her into an embrace. "I'm Eva, sweetheart, and it's so nice to finally meet you."

"The chicken soup lady?" Martine said in disbelief.

Eva nodded and smiled at Martine. "Yep, that's me."

"Gram," Derrick interrupted. "So what happened to Africa and the Peace Corps?"

Now Escobar looked confused. "Peace Corps, Eva?"

Eva looked at all of them. "Well, I had to tell them *something*, darling. I couldn't tell them that we were off fighting a curse, now could I?"

Derrick wanted an answer and he wanted one now. "Curse? Okay, Gram, fess up. Tell me all about this curse because I have a funny feeling you have something to do with it."

Escobar stepped forward and put his arm around Eva's shoulders. "Yes, she helped me break the curse. Your grandmother is quite the tiger."

Eva smiled coyly up at Escobar and blushed. "You tell them, darling. I'm plum bushed."

"Martine, sweetheart, you know you were sent to me so that I could protect you, right?"

Martine nodded with a slow bob of her head. "Yes."

Escobar smiled. "Well, you know you were given to me by your parents. I was your father's best friend and his dying wish was that I be your guardian. There was a witch named Giselle and she wanted your father at all costs. She was responsible for your parents' deaths… She was a jealous old hag who hated your mother. She cursed you as a result. It was very ugly to say the least. You were cursed to spend your life as a cat, but I managed to intervene to a degree and give you back some of your life. The only trouble was, you could never leave me as a result. It was too much of a risk to let you out of my sight. Giselle could have found you and then I shudder to think of what might have happened, but we fixed that, didn't we, darling," he said to Eva.

Martine took a deep breath. Oh my God. She knew so little about her parents... and now to find this out? Martine grabbed the arm of the couch and Derrick came to wrap a protective arm around her, steadying her.

"Wanna tell me what this darling stuff is about, Gram?" Derrick asked.

Eva rolled her eyes. "Escobar and I are lovers, honey bunch. I've always known about Martine and I've always thought she'd be a perfect mate for you. So when the opportunity came about to break Giselle's spell, it was the perfect time to introduce you to Martine." Eva gave them a smug smile.

"Wait a minute!" Martine shouted. What the hell was going on? "What about the chicken soup?"

Eva waved her hand dismissively. "That's all just garbage to get you to do what I want," she chuckled.

Derrick's face went slack. "What?"

Eva laughed a short bark. "You don't really believe I read your prophecy from chicken soup, do you? You all are too much."

"But Max and JC and..."

Eva scoffed. "Just a bunch of bunk. JC did my hair for me once and I fell in love with her. So I decided she was perfect for Max. Nothing more and no chicken soup involved."

Martine blinked several times and then she managed to spit out, "And me?"

"Oh, sweetie, I've known you forever. You just don't know it. Escobar and I go way back. I knew you were perfect for my Derrick, so when the opportunity presented itself in the way of that bitch Giselle, Escobar walloped you with a spell, shoved you in the cat carrier and dropped you off on the turnpike. Simple. I knew Derrick wouldn't defy a chicken soup prophecy. You had to be somewhere safe. We knew Giselle wouldn't find you way out here. Everything just came together."

Martine knew she should be angry. She knew she should demand more answers, but she was just too stunned to do much but stare aghast at them. Derrick was the first to speak. "I should be really angry with you, Gram. Toying with us like that, but I just can't." He kissed the top of Martine's head and smiled at his grandmother.

"So you and Escobar… all this time?" Martine asked.

Escobar nodded his head. "Yes, Martine, and now you're free from Giselle. It took some doing, but Eva came up with a plan and we utilized it!"

Eva clapped her hands together. "We kicked her ass all over northern Europe, evil woman. So go on, now. You two go make happy and we'll split."

"Wait!" Martine stopped them. "What about my parents? What happens now? All those years I lived in the penthouse? Will I still be able to shift?" Martine had a million questions swirling in her head. They made her dizzy and tired.

Escobar held his arms out to Martine and she went to him and let him envelop her in an embrace. "It's all fine now, Martine. I did what I had to -- to protect you. I know it meant keeping you from the world, but that was just the way it had to be. I trusted no one until I met Eva. Your parents were good people and they loved you enough to entrust me with your care. I know you have lots of questions and I'll be happy to answer them when we have more time to visit."

"Will you go away now? Will I see much of you again?" Martine's throat was clogged with trepidation. She'd never been without Escobar and the world was pretty darn scary after last night.

"Yes, my spoiled one. I'm sure you'll see Eva and I often. For now you make nice with your handsome man."

Martine looked up into Escobar's mischievous eyes. "What were you thinking when you hooked me up with a wolf?"

Escobar laughed, hearty and rich to Martine's ears. "I was thinking someone had to take the spoiled out of you, young lady, and Derrick was just the man to do it."

Martine hugged him one last time. "Thanks, Escobar, for taking care of me, for keeping me from harm and *I guess*, for finding me Derrick."

Derrick stuck his hand out to Escobar and took Martine with the other. "Thanks, Escobar, and what do you mean, *you guess*? What kind of a thing is that to say to the man who saved your feline hide last night?"

Martine whirled around and faced Derrick, a gleam in her eye. "You ripped my hair out. Look at it!" Martine held up a strand that was ragged.

Derrick pulled her to him and said, "Let's shave it off. You could be like one of those hairless cats."

"Derrick Adams, shut up now!"

"But, baby, think about all the money we'll save on product," he teased.

"I'll product you, farm boy. I'd bet I can't even get product out here in Clampetville!"

Derrick tugged her by the hand toward the bedroom, waving to Escobar and Eva as he did. "C'mon and I'll show you *my* product." Derrick wiggled his eyebrows at her.

Martine's laughter rang out through the small cabin as she followed him down the hall.

"Well, darling," Escobar said to Eva, "I think you done good."

"Think they'll kill each other?"

Escobar ran his finger down Eva's nose. "I don't want to stay to find out. C'mon, let's go find another part of northern Europe to raise hell in."

Eva chuckled at Escobar. "Oh, darling, I love when you talk dirty to me..."

* * *

Derrick deposited Martine on the bed and stripped his clothes off. "C'mon, lifemate, let's get naked."

Martine giggled. "Oh, all right, but listen up, farm boy, there will be no more talk of me going without product out here in the hills, even if we have to airlift it in. Are we clear?"

Derrick shrugged out of his shirt and Martine gave him an appreciative look as he threw it to the floor. "Deal, feline. Now let's get busy."

Martine sat up and lifted her shirt over her head as Derrick tore at his jeans and flopped down beside her, pulling her into his embrace and kissing her soundly. Martine sighed into his mouth contentedly.

"What was that for, cat?"

Martine slid her body along his, letting the heat of his skin seep into hers. "It was a happy sigh, so shut up, farm boy, and like it." She grinned at him.

Derrick slid his tongue over her lower lip and cupped her breast, thumbing her throbbing nipple to a stiff peak. Martine squirmed beneath his touch and let her hand stray to his cock, stiff and hot. She grasped him firmly and stroked him in long pulls, pulling from his mouth and nipping her way along his rippled abdomen to graze her lips over his shaft.

Derrick's hips pushed upward, seeking her mouth, and Martine smiled the smile of the utterly wicked as she took him in her mouth as far as her throat would allow and closed her lips around his silken length.

Derrick's hands found her hair and clutched it as she moved her lips in long passes over him, kneading his balls, tightened in anticipation, with slight pressure. Derrick hissed as her teeth grazed him, murmuring her name as she turned to straddle him, bracketing his strong thighs with her hands.

Derrick's hands ran over her legs, kneading them, caressing the sensitive skin of her inner thighs as he pulled her to his mouth.

His tongue connected with her pussy and sharp arrows of heat lit their way along her exposed flesh as Martine sank into the warmth of his mouth, gliding over his tongue as they pleasured each other.

A sharp tide of sweet heat wove its way over her nerve endings as Derrick suckled her clit, alternately licking it, then nibbling her until Martine's muscles clenched and a growl came from deep in her throat. When Derrick slipped a thick finger inside of her, plunging deeply into her slick passage, Martine bucked, riding it as her hips rolled toward the slide of them.

When Martine came it slithered over her, picking up a pace she couldn't keep up with as her skin burned and Derrick's tongue brought her to orgasm. Her mouth clamped around him and he shuddered beneath her, pulling at her hips until she released him, sagging against his hard body.

He soothed her with hot hands, strong and sure, until Martine was able to breathe.

Derrick sat up, pulling Martine to him so that her back was against his chest, cupping her breasts as he held her to him. Martine's eyes slid shut as a new heat rose in her.

The need to have Derrick imbedded in her deep, hard, fast.

Martine rolled away from him and lay on her belly, lifting herself high in the air, begging Derrick to enter her.

Derrick complied and soon she felt the hot press of his cock between the folds of her pussy, his big hands gripping her hips as he lay flush against her.

"Christ, Martine, I need to fuck you."

Martine gritted her teeth at his words, beguiling, sensuous. "Then fuck me, Derrick," she demanded, husky and low, her throat raw from pent up need.

Her thighs trembled as she braced herself for his thick entry. Derrick sat between her thighs and drove into her in one fluid thrust.

Martine's cry was sharp upon entry and she pushed her hips back at him with force, so he knew she wanted this as much, if not more, than he did.

Derrick growled, low and eerily feral as his hips moved to match Martine's thrusts. The clap of sticky flesh further pushed Martine to an edge she'd yet to stand at. An army of chills skittered up her spine and when he spread her flesh, dipping into it to caress her clit Martine could no longer hold back. She reared her head up and reached around to grab his neck as she came yet again.

Derrick tensed. His cock pumping into her grew harder with each stroke until he too let go, a hot stream of release that flooded Martine and had her groaning along with him. They fell forward together on the bed, heaving for breath. Derrick ran his hand over her head, brushing her hair from her face as he held her securely against him.

"Well, cat, that was really something, huh?" Derrick asked on a fresh gasp for breath.

Martine chuckled from beneath him. "Yeah, you're all right, farm boy."

He pinched her ass playfully. "This would be the part where you tell me you love me, Garfield."

Martine lifted her head to find Derrick's gaze intent and waiting. "Really, wolf man? I don't remember you telling me you loved me..."

He kissed the tip of her nose and grinned. "Nope, I didn't."

Martine pursed her lips and shot him a dirty look. "Nope, you didn't."

"Oh, fine, I'll go first. I love you, feline. I don't know why and I don't know how, but I do. There, how was that?"

"Oh, okaaaay, I love you too, farm boy."

Derrick withdrew from her and dragged her into his strong embrace as Martine snuggled against him, and then she had a thought. "You know, if we have children..."

"Yeah?"

Martine giggled. "We can call them cat dog, you know like the cartoon."

Derrick's laughter rumbled in his chest, vibrating against her own. "My pack just keeps getting weirder and weirder."

"Well, now that I'm here we'll have to see what I can do about that. I'll introduce them to caviar and the finer things in life like penthouse shopping and --"

"Sweetheart. There will be absolutely no catnip involved, will there?"

Martine chuckled as she kissed his lips. "I swear on my multiple formula cat litter..."

Wolf Mates: Moon Over Manhasset

Dakota Cassidy

Chapter One

Okay, so she had a tail.

Big, damn deal.

Well, it became a big deal if it scared off your potential one time boinks -- especially when the moon was full.

It was hard to contain said tail then.

Julia Lawrence whistled a tune as she stared with disdain down at the man she'd just attempted to boink.

God, what a chicken shit.

So she was a werewolf. A carnivore -- lupine, thank you. Why was that so damn scary to a guy?

Because he's a human guy and tails tend to frighten even the biggest of bad-asses... But didn't guys like big dogs? Like German shepherds and rottweilers?

Human men want to own them as pets, not play hanky panky with them, Julia.

Julia stroked her tail thoughtfully... She liked human men far more than she liked werewolves.

She didn't like the men in her pack. They were dirty and smelly, well, most were, anyway. She didn't like the men she was offered as potential mates either... Julia got a chill right up her spine when she thought of Boris -- the last man her family had tried to pawn her off on.

Talk about hairy. Boris wasn't just hairy when he shifted. He was hairy in human form too. Julia had been tempted to ask if an entire vat of wax might not be something he'd consider dipping head over heels into.

Julia scratched her ear and hoped to hell she didn't have fleas. That would just be icky. She had so damn much hair it was hard to avoid sometimes when she was running with her pack. Julia tried to do that whenever time allowed and pressure from her pack members forced her to.

Fricken' bunch of tree huggers.

It was simply disgusting, this shifting to howl at the moon as one big happy family, but Julia did what she must to remain a part of her pack even if she wasn't a bit like them. Black sheep or not, never let it be said Julia didn't play nice with her family members -- from a distance.

They accepted that because really, who could talk when you had pack members that were vegetarians and liked wee, fuzzy bunnies? Pack members who married friggin' cats, for God's sake. No one could cast a stone at Julia. So she owned a high-fashion pet boutique? Julia was the least of their worries. The pack needed to focus more on Max and Derrick and their penchant for adopting stray women who did hair and meowed. Though, Julia had to admit, Max's wife JC was a great hairdresser.

For the most part, her pack let Julia live the lifestyle to which she'd chosen to accustom herself to and that was that.

Looking down at her expensively high-heeled feet, Julia snorted.

What to do about the stud muffin who'd keeled over in a New York minute when she'd gotten a bit amorous while the moon was full. It was beautiful -- the moon that is -- and it turned Julia on... and her shifting got a little out of control and well... her tail came out. It was really quite an attractive tail -- as tails went -- but human males didn't always think so.

Hence the passed out hunk. A hunk who was a pansy-assed sissy.

Julia scooped him up and sat him on the park bench, huffing as she blew a strand of thick hair out of her face.

Damn, he was cute too, David was.

Was it David?

Er, David, Darren, Darrell... *whatever*. She couldn't remember now. The only thing Julia could remember was eyeing him from across the bar and feeling the call of the wild.

He was yummy indeed and Julia set about having him the way she did most of the guys she'd had. She just *had* them, let them believe they'd had her and mostly, Julia walked away unscathed. There was always the exception to the five hundred cotton thread count mambo.

A screamer.

What's-his-name here was obviously a *screamer*.

He'd definitely screamed when she'd wrapped her tail around his leg.

Sometimes they did that. Ah, well, ya win some, ya lose some.

Julia sighed in resignation. *Chicken shit.*

Covering him with his suit jacket, Julia decided home was the best place for her right now. Kitten would be waiting and hungry for her tender vittles and whatshisname wasn't going to be getting up anytime soon.

Or getting *it* up.

God, human men were so -- so *simple.*

Sometimes a girl just wanted to fuck. Julia just didn't want to do it with another *werewolf*; however, that presented a real problem because she was hormonally worked into a lather when the moon was full and when the moon was full, shifting couldn't always be controlled. So her tail popped out. Another werewolf would appreciate the beauty of her tail. Not so with humans.

Life as a werewolf was indeed, sometimes, the proverbial bitch.

And this meant no nookie, cookie.

Tucking his suit jacket around him, Julia figured he'd be all right. This was Manhasset, after all. Not much happened here. He'd wake up, probably freak, and then scurry back home never whispering a word about what he'd seen, because he probably wouldn't want to believe what he'd seen. She shrugged and thought about looking through his wallet for his address, then decided this was best.

Julia turned and strolled under the moonlight, basking in the scent of freshly cut grass as she made her way along the narrow path back toward the parking lot of the bar.

Oh, God, she loved the full moon -- it made her insane with gluttonous joy. Gloriously yellow tonight, it shone like a bright ball of pale butter.

Julia couldn't help it.

The need for release was greater than she was sometimes. Her forehead beaded with sweat as she fought her desires, relentless in their pursuits. Her legs trembled with need; sharp pricks of heat assailed her spine.

Julia paused for a moment, allowing the rush of frenzied heat to envelop her, overwhelm her, carry her away.

It happened then.

In all its magnificent, stupendous glory.

The tidal wave of joyous sensation raced within her, clutching madly at her throat.

She threw her head back, closing her eyes in utter bliss, arching her neck as she howled: "Dooobee-doobee-dooooooooooooooooo. Straaaaaangers in the niiiiight. Two lonely peeeeople, we were strangers in the niiiight... Love was just a glance away. A warm embracing chance -- dance -- chance... awaaaaaaay."

Was it *chance* or *dance*? She could never remember the words.

Julia shook her head as she waltzed her way back to her car, belting out Frank Sinatra as she did.

Christ, she loved to sing.

Especially when the moon was full and boffing was no longer a part of the equation.

* * *

Xavier Wolf slammed the door of his overpriced sports car and stomped down the sidewalk filled to overflowing with trendy boutiques. Christ, he hated meeting clients in this part of town. They were a bunch of stuck up, affluent, pretentious assholes with too much cash to burn.

Worse still, he was going to a pet boutique. A fucking *pet boutique* where they sold stupid crap like overpriced diamond studded collars and booties to keep their widdle furry companions' feet dry.

This offended his innate sense of right and wrong.

Like seriously.

However, the client and her money did not offend Xavier. She intrigued him with the fortune she'd managed to amass in such a short time with her designer puppy pants or whatever she made, and she had plenty of cash to invest. Xavier certainly wasn't going to let that pass him by. A coup was a coup as they said, and his investment firm was coup-ing left and right. Life as an investment counselor was damned good.

As he stood in front of the trendy boutique, his nose was assaulted by the smell of animals. Many animals. He covertly sniffed the air, narrowing his eyes.

Was that a poodle?

Little motherfuckers.

He hated those damn dogs. There'd better not be a Chihuahua in there or he was going to be picking bony fur out of his teeth for weeks to come.

Now, now, Xavier scolded himself. Living in polite society meant behaving himself *and* fighting the urge to devour small animals. He survived just fine on raw meat. No small animals were harmed in the making of a meal at his house.

Okay. Think money, Xavier, lots and lots of money.

Like a Brinks truck backing up to your house and dumping the lovely greenbacks at your doorstep.

Tucking his briefcase under his arm, Xavier pushed his way into the very pink and gold boutique, head down and calculating numbers in his overactive brain when his senses exploded.

His eyes rolled to the back of his head and he closed them briefly to stop the dizzying rush of scents that attacked his nostrils. Sharp, tangy, undeniably sweet, latent sexuality, a thick, churning hunger.

The scent of a woman...

A rumble, low and deep, sounded in his chest, but Xavier managed to fight it as he grabbed blindly for what he hoped was the edge of the counter. His white knuckled grasp held him steady. He took a deep breath and lifted his head with a slow, precise movement.

Jesus Christ... what the hell was that about? It swept over him in hard waves that crashed in his ears and pounded in his head.

As he scanned the small boutique filled with racks of stupid, fluffy outerwear for one's pet, he couldn't locate where the scent was coming from, but it was pounding through his veins in rapid bolts of heat.

A white, long haired cat sat on a fluffy pink and gold pillow, eyeing him with obvious disdain from the far right corner of the store.

Xavier eyed it back -- King of the Jungle that he was -- with a hard stare, letting Miss Kitten Chow know exactly who was in charge here.

She promptly turned her nose up at him and arched her back, stretching with a lazy deliberateness. Her mouth opened wide in a yawn of utter boredom.

Yeah, yeah, so he wasn't scaring her. She'd made her point.

The cat hopped down off her perch with a graceful thump and on soft cat paws, scurried off to somewhere beyond his vision.

Xavier inhaled with a long, ragged breath as the moment passed and he regained his focus.

What the fuck was that about?

And then he knew because the scent -- the scent of a *lifetime* -- walked from the back of the store somewhere and stood before him, tall and slender with a head of thick auburn hair that had his cock raging against the silk of his Armani trousers.

Hookay, this wasn't good.

Nope, not good at all, because for the first time in Xavier Wolf's life, he wasn't thinking about the greenbacks he would make off this possible deal. That in and of itself was totally out of the ordinary for him. Money was good. Money made Xavier happy. Hell, it made him ecstatic, but it didn't make him feel like *this*.

He was thinking that if he didn't rip this woman's clothes off this instant and fuck her senseless, his trousers would do the Incredible Hulk thing.

Well, hell.

Houston, we have a problem and it ain't of the financial variety.

"Can I help you?" her silky smooth voice queried. Her hazel eyes held a question Xavier hoped didn't involve the bulge in his drawers.

Can you help me? Yeah, first can I get ya to unload some cash and second, can I get you to help me unload a load...

Chapter Two

Julia cocked her head at the rather large man with the tawny hair who stood in her boutique looking utterly ridiculous amongst the pink and gold setting. His broad shoulders were clad in a black suit that her cat Kitten's hair was sure to find. A crisp white shirt and red tie complemented the dark ensemble. Julia admired his tapered waist from a clinical distance. He really had some nice hair on that head... thick and full, it grazed his collar in streaky blond waves. It was the only thing about him that didn't scream conservative.

Julia wondered vaguely what kind of product he used for styling...

He held a briefcase and the edge of her countertop like it was the only thing between him and the floor. He wasn't answering her and his green eyes had a kind of glazed look about them as he scanned Julia from head to toe.

He cleared his throat, swallowing hard as he did. Julia noted the muscles in his throat bulge and flex as he attempted to speak. "Jul -- um, Julia Lawrence?"

Yep, that was her. "Yes," she answered with some hesitation because now he had a wild look in his eyes that was freakin' her out a little.

Maybe he was sick?

He squared his big shoulders and held his hand out. "Xavier Wolf. We have an appointment today to talk about your mon -- um, I mean your financial future."

Ahhh. Recognition dawned on Julia. Yes, her money. She had lots of that and it needed to do something other than sit in the bank. It was just a matter of finding the right investment firm. Placing her hand in his, she said, "I'm sorry, you caught me off guard. Yes, I'm Julia Lawrence and yes, I have money that I need to invest. *You* are the nice investment banker my friend Bonita told me about. Why don't we go to my office so we can discuss my money?" Julia turned on her Prada heel, glancing briefly at her hand -- a hand that now was experiencing this odd tingle thing -- and made her way to the back of the store. She heard the confident shuffle of Xavier Wolf's feet and an odd rumble she couldn't quite pinpoint.

Kitten, her white Persian cat, was on her desk, basking in the sunlight. Julia sat behind the desk, motioning to Xavier to have a seat as well. He took the soft backed leather chair to her right and sat stiffly.

Julia's nose caught a whiff of his cologne and something else that was unrecognizable, yet familiar. It sent a fissure of awareness up her spine. Cocking her head, Julia watched as Kitten strolled across her desktop and planted herself firmly in Xavier's line of vision. She arched her back and swished her tail, preening for Xavier.

Huh. How odd. Kitten *hated* men…

Kitten rolled to her back and rubbed along the smooth oak of Julia's desk, giving Xavier a come hither look. She cocked her head, fully expecting Xavier to be completely besotted with her now.

Xavier Wolf narrowed his eyes at Kitten and tapped his finger on the pad he'd put in his lap. Obviously he didn't like animals.

Neanderthal…

"So, Ms. Lawrence, how about we talk investments?" Mr. Wolf's tone was curt and crisp with the impatience to begin doing business.

Julia leaned back in her chair and clasped her hands together. "Sure, let's talk money. How are you going to make me *more* money?" Because really, a girl could never have enough.

Xavier cleared his throat and pulled out a vinyl folder from his briefcase with Julia's name on it. He placed it on the desk, sliding Kitten out of the way. Kitten, refusing to be ignored, flopped over the folder with a thunk and rolled onto her back dramatically, putting her paws in the air with a playful jab.

Xavier brushed Kitten's fluffy tail out of the way, trying to ignore the cloud of hair she created, and focused on his paperwork.

Not to be outdone, Kitten stretched her body, flexing seductively, and rolled just a bit too far south. She fell into Xavier's lap unceremoniously, catching Xavier by surprise. Kitten curled into a ball and purred, arching her neck against the lovely black of Xavier's suit.

Oh, hell. She was making a mess of his crisp, perfect suit. Julia snickered as Xavier tried to work around the lump of butter Kitten had become.

He looked helplessly at Julia, who was rather enjoying the docile, all of a sudden coy side to Kitten.

"It seems Kitten is rather fond of you. You should be pleased, Mr. Wolf. She doesn't normally take to men." That was an understatement of the millennium. Kitten despised men in all shapes and sizes. However, Xavier seemed to have something none of the others did.

A really hot butt.

Julia shook her head and shifted in her office chair to clear the sharp stab of lust from her loins.

Xavier tightened his jaw and said between his teeth, "That's nice, but I don't think we'll accomplish much if our love affair continues."

Julia leaned forward, watching the flare of Xavier's nostrils as she did. "Don't you like animals, Mr. Wolf?"

"Love them." The words flowed off his tongue, but somehow he didn't sound sincere to Julia's ears. They were short and choppy, tight with reserve.

Julia pushed her office chair back and moved around the desk to scoop Kitten off of Xavier's lap. As she bent over him, her sensitive nose caught the sharp, yet distinct smell of Xavier Wolf.

Um, like *whoa*… Julia's legs trembled a bit in her high heels and she clung to Kitten for support.

Julia shivered. *Who's fierce?*

Their eyes met over Kitten and Julia's widened as she gazed into Xavier's. The air grew stifling and thick. Julia could almost taste it, thick like pea soup.

Kitten clawed at Julia's knit sweater, trying to get out of her grip and back into Xavier's lap. Julia backed away from the sight and scent of Xavier, reaching behind her to find the knob to her office door and clinging to the cat. She grabbed onto the cool brass with gratitude and shoved Kitten out the door, clamping it shut with a firm push.

Brushing her sweater off, Julia straightened her shoulders and took her place again behind her desk. Folding her hands together on the top of it, Julia smiled at Xavier Wolf. "Now, where were we?"

"Your financial future."

Julia nodded. "Right. So what do you recommend --"

Kitten's paw, swiping at the air under her office door, caught Julia's attention and interrupted her train of thought. The door shook with a violent tremble as Kitten wedged her paw under it and gave an ear piercing howl as she jiggled.

Hookay. This was going well. What the hell was wrong with the damn cat? Kitten hated men. Hated them... despised them.

Xavier was fighting a smirk as he quietly rifled through more papers in his folder.

Kitten jiggled the door with another pitiful wail and began throwing her body up against the door full force.

Julia rolled her head on her neck. "Obviously, this isn't working out, Mr. Wolf. Possibly we might consider rescheduling, er, somewhere more quiet?" Julia said over the noise of yet another howl from Kitten.

Xavier glanced with obvious impatience at his watch, as if her money wasn't good enough to warrant another meeting. If he was this way with a first impression, what would he be like long term when she called to ask if, in fact, buying into lip gloss that made your lips look ten years younger was a good investment?

"I suppose I could, yes."

Suppose? Who was this guy? She had the Brinks truck backing up to her house, dumping cash and he *supposed* he could help her invest it? She could go to the investment department of the 7-Eleven and be treated like this over a fricken' slushie.

"Well, then, I *suppose* I'll have to see if I can work you in. I'm a busy woman, Mr. Wolf. That's one of the very reasons I have so much *cash*." *Cash being the operative word to this equation, stupidhead. See if you can suppose that!*

Kitten began a rhythmic thump against the door, howling and clawing at it with sharp rakes of her nails. It was like she was possessed...

Julia pinched her temple to thwart the beginnings of a headache.

"Why don't you come to my office later this evening, Ms. Lawrence? We can further discuss this without disturbance. I think all of my associates will have left their pets with the sitter this week."

A glimmer of a smile in his tone made Julia chuckle and relieved some of the tension she was feeling. "I think that might be a good idea. How's seven for you?"

"That's fine. I look forward to it."

Kitten's yowling grew insistent, desperate. Julia was almost afraid to open the door.

"Do you have a back entrance from your office?"

Julia nodded. "I do, it's a fire escape out the bathroom window. It might be a bit small for someone of your, er, size…"

Xavier smiled. It came across as arrogant and cocky. "I think I can manage. This way?" He pointed over her shoulder to the right.

Julia nodded as she sucked in her gut. He slid between her and the chair in the corner with the merest of brushes, yet the contact sent waves of jitters along her arms.

"I'll see you tonight, Ms. Lawrence," he said almost against her ear as he slipped beyond her and headed toward the bathroom.

Julia bit her lower lip, trying to shake off the rush of heat lingering in her ear.

Yee and haw, he was hot.

Was it wrong to lust for the man who might potentially handle your money?

Was it wrong to want him to handle your fun stuff too?

* * *

Julia strode into Xavier's suite of offices at six fifty-five sharp. Minus Kitten as interference, she'd had time to think about her reaction to mm-mm-good's craggy beauty.

It was a clear deduction. That he might invest her money made little difference now. Lust was calling and who was she to deny it?

No doubt, he was delicious and Julia wanted to bang his drum. No doubt, he should be off limits because money was involved and the two never mixed. No doubt, Julia cared little at this point.

She wanted to explore what it was about Xavier that made her nipples bore a hole in her bra and her mouth as dry as a desert landscape.

Whether that was a good idea or not remained to be seen.

Her heels clacked on the fine Italian marble of the outer office as she passed through and located his office. A sharp knock later, he was standing in front of her, just as hot as he'd been earlier in the day. The deep grooves on either side of his face gave his face a granite look, softened only by the hint of a twinkle in his eyes.

"Ms. Lawrence."

He could call her Julia, seeing as she intended to mount and ride him like the stud he was. First name basis might be a good thing.

When she'd come to that conclusion, she didn't know. She did know her loins felt like gasoline had been poured on them and Xavier Wolf had just thrown the match.

Julia would have him. She *had* to have him.

Christ, she hoped her tail cooperated in the having process.

Xavier's nostrils flared and his jaw clenched.

"Mr. Wolf." Julia nodded and smiled with a slight turn upward of her freshly glossed lips as she made her way into the gray and black, very modern office. Leaning back against his desk, she crossed her ankles. Julia heard the sharp pop as Xavier flipped the lock on the heavy black door.

His approach was quick, graceful, and in a mere second, he was standing in front of her. "I'm going to take a wild stab here and guess we can wait for the business aspect of this meeting."

"I'm going to take a wild stab here too and guess you'd like to screw as much as I would."

His stance straddled hers, his thighs lingered near her own. His chest was mere inches from hers, making her fight not to squirm. "Oh, yes, Ms. Lawrence. I'd say you were right on target."

Julia leaned further back as he leaned further in, pulling out the clip that held her hair and letting it fall down her back. "Then, bring it," she demanded, the air now pungent with desire. Her nostrils flared too now, in response to that smell she couldn't quite put her finger on and chalked up to desire.

"Oh, I can bring it, all right." His whisper was almost a growl.

"Can you? Like you brought me tips on how to invest my money?"

"Are you mocking my abilities to invest your money wisely, Ms. Lawrence?"

"I've yet to see your *abilities*, Mr. Wolf."

"Is that a challenge?"

"Are you up to one?"

"I'm always *up*, Ms. Lawrence."

"Like I said, bring it," she commanded again on a hiss of barely controlled breath.

Xavier's eyes rolled back in his head before he caught himself and narrowed his gaze at her, shoving a hand into her long mane and gripping it, tugging her head backward.

Julia's neck arched and he took the opportunity to run his lips over it, skimming the sensitive skin, creating a sinfully slow shiver of need in her. He pulled her flush against him and ground with a slow twist of his hips.

She fought a groan, figuring it would be exactly what a man like Xavier wanted. To hear her beg for the mercy of his cock driving into her. Instead, she gripped his wrists and thrust back with her pelvis toward him. The thin material of her skirt allowed her to feel the thick ridge of his cock, bulging beneath his trousers. Julia wasn't afraid to share her needs with anyone. She did the picking when it came time to fuck and fucking was exactly what she intended to do.

His hand strayed under her skirt, slipping up her thigh and caressing the skin between the top of her thigh-high nylons and the crease between hip and leg.

His fingers burned her, setting off explosions of tiny points of heat along the way. Her cunt was instantly wet, throbbing and pulsing to be touched, but she held still, waiting. No man had ever excited her quite this way with just the hint of foreplay, but no man would ever have the kind of power to make her express that either.

Xavier moved to her lips, lingering over them, staring down at her as his hand continued to stroke her, avoiding her needy pussy. Julia could no longer fight the wish to have his hands buried in the front of her panties, so she did what she did best.

Took control.

Grabbing his wrist, Julia jammed his hand down the front of her silk thong on a gasp of surprised air. Just his hand, unmoving and touching her most intimate place, made Julia's knees weak, her mouth drier than before.

His chuckle was husky as he said, "I think you want me, Ms. Lawrence." His statement was plain, matter-of fact.

She'd agree if her throat hadn't clenched shut when he spread the lips of her burning flesh and trailed a thick finger between them, dragging it over her clit. Julia bucked not only at the touch of a finger that was slightly callused, but over his words.

Yeah, she wanted him and she wanted him instantly. The sooner she could feel the press of his thighs against her ass, the sooner she'd relieve this itch, and she wanted Xavier to scratch it.

Now.

Julia let her hand roam over his thigh, muscled and sleek. Placing a hand between them, she cupped him between his legs, letting the heel of her hand roam over his shaft.

Xavier jolted against her, hissed a fan of heated breath across her face as he clutched the back of her head and drew her lips to his. Placing his mouth over hers, he flicked his tongue over her lower lip, tracing the flesh, but not quite kissing her.

Julia's one hand worked his cock while the other easily unzipped his fly and let his trousers fall to the floor. Sliding into his underwear, she let the silken feel of his hardened flesh caress her hand. He was long enough to make an impression, fabulously thick enough that her hand just wrapped around his cock as she freed it from his boxer briefs.

Groaning for the first time since they'd touched, Xavier attached his lips to hers. He pressed against them hard, driving his tongue into her mouth so deep Julia felt the steam literally bond their lips. Her heart thrashed against her chest as they dueled with hands, lips, tongues. They touched, tasted, teased until she ripped her mouth from his, her breathing ragged and harsh.

There was only one thing she wanted now. The preliminaries seemed to matter little. Foreplay was simply out of the question.

The cock that she held in her hand, stroked with firm passes, had to be in her or she'd die with the need for it.

Turning, she tugged her skirt up with rushed hands, spreading her legs and lifting her ass. "I want you in me," she said over her shoulder with half demand, half invitation.

In seconds his hard body pushed against her softer one, molding to hers. Taking handfuls of her hair, he dragged them against his face.

"You'll wait until I'm ready," he rasped against her shoulder, which was still clad in her silk shirt.

Julia ignored his comment and the flush of instant heat that kissed her cheeks. The tension in his thighs told her his cock felt differently. Instead, she rolled her hips against his, and leaned forward on the smooth surface of his desk, reaching her arms up to grip the edge of it.

Daring him to enter her.

Wrapping her hair around his fist, Xavier teased her clit with the head of his cock, gliding it between the lips of her swollen cunt, and she clamped her legs together in response, capturing him there.

Her back arched, her hips rotated, and a fire burned deep in the pit of her belly as Xavier finally nudged her entrance. Slick and needy, Julia greedily spread her legs wider, yearning for his hard width to enter.

His grunt was thick and audible as he yanked her thong aside and drove into her, sinking balls deep. Julia's muscles contracted around him as they adjusted to the new, heady sensation of Xavier's thick, hot cock.

Xavier stilled for a moment, stroking her back with his hand as the other gripped her hair tighter. Her nipples beaded, sliding along the smooth desk top as his hand curved into her hip and she waited with impatience for him to douse the raging heat that clung to her pussy.

His first stroke made Julia cry out from the sheer exquisiteness of it. He filled her to capacity, stretching her with the width of his cock. His hiss was music to her ears as he plunged into her once again, rocking against her, tugging her head back with each stroke as she clung to the desk.

Her fingers grew numb and her knuckles white, but nothing stopped her from driving back against his cock, silently begging him to go deeper, harder. Their bodies made a rhythmic clap of flesh against flesh, hypnotizing, erotic, carnal. Each thrust he made lifted her hips from the desk and he let go of her hair, clenching her hips, crashing against them as he rode her.

The swell of orgasm rose, faded, eluded her for mere moments, only to resume with an intensity so fierce it threatened to break her. Julia's hand let go of the desk and found her clit of its own volition, stroking her swollen, tender, flesh. Julia gasped when Xavier fell forward on her back.

The sizzling heat of his heavy weight created a delicious sense of refuge. Then Xavier put his hand over hers, thumbing her clit with her, allowing her to guide him. Her fingers strayed further down her pussy as she found the base of his cock, slick with her juices, still driving into her.

Julia caressed him with her finger, feeling the juice of her cunt coating his cock, circling the base of his shaft, sliding further still to feel his balls draw up and tighten.

When release came crashing around them, it was like the jagged, hard end of a knife ripping through her and then Xavier simultaneously, connecting them for a brief and fleeting moment.

The current of electricity seared her cunt, grabbed her with hard fingers, wound around her until her scream was only diminished because Xavier literally growled.

His muscles tensed, his thighs bulged against the back of hers, and his cock jolted violently within her as his body slammed against her. It was, without a shadow of a doubt, the longest, hottest orgasm Julia had ever experienced.

A bead of sweat trickled between her breasts as they both struggled to breathe. Julia tried to swallow, but all she could manage was to slump against the top of the desk and fight off the dizzying aftereffects.

Xavier rose first, pulling out of her body, leaving her with brief regret, feeling like something was now missing. He ran a hand over Julia's spine in a gentler caress than before, pulling her thong back into place and smoothing her skirt over her hips.

Julia smiled a weak smile and stood too, swinging precariously around on her heels to be enveloped in those arms that had held her to him so close.

That was when she saw it.

It almost didn't catch her by surprise because she had the very same predicament sometimes and for a brief moment, she felt a kinship to him.

It really was kind of a bitch when it happened too.

Xavier Wolf had a tail.

And it sure as snot didn't look like hers.

Chapter Three

Well, fuck.

Of all the times to reveal something so goddamned personal.

Xavier waited for the typical shrill scream that ensued shortly after his tail became an issue, already preparing his pat alibi.

However, Julia remained silent.

Oddly, eerily so.

So she wasn't a screamer?

How refreshing.

Upon tilting her head back, Julia said, "What the fuck are you? I've never seen a tail quite like yours."

He'd have laughed if he wasn't curiously fascinated by the idea that she hadn't completely flipped. "You ask that as if seeing a tail pop out on a man is something that's quite common in your sexual adventures."

She wrinkled her pert nose. "You've ripped your pants, I think. This must wreak havoc on your clothing allowance."

Xavier hadn't heard the very familiar sound of material shredding. He'd been too caught up in the tight, sleek cunt of one Julia Lawrence. In fact, he'd never been quite as caught up as he'd been these past moments. "Sometimes," he said as nonchalantly as he could.

Was she in shock? It could explain why she wasn't a screaming lunatic.

"You haven't answered the question. *What* are you?"

"Actually, you asked what the *fuck* are you?"

"Yeah, so why don't you tell me what *fuck* is?"

"Are you well?"

"Like well as in physically? Or do you mean mentally?"

"I think mentally is the road I'll take."

"Mentally is all on a case-by-case basis, I guess." She frowned. "Oh yes, you're wondering about the shock and surprise thing, right? Or my lack thereof?"

He looked down at her. "Well, yes…"

"I'm not some chicken shit, you know, and I'm not afraid of a tail."

"Then now, I think the question is what the fuck are *you*?"

Julia's giggle was light and airy. "I asked first."

Why the hell wasn't she freaking out? By now they should be at the stage where she was hyperventilating and calling the Lord's name in vain, while alternately covering her eyes and peeking between her fingers. "Do you want to sit down while I tell you?"

Her green eyes glittered. "Only if you're an armadillo."

"I'm a lion. A werelion."

"Really? Like rooooar and Simba and all?"

"Why would I lie?"

"Well, I dunno. A lion?"

"Yep, a lion." Okay, *now* she was going to pop her cork, Xavier was convinced.

"Right here in Manhasset?"

"Right here in your quiet, snooty town."

"How interesting to meet other shifters. I've heard about prides, but I've only seen them on the Discovery Channel or at the Bronx Zoo."

Meet other shifters? "Care to explain what the fuck *you* are?"

"Nope." She grinned at him from down below. Julia reached around him and grabbed his tail, stroking the plumed end. "It really is beautiful."

Xavier's groin tightened again and he put a hand over hers to stop her from pushing his arousal any further. "Tell me what breed you are."

"I have a tail too, if that helps any."

He'd laugh if it weren't so not funny. How could he possibly be *this* attracted to someone who wasn't of his kind? "That could mean many things. You could be a hippo for all I know."

Her snort crackled in the air. "Yeah, I could." Julia sighed, obviously resigned to share her shifter form too. "I'm a wolf. Werewolf, precisely. However, I prefer *she-wolf*. You know, like that movie? The one in London? Only not quite as vicious. I don't think I've ever killed anyone. Nope." She shook her head. "As a matter of fact, I know I haven't. My pack is all into peace and junk. I even have a cousin Hector who loves fuzzy bunnies."

A *werewolf*… she might as well be a dog! But for Christ's sake, that hair -- it was irresistible… It also explained why he'd smelled her at the boutique. Lest he forget how friggen' intoxicating said smell was. "A werewolf…"

"Yeah, a werewolf. Want me to howl at the moon to prove it?"

"Uh, no. Not a lot."

Pushing away from him, she went to sit on the long black, leather couch, primly crossing her legs. "Okay, so my investment banker slash one-night stand is a lion. I swear, the shit that happens to me sometimes. No one would ever believe it. It doesn't matter. All that matters is you treat my money with care and make me more. Come sit down and show me how you're going to do that."

Julia smiled, pretty as the picture she was and as if she hadn't just called him a one-night stand. That was some crazy hot sex they'd just had and now she wanted to talk money?

Xavier didn't know if he could switch from Avenue Lust to Money and Investments on Thirty-third and Third just like that.

Apparently, she could.

As she crossed her legs and leaned back, Xavier fought a growl. Her hair, now tousled and falling past her pert breasts, made his mouth water and his cock salute the beauty that was her.

He was supposed to just forget about the best fuck he'd had, pretty much ever, and talk money? Just like that?

He had to.

She wasn't one of his kind.

* * *

Julia fought to maintain her composure as Xavier came to sit beside her and he began to explain the tedious, boring details about investing with Pride Investments.

Well, the name made sense now, anyway.

He babbled about stocks and bonds and her mind raced to keep up. Christ, he was gorgeous and the best sex she'd ever had. Powerful, forceful, domineering, demanding, fricken' hotter than jalapeños sex.

And he's a *lion*.

Like the kind from Africa.

Like the kind that roars.

Like in the Disney movie. Not to mention a Broadway play.

Like the kind that's supposed to be in a *cage*.

Hoo boy, she knew how to pick 'em. It also explained the unfamiliar scent of him. Julia should have known he wasn't human.

As his voice droned on, Julia's mind tried to wrap around another shifter living right here in Manhasset. Xavier was sinfully delicious, a powerfully commanding lover, and he wouldn't freak out if her tail popped out too.

It was just too perfect and Julia made a decision on the spot. She wanted more.

Lots more.

Wee doggie.

His proposal for investing her money seemed sound enough, even if she knew little about the initial dealings. Xavier patiently explained the good and bad, risky and not so risky while Julia eyeballed him, soaking up his superior beauty.

"So, I think that should cover everything and explain in detail our formula for sound investing." He ended with a confident smile and handed her the pen.

Julia smiled too, but she didn't take the pen from him, deciding rather to wait to have another reason to contact him. "I'd like to think this over, if you don't mind. A lot has happened tonight. I need some time to digest. Besides, I have interviews with other firms as well."

Xavier's eyes glowed in the dim light of his office. "I understand. I don't think you'll find a more sound choice than Pride Investments, but you go right ahead and do your research. We'll be waiting when you choose us."

Well, well. Nothing like a dose of confidence, huh? It made Julia tingle from head to tail. Rising, she stuck out her hand and smoothed the other over her skirt. "Thanks... um, for *everything*. I'll be in touch."

With a smug smile on her face, she left Xavier sitting in his office, clothes askew, eyes narrowed.

Way to love 'em and leave 'em.

Something in Julia told her that playing this cool would be what ended up working in her favor. Not the investment part of their newfound deal, but the sexual aspect.

So she walked away as if nothing had happened that was all that extraordinary. If Xavier thought for one minute he had her hooked, he'd use it to his advantage and Julia never let anyone have the upper hand.

Cool as a cucumber, she slid into her small sports car and drove home through the quiet streets of Manhasset. As she pulled into the driveway of her townhouse, it was then that she leaned forward and took deep, cleansing breaths.

A lion.

Xavier was a lion.

She was a wolf.

And they'd just had the best knock down, drag out schtupping she'd ever experienced.

That meant Xavier was going to be hers.

Until she didn't want him anymore.

Oy.

Vay even.

Julia was suddenly bone weary as she climbed out of her car and headed up the front steps of her pristine townhouse. She threw the portfolio of options Xavier had made up in the glossy folder on her entryway table and climbed the stairs to her bedroom.

Kitten greeted her with a very sedate meow. Stooping down, Julia cupped her chin. "What the hell got into you today, miss? Never mind, it was probably the same thing that got into me. He *is* hot, huh? I almost don't blame you."

Kitten nudged her hand, prodding Julia to pet her, arching her back as she ran her fingers along Kitten's spine before skittering off to do kitty things.

Stripping her clothes off, Julia concentrated on her werewolf form, allowing the shift of bone and flesh to take over. Sometimes it helped to think more freely, unencumbered by her human form. She didn't do it often, unless the moon called or her pack forced her to and it troubled her that she spent so much time denying this half of her.

The half of her that allowed her the freedom to race across moonlit fields and feel the rush of wind against her fur.

She stood in front of her full length mirror and observed her shape.

Her color was a muted chocolate, certainly not the red her hair took on when she was in human form.

What would Xavier think of her werewolf form?

What would she think of his lion form?

There surely couldn't be any boinking when they were in shifted status.

Could there?

No, not according to Martine and Derrick, her cousin and his wife. Derrick, a wolf, and Martine, a cat, said they couldn't mate when they shifted.

But somehow they'd made their odd union work.

Stretching out in front of her mirror, she watched her reflection and her ears perked up. What the hell was she thinking? There was nothing to *work*. No one held her attention for very long. While Xavier might be the cat's meow in bed, up against a desk, whatever, it was probably going to wear thin when he began to bore her.

However, until then, Julia planned to have him in as many different ways as she could manage and then, enjoy all the lovely money he was going to make her.

She'd smile if she could as she gazed in the mirror. Her wolf form really was pretty.

She had a nice tail, too…

Chapter Four

A werewolf.

Not a lion.

Not even a tiger.

Not even a Siamese cat.

Not even remotely in the same feline family.

And Xavier Wolf wanted the werewolf.

How ironic *his* last name should reflect *her* shifter form.

Running a hand over his chest, he lay in his big, king-sized bed, tossing and turning, while he thought lustful thoughts of Julia Lawrence. A tall, curvy redhead with full breasts, rounded and plump, and a scent like nothing and no one before her.

Her hair, that long mane of red hair, was enough to kill a lesser lion.

How the hell could he be attracted to a werewolf? Oh, and it was more than just attracted to her. It roared through his veins, singed his loins, made every one of his five senses scream. And it was keeping him awake right now.

This was unacceptable. It was outrageous.

Kitties and doggies didn't play well together.

Though admittedly, he'd grown up in polite society, joined his father's investment firm and managed, thus far, to keep from killing their neighbor's poodle, he didn't want to screw it either.

Xavier was supposed to like cats, at the very least. Not big, hairy dogs with gnashing teeth and a penchant for small tree animals.

Rolling over, he pulled the blanket around him and forced himself to think calming, soothing thoughts.

Tomorrow, when he woke up, he'd forget all about Julia Lawrence.

* * *

Upon awakening the next morning, Xavier might have chuckled at that thought just before sleep if it wasn't such an irritation now. His cock sure as hell didn't forget about her. It stood ramrod straight under the covers. Apparently, her scent lingered.

How was he going to do business with her if he couldn't keep his nether regions quiet?

As he showered and shaved, it gnawed at him. Losing Julia's business wasn't the worst thing that could happen. Losing the opportunity to feel her beneath him again might be.

Xavier realized what was really pissing him off here. Julia had left his office like they hadn't screwed with their clothes still half on, slapped up against his desk, as if nothing out of the ordinary had happened.

If nothing else, he was a memorable lay...

All morning long it distracted him to the point that he'd snapped at his secretary until the phone rang. When Xavier heard her voice, the tension seeped from his body and the world at large didn't seem so grating.

"Ms. Lawrence?"

* * *

"Mr. Wolf." Julia smiled into the phone against her will and fought the stupid, giddy rush of heat he created with his deep, raspy voice.

"What can I do for you today?"

Well, I was thinking, seeing as we already nailed your office desk, how about we try mine? Eyeing Kitten, sitting on her kitty condo across the room, Julia realized that would never work. Kitten would have to spend the night here tonight. "Well, I've decided to invest with your firm and I'd like to discuss that with you. Obviously, there's paperwork, so why don't we get together for a drink and go over it?"

"Is drinking a necessity with all of your business deals?"

It is if I intend to get you somewhere I can safely rip your clothes off without being arrested for public nudity. "I find that sometimes it's easier to part with large sums of money after I've relaxed with some wine," Julia said coolly.

"When and where, Ms. Lawrence?"

"My place. Is eight good for you?"

"That's fine. I'll bring the papers."

Yeah and bring that mighty fuck stick of yours too, she thought, then shook her head and gave him her address. "I'll see you then," she said with a clipped goodbye, hanging up the phone and twirling around in her office chair.

She had a long day ahead of her, but an even longer night if she accomplished what she hoped to. That meant she had to focus on something other than the King of the Jungle.

That wasn't easy to do when all she could think about was his thick cock and his heavy weight, pressing into her as he drove his shaft into her.

For fuck's sake. She had work to do and no one, not even the hottest man she'd encountered in a long time, would keep her from it.

Her new designs lay right where she'd left them yesterday and she attacked them with vigor. A call on her personal line roused her from her work and as she looked at her watch, she realized she'd whiled away four hours. "Hello?"

"Julia?"

"Hector? Is everything all right?" Her surprise was evident. What could Hector want? He hardly ever left his bunnies to do much else but eat. And he didn't eat what werewolves did. Hector was a vegetarian... Julia loved him and she loved her extended family, but sometimes, her pack was just too odd. Werewolves married to cats, humans. What was next? Parakeets? Werewolves who didn't want to hunt, but rather wanted to keep the small prey as pets. Like Hector. He loved rabbits and as a result, no one in the pack hunted them out of respect for him. He was a *sensitive* soul.

It was lunacy.

On more than one occasion, her cousins Max and Derrick had balked at the "one flew over the cuckoo's nest" pack they came from. That had all changed when they'd found their lifemates. Julia was virtually the only member left who still struggled with the oddities her pack members displayed.

"Julia, I *need* to talk to you." Hector's voice was urgent, almost pleading.

"You can always talk to me, Hector. What's wrong?"

"Builders."

"Builders?"

"Yes, they're coming here to the farm."

"Hector, honey... what builders?"

"Biiiig builders." His voice was filled with anxiety. She could almost see him pacing in his awkward shuffle across her aunt's kitchen floor.

Julia's impatience grew, but she kept as much of her exasperation out of her voice as she could. "To build what, Hector?"

"Condos."

"Condos? On Adams land?" Just who the fuck did they think they were?

"Well, sort of. There's some kind of fight over who owns the land, but do you know what that means?"

Posh apartments with swimming pools and sunken tubs in a Clampett-like setting? "What does that mean, Hector?"

"It means that all the creatures of the forest will die!" Hector's voice rose with evident fear. He so loved his cage full of rabbits.

"Hector, honey? Sometimes that happens. You can't save them all, you know."

"But I can, if you loan me some money."

Um, no. Julia loved Hector, she even loved his gentle, sweet nature, but she didn't love him enough to loan him money. "What can my money do? I don't have enough to fight a corporation of builders, Hector."

Someone wrestled the phone away from Hector and his protest squawked in her ear. "Julia?"

"Max, is that you?"

"Yeah. How are you?"

"I'm fine. The question is, how are all of *you*?" Now she was concerned. She didn't spend much time on the farm in Jersey with them, but she loved them just the same. She just didn't love to flea dip with them.

"We're fine, Julia. Hector is just jumping the gun. Don't worry about us." Max's voice almost convinced her nothing was wrong, but a niggle of doubt tore at her.

"Max, you know if you need me, all you have to do is say the word."

His laugh had a bark to it when he teased her with, "We all know how much you love to have your fancy high heels stuck in the mud up here. We're fine, Julia, really."

"Is Hector okay? He really loves those rabbits, Max. He sounds so upset."

"He'll be fine, Julia. I promise. Now go make some designer doggy trench coats or something and make us all here in the backwoods proud." Max said it with affection, but Julia knew that her pack didn't always approve of her choice to see them only occasionally. It didn't mean she didn't care…

She heard a rustle on the other end of the phone as Hector apparently tried to wrest the phone from Max. "Hec…" more rustling and then, "Hector! Stop it! Everything is fine. Julia? I have to go. It was good to talk to you. Bye."

The line went dead.

Julia sighed and blew at a strand of hair that had come undone from her ponytail. Something about the phone call left the residue of a bad juju in the pit of her belly. It wasn't just that she knew Max and the rest of her family thought she was a snob, but that something was brewing that she needed to know as a family member and was being left out of because they didn't want her and her fancy New York money -- as her aunt called it -- involved.

Her love of her independence and a good human male had set her apart from her family. Created a chasm that she wanted to fill, but didn't know how because her time was devoted to her business and the almighty dollar as of late. No one seemed to care that Max's mate was human… However, the quest to expand the pack and have full breed pups was something her family desperately hoped for.

God only knew how they'd feel about her latest conquest, Simba.

A lion probably wouldn't make much of a difference in light of the fact that humans and cats had joined the pack. Julia chuckled. If she and Xavier had children they'd look like chia pets with all of her hair and his mane. She wondered briefly what he looked like in his lion form.

Christ, it was like *Born Free*.

Julia grabbed a sticky note and wrote a reminder to call her family and check on Hector next week. The simple gesture only made her feel a bit better.

Deciding to focus on her money and the upcoming seduction of Xavier, she tucked her worries away on the hope that Max would call her if he needed her.

It was time to make a meal of Xavier Wolf.

* * *

Business -- money -- more business -- more money. Xavier chanted those words in his head as he climbed the steps of Julia Lawrence's very classy townhouse.

Shit, he could smell her from half a block away and unfortunately, so could his cock.

Business. This was business. Nothing more, nothing less. He'd let the sight and scent of her get the best of him last night. Xavier wasn't going to do that again. From here on out, he was going to try and salvage the remainder of their working relationship together, minus the banging.

Well, okay, maybe they could be *friends*...

As Julia opened the door and stood before him in just jeans and a figure hugging, green sweater, his mouth went dry and his reservations out the window.

Fuck, he thought as she invited him into her classically decorated townhouse, giving him an eyeful of her ass. An ass that was lush and full and curvy.

Fuck again, he thought when she turned to him and offered him a glass of wine. Raising her arm like that made the sweater she wore stretch across her breasts. Also lush and full and in need of a mouth to covet them.

"Mr. Wolf?" Julia cocked her head at him as she held out the wine glass, giving him a quizzical glance.

"Thank you," was all he managed as he fought to stave off the roar of blood rushing to his crotch. Again, he found himself setting his briefcase down and gripping the edge of her kitchen counter.

"So, now that I've decided to give your firm my business, tell me how you're going to make me *lots* more money." She smiled, her green eyes full of what he'd pinpoint as amusement.

Did she have to wear her hair like that? All floating around her shoulders and freshly washed? Was that Pantene she'd used? Of all the fricken' shampoos to use, she had to use Pantene? He loved that scent...

Where were they?

Money. How to make more. Yes, that was why he was here. No hanky-panky.

Moving closer to him, she stood on tippy-toe and looked up at him. "Wanna just get the messy stuff out of the way first, then talk money?"

Huh? "The messy stuff?"

Her giggle was light and airy. "Yeah, you know, the *fucking.*"

Oh.

Yes.

The fucking.

Fuck it.

"Could we do that? I can't seem to think of anything else." A very unmanly admission, no doubt, but who gave a flying fuck when your cock was pounding a hole into your thigh and threatening to rip your man panties?

"We can," she agreed, her voice husky, forbidden music to his ears. "Let's go upstairs," Julia suggested and he found himself turning to follow her like a stray puppy, er, cat.

Putting the wine down on the counter, Xavier was right behind her. So close in fact, that he didn't even bother to resist grabbing her around the waist as she began to climb the staircase.

Burying his face in the back of her neck, he took a deep breath and warred with his body for control, clamping her to him in a tight press of body against body. Splaying his hands over her curves, roaming them over the tightly packed jeans she wore.

Xavier's control teetered, then crumbled.

And then -- it was on.

Clothes came off with rushed, fumbling fingers.

Lips met and devoured one another as they each tugged off their jeans.

Giggles from Julia ensued as she fought to get her sweater over her head.

A grunt came from Xavier's throat as he tore at his tie.

Then, they were naked and Julia was leaning back on the steps.

Her breasts, nipples rosy and tight, hardened as she cupped them.

Her lips, full and glossed, pouted.

Her creamy skin glowed in the dim light of the stairwell.

Her thighs, long and full, parted for him

Xavier was between them before he knew better, pressing his length to hers, pulling her as close as he could without crushing her. Julia's arms went around him, clinging to his neck, burrowing her hands in his hair.

Vaguely, he realized they should go upstairs where she'd be comfortable, but he couldn't wrap his head around leaving the heat of her skin for even a mere second.

His head said, *slow down*, but his cock said, *"Get the fuck in there, my man."* With a rasp of breath, Xavier drew her lips to his, licking them, before tempting her tongue to meet his. Her sigh was soft against his mouth and his cock raged in response. Angling his head over hers, he continued to taste her as his hands ran greedily over her smooth skin, caressing the valleys and lingering on her breasts.

Julia slipped her hand between them and captured his cock, stroking it from top to bottom, making a warm canal of her fingers. He bucked against her, driving his stiff rod against her hot palm, relishing the stroke of her soft hands.

Before this went any further, Xavier had to taste her, lap at the scent that made him dizzy, devour the juices that flowed between her legs with his tongue. Pulling away from her with a jerk, Xavier moved along her body, arched against the steps now and settled between her thighs, focusing on the wet lips of her shaved cunt.

Gripping her thighs, he held onto them for support. The scent of her, musky and tangy, lay in his nostrils like Utopia. Xavier gritted his teeth to keep from ramming his tongue into her, jamming his fingers deep inside the slickness of her pussy.

Julia lifted her hips as he slid his hands under them, kneeling between her legs and resting his head on her belly. He fought the rise of a hoarse cry in his throat.

A shudder coursed through his veins, hot and thick. It rumbled with the beginnings of the roar for release. Xavier took a deep breath through his nose, absorbing the heat of Julia, inhaling her uniqueness, fending off this crazy need to consume her. Tentatively, he let his tongue touch the outer lips of her swollen cunt, running it over the outline of her pussy with a slow stroke, making small passes of his lips, teasing her swollen clit.

Julia's hands drove into his hair, pulling him flush with her pussy, arching into his lips. With a small moan, she lifting her hips and spreading her legs wider. It was a carnal invitation and Xavier accepted it with the greed of a small child being offered a thick slice of chocolate cake.

Using thumb and forefinger, he spread her flesh, wet and inviting, her juices beckoned him. The first stroke of his tongue rasped along her clit and Julia's groan from above was low, long, feral. Capturing her clit with his lips, Xavier suckled the nub, swirling his tongue over it, around it.

Julia's hands slipped away from his head and she let a finger, long and red-tipped, join his lips in pleasuring her. She ran her forefinger over the outline of his mouth, following his tongue's path as he licked her, laving her cunt, now hot and slick with her own unique scent.

It was heady and humbling to lay his head between the legs of this woman and as her cries became more insistent, Xavier's gut burned, his tongue tasted euphoria, his cock strained against his thigh, persistent with the desperate need to plunge into Julia.

Her hands cupped his jaw as he began to run his tongue along her exposed flesh in long draws, working a finger into her, clenching the smooth globe of her ass, burying his face deeper against her cunt.

Julia's scream was hoarse, rumbling deep in her belly when Xavier delivered the final blow, dragging his finger over her G-spot.

Her words came from between clenched teeth. "God, I'm going to -- come…" she almost snarled with a short yelp as she rammed her hips upward in short pumps.

Xavier couldn't help but smile against her flesh, soaked and fresh with the possession of his lips. Julia came, the rush of her juices coating his tongue, tangy and sharp. He had to dig his fingers into the flesh of her ass to keep from crying out his victory.

Then, he was withdrawing his finger from the warmth of her body, pulling her arms up over her head to cuff her wrists in his hand, positioning himself at her entrance, preparing to satiate his throbbing cock.

With a swift jerk of his hips, he sank into Julia with a grunt of completeness. For a mere moment, it was as if being inside Julia was the only place on earth he could find this kind of pleasure.

In that moment, Xavier stilled, trying to shove aside the thought and focus on the physical act alone. Yet, everything about this moment told him he had never experienced this sort of oneness with anyone before her.

Then, Julia lifted her hips impatiently, wrapping her legs around him, grinding against him, straining against his hands at her wrists, and he was lost.

Lost in the tight, wet heat of her, clenching his pulsing cock with fierce possession.

Xavier moved in slow, long glides, pulling out to almost the tip of his shaft, then driving back into her.

She whimpered and it was then that he took in her beauty, writhing beneath him. A fine sheen of perspiration glossed her forehead. Her cheeks were flushed with the color of a ripe peach, her eyes closed and the dark fringe of lashes grazed her creamy skin.

It drove Xavier to near madness with wanting her.

Owning her.

Letting Julia's hands free, he thrust his beneath her, shielding her from the fibers of the carpet, pulling her up until their ribs crashed together and her back was relieved of the sharp edges of the stairs.

Julia hung on him, her face buried in his neck as he ground against her pelvis, rolling his hips, instead of driving mindlessly into her.

They were so tightly woven together he felt the hard nub of her clit scrape against his lower abdomen.

The harsh intakes of breath in his ear told Xavier he'd found what pleased Julia most.

"Don't stop, Xavier... I need to come. I *need* to..." Her plea made his senses explode and so he ground against her harder. Rocking in her until he too was almost on the brink of losing the control he never gave away to anyone.

The slow burn of release captured his balls, drawing them tight against his body and when she clenched his ass in her soft, small hands, Xavier demanded she take the ride with him. "Come, Julia. Come for me. Come on my cock."

In a last crash of hips and sweat soaked bodies, Julia moaned a "yes" into his ear as she nibbled it with sharp teeth and then Xavier let go too as semen roared through his cock. Every muscle in his body tense and rigid, he let his seed flood her body. It came in heart pounding jolts that made his shaft swell and jerk.

Blessed relief followed as they both struggled to breathe and clung to one another.

"Wow," escaped Xavier's big mouth before he could stop it.

"Indeed, Lion King. Wow," Julia muttered back.

He laughed at her Lion King crack. Whatever this was, Julia had felt it too. It was in the way she was now unwrapping her legs from their vice grip and taking her arms from around his neck.

It was in the way she was posturing her body language.

Julia Lawrence didn't want to like him. She didn't want to want him this way either.

But she did.

So did he.

Wasn't this a quandary, when the King of the Jungle wanted a dog more than he'd ever wanted one of his own kind?

Chapter Five

"I think I have rug burn," Julia said on a shaky laugh as she squirmed from beneath Xavier's rugged form. His bulk, pressed to hers, was intoxicating. Their lovemaking had been far more intense than the last encounter and it left Julia fearful.

She didn't want entanglements -- attachments.

Oh, but from the way you just screwed him like he was the last man on earth, I'd say you were pretty entangled.

God, this could only get worse. She'd liked that waaaay too much.

Oh, hell, she'd *loved* it. Every bloody, riveting, heart pounding moment.

"Let me see your back," Xavier said, pulling Julia from her inner battle.

"I'm fine, really. I'll just go upstairs and wash up, and then we'll get down to business." Scurrying away from him, she gathered her clothes and flew up the stairs, hitting her bathroom with breakneck speed.

Clinging to the doorknob as she closed the bathroom door, Julia took deep breaths.

What made Xavier so damn enticing? What made him a better lover than anyone else?

Pressing her face to the enameled door, Julia scrunched her eyes shut, then opened them. She prided herself on her composure and that's exactly what she'd do now. Compose herself, pronto.

Straightening, Julia went to the sink and grabbed a washcloth, then dried and threw her clothes on. A last glance at her mirror told her she had that "you've just done something naughty" look. Her lips were swollen, her hair was a tangled mess of flame red, and her cheeks were flushed. Angrily, she grabbed her brush and ran it over her hair, smoothing the massive heap of knots.

Stomping out of the bathroom, she headed into the living room, where Xavier sat on her couch, looking out of place and too big for the fancy, floral pattern of it.

He had not a hair out of place and he'd put his tie back on. Damn man...

"So, let's get started. Tell me what we're going to invest my money in and how we're going to make me lots more?" Her voice sounded a bit shrill, but she'd managed to get the words out without throwing herself at his big, stupid feet and begging to be taken again.

Xavier's eyes glittered in the light on the end table. "Don't you want to talk?"

"Yeah. I want to talk about my money."

He shook his tawny head. "No, I mean about what just happened."

"Um... nope."

"Julia? We just had sex on your stairs. Don't you think that warrants a little acknowledgement?"

"Is this the afterglow part, Xavier? Ya know, where we talk about what an orgasmitron you are? I stroke your ego -- you go home feeling like you da man?"

His grin was snarky. "No, it's where we talk about why this keeps happening and if we should stop."

"Stop?"

"Yes, Julia. Should we stop having sex?"

Okay, here came the big kiss-off. She had to blow him off or she'd become too involved. If he was wondering whether they should stop -- in all likelihood, they should. It meant Xavier didn't want to become emotionally involved. Hell, neither did she.

Did she?

No. He was the best lay she'd ever had, but it sure as fuck didn't mean there weren't better.

Somewhere...

Swallowing hard, Julia went for the kill she wasn't sure she wanted to reap the benefits of. "Well, I would assume after you tell me how we'll invest my money, the only time we'll need to see each other is never. All of our communications can be based via phone or e-mail, yes?" Niiiice. Very smooth, not too cold, but cold enough that he won't think he was *that* important in the long run.

Xavier's eyes grew cold and his back stiffened. "Right. So let's talk about *money*, Julia, and how we can make you a boatload more. It would seem that's the way to your heart."

Don't take the bait, Julia. Do not --

"There are plenty of ways to my heart, Mr. Wolf. Money is most assuredly just *one* of them." *Oh! Shut the fuck up already, Julia. He wants to get under your skin -- don't let him.* She'd slap herself if Xavier didn't already look like he'd like to hold her hand and help her do it.

"Great," he said stiffly.

"Good," she shot back.

"Let's do it, then."

"I'm all ears." Julia sat on the other end of the couch from him, ignoring the heat he radiated and the smooth ripple of muscle in his back under his tailored shirt.

Jackass.

Xavier spread out a bunch of pamphlets and assorted papers for her to look over. Prospectuses on companies that were new and looking for investors, the rise and fall of the stock market over the past few years.

Julia swiped her hair from her eyes. Christ, she couldn't think with all of this hair. There wasn't a single word she understood about any of it, other than all of this was a potential way to make more money and find tax shelters.

An hour later, Julia signed on the dotted line, no less befuddled than she was when they'd begun.

Innately, she sensed Xavier wouldn't take her money and invest it unwisely. His firm had a solid reputation -- that much she knew from her research. Secretly, she was feeling too stupid to admit she didn't get a word he'd said and had no clue as to what exactly all this investing entailed. She'd figure it out on her own -- who needed some brick shithouse lion to help her?

Xavier gathered up his papers, handing her an e-mail account address and a password so she could see her money grow via the magic of the Internet. He shoved the rest of the paperwork into his briefcase and rose. "This is how you'll keep track of where your money is going. You can check it at anytime." His curt words were short and measured, making Julia bristle.

She took the paper and held out her hand to him. "I'll do that."

Xavier took the hand she offered and shook it with a hard grip. "See that you do. Goodbye, Ms. Lawrence."

Julia gripped his hand back and fought the image of that very hand between her legs. "Goodbye, Mr. Wolf."

Xavier strode to the front door and slipped out of it without another word.

Julia stuck her tongue out at him behind his back.

Childish?

Maybe.

Warranted?

Maybe not.

He had wanted to talk about what they'd done.

She didn't.

It was reflex. Self preservation, in fact.

It wasn't necessary to talk about something that could never be.

Tomorrow, she'd wake up and find she'd forgotten all about Xavier Wolf.

Julia stuck her tongue out again for good measure at his now disappeared back.

So there.

* * *

Xavier sat at his desk, staring at Julia Lawrence's account on his computer screen. She'd given him the biggest fuck off he'd ever had and it was driving him up a wall. Who the hell did she think she was, blowing him off like he was some toy to be played with?

It'd been a week, for Christ's sake, and she hadn't made a peep.

Neither had he, but he'd thought about her every waking moment.

And why the hell couldn't he just get the frig over her kissing him off?

Because he wanted her and it went against everything he believed in, everything he'd been taught. Xavier didn't believe in inter-species mating.

Well, not until Julia and her incredible scent anyway.

Hadn't his now deceased father told him that scent was everything?

But the scent of a werewolf?

On all levels it was preposterous. However, his cock didn't think so. It rose to the tune of Julia's name every chance it had. His cock wasn't just intrigued either. Xavier was too. He wanted to know more about the woman who acted like she was a hard ass, yet, according to her tax donations, gave money to the local ASPCA in enormous sums.

Toying with any excuse to call her, Xavier tried to formulate a plausible plan of attack. He hit the speed dial on his phone and waited for her to pick up, caring little that he had nothing in the way of ideas as to why he was calling her.

"Julia Lawrence."

"Ms. Lawrence," he said into the phone.

"This is she." The hitch in her voice told him she knew exactly who it was.

Okay, he'd play along. "Xavier Wolf." *Your serve.*

"How are you, Mr. Wolf?"

"Good thanks and yourself?"

"Good."

Good, then. "I'm glad to hear it." And he was. He was also glad inspiration had just struck him in the form of a new computer company he'd just gotten a prospectus on. It was the perfect excuse to call her.

"Okay, so we've established that we're both good. Is this a ray of sunshine call, Mr. Wolf? Or is there something you wish to discuss?"

Yeah, let's discuss the quickest avenue to your panties. I'd like to take the detour, please. Xavier chuckled into the phone. "I've come across a new computer firm that I think shows great potential. I thought we might get together and discuss it." Aha! Well executed if he did say so himself.

"Get together?"

"Well, yes, Ms. Lawrence. It involves paperwork you can't see over the phone."

Julia finally snickered in his ear. "I guess that would be fine. When and where?"

"How about coffee at the café around the corner from your store at seven?"

"Coffee is grea -- I mean, that's fine. Tonight?"

"Tonight."

"Are we having sex too?"

Xavier couldn't stop himself from laughing a sharp bark into the phone at her bold question. "I'll see you at seven, Julia." His cock, however, was not laughing. Not *with* him, anyway.

"I'll see you then, Xavier," she all but whispered into the phone as she hung up.

Tonight, in the safety of a café, he'd find out if Julia Lawrence was as interesting out of bed as she was in it.

Had they done it in a bed yet?

No.

Not for lack of wanting to, Xavier decided. He couldn't figure out why it was so important to know if she could carry on a conversation that had nothing to do with money. It just was. He needed to get Julia Lawrence and the vision of her beneath him out of his system.

A coffee shop was safe and harmless and well lit. One could hardly rip the clothes off of a woman in a coffee shop over caramel cappuccino.

His cock begged to differ.

* * *

Julia cleared her desk and headed off to her bathroom in her office to freshen up for her meeting with Xavier.

He didn't really want to talk money, did he?

Was it just a scheme to get her to see him because he'd been thinking about her in much the same way she'd been thinking about him?

Was coffee and investing going to be the only thing on the agenda?

She hoped to hell not. There hadn't been a moment this week that she hadn't thought about him and it had nothing to do with stocks and bonds.

A million times she'd wanted to pick up the phone and say, "Hey, wanna fuck?" It was crude and direct and exactly how she felt. The very idea of him had her panties wet and her nipples making her bra feel like an iron maiden.

Julia was curious about the man who'd set her libido on a rampage like no one before him. She'd had a lover or two... okay, maybe twenty in her lifetime, but they didn't do to her body what Xavier did.

Julia stared at her reflection. Her hair fell in thick tangles of flame around her breasts and she ran her fingers through the wild mass to smooth it out, then ran her hands into it in frustration.

Who could think with all this hair?

According to the National Geographic channel, her hair was what Xavier found most attractive about her.

It was like kryptonite to a lion.

It was part of the mate choosing process for them.

She intended to make sure she used that to her advantage tonight.

Fluffing her hair one last time, Julia threw on some lipstick, pressing her lips together before turning off the light and locking up.

As she strolled down the sidewalk her confidence wavered. So did her legs when she saw him sitting inside the small café, the dim lights casting a glow over his tawny head. Pausing for a moment, Julia leaned against the brick building trying to gain some composure.

For fuck's sake, he was just a man.

She'd had many in her lifetime.

What was one more?

With a deep breath, Julia pushed open the glass door of the coffee shop and strolled over to where Xavier was sitting, sliding into a chair.

"Ms. Lawrence," he nodded.

"Mr. Wolf," she nodded back

"Coffee?"

"Please. Just the plain old kind. Black, no sugar."

"Why don't you look over this prospectus while I get that for you?" He handed her a paper with numbers and junk on it that swam before her eyes. Did he have to smell so fucking good?

As he rose to place her order, Julia snuck a peek at his ass. He'd worn jeans tonight, snug and faded. They hugged his thighs, rippled with muscle.

Julia swallowed hard. She needed air. Who the fuck could breathe when he wore jeans like that?

Deep breaths, Julia. In with the good, out with the bad…

She was busy hyperventilating when Xavier plunked down a Styrofoam cup in front of her. He sat back down in his chair that was inches from her. The small mosaic tiled table was intimate, their knees almost touched.

"So, what do you think?"

Think? She couldn't think if she couldn't breathe, now could she? It was time to be honest. "I have not a clue on earth what any of this means. I'm good at making money. I'm not very good at what happens to it afterward. That's why I hired you. What do *you* think?"

He stared at her.

Julia stared back.

It was almost as if he was challenging her not to back down, but she didn't know from what.

She didn't back down, but it wasn't without effort.

"I think I have to have you, Julia Lawrence. I think I don't care about money right now. Yours or mine."

Wee doggie. Now we're talkin'. However, Julia decided to test him. "Where is this going, Mr. Wolf?"

"To your bedroom. Or at the very least, to your boutique."

"And then what? We bang each other senseless, you go home and question your attraction to a wolf until you tire of me?" Why did she want to know the answer to that? It was like inviting heartache. And who the fuck said her heart was in this to end up aching? Why was it so important that Xavier like her on all levels? She'd treated him like he was nothing more than a one-night stand. What else could she expect if he did the same?

"I can't see myself ever tiring of you, but something like that," he said with a wry, teasing smile.

"So the wolf thing *does* bother you, huh?" She said the word wolf on a whisper so the other patrons in the cafe couldn't hear her.

"It makes no sense."

"Does it have to, Xavier? Chemistry is chemistry," Julia said bluntly.

"No, Julia, I don't think you understand. You're a wolf. I'm a lion. There's a big difference in the two. Like essentially, I'm a cat and you're a dog. They don't mix."

Julia tilted her head, brushing her hair from her shoulders as she sipped her coffee. "You know, Xavier, here's where I think my family has a pretty good thing going on. Who said the laws of nature demand that we mate with our own species? Why does everything have to be so rigid because we're half shifter?"

Xavier scowled at her. "Have you ever watched a documentary on the Discovery channel about lions and even once seen them mate with anything other than a lion? Hell, I've never seen them eye up a llama with lascivious intentions, have you?"

Julia shook her head at him. "But the lions on Animal Planet aren't half *human*, Xavier. You are. It's like saying interracial couples can't be attracted to one another. It is what it is. We are both half human."

"What did you mean about your family having a good thing going on?"

Julia threw her head back and laughed. She couldn't believe she'd said that out loud. She spent most of her time telling herself how nuts they were, but truth be told, when it came to matters of the heart and emotions, her family had it all sewn up. They didn't see species or color or anything much else but the rawest, most pure form of love. "I meant that my family has a very eclectic view on lifemates and it has nothing to do with what species you are." *Boy, if that ain't the truth*, she thought.

"Care to explain?" he asked, his voice warmer now than Julia could remember it being since they'd met.

Chuckling, she smiled at him. "Let's see… my cousin Max is married to JC and JC is human. Max is our Alpha of the pack. The beta of our pack, my cousin Derrick, is going to marry a cat. Her name is Martine. My cousin Hector is a vegetarian and loves rabbits. The peculiarity list is endless and at one time, I thought they were a bunch of kooks. I wanted to be like everyone else's pack and have what another werewolf might call a *normal* family, but I just realized something very important. What is normal? If normal means you have to deny yourself the opportunity to end up with the person you love most, then fuck normal!"

Whoa… and whoa again. Where had that rant appeared from? Maybe she was sick and tired of denying who and what she was. Where she came from…

"Your cousin has a *cat* for a lifemate?" His question was laced with incredulity.

"Yep and she's good for Derrick. He was a shallow pig before he met her. She's also gorgeous to boot and they love one another. What else should matter?"

"I should think carrying on the line of the pack would matter. At least to *someone*. Cats and dogs mating don't make werewolves." Xavier's tone had taken that hard edge again and it made Julia bristle.

No shit, genius. Julia rolled her eyes at him. "Of course it matters. Who doesn't want to find their pack strong and eternal? But what matters more is that they weren't forced to marry someone of their own species because they weren't happy. Thus we'd end up with a bunch of miserable pack members. I'd say, in the long run, spending a lifetime with a mate you love and enjoy is far more important than making little wolfies or for that matter, baby lion kings."

Xavier tilted his chair back and the low lights of the café bounced off his T-shirt, highlighting his rippled abdomen beneath. "All of this free love and new millennium thinking is what's going to be the death of any pack."

Her eyebrow cocked upward and her hands gripped the edge of the table. "Really? Maybe it's narrow minded, pig headed jackasses like you that will be the death of packs in general?"

"Maybe that's true," he countered.

"You don't have anyone else in your pride that has another species for a mate? Not even a dirty little secret somewhere in the Wolf closet?"

"If I do, no one has shared it with me. The Wolfs are strictly into their own kind."

Their own kind. Like being anything but a lion was okay. Well, this werewolf kind had had enough. "You know, Xavier, I vote we do this. You give my account to someone else so I don't have to deal with the sight of you," Julia said as she rose from the chair, leaning over to look him right in the eye. "Then, you can skip on off to the Bronx Zoo and see if maybe you're attracted to a nice *lion*. This werewolf, or she-wolf as I prefer to be called, isn't going to be your what-the-fuck-am-I-doing fling!" she hissed into his face.

With that, she grabbed her purse and stomped out of the coffee shop, letting the door swing behind her. Flying down the sidewalk, she headed back to her shop as she dug in her purse for the key.

Fucking bigot. Who the hell did he think he was, insulting her pack? Julia Lawrence was no one's fly-by-night romp.

Ahh, but wasn't that what you intended Xavier to be?

It had nothing to do with the fact that he was a lion and everything to do with the fact that she didn't want emotional attachments.

"Julia! Wait!"

She heard Xavier call from behind her, but she had no intention of indulging in any more of his bullshit theories tonight. The trouble here was, Xavier wanted her, but he didn't want her for much else but fucking.

So when had she decided that she wanted him for anything else but the same?

A large hand circled her upper arm. "I said, wait!"

Julia spun around, yanking her arm out of Xavier's grip, and narrowed her eyes at him. "Don't make me go all werewolf on ya, Xavier. You don't want a *girl* to kick your ass do you? Especially a girl *werewolf*."

He pulled her to him by her waist, wrapping his arms around her and dragging her to him. "I dare you," he challenged, the hard tint to his eyes now gone and replaced with amusement.

Oh, really?

A dare was a dare, after all...

Chapter Six

Julia struggled out of his grip and jammed the key into the door of her shop, fighting what she knew shouldn't be viewed by Manhasset residents unless she wanted a good old fashioned burning at the stake.

She squeaked in the dark of the shop as her anger took on the beginnings of a shift.

Fuck, now she'd ruined another outfit, she seethed as her tail thrust through her skirt, shredding the fine linen of it. "God damn it, Xavier! Now look what you made me do!"

Xavier shut the door and the bell on it jingled as he strode over to her and peered around her waist. "Damn impressive tail you got there, Julia." His words were filled with his obvious amusement.

Julia, now furious, flipped him the bird as she threw her purse and keys onto the counter by the cash register. "Go home, Xavier," she said through clenched teeth. "Go mate with a nice chick from the jungle and leave me the hell alone."

His sigh sliced through the air as he hovered over her, looming and dark. "I can't do that, Julia. It would appear I don't want a chick from the jungle. I want one from the *woods*."

The words washed over Julia, leaving behind the roar of her need in her ears. It pulsed between them, almost like a question for acquiescence. Julia had no answer for when this had become a need for something more than a good lay. She had no answer for when her family's eccentricities had become a way of life she'd defend, versus scorn. She had no answer for why she'd so vehemently defended Max and Derrick's right to choose a lifemate of another species to Xavier. "You want to fuck, Xavier, that's all it is. If you go home you can get almost the same effect in the privacy of your own bathroom with your *hand*."

Oh! Slam dunk, Julia. Good way to rile the pussycat.

The heat of his frame so close to her own made Julia take a deep breath as he spoke. "Yes," he hissed, the air of it fanning her face. "I want to fuck, but I've never wanted to fuck anyone like I want to fuck you." His anger over wanting her took the wind out of Julia's sails. His nostrils flared and his eyes flashed.

It was actually kinda yummy.

Oh, and funny as hell.

Julia gulped as her tail all but disappeared and her irritation subsided. "It's just sex, Xavier. Looking the way you do, that's something you could get at any bar in Manhasset. Go do that." She couldn't believe she was throwing away perfectly good sex like a handy wipe, but for some messed up reason, it seemed like the right thing to do.

You have been dismissed.

Suddenly, Julia didn't just want to toy with anyone and she'd be boiled in oil before she let anyone toy with her.

His fingers circled her wrist, running a finger over the tender flesh of her palm. "I don't want just anyone, Julia. I want *you* and it's driving me fucking crazy."

Julia basked in the moment. *Neener, neener, neener.* Too bad, so sad -- even if it was driving her crazy too. "Why would you want a werewolf, Xavier? I believe essentially, I'm what you called a *dog*." She looked up at him and gave him her slyest of smiles as she mocked, "Woof-woof."

"You want me too," he said with superiority.

"Your point?"

He dragged her hand over the bulge in his pants. "*That's* my point."

"Wow, you got a real problem there, huh?" She took her hand and replaced it with his. "Hand -- meet cock. Cock -- meet hand. Make friends."

Pulling his hand from her grasp, Xavier chuckled as he moved with the grace and speed of the cat he was, enveloping her in his arms. "All you have to do is say, 'Go away, Xavier. I don't want you like you want me,' and I will." He splayed one of those big hands over the curve of her ass, molding her to him. The rigid outline of his cock pressed against her pussy. A pussy that had now turned traitorous and ached for his touch.

Well, for fuck's sake, when ya put it like that... Julia warred with the words that sat on the tip of her tongue, fighting like hell to bungee jump out of her mouth.

Xavier's lips roamed over the arch in her neck, grazing the sensitive spot just under her chin. "Say no, Julia, and I'll walk away."

Julia's arms wrapped around his broad shoulders of their own volition, kneading the muscles, tense and thick beneath her hands. "I'm not sure if I want to say no. So convince me otherwise." *Jeez, that was really good*, she mentally patted herself on the back. She might give some thought to giving classes on saving face one-oh-one.

"I don't think you need convincing, Julia."

"I beg to differ."

He slid a hand between them and hiked up her skirt, slipping into her panties, panties that were undeniably wet. He stroked a finger between the lips of her cunt and Julia had to catch herself to keep from moaning. "You don't have to beg at all, just say you want me too," he murmured as he let his lips roam over the open vee in her shirt. His tongue skirted the swell of her breasts, dipping into the top of her lace bra, moving closer to her nipple until Julia clung to him for support.

"This gets us nowhere, Xavier," Julia reminded him as his tawny head buried itself between her breasts, lapping at the smooth, heated skin. Her breathing was ragged and sharp, whistling from her mouth, but she lifted his head and forced him to look at her. "You'll just go home afterwards and regret it, then we'll repeat this cycle. You'll spend a week thinking you can forget this incredible sex we seem to have and by week's end, you'll be finding some new, lame excuse to contact me. You'll kick yourself three ways till Sunday because you don't want to, but you're compelled to nonetheless. How long do you suppose we can do this before one of us breaks?"

Xavier's eyes seemed to clear and he eyed her with a penetrating stare.

Julia let her hands drop to her sides. "I'm right and you know it. It's better you go home now and work on forgetting about this instead of working yourself up into a frenzy about how wrong it is. Seeing as I'm a dog and all..." She let her words, clear and concise, trail off into the dark.

"Look, I didn't mean to insult you. I just meant that we're two completely different kinds of shifters and it makes no sense to me that I find you *this* attractive."

"Was that an apology? Cuz if so, it sucked."

"No, it was an explanation."

"Well then, now you can really forget it. You owe me an apology."

His lips compressed into a thin line.

"Are you just looking for a fuck buddy, Xavier?" Julia prompted him.

"No. I mean, I wasn't. Hell, I don't know. I only know you drive me crazy. Okay, how's that for your ego?"

Julia chuckled. Xavier was curious about more than just her body and Julia intended to use this to her advantage. "Have you had any serious relationships, Lion King? Or are they all flybys?"

"Have you?"

Oy. Define serious. "Serious means different things to different people. I had one that was long term, but I wasn't in love, if that's what you mean."

"Was he a shifter?"

Julia shook her head. "No. He wasn't and when he found out I was, quite by accident, mind you, he freaked out. You still didn't answer the question. Have you had any serious relationships?"

Xavier straightened, but didn't leave her proximity. "No. Well, I had a girlfriend a few months back, but she wasn't so much into me as she was into my money. It was just as well. It meant I didn't have to tell her the truth."

"Truth? You mean that you're a lion? She was a human?"

"Oh, yeah. She was very human," he said with a laugh.

"So you've never been attracted to another shifter?"

Cocking his head, his eyebrow rose. "You know, I don't think so…"

"Me neither. I don't think it has to do with the fact that I don't like werewolves per se. I think it's more that I just didn't find one that blew me away."

"Unlike the way I blow you away."

Well, there was a statement, if ever there was one. "Yes, Xavier, I find you physically very attractive. No, I'm not willing to be your fuck buddy. I say, we walk away now so no one gets hurt." Namely her.

Pulling Julia to him again, he smiled. "I say, I can't walk away because what's between my legs won't let me."

"I say, what's between your legs can be satisfied by any orifice. Go find a keyhole or something."

"I say, you know that's not true," he mocked.

Julia sighed. *So?* "I say, we stop this madness before it goes any further."

"I say, sometimes a little madness is a good thing."

Julia placed her hands on his forearms. "I say, define right now what you want from me. If it's just sex, be man enough to say it and don't come to me later with the sticky emotions that sometimes arise from something that began as purely physical and ended up a matter of the heart."

"I say, I can't define you and what it is that I want from you and we should have sex while we try to figure it out."

"I say, *no more sex* until you know. Then I'm all in the know too and we can go from there."

"Is that your final answer?"

"Yes, Regis. It is."

Xavier laughed again. "So you want to get to know me?"

"Do you want to get to know me?" she countered.

"Yeah. Yeah, I think I do."

Pushing out of his arms, Julia smiled because it looked like she might have just gotten what she wanted. Maybe. "Okay, we can do that, but no sex until we have a frame of reference, Simba."

"Can I cop a feel?" he teased as he moved in closer to her.

"No. No copping anything. You already know my body. You'll either like my mind too, or you won't. We find out if this is purely physical and we'll just screw until we get this out of our systems and you won't have to worry about hooking up with some *dog* long term."

"So, you want to date?"

"I want to do whatever people call it when they aren't having one-night stands."

"Dinner, movies, coffee -- that kind of thing?" He sounded like he didn't have the first clue about how to woo a woman when it didn't entail bedding her.

"Yeah, Xavier. *That* kind of thing."

"How many dates do we have to have before we can have sex?"

"Arghhhhhhhhhhhh! You'd think buying me a cup of coffee was going to kill you if the coffee doesn't include sex. This is about exploring what's going on here between us! Getting to know each other and if we like anything else about each other besides the sex! Jesus! Forget it. Forget I mentioned it. Let's just go back to being client and investor, okay?"

"Why do I always have to buy the coffee? You're rich. You can buy the coffee too, you know."

Julia cracked up, laughing as she decided to give in. "Fine, I'll buy some coffee too. How's that?"

"It's a date. When?"

"Tomorrow. You can come to my place -- we'll avoid the stairwell like the plague and we'll have coffee, maybe rent a movie or something."

"Do I have to rent the movie?"

Sighing in exasperation, Julia said, "No, I'll get the damn movie. I hope you like chick-flicks."

"Um, no. No, I don't."

"Well, I guess that's too bad, seeing as it's my house you're coming to, isn't it?"

His cackle was brittle and sharp. "I don't know if I like this dating thing so much."

Julia crossed the room and opened her shop door. "Too bad. If you want into these panties ever again, it won't be without some effort on your part."

Xavier sauntered over to her with a slow stroll and shrugged his shoulders. "Fine. Can I have a kiss goodnight?"

"No. I don't kiss on the first date -- maybe not even the second or third."

Xavier leaned forward and pressed a kiss to her nose. "Wow, you drive a hard bargain. Okay, no kiss. I'll see ya tomorrow." He patted her on the back with a thump. "Hope eight is good for you. Bye." On that note, Xavier strolled out of her shop and off into the darkness, whistling a tune Julia didn't recognize. Running her hands through her hair, Julia watched his broad back until he was gone.

Fucktard.

Julia closed the shop door with a slow hand and leaned back against it.

She didn't have a clue as to what happened now, she only knew she really didn't want to be Xavier's plaything.

Why that was?

Why the hell should she care if Xavier *liked* her?

She'd had plenty of playthings in her time. He could be another block in her box of Legos.

But that wasn't what she wanted and she couldn't figure out why.

Sighing, Julia thought it again.

Fucktard.

Chapter Seven

Julia popped the DVD into her bad-ass electronics setup and drummed her fingers on the shiny black surface.

A date.

She and Xavier had a date.

To get to know one another.

No sex.

Absolutely none.

They were going to get to know each other.

Yee and haw.

Glancing at the clock on the mantel of her marble fireplace, Julia noted his ass better be waiting at the door in five minutes or she was starting without him.

Watching the movie, that is.

Not the sex.

Because they weren't having sex.

She'd spent a long day at her shop, looking up investment banking and trying to make heads or tails of this investing thing. All she'd figured out was this, she had a lot of money and it was sitting in the account Xavier had given her at his investment firm. There were lots and lots of numbers and columns and some names listed in those nice columns.

She didn't get it and she'd be fucked and feathered if she'd ask Xavier what it meant. There were plenty of ways to understand investing online. Julia decided she'd just look them up.

But not tonight.

Xavier was coming over.

They were going to watch a movie.

And *not* have sex.

Puckering her lips, she blew a breath of air out when the doorbell rang. Julia didn't know the first thing about dating and relationships and she had no earthly idea why she all of a sudden had a hankering to now. Her suspicion was that it had to do with

Xavier merely thinking he could get away with using her body and she was out to prove that no one used it unless she allowed them to.

So why not just use him back, get yourself a fuck buddy and call it a day, her conscience called to her.

Placing her hands on her hips, she decided she didn't know.

Xavier rang the doorbell again. This time he held it.

Flinging the door open, Julia found a smiling Xavier in jeans and a pullover sweater. Why did his chest have to be so fricken' appealing? "Hi, Julia. I brought you some flowers." He held up the cellophane wrapped assorted mix bouquet, looking very pleased with himself.

He'd brought her flowers...

Was that warmth she felt in her heart?

No. No, the Grinch's heart never experienced warmth. It was just some misplaced loin heat.

However, she found herself smiling anyway and taking them from him, burying her nose in the plastic wrap. "Thanks. That was very sweet."

He rocked back on his heels. "Yeah, and date-like, huh?"

Chuckling she waved him in and pointed to the couch. "Yes, indeed. Very date-like. Have a seat and I'll put these in water, then we'll watch the movie."

Julia dug in her fancy kitchen cabinets that she hardly ever looked in and found a vase. Placing the flowers in it, she smiled again as she let her fingers trail over the soft petals of the single red rose in the center of the mix.

Damn it, he was being too nice.

Scooping it up, Julia stalked out into the living room and plopped them on her coffee table.

Xavier smiled again. "They look nice there," he stated, again reminding her he'd done a good deed.

Julia sat at the other end of the couch purposely. "Yes, Xavier, they're lovely. Thanks again."

Xavier sat back and put his hands on his thighs, rubbing them. "So, what are we watching?"

Some bullshit romantic comedy. Boy meets girl, they're hot for one another, but oh no, a conflict arises. They manage to screw each other blind between said conflict and then, good conquers evil and they end up happily ever after. "A romantic comedy."

Xavier's face began to frown, but he stopped it, rolled his shoulders and looked at her with another one of those stupid smiles. "Cool."

Julia palmed the remote and pressed play. *Good.* She settled back against the couch and tried not to notice that he was mere cushions away from her.

As the credits began to roll, Julia twitched her nose.

Lawd, he smelled like sin and sex.

Nervously, she smoothed her cute new skirt over her thighs and tried to focus on the fact that Xavier seemed completely unaffected by her ensemble.

The word *shithead* floated through her head as Xavier settled in too and slumped down on the sofa.

"I like your skirt," he said from the corner of his mouth, never taking his eyes off the wide screen television.

His remark appeased her somewhat and made her secretly smile. "Thanks. I got it half price at a bargain basement sale in Macy's. It's Calvin Klein. Can you believe the luck?"

Xavier's eyes remained glued to the movie. "How very lucky of you. I'm sure your purse thanks you too."

Julia primly crossed her legs and straightened her camisole. It showed off all of what little cleavage she had. The buttons down the front had purposely been left open to expose just the top of her cleavage. Cleavage that Xavier didn't much seem to care about. "I got this little thing half off too," Julia commented as she ran a hand over the clingy rayon of her top, stressing the word little.

"That's nice too."

If it was so fricken' nice, why the hell aren't you looking at it? What are ya, blind or something? "Thank you."

This was beginning to frig with her brain cell reproduction. When you "dated," weren't you supposed to like actually look at each other? Maybe charming wasn't her bag? Her flirting, coy skills were sorely lacking? She needed to be more complimentary and less abrasive. Julia searched her mind to find one single flirtatious, playful thing to do to capture his attention.

Sliding to the end of the couch, Julia grabbed the rose from the center of the bouquet and took a deep whiff. "These are really beautiful, Xavier. Thanks again." Tipping the rose toward him, she smiled and let her eyes do the talking.

"Yeah. I got a good deal on those too. The supermarket up the road was selling them half price because it was the end of the day."

How lovely. Bargain basement flowers, bought in the supermarket. Julia wasn't going to let it spoil her attempts to woo Xavier. Under normal circumstances, she'd have told him to piss off. Tonight, she just wouldn't play into his game. Whatever it was.

Running the rose over her cheek, Julia faced him. "It was still a nice gesture and I appreciate it."

Finally, Xavier turned to look at her. He lifted his jaw, square and firm under the dim light of the lamp. "I'm glad you like them. You wouldn't think red would suit you because of the color of your hair, but it looks nice against your skin." His nostrils flared a bit then. Ever so slightly.

"Smell it." Julia held it out for him to sniff. "It's really beautiful, even if it did come from a grocery store."

Xavier's hand wrapped around hers as he brought it to his nose and took a deep breath. "I can pick 'em, huh?"

With a trembling hand, Julia nodded as the heat of his skin seared hers. Oh, yeah, he was good at the picking. Her lips parted as she began to answer, then she decided it was better to zip her lip.

Xavier took the rose from her and caressed her cheek with it. The soft petals kissed her skin. Moving lower to the hollow of her throat, he brushed it over the top of her exposed breasts.

Julia's breathing hitched, becoming slow and shallow.

Xavier leaned into her, but never took his eyes off of hers. "I like this little whatever you call it -- top too," he murmured, dragging the rose along her collarbone, over her shoulders and dipping back between her breasts again.

"Thank you," Julia whispered, mesmerized, wet, needy. The tiny scrap of thong she wore chafed between her legs.

Xavier leaned in further, forcing Julia to lean back on her elbows, his daunting frame becoming even more so as he loomed over her.

He smiled then, with a slow wickedness, letting the rose brush against her flesh that was now, like a landscape of nerves, acutely aware and hypersensitive.

Julia's nipples grew tight and beaded, pressing against her top as the sounds from the movie became muted and all she could hear was her own breath in her ears.

It grew ragged, thick, and the tight band of tension around her chest gripped her, pushing her exhale of breath out with a forced rasp.

Xavier draped his body over hers, never touching her, but allowing the smell of him to permeate her senses, the heat of his solid weight to entice her, call her. His lips were so close to Julia's she found herself straining to meet them, yet refusing to initiate the contact.

Nor did Xavier. Instead, his eyes held hers as he rested his weight on his forearm beside her on the couch. They glittered when her tongue slid over her mouth, hoping to wet the dry surface of her lips. The rose glided over her still covered nipple, making it tighter, harder, greedy to be caressed. Xavier drew it across her breasts in a sweeping motion and Julia finally closed her eyes, arching into the gentle motion, allowing only her imagination and her senses to guide her.

Hot breath fanned her face, sweet with the scent of mint, filled with a hint of lust. Julia licked her lips again and felt the silken petal of the rose on the tip of her tongue. Xavier outlined her mouth with it and she gripped the sofa cushions as he again strayed downward, over her shoulders, along her breasts, brushing her belly through her thin skirt.

A simple flower had become a tool given the power to wreak havoc on her. It was suddenly a finger, tracing her inner thighs. A hand, slipping between them. A tongue stroking her aching flesh with the soft touch of a lover.

Julia moaned, long and desperate, breathy and wanton when Xavier's hair fell across her cheek as his lips brushed her neck and she strained upward, reveling in the silky soft strands. Still, his body didn't touch hers. She craved the steel length of him, pushing her into the sofa, but he continued his exploration, and then Xavier whispered with his deep baritone, "Take off your panties, Julia."

With a shaky breath, Julia hooked her thumbs at the top of her panties and slid them off, leaving them to fall from her feet. Raising her legs, she parted them with ease and the cool air of the room on her soaked, fiery flesh made her writhe.

Xavier's chuckle was triumphant in her ear, but Julia cared little as she held her breath and waited, fighting for patience.

The first touch of the rose on the folds of her pussy had Julia seeing flashes of light behind her closed eyes. The silk of it stroking over her swollen clit brought a sizzling, sharp bolt of electricity that settled in her belly and gripped her with iron claws, refusing to let go.

Her legs fell open, allowing him full access. Xavier's breath became more rapid as he stroked her cunt with the petals of the rose, sliding it back and forth over her clit and for the first time since he'd begun to tempt her with the power of suggestion, he put his lips to her ear, resting them there, letting her hear the speed of his intake of air.

Julia's pussy clenched, the muscles tightening, seeking respite, reaching for satisfaction. She whimpered when he drew the rose in a circular motion, making each pass tighter until all movement was focused on her clit. Julia cried out at the tendrils of sweet flames licking at her, building to a hot release.

Realizing Julia was on the brink of orgasm, he slowed. He pulled away, caressing her inner thighs with the lightly scented blossom, leaving Julia on the verge of begging. Xavier dragged the flower over her lower abdomen and once more dipped it back into her cunt.

All thought was now gone. Julia simply wanted nothing but release from the madness of Xavier's ability to seduce her without even touching her. His lips grazed her earlobe, yet he spoke no words while he let the rose work a magic all its own.

When the frenzy of orgasm could no longer be held back, Julia lifted her hips, using her hands to press upward against the silken texture of the rose. Her back bowed. Her head swam. Her focus was solely on the hand that guided the flower over the slick folds of her flesh again and again. Pressure surged in a tidal wave, tension forcing her to cling to the cushions of the couch. A coil of pent up fire soared along her skin, skipping over it and randomly touching all of her nerves.

Julia's orgasm was sharp, resonant, a sensual melody of nothing more than the merest of touches, rippling over her in waves of quivers. The sigh that escaped her lips was gentle, hushed, filled with a shudder of relief.

Letting her hips rest again on the couch, Julia took a long, deep breath, opening her eyes.

Xavier sat up and looked down at her. His face looked thoughtful rather than smug, which was just what Julia was expecting. "That beat a chick flick, wouldn't you agree?"

Her giggle bubbled out of her mouth before she had the chance to stop it. "Yes, that beat a chick flick." It was the most erotic experience she'd ever had.

However, he didn't need to know that, did he? Because certainly, he'd jam that into his arsenal of weapons bag and prepare to launch a new attack with it. What was next? Vegetables and a potato peeler? Who had earth shattering orgasms with a supermarket flower?

"You got any popcorn?" he asked with a grin. The only hint of what had just passed between them was the gleam in his eyes.

Yeah, ya think we can jerk me off with some of Orville's finest while we're at it? "I do."

"So how about you pop some and we'll start this movie from the beginning?"

Julia didn't have time to be embarrassed about her display. Not until after Xavier had gone home and she was alone in her bed. He'd left with the promise to call her and a quick peck on the tip of her nose.

In the dark of her bedroom, Julia's cheeks flamed. Her behavior on that couch had been wanton, wicked, downright shameful.

Then, she smiled. The romance of it all left her breathless as she struggled to figure out what Xavier's motive could be. He hadn't gained anything from it.

Pulling the thick comforter over her head, Julia burrowed deep beneath it and focused on turning off her brain.

Xavier Wolf was going to be the death of her and her out of control libido.

Still, her heart warmed and it wasn't tweaking her quite the way one would think for a cynic like her.

Her last thought before drifting off to sleep was of Xavier's lips flush against her ear and the scent of roses filling her nose.

Damn bargain basement flowers...

* * *

Xavier worked the length of his cock with a soapy hand. His strokes were hard, firm and done with the imaginings of someone else's hand. A softer, smaller version of his own.

Cheerist, this woman was going to drive him fucking insane.

The image of Julia half dressed on her couch, writhing beneath the ministrations of a rose drove Xavier over the edge to orgasm. Her skin, creamy under the glow of the lamp. Her full lips parted and plump. The red of her hair glistening around her shoulders coupled with the raw, sweet scent of her remained vivid, plowing through his mind's eye.

He gasped and blew at the water dripping into his mouth from the spray of the shower.

Xavier watched as his seed spilled over his hand and circled the drain at his feet below with a distant gaze.

He was losing his focus and it was all because of a friggen' dog. *She-wolf, thank you.*

They'd talked well into the night after the movie and now, two weeks later, Xavier found he wanted to know even more about Julia. He wanted to see her again, hear her laugh, wrap himself into a tight ball around her slinky, sexy body and never let her out from under him.

He spent far too much time thinking about her and far too little doing much else.

Did this a relationship make? Was this the dating bullshit he'd scorned?

Xavier leaned a muscled arm against the tile of the shower and rested his head on his forearm. It must be what it was because he sure as hell hadn't experienced this with his last girlfriend. Half of the time he couldn't wait to get away from her and the rest of the time, he'd spent buying her pretty things to keep her off his back. Xavier had rapidly discovered it *was* just the sex and even that made no comparison to Julia.

But Julia didn't want anything. Not monetary gain because the financial gods knew she didn't need his money. She didn't seem terribly interested in being seen at social functions with him, of which he was invited aplenty and a regular feature in the local society pages. So what did she want?

His first assumption had been that she'd just wanted to bang and he'd been more than happy to accommodate.

Now, she was talking crazy stuff about getting to know one another and relationships and Xavier was finding that he wanted to explore what she was so vehemently demanding. But he didn't want to do it without making Julia wish she hadn't excluded the physical liberties they could be taking.

He grinned.

He'd had her a couple of weeks ago. Lock, stock and supermarket flowers.

Yeah, he was feeling pretty damn smug as of late.

Stepping out of the shower, Xavier toweled off and wrapped it around his waist as he headed for his laptop in his bedroom. He clicked on Julia's account and smiled again. Things were going well. He'd advised her in making smart choices by the looks of her ever growing account.

This was cause for celebration, yes?

Chapter Eight

Julia smiled at her phone and let go of a breathless giggle. Xavier wanted to celebrate the fat numbers of her investments by taking her to dinner. Her heart skipped a beat and her stomach did a nosedive.

Catching a glimpse of her sickly, stupid smile in her computer screen, Julia frowned.

Shaking her head, she reached for the phone and dialed up the only other two people in the world she'd seen look just like she did right now. "Martine?"

"Hey, Julia! How are you?"

Infatuated, indescribably giddy, infectiously happy… in deep. "I'm okay and you? Derrick? The baby?"

A small, dreamy sigh blew over the phone line. Much like the one Julia caught herself doing when she talked to Xavier. "Everything is great! I'm due soon. I wasn't sure how long the pregnancy would last because, well, because you know, the cat/wolf thing, but it seems it won't be long now."

Julia giggled. Julia had wondered, too, if Martine being a cat and Derrick being a werewolf would not only be bizarre spawn, but the strangest of pregnancies. "I can see where that could cause some gestation questions. Hey, is JC around too? I know you guys do lunch on Fridays together."

"She is. Hang on and I'll put you on speaker."

Julia twirled a stray strand of hair as she listened to the rustle and JC's cheerful hello. "Okay, ladies. I have a problem."

"Are you all right?" The concern in JC's voice touched Julia. She really did need to spend more time at the farm with them and she didn't deserve their sympathy when all she did was bitch about the lack of a Starbucks when she visited.

"Oh, I'm fine, really. This is nothing serious. It's girl talk."

Julia could picture both Martine and JC giving each other "the look." "Er, girl talk. Okay, I'm going to be real honest here, Julia. You don't do 'girl talk'."

"Well, I meant *man* talk."

"Man talk?" they said in unison.

"Like serious man talk?" Martine asked.

"Yes," she responded. "Serious man talk."

"You don't do *man* talk, Julia. You do man *du jour* talk," JC quipped.

"Yeah," Martine chimed in. "What the hell is going on?"

"Okay, look. I know I'm what you both consider a man eater --
"

A simultaneous snort reverberated in her ear.

"But I've met someone and well -- I --"

"You like him. C'mon, Julia, say it with me. If I were there, I'd help you move your lips. You *like* him. He's interested you in something more than a little slap and tickle and you don't know what to do about it, right?" JC cajoled.

Fuck... "Yes. Yes, I'm interested in pursuing something... I don't know what, but something."

"Aw, c'mon, Julia. Stop talking about this like it's some business deal. You want him and you want him bad. What's his name?"

"Xaaaaavierrrrr," Julia gushed. Did she just gush? Oh, Christ, she was gushing. She clamped a hand firmly over her mouth.

A collective squeak bounced over the line. "Oh! Julia, that's wonderful! Tell us all about him. I want to know every last detail about the man that's finally roped your loose ass --"

"Martine!" JC chastised with a shout.

"Oh, Julia! I'm so sorry. It's just that -- it's just that -- you *do*, well, you know, get around. I didn't mean that you weren't careful. I just meant that you've been ditching guys --"

Julia interrupted her. "It's okay, Martine. You're right. I've had a man or two in my time. That's not the point. The point is, this man, this irritatingly, frustratingly, sexy as all hell man, is making me crazy. I can't stop thinking about him. I can't keep myself from finding any stupid excuse to call him. I don't much like this. It's uncomfortable for me. It's a foreign land where I don't speak the language."

"Didja do him yet?" Martine asked blatantly.

"Yeah, I did him and then I didn't and it's driving me out of my mind."

"Huh?" JC said.

Julia explained her lame brain idea to not boink to the both of them and then she said, "I don't know why I didn't want it to be another one-night stand. There's just something about him that made me want more and quite frankly, it's freaking me the hell out. We've only known each other just a little less than a month, but..." Julia drifted off.

"But when it's right, it's right, Julia. It's called l-o-v-e and you got it bad. It doesn't matter how long you've known him, just that it is. I didn't know Max for more than that and look at us," JC pointed out.

"Oh, noooooo. I did *not* use the word love. I said I like him. Like. As in a serious case of like." Julia shifted uncomfortably in her office chair.

"Yeah? Tell me something, Julia?" Martine asked. "And don't analyze, just answer the questions honestly. Does your stomach kinda get all funky when you see him, even if you just saw him the day before?"

Ugh. "Yes," Julia answered truthfully.

"Do you smile and sigh when he calls?"

So the fuck what? "Y-yes."

"Do you think about him constantly? No matter what you're doing?"

Define constantly. All the time? Every second of the waking day? A lot? Sure. Fine. Okay. Call that constantly. What-everrrr. "Um, yeah..."

"Have you *twirled* your hair?"

Julia's hand dropped guiltily to her desk.

"I'll take your silence as a yes. You got it bad, baby."

Julia's stomach did a nosedive. "Well, what's bad? I mean, we've been dating and keeping our hands to ourselves. Come to think of it, he hasn't laid a single finger on me since I told him hands off."

JC and Martine sqeeeeeed. Long and all giggly. Julia squinted her eyes at the sharp sound, now ringing in her ears. "Oh, he's got it bad too!" JC yelped.

"If he has it so bad, why hasn't he touched me since we decided to 'date'? I don't see your logic."

"Here's the thing. He's doing just as you asked. No touchy feely. If he weren't nuts about you too, why would he wait around for you to give in? Why bother to woo you and go along with your stupid plan? He'd just slink off and find some other chick to stroke his yoke. He's putting the effort into doing exactly what you asked for and it wouldn't surprise me if he's also giving you a good dose of reverse psychology. I say, if he can get your attention, he's halfway there."

"Oooh, I agree with Martine," JC said. "He's in."

"I don't know if I like this," Julia offered. Her uneasiness grew at the idea of love. She loved raw steak. She loved her business. She loved her money that came from her business, but she didn't know about Xavier. He sure as hell didn't make her feel like a piece of raw meat did. Or did he?

"Hey, Julia? Is he a human?"

Julia grinned at JC's question. "You'd like that, wouldn't you? It'd mean you weren't the only human out there in Clampetville as you so fondly call it, huh?"

"Well, sometimes I think it would be nice to have someone to sit with while you all go off and do lunar things."

Julia chuckled. "No, he's not human."

"Oh, hell. Is he like a cockatiel or something?" Martine teased.

"What makes you think he isn't a werewolf?" Julia asked.

"Hmmmm, my first clue was you don't like them?" JC joked.

"You're right. He isn't a werewolf."

"What is this, *Jeopardy*? Don't keep us in suspense. *What* is he?"

"He's kinda in Martine's area of expertise…"

"A cat? Oh, God, wouldn't that be glorious. We could share bowls of cream."

"Not exactly. Think *bigger* than a house cat."

"C'mon, Julia, just tell us. It isn't like it's going to make a difference anyway. Surely you know that in this family, anything goes!" JC reminded her with an edge of frustration.

"A lion… he's a lion."

"Shut the fuck up!" Martine screamed. "How is it that you, a werewolf, get a damn lion and I, a cat, end up with a freakin' dog?"

Julia knew Martine was just joking, but the dog comment from Xavier had tweaked her. "He called me a dog..."

"Shit, Julia, I'm sorry," Martine apologized. "I tease Derrick all the time and he teases me too. I didn't mean to insult you. Is this Xavier a discriminatory kind of shifter?"

Julia frowned. "He claims no one in his family has ever mated with anything else other than another lion."

JC harrumphed. "Well, I guess they're in for a surprise then, eh?"

"No one said anything about lifemates. We're dating..."

"Yeah, so was I. Look at me now. I live in Hooterville and I'm madly in love. Don't rule it out, Julia." JC's tone was light, but Julia knew what she said was true.

"Hey," Julia interrupted JC's musings. "How's Hector?"

There was a silence, before Martine piped up. "He's fine, Julia. You know how dramatic he can be. He's off playing with the wildlife. Everything is okay, really."

Julia dismissed it for now because she was too distracted with thoughts of the King of the Jungle. "Well, girls, as always, it's been informative. I'm glad I called."

"Hey, Julia?"

"What, Martine?"

"Could you get preggers too so we can have a were-lion for our cat-dog to play with?"

Julia threw her head back and laughed into the silence of her office.

She really needed to go home soon and see these people she called family.

* * *

Xavier picked her up for dinner at seven sharp with a peck on the cheek. Julia contained a roll of her eyes. She'd decided that tonight was the night. Xavier was going to get lucky tonight whether he liked it or not, therefore, so was she.

"Did you have a good day, Julia?" Xavier asked from the driver's seat of his car.

"Yeah, I did. You?" His handsome face in the evening light was sharp and the contours defined by the passing street lamps.

Julia's toes tingled, followed shortly thereafter by anything else on her body that could tingle.

"Well, I have to say that all that money you made was a nice way to start it."

Her chuckle was girlish and she leaned over his arm that lay on the cushion between them, letting her breasts rest on it. "I have to admit, it made me smile too. I'm glad I chose your company."

He flashed her a devilish grin. "Me too."

Xavier pulled into a parking lot of a local restaurant Julia had known was closed for renovations when he'd asked her to choose a place to eat. "Hey, what gives? Where is everyone?"

Julia flipped up the arm cushion and sat forward on the leather seat. "It's closed." She smiled at him and unbuttoned her long jacket.

"Well, how the hell can we have a date for dinner if the place is closed and apparently you knew it was?"

Throwing her coat to the backseat she replied, "Because we're not having dinner. I'm having *you*…"

Xavier cocked an eyebrow at her as he scanned her outfit. What there was of it, anyway. "Is this what happens on a date?"

"That's what's going to happen on *this* date," Julia assured him as she reached down and pulled the lever to move his seat back. She slung a leg over his waist and settled on his lap. Xavier's cock brushed between her panty-less legs, hard and thrusting upward, nestling exactly where it should be as far as Julia was concerned.

"I thought we had a no sex rule?" he asked, his voice hoarse and rough.

"We did," Julia agreed as she brushed kisses along his jaw, tugging on his ear. His hands went instantly to cup her breasts, now peeking out of her laced, satin corset.

"Um, what happened? Did we peak? Have we gotten to know each other well enough to allow for *this*?"

Julia captured his bottom lip and lined it with her tongue as she ground against him with her hips. "I know your favorite color, your favorite food and what you like to watch on television. I think we can resume having sex."

"Really?" He sounded like he didn't believe her.

"Really."

"Oh," he muttered as his lips wandered over her mouth, meeting her tongue as she dipped it between his lips.

"Oh? You don't sound too thrilled." But his body said he was, Julia thought as she unzipped his pants and freed the cock she longed to have inside her.

His thumbs rubbed her nipples, tight and hard. "Well… I don't know your favorite color yet…"

"Green," she answered as she stroked his cock, letting the back of her hand rub against her swollen clit.

"That's a nice color."

"Thanks."

"I like green."

"Me too, it's why I picked it."

"What's mine?"

"Navy blue."

"Right. Not the pastel girlie, sky-blue shit."

"Right. No girlie shit."

"My favorite food?"

"Gazelle."

"Right. I don't care much for the older ones, though."

"Right."

"My favorite television show?"

"*Who Wants To Be A Millionaire.*"

"Right. I think Regis is funny and I like the money part."

"I know. Are we done?"

"I think so."

"Can we mess each other's hair up now?"

"Yes. I think that would be beneficial to both of us."

"Good, then be quiet and let your uberdick do the talking."

He chuckled, but pulled his mouth from hers. "Wait. I want to say one thing before we do this."

Julia fought a frustrated sigh. "What?"

"I like you. I like you a lot. I want to see you on a regular basis from now on. This isn't just about getting into your pants."

"I don't have any pants on."

"Oh. Right. Deal?"

"Deal. Ready?"

Xavier was obviously tired of fighting her off and his hands picked up their pace, fondling her breasts. "Yessss," was his answer, hushed and thick, sending a ripple of fire along Julia's spine.

"Good. Now be quiet," Julia demanded as she positioned him at her passage and sunk onto his cock, hard. Her muscles clung to his length, clenching it.

A resounding, raspy sigh echoed in Xavier's car. A sigh of completion, unification, fulfillment.

Julia rolled her hips as Xavier's lips made their way over her throat and along her exposed shoulders, finally settling on a pink, hard nipple. He laved it, cupping her breasts, bringing them together and licking each nipple alternately.

Julia clutched at Xavier's head, threading her fingers in his hair, rising and falling on his cock that now, with each stroke, grew within her.

Xavier thrust upward, his hips gaining a faster rhythm while his mouth slid over her breasts.

Julia groaned as her clit scraped his crisp pubic hair, the delicious friction making her cry out as she bucked against him.

Xavier's body grew tense and rigid as he gripped her hips and once again sought her mouth. His tongue thrust against hers like their joining, in tune with each stroke.

The onslaught of climax roared through her, leaving her no time to fight it off. Julia came with a satisfied scream tearing from her throat before she could stop it. Her pussy contracted and the flood of her juices bathed Xavier's cock. Xavier too, rammed his hips upward, driving into her, touching her G-spot and spewing his hot seed with a series of jerks.

Julia flopped against him, taking air into her lungs and Xavier's arms went around her, smoothing his hands over her back as he held her close.

It dawned on Julia that with Xavier's arms around her, she felt protected, safe, *content*.

Maybe this was much more than a serious case of like…

"Hey," Xavier nudged her with his shoulder. "Do I know your favorite television show?"

Laughing, Julia kissed his lips. "Does it make a difference?"

"Hell, yeah, it makes a difference. You know mine."

"I really like *CSI*."

"Oh. Well, okay, then."

"Anything else?" she asked as she smiled down at him.

"Yeah, is this something we can do all the time or do I have to marry you now?"

"Oh, we definitely have to get married now. All of my pack members would insist upon it. I mean, we did do the official boink in a deserted parking lot sacrificial rite of passage. That's some serious shit where I come from."

Xavier's laugh made his chest vibrate beneath hers. "Then, I think you'd better consent to be my woman -- at least, my girlfriend. Oh, and you'd better tell me what your favorite food is. So we can claim we *really know* each other," he teased as he kissed the tip of her nose.

Julia dissolved into giggles.

Xavier's girlfriend, huh?

Not bad for a night's work.

Chapter Nine

Pink?

Oh, fuck it was pink.

Whatever happened to good old fashioned blue?

Blue was negative, yes?

Julia reread the stupid box again, fumbling with it as she squinted at the tiny print on the package.

Pink.

Yes, that was the dreaded color.

Oh my God, oh my God, oh, my flippin' God, were the only thoughts she had as she rifled through her walk-in closet and found her overnight bag.

Rummaging through her dresser drawers, Julia threw some underwear and T-shirts, along with a few pairs of jeans, into the case. She dragged it over to the bed and flopped down, trying to control her shaking limbs.

Think, she needed to think. She was all about organizing.

Money, she needed money.

Locating her laptop, Julia clicked on her account with Pride Investments and punched in her password. Julia's eyes flew open wide and her stomach sank like the Titanic, but she forced herself to look at the empty account.

Gone.

It was all gone.

Not a penny left. That had to be wrong. It must be a computer glitch and she didn't have time to fuck around finding out. It would mean she'd have to call Xavier and she just couldn't do that right now.

Fueled by her recent "pink" findings, Julia fled, with but a call to her store clerk to hold down the fort and look after Kitten. Julia went where she knew, no matter what, she'd be welcomed with open arms and a bowl of chicken soup.

Home.

To New Jersey and her grandmother and a shoulder to cry on.

* * *

Julia's eyes were red and puffy from crying. JC handed her another tissue and Martine brought a blanket to cover her with, brushing back the hair from her eyes.

"I'm sorry, Julia. I wish there were something I could say to make you feel better," Martine offered as she waddled over to the rocking chair in her aunt's big family room.

"Have you called Xavier, Julia? Maybe he can answer some of the questions you have. I hate to say it, but you just might be jumping to conclusions here," JC said as she rubbed Julia's arm comfortingly.

"Yeah? Ya think he can tell me how he plans to spend all of my fucking money?" Sure enough, when Julia had checked her account again, her money was gone. It wasn't a matter of proving Pride Investments had her money, it was that the only person who could have taken it was Xavier.

The motherfucker.

She'd sue the snot out of him, once she had her wits about her.

Martine winced. "We don't know what happened to your money, Julia, and it isn't like you're giving Xavier a chance to tell you."

Julia snapped like a dry twig. "He hasn't called me in a week, Martine, and besides, if I talk to him now, I'll stuff my fist down his throat and look who's talking! Since when did you become all reasonable and easygoing, Ms. Fancy Feast?"

"Stop it right now, Julia! You're angry and your hormones are all out of whack. It's making you say things you don't mean. I'll take that into consideration after you apologize to my wife," Derrick said as he hovered over Julia, his tall, looming presence almost sweet and endearing in defense of Martine.

Martine jumped up and grabbed Derrick's arm. "It's okay, farm boy. Relax. Julia is right to a degree. I wasn't always this easy to get along with. Pregnancy has mellowed me. It will Julia too."

Oh, God, she was fucking *pregnant*. How had this all happened? *Could it be the part where you were naked and bumping uglies? Sometimes pregnancy happens that way, you know. It isn't all just a rumor...* Julia Lawrence was pregnant and expecting the child of a lion.

Roar.

Julia ran a hand over her hair and looked up at Derrick with red, swollen eyes. "You're right, Derrick, and I'm sorry, Martine. I'm tired and frazzled and puking my guts up. I'm poor, thanks to the King of the Jungle and I just seem to be taking it out on anyone within striking distance."

"So where can we find this asshole?" Max asked as he stalked into the room, his handsome face a mask of fury.

"You don't." JC stood and put a soothing hand on her husband's chest. "I'm a firm believer in hurry up and wait and right now, it doesn't feel right to do anything else. We need to contact the authorities and let them handle the money aspect."

Instantly, Max's hand went to JC's and he held it to his chest as he gritted his teeth. "I'm a firm believer in kicking the shit out of him and asking him what happened later. Do you need any more proof other than Julia's money is gone, she hasn't heard a word from him in a week, and she's knocked up?"

JC took a deep breath and shot Max a look that was appeasing. "Look, Max, I know it doesn't look good for Xavier right now, but he doesn't even know where Julia is. It's not like she called him to tell him she'd come to the farm. I just have a feeling that he's missing something and he doesn't even know it."

"Damn right, he'll be missing his esophagus when I'm done."

Julia couldn't take anymore. She just wanted to crawl into her bed, pull the covers over her head and wonder what the hell kind of child she and Xavier would produce.

Fucking lying, I want you to be my girlfriend, money stealing, expert love making, fricken' lion!

"Please guys. I can't do this right now. I'm tired and my stomach is in a knot and I don't care if I never hear from Xavier again. I think I have bigger fish to fry now." Julia absently rubbed her belly.

Max's look instantly softened. "I'm sorry for upsetting you, sweetheart. I only want to look out for you."

Hector shuffled into the room, carrying one of his beloved bunnies and a plate of warm cookies. He held both out to Julia. "Here, Julia. I thought this might make you feel better. I'm sorry you're so sad about your boyfriend."

Hector's sweet, genuine face showed great concern. "It's okay, Hector. Come sit with me and we'll share the cookies." Julia took the bunny from him and absently stroked the soft fur on its back.

Lights in the driveway flashed past the big picture window and Derrick frowned. "Who the hell…"

Martine shuffled over to the window and chuckled softly. "I guess you'll see, cuz here he comes, stomping up the front steps like someone owes him money." The pounding on the door began almost immediately.

"Him?" Julia asked.

"Oh, indeed, it is him. *The* him. The him that better have some really good explanations to throw out into the Adams' universe."

It was Xavier. Julia handed the bunny to Hector and flew off the couch. "I don't want to see him. Tell him to go away, now!"

JC tugged a lock of Julia's long hair. "Yeah, ya do. You want to know how he plans to support his baby and you want to know where your money is. This isn't like you, Julia. You never run away from a problem. So how about we find this out together instead of turning tail and running, so to speak."

Julia's anger brimmed, steadily boiling to the surface. She wanted to yank his tail right off, is what she wanted to do. "Open the door, Max," Julia ordered, narrowing her eyes.

Max popped the door open, letting it swing wide. Xavier almost fell through it, fists clenched and jaw locked. "Where is Julia?" he growled at Max. No remorse for the intrusion. No preamble about what he was there for.

Max thumped Xavier on the shoulder. "I dunno, where's her money?"

Xavier lifted his chin and looked Max squarely in the eye. They stood almost nose to nose. "I'd like to talk to Julia," he said again, his tone tight and measured.

Max hissed a laugh. "I'll bet you would."

JC slithered between them and used her back to push Max away from Xavier. She held out her hand. "Hi, Xavier. I'm JC. So nice to meet you. Boy, are you in a shitload of trouble." She smiled at him, her pretty eyes glancing upward at his large frame.

Xavier enveloped JC's small hand. "Nice to meet you. Now where is she?"

"Oh, unclench your teeth there, Safari Man," Martine said as she sashayed up to him. "I'm Martine and it would seem we come from the same kitty family. Nice to meet you."

Xavier's look was that of the bewildered. "Um, nice to meet you too. Now can someone please tell me where Julia is? I need to speak to her, *now*."

"Here I am, you lying, stealing, bullshit artist!" Julia yelled.

Xavier whipped around for the first time, facing the room. He appeared relieved, genuinely glad to finally see her. "Julia, I've been trying to find you for over a week, for Christ's sake!"

"I'll just bet you have. Need some more money, Xavier? Maybe a nice trip to Cancun, you shit!"

"Look, we have a lot to talk about. Can we go somewhere quiet and sit down?" Xavier approached her with his typical, give-me-what-I-demand attitude and Julia was having none of it. When he reached for her hand, Julia snatched it back.

"Quiet? Do you need to go somewhere quiet to concoct more bullshit?"

"Julia." His voice warned her he was growing more and more agitated.

"Don't you Julia me, you liar! You stole my fucking money and I want it back!"

With great calm, Xavier said, "Would I be here if I stole your money, Julia? Does that even make a little sense to you? Are you thinking with all of that hair?"

Well, okay, so it didn't make a lot of sense. Why hadn't he just taken the money and run? Her theory about it helping to save his company with her money no longer made sense, but she threw it out there anyway. "You leave my hair out of this, Lion King! You took my money to save your failing company!" she accused.

Xavier's bark of laughter crackled in the air. "You may have a lot of money in the scheme of things, Julia, but it wouldn't be enough to save a firm like Pride Investments, even if we needed saving."

Julia cocked her head. "Oh, really? Then where the fuck is my goddamned money!"

Max moved in on Xavier and pinned him with his eyes. "Yeah, city boy. Why don't you explain what happened to Julia's money and you'd better make it fast or I'm going to have to beat it out of you," Max seethed in Xavier's face.

Xavier didn't back down either. He thrust his broad chest forward and spewed back. "I don't know, but I'd hardly think the two of us brawling over it is going to help the situation much."

Max's hand moved with lightning speed, grabbing Xavier by his throat and shoving him against the wall. "Nah, probably not, but it'll make me feel better just the same."

"Max!" JC roared. "Let go of him right now!" JC tugged on Max's arm. "Stop behaving like a Neanderthal, for crap's sake. Jesus, why is it that you all have to solve everything with force?"

Yeah, can't we all just go hug a tree together? As much as Julia would have liked to nail Xavier right in the chops, she had to agree. Max's beating up Xavier wasn't going to make matters better. "Max, let him go," Julia said with a calm that came out of nowhere.

Max didn't budge.

Neither did Xavier.

"Max, stop!"

Everyone turned with surprise to see Hector rushing at Max and Xavier. "I'm sorry, Julia. I'm really sorry." Hector let his head hang as he stood in front of Julia.

"Why are you sorry, honey?" Julia asked with concern.

"I did something bad, Julia. Really bad. But I did it for a good cause. Honest."

Julia was perplexed, stunned. "What's wrong, Hector? What are you talking about?"

Hector clung to the rabbit and said, "I took your money, Julia."

"Whaaaat?" Julia took Hector by the shoulders and gripped them. "How could you take my money?"

Xavier shoved Max off of him with a grunt and went to stand beside Julia. "You're Hector? Rabbitman@freedomfortheweeanimals.org, Hector?"

Hector shook his head and held out his hand, reaching over Julia's arm to shake Xavier's. "That's me. I'm really sorry, Julia. I didn't mean to take it all. I sorta screwed up and took too much. I wanted to make a bunny sanctuary… When I tried to put it back, well, I couldn't figure it out. It's a looong story, but I did it for a good reason and I had no idea you were going to have this guy's baby. I didn't even know he was your boyfriend. How was I supposed to know the father of your child was the guy you did all of your investing with?" Hector lifted his chin and stared right back at Julia.

"Baby?" Xavier yelled, looking at Julia, eyes wide, mouth set in a firm line.

"What reason could you possibly have for stealing, Hector Adams?" Derrick stormed.

Hector cringed. "I -- well -- you know that builder says he has a right to Adams land. He's going to build some stupid condos or something and that will kill off the wildlife. Where will all the bunnies live if not on Adams land? I couldn't let that happen and I knew Julia had gobs of money, so I took it."

Julia let Hector go and shook her head. She had a feeling that she owed Xavier an apology. "How the hell did you figure this out, Xavier?"

Hector shrugged his slender shoulders. "He traced me, I'll bet. I thought about it afterwards. I did it for the bunnies, Julia. I'm sorry. It just got out of control and when you showed up here on the farm and told everyone what was happening, I tried to put it back. I swear I did. Seems I'm much better at robbing the rich."

"Hector, why didn't you just come to me? And Max, you told me everything was all right. What the hell is going on?"

"Hector? You're in deep shit, buddy," Max threatened. "It was nothing for you to worry about. We don't want your money, Julia. It isn't right."

"Damn it, Max, how about you let me decide where my money goes and Hector, what you did was really sucky, but I understand... I think." Julia shook her head. All of a sudden, her rage dissipated, but obviously, Xavier's hadn't.

"Baby? What the hell is going on, Julia?"

"Hold on," Martine said. "Before you two start hurling things at each other, why don't we take Hector and this party elsewhere while he tells us how to get your money back, Julia. You two need time to talk. Julia? We'll be at our cabin if you need us. Hector? Bust a move."

JC latched onto Derrick and Max and ordered, "C'mon, caveman brothers, outta here."

As they filed out, Julia turned to face Xavier. Her heart cramped at how tired he looked. Julia took a deep breath. "I'm sorry."

"Sorry? Sorry? You thought I embezzled your money and you're sorry? You left Manhasset without a single 'fuck you' and you're sorry?"

Wee doggie, he was fuming. "I know it looks bad, but imagine it from my end, huh? I look at my account and it's empty. What was I supposed to think, Xavier? Some money is better than no money. I sure as hell didn't hear from you..."

"How the hell am I supposed to call you when you don't goddamned well answer your cell phone? I left you at least fifty messages, Julia Lawrence!"

Oh, maybe mad was the wrong word to use here. Livid? Yes, that suited his purple face and the mottled color on his cheeks. "My cell phone doesn't work in Hooterville," she joked, hoping he'd relax.

"Ooooooh, well isn't that nice to know while I hunt for you high and low in fucking Manhasset!" he yelled as he glared at her, wild eyed and well, still kinda cute.

"Are you really mad?" Julia smiled prettily and clucked her tongue.

"Yes, I'm *really* mad, Julia!"

"Like really, really mad?"

"Julia? I'm as many reallys as you can tack onto mad. You didn't even give me a chance to explain. You just took off like a shot. How the hell can we date if you do that? Your communication skills sorely lack."

Okay, she'd give him that. She'd been frazzled and pissed and scared all at once and she'd done the only thing she knew how to do. Run away. "You're right. I said I was sorry. Ya want a lung now?"

"No, Julia. I want an explanation. Several as a matter of fact."

"It was a pretty bad day?"

"No, no. That's not good enough, Ms. Werewolf. I want to know why it was so bad a day, you couldn't tell me. I get the money part. I don't get why you jumped to conclusions. I don't get the baby part..."

Oh, yeah. The wee were-cub they were going to have. "I took a pregnancy test. It was a very pretty shade of pink. I didn't think I could get pregnant out of mating season, but it would seem the cross shifter thing must have gone awry."

"A baby…" he muttered. Xavier's eyes were weary and his jaw went slack.

"I don't need anything from you, Xavier. Not your money, not your support. So you can just go on home to Manhasset and never have to tell your family a thing." *Jackass.*

"Forget my family, Julia. I don't care how they feel about us."

"You don't?" *Are you on crack, Mr. my family has never mated outside of its own kind?*

"No, I don't. I do care about this baby and forgive me if I take a moment to adjust to becoming a father."

Julia snickered. She couldn't imagine Xavier as a father. Jeez. She couldn't even imagine herself as a mother. "This wasn't something I planned. We didn't use protection from the get go and I thought you were human when we nailed each other the first time…"

Xavier ran a hand over his tawny hair and pulled her to him. "I'm not blaming you, honey. I'm just overwhelmed. I expected to have to prove to you that I didn't steal your money and instead, Hector stole my thunder."

"You weren't expecting a baby either…" Julia bit the inside of her cheek. She'd had a week to adjust to the possibility of motherhood and she'd done it without considering Xavier.

"No, I sure as hell wasn't, but I won't say I'm unhappy. Just a little -- a little --"

"Freaked out," Julia finished for him. "I know. I was too. You can take all the time you need to think, Xavier. I would never pressure you into anything you didn't want. You were a swinging bachelor, going through women like fast food. I obviously don't need anything from you to raise a child. So go back to Manhasset and give yourself a chance to get your thoughts together." And she meant those words. As much as she wanted Xavier, she'd never ask him to do something he wasn't up for one hundred percent. Julia tried to squirm out of his arms, but Xavier tightened them around her.

"I'd never met a woman quite like you at any of the drive thrus I hit either, Julia. I have no intention of letting that go. I was serious when I said we should see each other exclusively. Exclusive just got a whole new meaning," he teased as he kissed her cheek.

"How about we take this slowly. I'm not talking marriage or anything of the kind. I'm talking about us staying on the path we originally intended. We just have an added bonus with junior here. I'm sure we'll discover soon enough if what we have is long term. Plus, I think I'd better work on my communication skills, huh?"

Xavier splayed his hand over her still flat belly and chuckled. "Uh, yeah. They could use some help. I say, deal." Xavier kissed her then, and Julia found herself pressing into his hard frame, wrapping her arms around his lean waist.

"I say, okay and I guess I should let you meet the family minus the possibility of having the shit kicked out of you, huh?"

"I say, can we do that later?"

"I say, it depends on what later involves."

"I say, it involves you and me naked anywhere but here in the living room."

"I say, you tell me how you found me first."

"I say, you've got a really nice store clerk named Rachel and she was a hard cookie to crumble."

Julia smiled. "You knew about Hector? Why didn't you call the money police on him?"

"Let's just say I made the connection and I figured his intentions were good, whatever they were."

"You know, Simba?"

"What?"

"I like you a lot too."

"Good. Don't ever run off on me like that again, Julia. Now, whaddya say we go consummate that like?"

"I say, I want to see you in lion form."

"I think I can arrange that, but only after we go make like."

Julia pressed a quick kiss to his lips. "I'll race you to my room."

Julia zipped out of the big family room and off to her bedroom, Xavier's laughter filling her ears.

The End...
Well, almost...

Epilogue

Xavier smiled up at Julia and she curled her arms around his neck, arching into the last stroke of his cock with a whimper.

He scratched his back on the tree he was leaning against in a sitting position. "Woman, you'll kill me with these romps in the woods."

"You love our romps as much as you love me and you know it."

"Yeah, yeah. What I don't love is these damn burrs stuck in my ass."

Julia reached under them and tweaked that ass, hard and supple, and giggled. "It's a small price to pay for my feminine wiles."

They'd spent many weekends here at her family's farm and the more she came home, the more she felt her roots strengthen. The Adams clan had also welcomed Xavier exactly as Julia expected they would.

"You been thinking about that marriage thing?" Xavier asked.

"Oh, yeah. I thought about it."

"And?"

"And, okay."

"Damn, that was way too easy for a woman who didn't want any sticky relationships."

"Don't get too complacent here. You felt much the same way."

"Well, I changed my mind."

Julia stuck her tongue out at him. "So did I."

"Good thing or junior might be illegitimate."

Julia laughed and snuggled closer to Xavier. "I guess he won't be now."

"Not if I have anything to say about it."

"I only let you have a say --"

A loud voice cut Julia off, forcing them to pull apart and rush to gather their clothes.

As both she and Xavier hit the clearing, they found a large man standing with a clipboard. His dark head was bent over it and he massaged the back of his neck.

Julia rushed toward him and confronted him. "Who the hell are you? This is Adams land."

With an eerie calm, he looked up and said, "I know." His pale blue eyes penetrated hers.

"Then get the hell off of it!" Julia yelled up at him. Cheerist he was pale, freakishly so, but he was fabulously sculpted and chiseled like fine marble.

Xavier came to stand beside her, putting an arm around her thickening waist. "How about you tell us why you're on Adams land and then you get the hell off it?"

"No," the stranger said staunchly.

"Did you just say *no*?" Julia screeched in disbelief.

He shook his head. "Yes."

Julia looked at Xavier with wild eyes. "Did he just say no to *me*? *Me*?"

"He did."

"To *me*," she reiterated.

"Yes, honey. You."

Xavier backed away from the tall, dark stranger and said, "If I were you, I'd tread lightly. That's all I gotta say." Leaning into Julia's ear, he whispered, "Go easy on him, honey."

"Who the hell do you think you are, telling -- *me* -- no?!" Julia pointed her finger at him as she frothed at the mouth, noting once again how pale he was.

"I have every right to tell you *no*."

"Really, Casper? Says who?"

"Me."

"And *who* are you?"

Towering over her, his condescending look was the last thing he gave her before he said, "I'm an Adams…"

Wolf Mates: Ruff & Ready

Dakota Cassidy

Chapter One

"Fucktaaaaard!"

"Tree hugger!"

"Jack off!"

"Grow up, Emerson!" was the heated return response, followed by mocking laughter.

"Grow *this*!" she yelled back to the slam of the flimsy trailer door.

"Oh, Emerson! I don't see how being a potty mouth is going to help us here. I mean, we want to be civilized, don't we? Who's going to take us seriously if we resort to name calling? It's petty and well... sooooo kindergarten."

Emerson Palmer gave Hector Adams a pointed look and then hung her head, rubbing her temples. "You're right, Hector. That *was* childish of me." But hey, every once in awhile it was okay to let your inner child out Emerson decided, throwing a pine cone at Lassiter Adams' trailer window with fastball speed. "You hear me, you needle dick? You're a condo loving, landfill snarfing, brick laying 'ho!"

The trailer door remained closed.

Palmer versus Adams, round one bazillion and one was officially over.

For the moment.

Emerson Palmer, environmental groupie, defender of all creatures great and small, had had this argument with Lassiter Adams for three months now -- ever since he'd parked his stupid construction trailer/bachelor pad on Adams land and declared it his.

Every bloody day for three months.

Emerson blew a strand of long, platinum blonde hair that had escaped from her ponytail out of her face. Her cheeks were flushed with anger and frustration as she stood, looking at Lassiter Adams' trailer door.

He peeked out of the small window along the right side of his temporary quarters and waved to Emerson with a smug smile, further infuriating her.

"Arghhhhhhhhhhhhh! He makes me insane! I just can't figure him, Hector, ya know? He's been here for three months, digging stuff up, and not a single apartment complex to show for it. You'd think he'd want to get moving. Yet, he does the same thing day after day. Dig holes and cover them back up. He's like a dog looking for a bone and he can't remember where it's buried."

Hector smiled at Emerson, snickering while petting his beloved rabbit with a gentle hand. "Well, that *dog* likes your butt."

She snorted. Lassiter Adams didn't like anything but money. The money building an apartment complex in the middle of nowhere would bring him. Young city dwellers looking for a bit of suburbia would swarm here for a taste of town and country. Thus killing the animals Emerson fought so hard to protect.

Defeated for today, she began the long walk back to the Adams house with Hector close behind her.

Once more, for posterity, she shrieked into the now bulldozed clearing, "Animal killer!" Her vicious accusation echoed through the open space.

Hector clucked his tongue at her with reproach. "Emerson, I really don't think this has gotten us anywhere so far. Maybe you should try being nice to him? He doesn't hate animals. He has a parakeet. You saw him talking to it through the window when we spied on him. So he must not hate all animals."

Emerson's eyes flashed at Hector and he cringed ever so slightly. "If he didn't hate them, he wouldn't want to build stupid condos on their homes. If we don't stay tough, Hector, we're going to lose the fight."

His snort was all Emerson needed, but he went ahead and said the words out loud anyway. "I don't wanna be the bearer of bad news, but we *are* losing the fight, Em."

Turning on him, she threw her hands up in the air. "And so what? You want to just give up?"

"No." He shook his dark head vehemently. "I never want to give up, but how can we fight the back taxes owed on acreage this size, Em? Max didn't know about them and he couldn't come up with the money to pay it, so the town took what they were offered from Lassiter. He sure has plenty of money."

What a mess. How could it be that the taxes had been left unpaid for so long? The Adamses weren't rich -- well, maybe Julia was -- but they weren't poor either. So who forgot to check the little stub on the mortgage bill? According to Hector's cousin Max, no one had known the taxes hadn't been paid. Adams land had always been Adams land. Period. Which led Emerson to believe that the town of Columbia, in the fine state of New Jersey, was dicking the Adamses around for some cashola and they'd decided that the first person to come up with said money was as good as any -- and that money came from Lassiter Adams.

Greedy corporate bastard that he was, small town USA had let him grease their palms.

Yet, he hadn't built a single thing to date. He dug around with lots of machinery while Emerson and her group of environmental activists chained themselves to bulldozers and trees to protest. His answer to that was to simply choose another portion of the vast Adams acreage to dig up, surprising them each new day that dawned with a new location. It became like a daily game of cat and mouse to figure out where he'd dig next.

However, none of that explained his claim to be an Adams. Adams was a common last name -- as common as Jones or Smith. So where was the proof that Lassiter was an Adams? Of the *were* variety, no less?

There wasn't any proof like documentation, other than he shared the same last name. And, due to the fact that asking Lassiter might reveal a secret about the Adamses they didn't want to reveal -- no one said anything. They grumbled, they shook their fists at him, but they didn't make him prove he was really an Adams from the infamous werewolf pack, better known as One Flew Over the Cuckoo's Nest.

Yes, the Adams family was rare and unusual. They didn't care if your mate was a penguin, so long as you'd found love. They didn't care if you didn't like to hunt and run with the full moon or lived on a strictly vegetarian diet and married a cat. They loved you for *who* you were, not what the typical werewolf pack thought you should be. That was what made Emerson fight even harder on behalf of the

Adams, because they accepted her for who she was -- an avenger of small creatures and animal lover extraordinaire.

Emerson's family couldn't accept what they considered her quirks and so, at the age of twenty-one, she'd left. Now she only saw them occasionally, because she couldn't accept their rigid werewolf rules and regulations.

That might have made her a rebel in the eyes of most wolf packs. However, not in the eyes of the Adams family. The Adamses didn't care that the very idea of hunting a small animal made her queasy. Just because she was a werewolf it didn't mean eating meat was essential to her well-being. She was, after all, half human and found she shifted just fine on broccoli, thank you.

It was simply another factor in her quest to help the Adamses. Their unconditional acceptance of her.

And that brought her back to the stalemate they were in with the newest Adams and where this land ownership nonsense remained. Lassiter Adams dug up the surrounding acres like a kid in a sandbox and the Adams clan couldn't stop him.

But it wasn't for lack of trying. All of the Adamses, in one way or another, had attempted to drive Lassiter away.

Even Julia -- wealthy from her designer pet clothing boutique -- didn't have enough liquid assets to stop Lassiter.

He was a monster.

An ass-tastic monster, but still a monster.

Emerson ignored the call of her hormonal whining and the reminder that Lassiter was crazy hot, and set about focusing on her newest form of protest.

Maybe she could find all the keys to his stupid bulldozers and swallow them?

She'd shit brass for a week, but it might be worth it.

* * *

Lassiter Adams let the curtain of his window fall, shutting out Emerson Palmer, and set about looking once again at the map of vast Adams acreage. Shit, there was a boatload of land to cover, but he'd dig and dig until the twelfth of never if it meant that he'd find what he was looking for.

For the first time in the many years since he'd been searching, he felt hopeful. An end to this disaster in life he'd been dealt would be welcome.

Crossing the room, he looked into his parakeet Bud's cage and winked. "Well, little guy, I think we shut up that Emerson for today. Looks like she's off to fight another cause. Christ, I'm sick of her yap."

"Sickofheryap. Sickofheryap," Bud chirped back.

Though, she did have a hot yap. Lassiter rather liked to watch it move when she opened it and called him some of the most vile names he'd ever heard. It was full, lush, ripe and very red -- very kissable and in the three months since he'd been here at the Adams stead, he'd, on more than one occasion, wondered what it would be like to have them wrapped around his cock.

She was a feisty one.

A feisty pain in his long drawn out search for a needle-in-a-haystack ass.

He looked at Bud and chuckled. "You know, I feel lucky here, Bud. I think this just might be it."

"Ititit," Bud chirped back, fluttering his multi colored wings from his perch.

"Yeah," Lassiter said out loud, more to reassure himself than anything else, "it. We'd better hope this is it. We're running out of options." His stomach grumbled, making him momentarily forget the shitload of work ahead of him. It was feeding time.

Pausing for a moment, he wondered what Emerson would taste like. The creamy arch of her neck against his lips when he...

Rolling his head on his neck to relieve the tension Emerson never failed to create, Lassiter ignored the flare up from all points tropical just thinking of her evoked and went to his fridge for nourishment, planning the next day's dig.

And how, yet again, to outwit, outlast, outrun Emerson Palmer.

Chapter Two

Emerson cooed at baby Quinn and shoveled another spoonful of goop into his mouth. His gummy smile gave Emerson a reason to smile too, rather than hang onto her anger.

"He's a messy one, huh, Em?" Derrick Adams remarked while grabbing a roll of paper towels and cleaning the floor surrounding Quinn's high chair.

"He's definitely a team player when it comes to messy," she giggled, taking some of the paper towel and wiping at her jeans.

Derrick ran a hand over Quinn's head with fatherly affection. "He gets that from his mother. Have you seen her eat?" he joked.

"I heard that, Derrick Adams, and I'll have you know, cats are the cleanest creatures on earth. You dogs are another story altogether." Martine sat on the chair opposite Emerson and grinned at Quinn. Tucking her long, graceful legs under her, she folded her hands and placed them on the wooden table. "And even if his eating habits were from me, it's very obvious, wolf man, his looks are too."

Derrick put an arm around his wife's shoulder and kissed the top of her sleek black head. "Yeah, I guess I have to credit you with those."

They made a great couple, Derrick and Martine, Emerson mused. They were another example of how accepting the Adams pack could be. Quinn was proof that the Adamses were good people. He was, after all, half domestic cat and half werewolf.

Cat-dog, as Martine had explained with a laugh. Little Quinn was the apple of everyone's eye and certainly would grow up with a healthy attitude toward diversity.

"You're good at this, Emerson. You really ought to have one of your own," Martine said, taking Quinn from his high chair and bringing him to the sink for a cleaning.

Well, at this stage in the game, Immaculate Conception was her only alternative. Unless BOB could father children, Emerson was shit out of luck. A twinge of motherly dreams gone astray hit Emerson, but she shrugged it off in favor of being a pseudo aunt and caretaker of stray animals.

"Emerson? How did the rumble for wee animals in the jungle slash potential pay per view special go with you and Lassiter today?" JC asked, stirring something that smelled delicious on the stove.

Emerson's snort was derisive. "It went like it always does. He digs. I hurl epithets at him for being an animal killer while he does it. He doesn't budge, he doesn't flinch, he just keeps on going. *Nothing* ruffles that man --"

"And it's starting to piss you off, eh?" Max interrupted, kissing JC's cheek and cupping her burgeoning belly. "How's Max junior in there today?"

JC smiled warmly, but said, "We don't know if it's a junior or a juniorette, farm boy, and the baby is just fine."

Though it looked as if JC were due at any moment, her pregnancy wasn't quite what the alpha Adams, Max, had expected. In a human pregnancy, JC was but three months along. However, seeing as the sire of this particular offspring was a werewolf and the mother a human, no one knew what to expect. Apparently, each half human, half werewolf pregnancy was different.

"I can tell you this, snookums. It might be a while before I let ya knock me up again. I have human friends who were pregnant and they don't look like this --" she pointed to her belly and snorted, "-- when they're only three months along. What I don't get is how I feel like I've been pregnant forever. It's the damned pregnancy of the millennium, for crap's sake," she complained.

"It's sturdy seed I planted, eh, wench?" Max nudged Derrick and snickered.

Turning, both hands on her wide hips, JC narrowed her eyes and pointed the spoon she had in her hands at them. "Sturdy my eye, Don Juan. It's demon seed, buddy, and don't you forget it! It keeps me up at night. It makes me puke all day long and worse still, it's given me split ends!" JC stomped off to the freezer, waddling as she went.

"So, Emerson? Make any headway with Lassiter today? Or are we still where we were three months ago?" Max asked again.

Sadly, Max's defeated look made Emerson's daily report even bleaker. "Well, I did call him some new names today, if that makes you feel any better."

"Look, Emerson. You're not getting anywhere here. I feel like we're just wasting your time, not to mention the time of your organization. I don't want to give up but Lassiter is shredding our land acre by acre, and neither you nor I seem to be deterring him."

Emerson looked up into the handsome, rugged face of Max Adams and, for the first time since she'd begun this project to save his land, she felt all hope slipping away. "I can't give up, Max. I feel like it today, but I can't and neither can you. Don't you want your baby to someday be able to run under the moonlight on Adams land? Don't you want that too?" she asked Derrick pleadingly, turning to face him and Martine.

"Yes, Emerson," Max assured her. "It's what we all want, but we've used up a lot of your valuable time. There's no talking to the man, no reasoning with him. He bought our land right out from under us and with no explanation. It doesn't matter if he's an Adams, according to the town. They just like the fat account they have now because of him. So what else is there? You can't go on day after day calling him names and throwing foliage at him. You had a life before our cause and you should be able to go back to it."

If only the life part of that impassioned speech were true. Emerson's life was the animal rights organization she worked for. Save the Tails was all she had and, truth be told, she'd be really sad to leave the Adams, even if they did find a way to stop Lassiter. "So are ya kicking me out?" she half-joked, half-wondered out loud.

"Are you kidding? Who would teach us new and inventive ways to say shit stain, if not for you?" Martine asked. Her smile was sympathetic and so genuine it made Emerson's teeth hurt. "We just feel guilty, Emerson. We know the money for this cause you've taken on is long gone by now. Your paycheck stopped coming three weeks ago."

Foiled again. Indeed, her paycheck had stopped coming because Save the Tails couldn't justify the kind of money needed to stop a company as large as Lassiter Adams'. It was a non-profit organization. Their salaries came from donations. The pay was little, but the work was rewarding for Emerson.

It didn't matter that her pay was inconsequential. It was never very big to begin with. Emerson just got by on her salary as it was. She couldn't afford to live without it permanently. She'd be high and dry if not for her trust fund.

"I'm okay, Martine. I really am. I want you all to have what you deserve, and Lassiter Adams has to shit or get off the pot someday. He can't just keep digging forever. We have to figure out what he wants and try to offer him something."

Damn, she hated the failure of her voice in her own ears. Fuck Lassiter Adams. The defenseless animal killer! "Just give me a couple of more weeks and let's see what happens, okay? I've been in a tangle or two with the likes of worse than Lassiter. Unless I'm imposing..." She let her words trail off. Maybe they were just sick of her interfering in their lives? Emerson could be very single minded when it came to the environment. When she was off trying to preserve something, she forgot much else.

Like her nails.

Looking down at her hands, she realized they were in need of a good manicure. Everything went by the wayside when she had the environmental bug up her ass.

"Emerson can stay as long as she wants. Got that, Em?" JC called from inside the freezer. "She's the only other person in this house who hasn't made fun of me because I'm worried this baby created by my farm stud is going to be born with better hair than me."

Max's chuckle was playful when he crossed the kitchen to swat at JC's backside. "You can stay as long as you like, Emerson. You're no imposition. We feel like we're imposing on you."

If only Max Adams knew how good his family was for someone like Emerson. Someone like Emerson who didn't have the support of her own family, but had found it with these people.

Her reluctance to give up was bolstered.

Lassiter Adams could kiss her hairy lupine ass.

And why did the very thought of that give her chills?

And not the kind that were unpleasant.

* * *

Emerson rapped on the thin, white door of Lassiter's trailer. Trees whipped with the nippy breeze and the air was clean with the scent of freshly dug dirt. The night was chilly, calling to her to shift and roam freely over the hills and valleys of the Adams farm.

But ya can't do that if Lassiter Adams is going to be hot on your ass with his bulldozer, now can ya?

That was the very reason Emerson was here. To try one last ditch effort to talk Lassiter out of keeping the land. Maybe she could talk him into allowing Max and his family to pay back the money he'd forked over. Like easy lifetime installments on a monthly basis.

"Ah, the tree hugger," Lassiter mocked, opening the door to reveal the brick shithouse hard body he was. His voice was like brown sugar melted with butter, thick and bubbling sweet. He grinned in that smug, disarming way that made her furious and tingly at the same time.

Emerson let out a loud, exasperated sigh and bit her tongue. "Yes, it's me. The tree hugger. I'd like to talk, if we could." She was shooting for amicable, but saying the words through clamped teeth might ruin the effect she was aiming to achieve, so she loosened her face into an almost smile.

"Shouldn't you be off trying to save the almost extinct tsetse bat in Zimbabwe or something?"

Folding her hands in front of her, she clasped them together to keep from clocking him in his perfect chops. Pleasant. She could be pleasant. She had to be pleasant if she wanted to try and find a rational end to this. "I don't think Zimbabwe has tsetse bats. I could be wrong, but last I checked, no tsetse bats."

Lassiter's jaw twitched and his hands rested on his lean hips. "Well, there must be a better cause than this. Go find it, Emerson, and leave this cause alone. It's a dead issue. I'm not leaving."

Sucking in her cheeks, she tamped down the ire that swirled in her throat and worked its way to her sharp tongue. "What is it you want, Lassiter? You haven't built anything, but you keep digging up stuff and ruining perfectly good wilderness. Why can't you just let the Adams be and go dig somewhere else?"

"Because you'll just follow me to '*somewhere else.*' I figure I'm hiding in plain sight here." He chuckled, probably because he thought he was clever. When really, he was just a shithead.

Ohhhhhhhh, that smug, arrogant tone of his chewed at her ears, making them burn. Shoving her hands in the pockets of her jeans, she plodded on. "I don't follow you, Lassiter. I follow a cause," she said with a calm she didn't feel.

Rocking forward on his toes, Lassiter positioned his body close to hers without actually touching it. The heat he emanated was sexy and daring, and Emerson's nostrils responded in kind, flaring to the musky, male scent. "Your cause won't stop me from doing what I need to do, Emerson."

And what the fuck was that exactly? What did he need so desperately to do? Emerson looked into his dark brown eyes, staring down at her, and narrowed her own. "You never change, Lassiter Adams."

His breath fanned her cheeks, warm and smelling faintly of something sweet. "Neither do you, Emerson Palmer," he said with sinister glee before hauling her to him and pulling her into the trailer, then shoving the door shut with a booted foot.

Emerson hung in his arms, neither allowing nor preventing her capture. Calling Lassiter large was, by far, understating his bulk. The arms that held her tightened, holding her much smaller frame close, allowing her a sampling of his thickly muscled thighs.

And what hung between them.

Some things, like the hard thing between Lassiter's legs, never changed.

Chapter Three

"So when are we going to stop behaving as if we don't know each other, Em?"

Emerson leaned back and she braced herself on his hard forearms. His rugged face, always suspiciously pale for the amount of time he spent in the sun, loomed in front of hers. "I never said I didn't know you," she hissed, finally losing the control she'd promised herself she wouldn't.

"So then you've told the Adams you're privy to me in, er, the most carnal of ways?" he taunted, but didn't elaborate.

Her cheeks burned. "That's no one's business but mine. It has nothing to do with what's happening here at the Adams'. However, if you choose, you can give me up. Go crazy," she dared him, defiantly letting her gaze slip to his.

Lassiter's hand slid down her spine, resting on the curve of her ass. The hip hugger jeans she wore now seemed terribly tight, making the heat of his bulk an entity she wasn't willing to encounter. His tight, full body press was keeping Emerson from thinking clearly.

"So, that was just a weak moment for you last year in California? I meant nothing to you, is what you're saying? I'm some cheap lay to be discarded at whim?" His tone was light, but the underlying anger in it was there too. She sensed it in the way he said discarded. Eyes like melted chocolate stared into hers, daring her.

To do what, she didn't know.

To say what, she knew even less.

Oy. No, it hadn't been like that at all. It had, however, been very foolish on her part, and when all was said and done, she'd left California for less humiliating territory with her tail between her legs, literally. "I'm saying that it happened and it's over. What's happening here has nothing to do with California."

His head dipped and he rasped his tongue over the smooth column of her throat, evoking her raw nerves to dance to life. "Do you always fuck the men you hope to annihilate for your *cause*?"

"Do you fuck the women who hope to annihilate your cause to prevent them from coming out on top?" she shot back snidely.

"I *was* on top, as I recall."

Emerson's body trembled, not only with the memory of their one-time encounter, but with the idea that she wasn't trying very hard to keep another from occurring. "No, Lassiter. You know --"

"I know nothing, Emerson. I know we screwed our brains out and the next day you were gone. Your replacement didn't have nearly the ass you do, especially when he chained himself naked to a tree."

"I had business to attend to elsewhere. Now I'm here and we meet again. You on one side and me on another. That's not news. We had no business doing what we did. So could we forget that and move on like adults?"

His fingers swept over the underside of her breast and his mouth lingered over hers, the tip of his nose just touching her own. "Sure we can," he answered cockily before taking her lips to his and nibbling the soft flesh.

"Good," she muttered, more to herself than anyone else. Rotating her head away from his, she said brokenly, "That means -- well, it means -- that you have to -- Ohhhhh..." she murmured, distracted by the slither of his tongue, silky and hot, cool and sweet all at the same time, slipping between her lips and devouring her senses. Her mouth parted like the Great Divide, opening in acceptance, letting his tongue wreak havoc with her body.

His chuckle was low when Emerson responded, returning the kiss fully by arching into him.

Long fingers dipped into the top of her baggy sweater, trailed over the top of her cleavage, teasing her nipple with an elusive wisp of a swipe. He lingered, caressing the skin and kissing her with a greedy mouth that demanded she comply. Lassiter's hands delved deeper, popping a nipple out of her lace bra and rolling it between his fingers.

Emerson's groan was long, shuddering, tormented by the electric shots of pleasure that flew to her cunt with rapid fire. Liquid and like molten lava, she found herself wrapping her arms around his shoulders, pulling him in closer, inviting him to relieve the burning ache in her pussy.

His fingers found the buttons of her sweater and deftly opened them, parting the sweater and popping the clasp on the front of her bra. He roamed over the swell of each breast, moving from the soft texture of skin to the harder, rippled texture of her nipple.

The internal battle for supremacy was losing in the wake of Lassiter's hands. Strong, callused, expertly moving from breast to breast, massaging them in sensuous circles.

She shivered, relaxing into him, straddling Lassiter's thick thigh and rubbing against it with a slow slide. The friction of her jeans, coupled with his long fingers teasing her nipple, left Emerson wet, squirming, and she clung to him.

When he dove for her nipple, latching onto it and sliding his tongue along the rigid flesh, Emerson sighed, leaving a residual squeak to slip out in its wake. His mouth was heaven, his tongue raspy and hot, lapping at her aching nipple.

Her trembling was supported only by his solid hold on her, keeping her from melting on the spot. The sharp sound of the zipper on her jeans sliding down was mingled with her exhale. Lassiter sinuously slid a hot hand over her abdomen, circling her navel with his forefinger, trailing it over the top of her bikini underwear. Slipping under the silk, he wasted no time spreading her flesh, roaming over the lips of her cunt, wet and hungry for his touch. She bucked against his hand, letting the heat of it hold her captive, absorbing the delicious torment he stirred.

When his finger found the hard, swollen nub of her clit, she bit her lower lip to keep from howling. Lassiter fondled her clit with gentle passes, then slid a finger into her passage, allowing a moment for her to adjust before thrusting with firm strokes.

The rise of an orgasm Emerson shouldn't be having lashed at her with a careless abandon. Small tendrils of smoke gave way to an inferno of sensation, clawing at her gut and settling in her pussy.

She fucked his finger, focusing all of her attention on the rigid pleasure it brought, while his mouth tugged at her nipple. Her hands grabbed at the thick locks of hair on his head, clutching and driving them into his scalp as the wild need to come took over everything else.

When his teeth grazed her already sensitive nipple and the heel of his hand caressed her clit, Emerson whimpered, then let go with a heave of air. The pressure of her climax suspended and held her in its grip, then slammed into her with hurricane force, making her knees buckle.

Lassiter's firm hold on her never wavered. When his skillful ministrations seized Emerson, she collapsed against his rock-solid frame, blowing out a gush of air and clinging to him for support.

Dragging her upward, Lassiter stood her up to face him and smiled. "So, I guess we're going to do the 'this was a mistake' thing again, right?"

Emerson's lips wouldn't move and her throat was Sahara desert dry. She shook her head. Cheerist what was wrong with her? What was it about this man that had her one moment wanting to slice his balls up and serve them as pâté on a cracker, and the next melting like so much butter in his hot hands?

Gathering her focus, Emerson looked into his dark brown eyes and gave him a wan smile. "No. It's never a mistake if I come."

His eyebrow slid upward, but his impassive face remained calm, letting her know he wasn't going to be ruffled by her smart mouth. "Well, at least someone did."

"The right someone," she shot back through teeth that were clamped.

He stepped back from her, letting his arms fall to his sides. "That someone is still not going to get what she came here for. Whether she lets me play with her fun stuff or not."

"Yeah? Well, that street goes both ways, stud! Playing with my fun stuff doesn't mean that I'm going to stop harassing you until you go away."

The implication that she'd come to win by any means, even if that means was trolling, finished it for her. It simmered in her brain, and then boiled over. Her temper did what it always did. Flared, zinged to an all points bulletin, and then spilled out of her mouth. "Screw you, Lassiter! I don't give a shit how many bulldozers you have or how much money you throw around. I'll see you in hell before I'll let you trash any more of the Adams' land!"

Swinging around on her heel, Emerson clomped out of his shabby trailer and into the night, letting her fury allow her to shift.

The shift of bone led to the ripple of muscle and tufts of fur appeared on her arms as she bent to go with the flow of her change.

Her clothes fell away, pooling on the ground, shredding with the force of her growth.

She shook her now furry head, the snap of her ears satisfied her that she had indeed completed the shift. Once on all fours, Emerson lurched forward, hitting her stride with a light jog, then allowing her fury to fuel a fast paced trot.

The fucking son of a bitch.

The goddamned, thick haired, hard bodied, rippled abbed son of a bitch!

How dare he even imply she was willing to hock her wares for an environmental cause!

She just couldn't figure out why her cause didn't stop her from allowing him access to the wares in question.

* * *

"Screwyou. Screwyou," Bud chirped from his cage across the room.

"Okay, I get it. Shut up already," Lassiter warned testily. "Don't make me take your bird bath away, pal."

Damn it. He hadn't meant for things to get carried away. Emerson had a way about her that either had him cocked and at attention, or so pissed off he couldn't see straight. Her defiant arrogance, her flashing blue eyes, her rigid posture lent to a lust that took on a life of its own.

She wasn't typically what you'd call hot. Her lips were too full, her body almost too lean and her hair, always falling down around her heart shaped face in unruly, silken strands of blonde the color of wheat in the sunlight, was always a mess. Her nails were short and sometimes ragged -- most likely from all of the chaining herself to inanimate machinery. Her clothes were anything but what he'd seen on the average hottie in a bar or at the mall.

Emerson didn't much care for female finery, he supposed. She didn't wear what the current fashions were, according to what he saw on television, but it didn't stop him from wanting her just the same.

She did things to his nether parts that no woman should be allowed to do. It could be called indecent, and all she had to do was show up. After almost a year since their last meeting, he still warred with the urge to hunt her luscious ass down and make her submit to him. Yet, there she stood at his door, fresh faced and blonde, fighting the obvious urge to wallop him one and it started all over again.

She turned him on. Her scent made his nostrils flare and his unrelieved cock swell, straining against his jeans. She engaged every last sense he had, and it infuriated him to find that he couldn't keep his hands to himself.

Emerson smelled like a warm summer breeze laced with a hint of jasmine. It clung to his nose and lingered there. Bringing his hand to his face, he caught the remnants of her desire on his fingers. Tangy and sweetly laden with the thick cream of her satisfaction.

In exasperation, he shoved a hand in his pocket. Fingering the well-worn, rumpled piece of paper that never left his hands, the reminder of why he was on Adams land to begin with, Lassiter resolved to get a better grip on his loins.

No one, not even Emerson juicy lipped Palmer, was going to keep him from achieving that.

No one.

Chapter Four

Emerson ran with the chilled breeze at her back -- as if running could keep her ahead of Lassiter Adams -- as if his sensual invasion of her body could be run from.

She'd done just what she'd done in California.

Or, close to what she'd done in California.

Pausing under a barren oak tree, Emerson lay down. Paws in front of her, nose buried between them, hunkering into the cold ground.

Aren't you the little tart? her conscience called.

Indeed, she was. Throw a little weak and spineless into the pot, and she had a bubbling sauce of sissi-fied Emerson.

Lassiter had something, whatever that something was, that made her forget everything but her hormones. She had no other explanation. It was the only one she could come up with.

Especially after California.

Their encounter had happened quite unexpectedly and probably not the way most one-night stands do. One moment they were spewing fire and brimstone, the next, kissing the living shit out of each other and throwing down.

Oh, and they had thrown down.

In fact, it was the best throw down she'd ever had.

It all happened so quickly, after months of their ongoing battle, that when it was over, neither of them knew what to say.

So Emerson didn't say anything. She left without so much as a glance over her shoulder, slinking back off to the east coast and spending every waking moment trying to forget what had happened.

And now, she'd done it again. Well, almost.

Shitpissfuck.

What she couldn't understand was how Lassiter had become so hard-hearted. There'd been a time when he'd been on the same side as she.

* * *

As usual, seeing Lassiter sent Emerson's pulse soaring and her eyeballs floating off into the back of her head like she was possessed. Seeing him with Hector made her want to throw things.

A good night's sleep and some perspective about her personal relationships versus work had left Emerson feeling stronger. Her convictions were the same, no matter who she allowed to crawl between her legs.

Lassiter Adams had to go and he had to go without the personal joy it would bring him if she pitched another hissy fit. She'd resolved to remain as calm as possible and keep her name calling to herself.

Until she saw Lassiter with Hector, chatting like they were old fucking college roommates, reliving the good old days.

Was that what she thought she saw?

Was Lassiter really petting Hector's bunny?

Ohhhhhh that was a cheap play for Hector's emotions. There was no better way to his heart than to give him the opportunity to talk about his bunnies. Hector loved his bunnies. In fact, he loved them so much he'd once tried to steal money from his wealthy cousin Julia to save them.

Yet, there was big, tall, albeit a bit pale, muscled Lassiter, talking and laughing with Hector and not just holding, but petting his bunny. His lean, long tapered fingers stroked the fur with the ease of an animal lover.

But Lassiter wasn't an animal lover, or at least he wasn't anymore.

He was a defiler of them, ripping their homes to shreds, usurping their lives.

In general, fucking shit up on a daily basis so he could build condos with hot tubs and vaulted ceilings.

Emerson strode on lean legs to the clearing in front of Lassiter's trailer and stopped in front of the two men, waiting for them to acknowledge her.

Lassiter's head bobbed up, his sunglasses hiding whatever was behind them. "Morning, Emerson," was his casual "oh, it's you" greeting.

Ignoring Lassiter and his scent on the cold morning breeze, one that made Emerson's knees weak, she gave Hector a pointed look. "What's up this morning, Hector?"

Hector's grin was wide. "Lassiter said he'd help me rebuild the bunny house. I was having a lot of trouble with Pinky here." He pointed to the large, white bunny Lassiter held to his chest. "He kept getting out because the lock won't stay shut and Lassiter helped me find him."

Oh.

Well, wasn't Lassiter a real caped crusader?

The glee with which Hector spoke, his complete obliviousness to whatever Lassiter was cooking up, Lassiter's taking advantage of Hector's innocence, made Emerson's blood boil.

Emerson brushed her hair out of her eyes and faced Hector, who was a little too moony eyed for her taste. "I can help you, Hector."

He frowned, his eyes flashing confusion. "You cannot. You don't know how to use power tools."

Emerson sent him a signal with her expression that begged him to work with her, but Hector was having none of that.

Shaking his head, Hector said, "Lassiter knows how to use power tools."

Lassiter knows how to use all sorts of *tools* was Emerson's first thought.

"So… so do I," she muttered back. Well, okay, so she didn't know how to use a power tool, but that's what the Internet was for, right? Shit, she sure hoped JC had managed to convince Max that DSL was a necessity in Hooterville, as she called it.

"Really?" Lassiter drawled. "You've come a loooonng way since that trust fund, haven't you, Em?" His dark hair shone in the sun, dark hair that Emerson, just last night, had latched onto in passionate abandon. Leaning back against the shabby railed fencing that still remained after he'd dug the ground to China and back, Lassiter crossed his feet at the ankles and cradled the bunny. His T-shirt stretched over his pecs, enhancing their ripple.

And it was pissing her off. "Yeah, I have," she replied with as much calm as she could muster. "C'mon, Hector. Let's go see what we can do about Pinky's bunny hut."

Hector wasn't so convinced. "I dunno, Em. It has to be sturdy, otherwise Pinky'll get out again and I would be *very* upset if I lost him."

"We couldn't have Pinky running amok, now could we, Emerson?" Lassiter asked, turning his gaze to capture Emerson's. His question, laced with a taunt, increased her determination to build a freakin' bunny hut.

Hop, hop.

Emerson grabbed Hector's hand, staring up at Lassiter's dark, bespectacled eyes. "No, we couldn't have that. I can build a bunny hut. I will build a bunny hut. Now, c'mon, Hector," she commanded, pulling him behind her, before stopping momentarily.

Letting go of Hector's hand, Emerson took brisk strides back to Lassiter and shoved her hands in the cradle of his arms. "We'll take Pinky, thank you," she said stiffly, yanking Pinky, who was quite happy where he was, out of those fantastically bulging arms. Looking down at the silky white creature, Emerson said, "C'mon, Pinky. You're going to have a new home."

Emerson stomped off, Pinky and Hector in tow.

See me stick my tongue out at you, Lassiter Adams.

His chuckle drifted to her sensitive ears, mocking her.

* * *

Six hours later, a whole lot of chicken wire and piles of wasted wood, Emerson threw down the power drill with a scream of frustration. "Fucking piece of shit, useless, pointless, God damned waste of seventy-five bucks!" She closed her eyes and whirled around in a circle, kicking dirt as she went and dancing on the instructional sheet she'd printed from the Internet. In one last moment of fury, she kicked the long two-by-four that lay on the saw horse over, stubbing her toe.

"Mooootherfucker!" she yelped while hobbling on one foot.

"Uh-oh. Is that the potty mouthed, power tool wielding, 'I can do this myself' Emerson I hear?"

Fabulous.

Just what she needed.

Lassiter Adams up her ass, cracking on her for not being able to do something as simple as build a bunny hut.

Rubbing her foot through her sneaker, she retorted, "Shut the hell up, Lassiter, and go back to your trailer. I don't need your comments. I'm just experiencing a couple of technical difficulties is all."

Duct tape... nothing a little roll or twelve of duct tape wouldn't fix. She'd been smart when she bought the economy pack. Who needed a freakin' radial arm saw when you had duct tape?

Lassiter flicked a hand at the pile of wood she'd wasted and smiled. "So, ya need some help?"

Not if the world were to tip on its axis and she needed a reincarnation of Noah's Ark to sail 'round the tilted world, would she accept help from Lassiter Adams.

"Um, no thank you."

Walking toward her, all yummied out, he said, "That's the 'I'd rather be dead than take help from you, Lassiter' no thank you, huh?"

"No, actually, that was the 'I'd rather have my ovaries removed with rusty pliers and no anesthesia, Lassiter' no thank you." Emerson smiled smartly and gave Lassiter the evil eyeball. Damn him for interfering. She didn't need him to point out that she was fucking this up. She had a handle on that already.

It hadn't occurred to her that his trailer was in plain view of her bunny hut building site, and that he'd probably been watching her from his window and laughing his hot tookus off while she struggled.

"I don't need any help," she said again, pushing her hair out of her face with irritation.

His glance surveyed the mess she'd made and he toed some of the sawdust at her. "I beg to differ."

"I like it when you beg."

"Funny, I thought that was you doing the begging in California..."

Fucktard. "I don't need your help."

"Oh, but you do."

"No, no I don't."

"I build houses and apartment complexes, Emerson. You save trees, of which you've wasted many on this project. I think I can help."

Stupidhead. "I don't think Pinky and his fuzzy mates need a sauna and hot tub in their hut," she said dryly, turning her back to him to survey the mess she'd made. "Stick to ruining perfectly good forests so you can build swanky apartments, and I'll take care of the bunny hut."

Emerson felt the heat of his body behind her even before he spoke. "It doesn't have to be this way, Emerson. It wasn't always." His words were sentimental to her ears, said with the memory of familiarity, rife with what she'd call regret if she didn't know better.

"Sure it does, Lassiter. It has to be this way because we're no longer on the same side." Saying that out loud was almost physically painful for her. Her gut clenched, tightening and recoiling from the truth. Remembering what once had been was bittersweet and almost always hidden by her anger. They meshed with one another so perfectly now that she didn't know how to separate the two. It was a rare occurrence that allowed her to take Lassiter out of the box she labeled "forget about it already." When she did, it led to a void she couldn't fill with the jerk she'd run into ten years after they'd parted.

Anger with Lassiter was best. When she wasn't angry with him, she was throwing herself at him like a virgin in a whorehouse. Slapping herself against him like he was the last man on Earth.

Placing his hands on the top of her shoulders, Lassiter drew her to the wide expanse of his chest, curling his fingers into her collarbone. "We were friends for a long time, Em, and then, in California, we were lovers." The warmth his hands radiated soothed Emerson, seeping into her pores and turning into a liquid, electric current that skittered down her spine.

Who was this Lassiter? Not the one she'd seen after almost ten years in California. This Lassiter who sounded as if he regretted never looking back wasn't the one she'd become reacquainted with in California. That Lassiter was cold and angry. He was too busy making money with his big construction firm to regret much, in her estimation.

Yet this Lassiter, the one who stood behind her, encouraging her head to lie against his breastbone, didn't feel like the Lassiter from California. He didn't smell like him either. His scent was less harried. Less dark was the only way to describe it.

Lassiter didn't have an easy childhood, but instead of allowing it to hold him back, it had always seemed to fuel his desire to help others. However, the man she'd encountered in California was a man who lived strictly to exact some kind of weird revenge that Emerson was unable to understand.

On who or what he wanted revenge, Emerson was clueless. But the fact remained that Lassiter was here to do something she despised and that would always keep them from what "used to be."

"We don't have to pick sides when we're in bed," he whispered low against the shell of her ear, sensuous and inviting. It took all of her will and everything thereafter to keep from winding her arms around his neck.

"We aren't going to bed." No, no they weren't. And they weren't going to *ground* either, she thought, scrunching her eyes shut and staving off the impulse to throw him down on said *terra firma*, tear at his clothes and nail him.

Lassiter chuckled against her hair, the sound deep, vibrating against her back. "You know that's not what you want. You want me, Emerson, as much as I want you." He stated as much with his hands as with his words, roving over her ribs, running small circles against her thin shirt, skimming the underside of her breasts.

Her throat was closing and words were forming with sludge-like motion, but she was fighting it with everything she had. "Sex won't solve anything, Lassiter," she offered as a meek refusal.

"I disagree."

Yeah, so what else was new? They disagreed. Novel, huh?

"I think we can solve a lot of things if we just let happen what should happen on a frequent basis with you and I." A delicious tendril of a flame spiked her continual craving for him when he gathered her hair in his hand and tugged her head back.

"There's no solving this. You're not the man I once knew, Lassiter." Her protest grew less vehement when he nibbled at the side of her neck.

"No, Em, I'm not the *boy* you once knew."

Chapter Five

That was the truest statement he'd made thus far. No, he wasn't the boy she'd once known. The boy she'd once known didn't do this to her body. He didn't leave her weak and wanting more. She stiffened but Lassiter held her even tighter, running his tongue along her neck, against the lobe of her ear. Her head began to swim, her heart crashed against her ribs, her pussy throbbed with needing him.

"Why does it have to be this way, Lassiter?" she whispered to him, longing for something long since over.

Caressing the swell of her hip, he said hoarsely, "Let it go, Em. Let's just let it go for now. Let me touch you, lick you."

Her knees shook, her pulse quickened enough that she could hear it in her ears. The word 'no' was on the tip of her tongue, but the tip of his tongue held a different answer as it skimmed her ear, tracing small circles along the outer rim.

Spanning her waist, Lassiter pressed her to him, against the hardness of his chest and onto the bulge in his jeans.

With a will of their own, her hands wrapped around his neck and she arched into his hold, biting her lip as the heat of their bodies sizzled, searing an imprint on her spine. Skimming her sides, Lassiter dragged his hands over the swell of her hips, rounded the curve of her inner thigh, roaming in and out of her legs with a precise pattern.

The groan she omitted was low, feral. It caught in her throat and she swallowed the urge to claw at him with hands that rushed the process. Instead, she opted to let her head fall back and revel in the myriad of emotions he stirred in her, forgetting the anger between them.

The pop of the button on her jeans, the slide of the zipper went almost unnoticed to Emerson. Lassiter swung her around, gripping her shoulders and dragging her against him. His lips took hers possessively, plunging his tongue between them with rough insistence, gathering her closer until she almost couldn't breathe. Splaying his hand over her ass, he ground his hips into her. Emerson stood on tippey toe, trying to drive back at him, but Lassiter was stronger, scooping her up and laying her down on the ground.

Through her fuzzy haze of lust, she realized that they were out in the middle of the woods. It was cold and the ground, colder still. However, that didn't stop her from wanting him. It didn't stop her from needing to complete this act of sheer madness. It didn't allow her the time to think about it, or even want to reason with it.

Pushing her jacket off with hard hands, Lassiter groaned when his hand cupped her breast through her shirt. He pulled her to him, lodging her thigh between his own and thumbing her nipple. His callused skin caught on the material of her shirt, rasping over it, sending rippling waves of electric currents to her cunt.

Emerson pressed her palms to his chest, straddling his thigh and squeezing it to keep the wet heat between her legs from overwhelming her and she found her hands tearing at his waistband, pulling his shirt upward.

Her urgency led to impatience as she fumbled with his belt buckle and the zipper on his jeans. Her heart crashed with her impulsive need, her lungs begged for air, her breath coming in choppy breaths.

Emerson needed Lassiter inside her *now*, but Lassiter had other ideas. Ideas that had nothing to do with rushing their mating.

Yanking her arms over her head, he collared them in his hand and used his other hand to tug her shirt upward. Rolling Emerson to her back, he swiped her flesh with his tongue, circling her nipple, dancing around it, eliciting shivers of anticipation from her. Thrusting against him, she bowed her back, arching to invite him to lick her, but he followed a lazy path along her ribs instead. Nibbling at them. Caressing her skin, so hot now it literally burned. Placing delicate stabs of his tongue into her navel.

Her cunt throbbed, ached, swelled with the taunt of silk against her flesh. His muffled chuckle mocked her ears, but seared her senses.

Just when she thought she could no longer withstand the torture, Lassiter took her nipple in his mouth, rolling it between his lips, lapping at it with a snake like tongue. He unzipped her pants, settling a hand to rest in the curls at the top of her pussy.

Emerson's hips bucked against the warm invasion. Lassiter's hand was so big it spanned nearly the width of her slender hips, possessive in its progress to her cunt. The sound of her own breathing, labored and raspy, slithered to her ears and she squirmed against Lassiter's hand, awaiting his next move.

Removing her jeans with one hand, he pushed them down past her knees, still suckling her nipple, moving from one to the other with licks and strokes. Slipping a finger into her folds, Lassiter teased her clit, trailing his finger over the tip of it with a light pass.

The ground was cold on her back, but it didn't stop Emerson from kicking her jeans from her feet, taking her shoes with them and spreading her legs wide. Then she pushed up to meet the hand that brought with it such skilled ministrations.

A fire erupted in her groin when Lassiter let her hands go and lowered his body to her abdomen, continually stroking her, rubbing the lips of her labia, planting kisses along her hips and thighs. Leaning over her, he lay across her belly and took a deep breath. The inhalation was sharp, and a familiar act displayed when werewolves mated.

Scent was everything. Yet Lassiter wasn't a werewolf…

Emerson lost that vague, worrisome thought when he laid his head against her belly and stroked her inner thighs. Her hands threaded through his thick hair, luxuriating in its soft texture, pressing him close to her, letting the warmth of his breath so teasingly close to her cunt keep her walking the ledge of desire.

Over and over he drew his hands along her skin, setting patches of it on fire with need. Spreading her flesh with fingers that were assured and deft, Emerson caught her breath, holding it and waiting for the ecstasy she knew his tongue would bring.

Lassiter didn't dive into her the way most men had in her experience. He savored her, tasting her with light licks, stroking her with both tongue and lips. Dragging his finger along her slit to stop at her passage, he inserted a finger with a slow glide.

Her cunt wept and Lassiter groaned, licking the cream of her with a flat tongue, circling her clit, sucking it until she lifted herself on her heels to grind against him.

The sharp swirl of orgasm fluttered in her pussy and the last thrust of his finger had Emerson releasing Lassiter's head and shoving a fist in her mouth to keep from screaming out. It rocked her, shaking her entire body, left her trembling as it assaulted her again and again. Her gut was in a knot, her nipples tight and hard against the now chilled breeze.

Lassiter stayed between her thighs, letting her relax, kissing her with a gentle mouth. Moving back up to her lips, he kissed her. His tongue driving into her mouth, spicy and tingled her own. Cupping his jaw with both hands, Emerson opened her mouth wide, absorbing the heat of his lips.

Reaching between them, Lassiter pushed at his jeans and Emerson's hands followed right behind them to slip into his underwear and touch his cock.

He groaned into her mouth, a low, husky, growl when she rubbed the smooth tip of his shaft, playing over the head of it before grasping it and stroking its length.

He shoved his jeans down, kicking his sneakers off with them and straddled her narrow hips. Rising on her elbows, Emerson met his gaze, intense, dark and shadowed with lust. Still clad in his T-shirt, it fell over Lassiter's lean hips carelessly. The sharp definition of his hips, cut and hard, made Emerson's mouth water. She ran a hand over them, burrowing into the crisp hair just above his cock. Her fingers explored the ridges in his abdomen, kneading the flesh. Clutching his ass, she pulled him to her and lay back on the cold ground to let his cock hover over her mouth.

He ran a hand down the side of her cheek, caressing her jaw, cupping it, directing her to take him between her lips.

Scooting further down, Emerson rested her lips against his hard shaft, licking the flesh with tentative strokes. He was long, thick and so hot it seared her skin. His scent was musky, male. It smelled of sinful thoughts and carnal desires.

Swiping her tongue over the cap of smooth flesh made Lassiter buck. Cupping his balls, she licked him from stem to crown, at first with a flat, slow tongue, relishing the taste and texture of his skin, salty and hard. Her pace quickened, until she enveloped him between her lips, arching her neck to take all of him, letting his cock rest in her mouth before swirling her lips back up his length.

His hiss of satisfaction carried to her ears on the sharp wind, cool and thick with the smell of sex, desire, need.

Lassiter's hands found her head and with hips pumping, he thrust into her mouth furiously. She let her saliva moisten the passes she took, tightening her lips around his cock to form an O. His balls drew closer to his body, full and heavy, and Emerson cupped them, rolling them between her fingers, skating over the sacs with light touches.

Lassiter growled, "Stop. Stop *now*, Em." His demand was husky, ripping from his heaving chest and ending on a grunt.

Threading his hands into her hair, he pulled her close to his belly, obviously fighting for control. Palming her head, he dug his fingers into her scalp and took deep breaths.

Letting her go, he moved down her body, slipping between her legs and hauling her to him, enveloping her in arms that were like bands of steel.

Wrapping her legs around his waist, Emerson lifted her hips, allowing his thick cock to drag between her folds. Her heart raced with anticipation. It had been so long since they'd been together, and she found all of her reasoning crashing around her.

The swollen tip of his cock pressed against her. Lassiter was thickly girthed, not outrageously so but enough to make Emerson apprehensively expectant. It had been a long time since she'd mated with anyone and Lassiter sensed it.

"I'll take it slow, Em," he murmured, hot against her ear. "I want you enough to drive into you without reason, but I'd never hurt you. Relax against me, baby. Relax," he coaxed.

Emerson took his gentle, husky cue and gathered a breath, focusing on the heaven that was his body, flush with hers. She let each plane of his body sink into hers, every ridge and silken muscle join with hers, and then Lassiter took his first stroke.

The thrust, a wet, sensual glide of flaming heat, took the breath from her and she clung to Lassiter's shoulders, adjusting to the bulk of him.

His muscles were bunched with tension, but he held back until she shifted her hips and moaned, no longer able to contain the need. Holding her up to shield her from the cold ground, he took another deep plunge. Emerson moaned when her clit scraped against the crisp pubic hair at his belly. His thrusts brought their hips in sync, sealing them together. Sweat glued their hips, fusing them. Lassiter buried his face in her neck, his lips attaching to the smooth skin while he rolled against her, rocking them in a slow dance.

The weight of him, the sheer delicious pleasure of his skin against hers, was heady. Her nose flared with the scent of his sweat mingled with hers. Her cunt swallowed the length of him, inch by inch as he slid into her, convulsing around him until she thought she might cry out from the delirious pleasure.

Curling under him, she tightened her legs around his waist, mumbling incoherently when the fierce onslaught of orgasm touched the first nerve and set her on a path there was no turning back from. Emerson drove against him, pumping her hips upward, undulating with wild abandon, reaching to find the release that would end this burning climb to relief.

She felt the muscles in his back cord and bunch with tension, flexing against her own. Lassiter's neck arched back, the strong column of it tense.

As a myriad of sensations flooded her, Lassiter clenched his teeth, threw his head back and howled, long, eerily, sharp and resonant. It sang in her ears, leaving behind the vibration so familiar when she ran with her pack mates.

Yet her focus was lost when she came too, digging her fingers into his back and gritting her teeth when the undeniable pleasure he created exploded. Her juices ran, mingling with the hot spasms of come his cock ejected, jerking within her.

She couldn't hold onto him anymore, her arms ached and were weak from her release. Letting her arms fall away, she hung from his grip, trying to process what had just happened.

Lassiter panted for breath against her chest, keeping a tight hold on her.

When reality set in, Emerson realized her ass was numb from the hard ground beneath her and the cold was seeping into her bones.

She also realized they'd just boffed in the middle of a clearing, in the dead of night, buck, fricken' naked for all to see.

Howling like two dogs in heat.

Jesus Christ in a mini skirt.

Wait, her brow furrowed. *Howling...* Lassiter had howled. That high pitched keening only werewolves were capable of.

She lifted her head, grabbing the top of his by the hair and yanking it upward, looking directly into his eyes. "Wanna explain?"

His eyebrow crooked upward. "Explain what?"

She narrowed her eyes. "How can I put this delicately? When you were gettin' your rocks off, you howled. Stop right there," she said to his open mouth. "I know you want to protest, but save it. I know a howl when I hear one."

"It was good. I said so in the way of a *moan*. If you want to call it a howl, okay. I howled."

Emerson let go of his head with a quick hand and pushed at his chest, scrambling out from under him and pulling down her shirt. She dragged her jeans on and shook her head. "I work with animals all the time, Lassiter. You howled, like a -- like a --"

Sitting up he asked, "Like a *what*, Em?"

Well, fuck. Now here was a dilemma if there ever was one. She was outright accusing him of being exactly what she was. A werewolf. But if she did that, if she spoke the words and he wasn't a shifter, how the hell would she relate his howling to something that wasn't supposed to even exist?

Or something like that.

For fuck's sake. If he was a shifter, how did she miss that all those years ago? And how did she find out what he was without exposing the Adams too? How would she know the first thing about shifting if she wasn't a shifter herself? How retarded would she seem if she came out, guns blazing, accusing him of being a werewolf? Humans didn't like that sort of thing. They mostly didn't believe in that sort of thing. But she damned well knew a howl during mating when she heard one and if she didn't learn to stuff it, she'd out herself and the Adams pack.

Oh, the web of deceit she'd been ready to weave. Her big mouth, impulsive and always at the ready, would be the death of her.

"Forget it," she dismissed her accusation, hoping he'd let it go. "I have to go. It's cold and I need to get up early to finish this damned bunny hut." She turned to leave, but Lassiter grabbed her arm and spun her around.

"It doesn't have to be like this, Em."

"It doesn't? You keep saying that, Lassiter, but I disagree. What else could it be like? Just because we rutted like pigs doesn't change the fact that we're still on opposite sides of the fence." So there.

"But the fence dynamics change when we get in the same corral."

"This isn't going to happen again. No more sex, Lassiter. Not until we talk like adults."

He pulled her up against him and smiled cockily. "You sure about that?"

"As sure as I am that your motives for being here aren't what you'd like everyone to believe, and I intend to find out what they are. There was a time when I would have already known all of this because you would have told me, damn it," she yelled in regret.

Kissing the top of her head, he let her go by dropping his hands to his sides. "Knock yourself out, Em."

"I don't need your permission."

"No, you're right. You'll rush headlong into something before thinking it through. Much like that mouth of yours, you're impulsive. You always were." His sardonic response was laced with a chuckle.

Yeah, yeah. Whatevah. "Look, meat murderer. This --" she pointed to the space between them, "-- isn't going to happen again. Got that?"

He winked at her, his face splitting into a grin that enhanced his dimples and made her knees weak. "Yeah, I gotcha."

Placing her hands on her hips, she sneered. "Good. Now go away. Better yet, I'll go away," she yelled at him, sticking her neck out like a three-year-old and whirling around to stomp off toward the Adams house.

"Niiiiiight, Em," he called from behind her.

Arghhhhhh! He was so smug, so self assured.

Crashing her way back to the Adams house, she pushed the door open and tiptoed into her bedroom, resolving to never get close enough to Lassiter again that they'd find themselves wound around each other like tangled yarn.

Nosexnosexnosexnosex.

Her hormones protested. *But why? It was good. It was so good one might call it spectacular. How silly is it to deny yourself the small pleasures in life?*

Lassiter was anything but small.

Emerson blushed. No more Lassiter and no more sex and no more thinking about his damned enticingly gift wrapped package.

No matter how lip lickingly hot he was.

And he *had* howled.

Yes indeed.

Emerson intended to find out just what that meant.

Chapter Six

"Em! Em, get up!"

Emerson popped an eye open to get a blurry glimpse of Hector standing over her, stroking his favorite bunny, Pinky. "What's up, Hector?" she mumbled, pulling the covers around her and holding on to the cocoon of warmth she was in.

"You have to get dressed and come see! I can't believe you did it, but you did. Thank you, Em. Pinky thanks you too." Hector smiled and lifted Pinky's paw to wave at her.

"How about you gimme a sec and let me brush my teeth and get dressed, and then I'll come see. How's that?"

"Okay, but hurry!" Hector scurried out of her room, his broad back a stark contrast to his child-like behavior. Hector was sweet and innocent and nearing thirty years old. Sometimes, even Emerson couldn't believe he was a fully grown man. He was certainly as smart as one, but the maturity level he displayed was anything but manly.

Nonetheless, Emerson had found him irresistible when he'd come to ask for help from her animal rights group. His genuine concern, his knowledge about wildlife, coupled with his simple joy in living had given her all the reason she needed to support his cause.

And now, she needed to find out what had Hector so excited he'd come and woken her up. Dressed and washed up, she headed outside to find him waiting for her with a wide smile on his face.

He tugged her hand, enveloping her smaller one in his very large one. "Come with me. Oh, Em, you so rock!"

Oh, indeed, she had rocked. Or had rocks, stuck in her spine, that is. Her back was a bit tender from her overt display of uncontrollable lust in the middle of the wilds of Adams land, and as Hector dragged her back to the scene of the crime, she couldn't help but flush with guilt.

She was feeling very 'ho-like this morning.

No more encounters of the sexual kind, Miss I Want A Piece of That, she reminded herself.

Her resolve this morning was stronger than ever.

And the view that assaulted her eyes as Hector pulled her toward the clearing where she and Lassiter had banged each other senseless made that resolve weaken.

"See, Em? I can't believe you did it. After last night, when you were throwing stuff around and hacking up wood, I didn't think you could do it. But you did! It's really great, Em. Thank you. All of my bunnies thank you."

Oh, my.

Well, there it was in all its glory.

A bunny hut to rival Trump Towers.

It really was quite a sight with its multi-level tiers and chicken wire sides.

Lassiter. He'd done this and Emerson was baffled. What kind of a man, a man who willingly killed wildlife on a regular basis, built a bunny freakin' hut?

Hector scooped her up in a hug. "Thank you, Em. I love it."

Emerson rubbed her eyes and pinched the bridge of her nose. "It -- it wasn't me, Hector. I sucked at trying to make the bunny hut. I mean, I cut things wrong and in general made a big mess of things. I didn't do this." *I did, however, have an orgasm of cosmic proportions because of it.*

His head cocked in confusion. "Then who did?"

Rolling her eyes, she had to give kudos where they were due. "I think it was Lassiter…"

"Woooow. He really digs you, Em," Hector fairly squealed his delight.

"No, no he doesn't. I think he digs *you*, Hector. Or at least, he was trying to help you. Definitely not me." It was so much like the Lassiter of old to do something like this. She had no other explanation unless he'd done it for Hector.

Unless…

Unless he was going to take some ghoulish pleasure out of knocking the hut down when he trampled all over the rest of Adams land…

The fuck.

"Emmmmm." Hector's tone held a warning. "I see your wheels turning. Don't do it, Em. It always gets you in trouble!"

Hector's voice became a muffled haze, rather like the adults in a Charlie Brown cartoon. Her anger soared and her mouth began before she was even at his trailer door. "Lassiter! Get out here, you animal murderer! Destructor of all things sacred! I know what you're up to and it isn't going to wor --"

Hector slapped a hand over Emerson's mouth with a clap. "Emerson Palmer, shut up!"

Her eyes opened wide with surprise while Hector dragged her backwards, his arms like steel bands around her, leaving her immobile. "Mmmmm," she protested against his big hand.

"I said shut up, Emerson. Sometimes a gift is just that. A gift. It doesn't have to have any ulterior motive behind it. If Lassiter did this, and I can't think of whom else might have, then fine. I'll say thank you *myself*. You keep your big, out of control mouth shut. It might work when you're fighting bad guys who kill little animals for profit, but it isn't always necessary. You're so 'rage against the machine' all the time, Em. Like everything is a big conspiracy or something. Chill out." Hector let her go with a slight shove and put his finger to his lips. "Now, shhhhhhhhhh."

Rage against the machine? The world had gone mad and forgotten to send her the memo. Who was this Hector, all reasonable and forgiving of a man who wanted to trash his home? "He's trying to tear up the very land this hut is built on, Hector," she protested yet again, albeit weakly -- quietly.

"You know what, Em? I don't know that I'm so sure of that anymore. I know you think he built this so he could take some sort of sick pleasure in tearing it down when he builds his condos, but I just don't believe that anymore. I think he built it to impress you. I think it's his olive branch to you."

Yeah, and Emerson would bet he hoped the branch had thorns on it so he could stick it up her ass. "I doubt that, Hector."

"You doubt everything, Emerson. You're a real downer sometimes. I'm telling you, let this go for now and let's see what happens. Keep your mouth shut and let me thank Lassiter. You can go think up new ways to convince yourself he's evil."

Emerson was speechless. Stunned. Rooted to the spot, watching Hector's retreating back go off to thank the almighty Lassiter.

Her eyes narrowed. Lassiter was up to something and there was no time like the present to find out what it was. She wasn't falling for this Lassiter has a heart crap. He might have had one once, but not anymore.

* * *

Emerson stood by the large maple tree, just beyond Lassiter's trailer. Under the cover of night and the howl of the wind, Emerson was feeling safe. The position gave her a bird's eye view of his back door. The sliding glass door where she watched him talk to his pet parakeet.

She'd shifted as a precautionary measure. Now, in wolf form, she curled around the trunk of the tree, perking her ears to see if she might catch a phone conversation -- or anything that might lead her to understand what had brought Lassiter here.

I'm not the boy you once knew. Lassiter's words were as close to the truth as it got for Emerson. They had stung her ears the other night and the more she thought about them, the more regret lingered.

She and Lassiter had gone to school together. His last years in high school were spent mostly with her. Emerson, the awkward teenager, and Lassiter, the foster child of caretakers he just couldn't identify with but loved nonetheless. They'd met when she was in eighth grade and Lassiter in the tenth. She'd met him in an after school accelerated math class held at the local high school.

Lassiter had stopped a bunch of boys from picking on her and, for whatever reason, from that moment on they'd been friends. He was quiet much of the time, but when Lassiter spoke, it was like a kernel of wisdom Emerson clung to.

Meaning. It was always said with a purpose and with meaning. Lassiter's life hadn't been easy, shipped from foster home to foster home, until he'd come upon the Fullers. A kind, older couple who'd taken him in at twelve and loved him like their own.

Yet, Lassiter always had a dark side Emerson couldn't reach. It was deep and layered, rank with a smell Emerson could never quite pinpoint. He was as different as Emerson was and it bonded them.

Lassiter was a loner -- a loner no one screwed with. That didn't stop them from talking about his pale skin and sunglasses when he wasn't around, though. He wore them all the time, making Emerson want to tease him about it. But she didn't because Lassiter didn't tease her about her gangly, awkward body and her braces.

He'd treated her like his kid sister and, though Emerson had wished it differently, she'd respected their boundaries and kept her schoolgirl crush to herself. She'd had enough of a stigma already, hiding her half-were heritage. Yet she never felt like the dork everyone else thought she was when she was with him. Often, Lassiter had told her, her opinionated mouth would bring her trouble, but back then he'd chuckled more than he'd scowled over her rants about one thing or another.

Lassiter always said less was more.

They'd shared a common bond in their love of animals. At the time, Emerson was working after school at an animal shelter and she'd managed to wrangle a job for Lassiter too. He was diligent in his duties. The animals adored him and it'd seemed like he'd liked them right back. He had a way about him that drew them to him. Even the orneriest of domestics could be soothed by Lassiter. His low, honeyed tone of voice and his easy, gentle hands never failed to amaze Emerson when she watched him in action.

For two years, before Lassiter graduated and moved away, they'd been the best of friends. When he left to go to college, Emerson had cried herself to sleep every night for a month. Her parents had fretted over her and her mother had threatened to drag her into therapy if she didn't get over what she'd called Emerson's "bizarre attachment to the pale boy."

Sure, he'd called once in a while and she'd gotten a letter or two, but it would never be the same as sharing French fries on a park bench after work, watching the sun set. It would never be the same as the time he'd brought his portable radio to the park and slow danced with her after she'd gone to the ninth grade Spring Fling and no one asked her to shuffle off to Buffalo.

That moment, the moment when he'd held out his hand to her from her place on the park swing, would forever turn her insides out. She would always remember the warmth his arms around her had brought when she'd buried her face in his chest, fighting tears. The comfort he'd offered with no words but with a gesture, a gesture Emerson could still feel imprinted on her heart.

It would never be the same as being able to talk with him for hours on end about nothing in particular and everything that was important in her world.

After a year or so, Lassiter didn't call anymore and Emerson moved on, but she'd missed his presence for a long time thereafter. She'd lost track of her lifeline who'd been something so much more than a friend to her. He'd become an integral part of her life, and his leaving, something Emerson knew he'd eventually do, left a void that couldn't be filled by anyone else.

When next they met, it had been in California, and then nothing about Lassiter was the same.

Nothing.

He was cold and angry and bitter, but over what she didn't know. No longer the skinny geek she'd once known, their physical attraction was instantaneous, but Lassiter wasn't interested in strolling down memory lane.

If he'd been surprised to see Emerson picketing his condos, he hadn't shown it.

Refusing to be drawn back into the past by silly sentimental journeys, Emerson padded closer to Lassiter's sliding glass door. The steps leading up to it were rickety at best. Narrow and wooden, they creaked with each step she took. She could only hope that the roar of the wind hid her ascent.

Cocking her head, Emerson listened at the sliding glass door while Lassiter talked to his parakeet as if it were his only friend in the world.

"This is Adams land. It has to be the right Adams. I don't know what to do, Bud. I've looked and looked and nothing, but I can *feel* it's here. Damn it, I *know* it's here."

What the hell was here?

"Hereherehere," the parakeet mimicked back.

Lassiter put his hand in the cage and stuck a finger out for Bud to hop onto. Bud went willingly and Lassiter took care in taking him out and setting Bud on his shoulder. "I could use a little help here, my man. Wanna read the letter again?"

Letter?

"Nononononononono." Bud flapped his wings and squawked in protest, skittering from side to side on Lassiter's broad shoulders.

The parakeet nipped at Lassiter's ear and he chuckled. "Okay, so what you're telling me is we've been over it a million times, huh? Okay. No more letter."

It was as if the bird understood Lassiter. What kind of freaky nut had Lassiter turned into that he shared confidences with a parakeet? Talk about eccentric. Who did he think he was? Dr. Doolittle?

Leaning further toward the door, hoping to discover what this letter was about, she hit the banister of the stairs and scuffled to remain on the small landing. Her nails scratched the surface with a painful screech, echoing into the dark night. The sound bounced around the trees like a ping pong ball.

That's what she got for not getting a damned manicure.

Chapter Seven

No sooner had she righted herself than the back light came on, blinding her with its glare.

"What the hell?" was Lassiter's inquiry as the door whipped open and he stared down at Emerson in her wolf form.

Hooo boy, she was in the shits.

Foiled.

Caught.

Red handed even.

However, as she looked up at him, his face split into the first grin she'd seen him display since meeting him again.

His hand reached down with tentativeness, much like he'd done when he worked in the shelter with her and a new animal was brought in, frightened and leery.

Emerson decided she didn't have much of a choice. She could run away and not look back, but she could also gain some valuable information if she played this right.

It was sneaky.

It was covert.

It was sooooo despicable.

It was pure fricken' genius.

Things were looking up.

Score one for Emerson Palmer.

"Hey, puppy, aren't you pretty? Are you lost? What an unusual coat. You're almost white," he cooed, kneeling down and staring into her eyes.

Pretty. Yes, she was rather pretty in wolf form, wasn't she? Preening, Emerson sat back on her haunches and allowed Lassiter to run a strong hand over her muzzle. Oh, the man and his hands. Indeed they could be used as weapons of mass hormonal destruction.

Emerson had to remind herself that as a "puppy" she'd more than likely be very hesitant with a stranger. So she backed away from him and looked the other way.

"Ya hungry, puppy?" he asked in an obvious effort to tempt her in with food.

"Hungryhungryhungry," Bud twittered from his shoulder.

"Tell ya what. I'll leave the door open and if you're so inclined, you just come on in," he invited noncommittally, his voice swirling in her ears, husky, hot, calming.

"Comeonincomeonin."

Damn, that was some parakeet. Her experience was that they were difficult to train and rarely learned the variety of words this Bud spouted.

Well, she had nothing to lose by gaining access to the inner sanctum and everything to gain.

Poking her head around the corner, Emerson placed first one paw, then the next over the sliders. Lassiter, tall and firm stood by the kitchen sink, was tearing something up that he'd taken from the fridge.

Emerson's nose lifted, trying to catch the scent.

Ugh, beef. Steak maybe. Definitely steak. With onions. Bleh.

"I see the call of food wins," he said over his shoulder with satisfaction.

Crap. Well, if she was going to play the part, she was going to have to put up or shut up.

Setting the bowl down in front of her, Lassiter pulled a chair out from the small table, leaning forward on his elbows to watch her, and waited for her to approach the bowl.

Sniff! Yes, she should sniff the bowl. That was very dog-like and totally in character. Nudging the bowl with her nose, she swiped her tongue over the bits of meat he'd taken such care to shred. Her stomach lurched.

Lord, the humiliation when he said, "Gooood girl. See? I won't hurt you. I'm guessing you're a girl because you're so pretty. I'll look later to be sure."

No, no, no. She was not spreading her legs, er, paws for Lassiter Adams ever again. He was going to have to go with the assumption that she was a girl or she'd bite his hand off.

Her stomach rolled, looking at the bowl of meat. Definitely steak and decidedly a few days old. Licking at it with a light tongue, she found she had to grit her teeth to keep from yarking the meat right back up. Emerson silently sent an apology to all the animals she'd vowed never to eat.

Bud hopped from Lassiter's shoulder and onto her back, landing with his small talons digging into her spine. He dipped his head and nipped at her fur.

For the love of Pete.

"Bud, be nice. See how nice the puppy is? You be nice too," Lassiter warned in a high pitched, child-like voice.

Hookay, this was sorta freaking her out on a gazillion different levels. Closed mouthed, pissed off at the world, over the top manly-man was talking to her like she was a toddler. Coaxing her to eat, stroking her fur, talking to her all cutesy. It would be desperately funny if she could actually use it to mock him.

He'd spent far too much time alone in her estimation. What else made a man behave like this? It was a totally schizophrenic or bi-polar, or some crazy disorder that didn't have a name.

"Are you full, pretty girl?" Lassiter inquired, his entire face alight with complete serenity. "C'mon, you can do better than that. Eat up, Princess."

"Eatupeatupeatup," Bud seemed to encourage.

Princess? Princess? Oohhhh, this was ammunition to be used at a later date.

Now, onto the matter at hand. This letter... Where would Lassiter keep a letter and how was she going to find it?

Rising on all fours, Emerson decided some investigation was in order. Turning to get an idea of the layout of his trailer, Emerson made a beeline for the bedroom with Bud still clinging to her back. This letter, something that obviously held significance, would probably be there.

The hallway was short, covered in shag carpeting that was worn and fraying.

Lassiter's bedroom was small, merely enough to turn around in and not much more. It had a pile of dirty laundry she tried to delicately step over. Swooping her head down, she sniffed a stray sock.

"Ahhhh, I know what you want to do. You wanna play, don't you?"

Er, no. Not so much.

Lassiter stooped down and picked up the sock. The muscles in his arm flexed enticingly and Emerson had to look away from his yumminess. It blinded her to her mission.

The letter.

Dragging the sock beneath her snout, Lassiter teased her with it.

Oh, no, she was not putting his dirty ass sock in her mouth. Nuh uh.

"Get it, c'mon, girl, get the sock," he encouraged in that same stupid high pitch, smiling like a kid.

If she could roll her eyes right now, she would. For crap's sake. Making a halfhearted attempt at "playing," Emerson nipped the sock, successfully getting it between her teeth and giving it a slight tug.

Lassiter smiled broadly again.

What the hell was his gig?

He tugged back, swishing the other end of the sock around in circles playfully.

Bud flapped his wings at being jerked so suddenly when Emerson gave a small growl and pulled the other way. His wings flapped, carrying him to the tall dresser that was crammed in the corner. Digging her paws into the carpet, she got a hold of the sock and yanked hard, pitching Lassiter forward.

Girl werewolves rule, weird meat murderers drool, she thought with some satisfaction.

Plopping down beside her, Lassiter put an arm around her back and commented, "You know, I envy you, Princess. If I could stay like you all of the time, I'd bet life would be a whole lot easier."

Huh?

Stay like her?

He lifted her back leg and eyeballed her crotch. "You *are* a princess," he decided out loud.

A princess indeed.

Emerson yanked her leg back from his hand with a snort. How utterly degrading.

"Don't be offended, pretty. I was just checking," he assured her with an affectionate pat on the head.

Turning, Emerson gave him her back end and swished her tail in his face. Check *this*.

Emerson let her mouth open wide, pushing the sock to the floor with her tongue. It fell soundlessly to the carpet. She turned around again and sent Lassiter a disinterested glare, telling him playtime was over.

If he would just go away, she could rifle his bedroom. But Lassiter had other ideas.

"So what's your story, Princess? You lost? A stray?"

All righty then, Lassiter obviously wanted to bond. Sitting back on her haunches, she let him ramble, watching his delicious mouth move.

"Do you need a home? You could always stay here with Bud and me. We don't have a lot of room, but we can make adjustments. It's been a long time since I've had a pet. So, whaddya say? Wanna hang out with us?"

I'd rather walk over an acre of broken glass with my lips.

"You don't have to decide right away. I have plenty to keep me busy right now. Believe me, I got trouble and it comes in the way of another female that has nothing to do with the canine persuasion. In fact, it might be nice to have a female around these parts who isn't always such a pain in the ass and can't talk back."

Oh, really? I can't imagine who you might mean.

He ran a hand over his thick hair and chuckled. "Her name is Emerson, in case you're wondering who I mean. She's got a mouth the size of Canada and a cause just as big. She calls me a murderer. Can you believe that?" he asked her, looking into her eyes and chucking her under the chin. "She says I murder small animals. Me, an animal lover. If she only knew."

Only knew what, *you oversized hunk of meat loving studliness? Damn, spit it out already.*

"I would never hurt an animal, Princess. Emerson should know that by now. We knew each other when we were kids."

Yes, Emerson, all knowing and all seeing, clairvoyant, should just know what the fuck you mean. God, men could be such retards, but Emerson found his words touching the fringes of her heart. Much in the way the bunny hut had.

Stupidhead.

"We were good friends back then," he interrupted her thoughts. "She was skinny as hell and awkward, but she isn't

Dakota Cassidy: Wolf Mates

anymore…" Lassiter trailed off with a hitch in his voice Emerson couldn't say she'd ever heard when he referred to her in the past and especially now. It lingered between them, and he smiled at her in the way he once had when he was her friend so long ago. When he talked about where and who he'd wanted to be after high school.

"You know what, puppy? I don't think Emerson and I are friends anymore. No matter how I feel about her."

***

Lassiter! Hey, doofus. You're talking to the dog again. It can't be healthy to only spend your time with animals.

Lassiter frowned up at Bud in his bird cage and mentally sent him a shut up.

No, no, I won't shut up. You're talking to a dog. Get a grip on your emotions, my man.

Yeah? Well, I talk to a bird too.

I'm offended. I'm much smarter than a dog.

If you're so smart, why the hell can't you figure this out?

If I had a pair of legs, I just might. Now quit bitching and why don't you talk to Emerson? Ever since you ran into her again, you've been an ass.

Yeah, well Emerson can do that to a guy, he shot back mentally.

Emerson was your friend once, Lassiter, and don't give me shit about it. I was there, numbnuts. All those nights you talked about her, all those nights when you said you wished she were just a little older. You liked Emerson, Lassiter. She liked you. Now you won't even talk to her. You won't even tell her what's really going on here. It's bullshit and it's bullshit of your own making.

Lassiter sighed in resignation. Looking down at the dog, he thought, I *am* talking to a dog…

His world had narrowed to not much more than Bud and the mission to find what he was looking for. Companionship, especially of the animal variety, seemed to suit him best. If he didn't have to do much else but feed them and throw them the occasional bone, things worked out just fine. A pet didn't require sharing himself or emotions, something Lassiter didn't do easily. Except when he'd been with Emerson… He couldn't afford to think about Emerson now. No matter how much he wanted her -- and he wanted her.

Christ, he wanted her.

He wanted to talk to her again, like they used to. He wanted her slender body pressed to his. He wanted to tell her everything that had happened in the last ten years.

But he couldn't. How could he tell her something like this?

Oh, please, Lassiter, Bud scoffed in his head. *That's an easy way out for you. Hide behind me, why don't you? All these years you've been so determined to find the answer to this mess that you've forgotten about real, live people. Why don't you go get laid? Oh, wait, you did that. Why, I had to turn my wee parakeet eyes the other way when the two of you were all over each other.*

Bud?

What?

Shut up.

* * *

How he felt about her?

And how do you feel about Emerson?

"So, I could certainly use one," he went on. "A friend, that is." Pushing off on his heels, Lassiter rose and headed back toward the kitchen, opening the fridge door.

Emerson followed, hoping he'd talk to her some more, but she stopped dead in her tracks when she saw the contents of the fridge. The light from the refrigerator shone on his face, making his skin look eerily pale, but still as handsome as he'd always been to Emerson. His complexion was a rare blend of creamy beige, mixed with a dab of color on his cheeks. His cheeks were razor sharp and had dimples, deeply grooved on either side of his mouth.

She sniffed the air again. An unfamiliar, yet faintly copper smell assaulted her snout. Peering closer inside the fridge, she lifted her head and looked closer.

Um, unless she was mistaken, he had a whole lot of something that didn't look like the drink of champions in yon refrigerator.

It looked like blood.

Blood like one would find stored in a hospital blood bank.

Eek.

Well, then.

This was freaky beyond her expectations.

He shook the plastic bag of blood and took a small orange straw from the drawer, pushing it into the bag and sipped.

Like it was a fucking juice box or something.

But that sure as shit wasn't Hi-C Red Raspberry Splash.

Catching Emerson watching him, Lassiter grinned, his eyes glowing. "You can smell it, can't you, Princess? I know, you're thinking what the hell, right? All vampires drink blood, puppy." Winking, he smiled again, flashing his incisors, now long and gleaming in the dim light over the kitchen sink.

"Bloodbloodblood," Bud screeched, flying above her head and landing on Lassiter's broad shoulder.

Only vampires have fangs.

Of course they do silly.

Lassiter has fangs.

Very shiny, white ones too.

Only vampires drink blood.

Of course they do, silly.

Blood.

AB negative.

Or maybe he liked O positive?

Blood.

Vampires.

Jesus Christ in a mini skirt.

Lassiter Adams was a vampire.

Hookay, time to go.

Chapter Eight

Emerson scooted out the sliding glass door like a gang of rednecks in Hooterville were hot on her heels, threatening to marry her off to Bubba. She tried to be as nonchalant as she could about it, but when she scratched at the door, Lassiter asked if she had to "make potties." Emerson would have yelled a resounding, "Hell, yes," if she'd been in human form.

Her legs took the stretch of woods in harried urgency.

Memories from long ago rushed to her mind's eye. They crowded out everything but what she'd just seen. Every conversation they'd ever had, every secret they'd shared she could remember in vivid detail.

How could he have not told her he was a vampire?

Which spawned the question, why hadn't she told him she was a werewolf?

Because you just don't walk up to your best friend and school girl crush and say, "Oh and FYI, I'm a werewolf. Kinda like a dog, but not quite the same, ya feel me? You know, woof woof."

Why hadn't she smelled him and the difference between a human's scent and a vampire's?

Because your hormones were in overdrive?

What the hell did a vampire smell like anyway?

Ohmigod. It all made sense now. His pale skin, his sunglasses, his solitude. They both had their reasons for secreting away, spending little time with their own peers.

Their paranormal bond had drawn them together and neither one had ever been the wiser. Her worry that Lassiter would find out what she was had been for naught. Each full moon when she'd fretted if they were due to meet, she'd worried he'd find out. Lassiter must have been as worried she'd find out about him.

Had his foster parents known? If vampires needed blood to survive, how had he managed to make it all those years on just Mrs. Fuller's chicken fried steak?

But he'd had *food* in his refrigerator.

None of this was adding up and the more she thought about it, the more two plus two equaled something other than four.

Emerson pushed her way through a thicket of trees, panting from her getaway. She found the spot where she'd left her clothes and began to shift. A chill coursed down her spine when she shifted back to her human form.

Nothing could have prepared her for what she'd just seen. Nothing could have prepared her for the shock that Lassiter hadn't shared the single biggest secret he had with her.

Emerson wasn't sure which upset her more, finding out at all or finding out without the benefit of Lassiter telling her.

Pulling on her clothes and leaning against the trunk of the tree, she sank to the ground, wrapping her arms around her legs. Her head was a mixed up jumble of emotions. Lost in the memory of conversations they'd had that now had a whole new meaning. She felt confused and lost.

Yet, one thing remained predominant in her mind and it wouldn't let her go.

This situation also had another meaning.

A bigger meaning than she'd first thought.

Lassiter Adams was no Adams. Not of the werewolf kind anyway.

The liar.

However, that didn't make much of a difference now. Lassiter had the money it had cost to buy the Adams land. It mattered little that he wasn't kin.

And this letter. What did it mean? What did it say and why had it brought him here to this specific Adams-owned land?

The Adams name and whatever Lassiter wanted fit like two pieces of a puzzle.

They were tied together with some sort of significance and Emerson had to find out what that was. She also had to tell the Adamses.

Cold now from the wind and her shift, Emerson rose to make her way back to the Adams house. On stiff legs, she ran a hand over her mussed hair.

"Emerson?"

Her head whipped around. Startled, she faltered, tripping on a fallen branch. Lassiter's hand snaked out to catch her.

His vampire hand.

Where had he come from and how did he manage to always sneak up on her without her noticing?

"What are you doing out here?" he asked, keeping hold of her hand.

"What are you doing out here?" she volleyed back.

"Looking for a do -- Never mind. Why are you out here? It's cold."

"I'm admiring the trashed landscape," she snapped.

His sigh carried on the howl of the wind. It held exasperation. "Emerson --"

"Don't Emerson me, Lassiter. You're ruining this beautiful retreat for your own selfish purposes. So you can make a little money to put in your already fat bank account. Damn it, Lassiter, who the hell are you?" she yelled into his face. Vampire or not, she wasn't afraid to voice her opinion. As long as he wasn't into biting. Those fangs had looked pretty damned sharp. That was okay, she had incisors too. Grrrrr and all.

"I know you're angry with me, Em. It still isn't what you think."

No, no siree, it sure as hell wasn't what she thought anymore. She never in a millennium thought Lassiter was a vampire.

Looking down at her hand clasped in his own, Emerson yanked it away. "So, why don't you throw me a bone, Lassiter? What is it if it isn't what I think?"

"Forget it."

"I can't forget it."

"You'll have to."

"Exactly. Now we're back to square one again. I have to go. I'm cold."

"Don't…"

Hearing the regret in his voice, Emerson stopped cold, hoping he'd spill the beans. For a mere second, she'd heard the Lassiter that once sat on a park bench with her and told her it was no big deal that she was so skinny. Someday, boys would be crazy about her. The

Lassiter that held her hand when she'd cried because one of the animals she'd fallen in love with at the animal shelter had died.

"Don't what?" she asked, soft and almost hesitant to hear his answer.

His jaw ticked. "Nothing."

Being a vampire was nothing? Nothing?

Was being a werewolf? a voice whispered in her conscience.

Oh, the secrets and lies they'd created.

For some reason, tears stung her eyes. Tears for who they once had been, for who they were now. For all of the reasons they couldn't talk the way they'd once been so adept at.

On impulse, Emerson reached up, cupping his jaw, running her thumb over the rigid line, trying to smooth away the tension. Pulling his tall frame close, she gave him a brief kiss, skimming his lips with her own and moving away with haste before she said, "I don't know you anymore, Lassiter, but I'd like to."

His arms went to gather her close, but she pressed a finger to his lips and moved out of them, knowing what would happen if she let him hold her.

"For old time's sake, I'm ready whenever you are, Lassiter," she whispered, hearing the sad tinge to her words.

Squeezing his arm, Emerson turned and walked back toward the Adams house.

Her heart thrashed in a painful rhythm with each step she took. It hurt to breathe. It hurt to remember.

It hurt period.

* * *

"We have to talk," Emerson said to Max while they sat in the kitchen, sharing a cup of coffee. Her restless night's sleep had led to a morning filled with questions and still no answers. She did know one thing, she had to tell the Adams pack. No matter how she felt about Lassiter, they deserved to know the truth.

"Go for it," Max said with a congenial smile.

Licking her lips, Emerson took a breath of air. "Lassiter Adams can't be an Adams."

Max's chuckle was something Emerson hadn't expected. "I figured as much. How'd you find out for sure?"

"It doesn't matter. Can I ask you a question that's gonna seem way out of left field?"

Sipping his coffee, he nodded. "Of course. Shoot."

Well, there wasn't any beating around the bush about it. So she'd just ask and damn the consequences. "Do you believe in vampires?"

His dark eyebrows rose. "Well, I guess I can't say as I don't. I mean, it would be hypocritical if I said I didn't, seeing as I'm what JC calls a dog, right? I'm a werewolf. So are you. I exist, so I'm sure other paranormal beings exist too."

Emerson shifted in her chair and rubbed her neck. "Wanna know why I know Lassiter isn't related to you?"

Max's handsome face frowned. "If you two had some sort of kinky liaison and he confessed during a good round of hide the baloney, then, no, I don't think I want to know."

Emerson's jaw dropped. "What the hell does that mean?"

"It means I've seen you look at him when he's not looking. Even in the height of your frenzied protests, you looked like you kinda dug him. He looks at you the same way. It doesn't make me any less pissed that he's here, tearing the shit out of my land, but it's there just the same."

For fuck's sake. This was ridiculous. Did everyone think Lassiter had a thing for her?

"Yes."

"Yes, what," she spat, angry that he and his family had noticed.

"Yes, we all think Lassiter likes you. It's sort of bizarre, the vibes I get from you two. I haven't been able to pinpoint it."

"It's called lust, honey," JC answered for him, waddling into the kitchen. "It's what gave me this." She pointed to her belly and smiled. "I take it we're talking Lassiter and Emerson?" Lowering herself into a chair, JC sat down and folded her hands together.

Max's head bobbed up and down.

Emerson hopped up from her chair and thwarted any further conversation about her and Lassiter. "Do you want to know how I know Lassiter isn't really an Adams or not?"

"Oh, relax, Emerson," JC chided. "It really is okay to be hot for a bad boy. We've all done it once in our lives. Lassiter is pretty hot, even if he is kinda pale. Lassiter has some deeper issues than building condos, that's for sure. I just don't know what. But I've seen him with that bird and I know he's not a meat murderer, as you call it." Clucking her tongue, JC shook her dark, curly head. "I just can't figure him out."

"Well, I did."

"Pumpkin?" Max said to JC, smiling at her. "Emerson has something she'd like to say."

JC leaned back in her chair and looked toward Emerson with an expectant expression.

Shoving her hands into the pocket of her worn jeans, Emerson looked back at them both. "I know he's not an Adams because he's no werewolf."

"Well, we didn't know for sure," JC reminded her. "It's why we haven't beaten him up for ruining the land out there. If someone were to know about us, we'd be in far worse trouble than we are now. It's rather irritating to know Max could annihilate him and he hasn't for fear of being found out. Talk about your hands being tied behind your back, huh? So do tell. How'd you find out he's not a werewolf?"

"He's a *vampire*."

"Wow. Cool. Like drinks blood and sleeps in a coffin, vampire? How do you suppose he put a coffin in that little trailer out there?" JC wondered out loud, completely unfazed by what Emerson had just revealed.

"Did you hear me, JC? Lassiter Adams is a vampire," Emerson repeated, hopefully this time with effect.

Taking a long sigh, JC nodded. "I know this is the part where I'm supposed to freak out, but do remember where I found my lifemate, would ya? In the pound. And also remember, he's a freakin' dog. Just like you, Em. Nothing could faze me after that. I have no doubt that there are plenty of you critters around, and I have no doubt there are critters I know nothing about. I'm not egotistical enough to believe I'm the only life form that roams the planet. I'm good with it. It's really sorta *X-Files*, if you ask me."

"The point is, if he's a vampire, he can't be an Adams," Emerson stated.

JC cocked her head up at Emerson and giggled. "Er, I wouldn't be so sure about that, Em. The Adams are a busy bunch. Look at Max and I. I'm human. Martine is a cat. Hector is a vegetarian, Xavier is a lion. Why would it surprise you that a vampire might be related to them? Nothing surprises me when it comes to this bunch of nuts."

Emerson's brow furrowed. "You can't possibly believe that what he says is true!"

JC stood, pushing back from the table and placing a hand in the crook of her back. "After what I've seen, Em, I'd believe anything." Coming to stand near Emerson, she picked a lock of her shoulder length blonde hair up and examined it. "You know, Em. I've been thinking about your hair. It's so beautiful. Never been dyed, silky and the color is gorgeous. Why don't you let me trim it? You could use a trim."

She'd just told them that Lassiter was a vampire and JC was offering product tips and makeovers. "Are you people insane? Lassiter is a vampire. A vampire!"

Max barked a laugh. "Yeah and so?"

JC laughed too. "It doesn't change anything. He still bought the land and paid those trumped up back taxes. He owns it. Even if he's an alien with two packages. He has the right to dig it up."

"And he digs you, Emerson," Max teased.

Deflated, Emerson knew she was going to have to confess to them about her past relationship too. It would save the questions later if they found out. She'd rather they heard it from her than someone else, or maybe even Lassiter. "I also have a confession to make."

JC rolled her eyes. "Lord, Emerson! What else is there?" Throwing her hands up, she said, "Forget I asked that. Never mind. I can only imagine. Go ahead, tell us."

Crossing her arms over her chest, Emerson sighed. "Lassiter and I were once friends. We kind of spent some of our last years in high school together."

Rocking back on his chair, Max gave her a knowing smile. "I knew I felt something between you two. I knew it. Question is, why didn't you tell us before?"

Pushing her hair behind her ear, she looked Max directly in the eye. "I didn't think it was relevant, and he's not the man I once knew."

"So what do you know about Lassiter? If you spent some time in high school with him, you must know who he comes from. Where he comes from. What his parents are like," Max asked.

"Lassiter is adopted. Well, not adopted, he was a foster child for almost all of his life. We saw each other in California again about three years ago. I hadn't seen him in almost ten years by then. He was so different from the man I knew when I was a kid. Knowing him didn't change the fact that we had different beliefs, and it didn't change the fact that I was going to keep protesting his stupid condos."

"So you have unresolved feelings for him. Don't bother to deny it, it's written all over your face." She waved her hand, dismissing the thought. "Forget that for now. Even if he isn't really an Adams, he had the money to pay off those trumped up back taxes. That still brings us right back to where we were. No condos. He hasn't built a single thing. He's torn up a tree or five and made himself a nice little trailer park, but no condos. So what do you think he's up to?" JC asked, wrapping her arms around Max's shoulders.

"I did something pretty sneaky last night," Emerson said, almost more to herself than to Max and JC.

"I'll bet. I'd even bet that it was how you found out Lassiter was a vampire," Max mused.

"I showed up at his door in my werewolf form and he let me in. He thought I was a stray. He fed me..." she revealed, her face turning red from humiliation.

JC began to laugh so hard that tears streamed down her face. "Oh, do I know that story. Max did the same thing. I took Max to PETsMART and to the vet to be neutered."

Emerson couldn't help but laugh too. It was all too unbelievable.

"So what happened? Did he turn into a bat?" Max queried.

"No, nothing like that, but he's got a whole lotta blood in his refrigerator and he sorta confessed to Prince -- er, me, that he was a vampire."

"Any clue as to why he never told you, Emerson?" JC asked, smiling in sympathy at her.

Shrugging her shoulders, she shook her head. "I'd guess for the same reasons I didn't tell him. Who just walks up to their high school crush and says 'I'm a werewolf'?"

"Hell if I don't know that," Max commented wryly, sending JC a warm smile.

"He also mentioned a letter. A letter he was telling that parakeet Bud about."

"You know," JC said, looking directly at Emerson, "how bad can this guy be if he takes in stray dogs and has a parakeet? Nothing about him is fitting here."

Martine poked her long, elegant neck around the corner, silky strands of hair framed her face. "Speaking of that bird of his, I can't figure it. I want to wrap him in a crescent roll and eat him, but something keeps stopping me..."

"Hector would shit a bunny if he knew you wanted to eat another animal, Martine Adams! I'd control those impulses, if I were you," JC joked.

Martine grinned and stuck her tongue out. "I'm just saying he looks tasty. Under normal circumstances and if caviar weren't shipped to me by Escobar on a regular basis, I might be forced to give in to temptation and it could get ugly."

Just then the phone rang, bringing both JC and Emerson back to the situation at hand. Max jumped up to grab it and a smile spread over his face, making him look worry free for the moment. "That's great news, guys. I'll pass it on and the troops will be there soon. Did you call Eva? She'll flip. Okay, see you soon, Xavier."

He winked at JC. "Guess who just had a little girl?"

"Oh! Julia had the baby. A girl... how fabulous!" JC squealed. "But wait. Is it a cat or a dog? And hang on just a second. I was pregnant before Julia! Why did she have a baby in just a few months and my pregnancy just goes on and on like *War and Peace*?" she asked Max. "It's not fair, damn it!"

Max laughed, shuffling her out of the room while JC moaned in between gabbing excitedly. Emerson guessed they were going to prepare for a trip to Manhasset to visit Julia and Xavier and the new baby.

A little girl.

Emerson's heart clutched with just a smidge of envy, but she pushed it aside in favor of the sleuthing that had to be done.

She had a vampire to catch.

Chapter Nine

The Adams house was quiet, too quiet with everyone off seeing Julia and Xavier's new baby in Manhasset. They'd named her Catalina and, according to JC after her phone call to Emerson, she didn't appear to be lion or werewolf. The nature of little Catalina's shifter form might take years to develop.

Emerson decided one last trip to Lassiter's in her wolf form was in order. For whatever reason, he seemed to feel comfortable talking to "Princess," and finding out about this letter was essential to finding out what Lassiter was doing here.

She didn't know why it was so important, but it had to be the key to unlock this last door. It was also the key to finding the old Lassiter and that had become as important as stopping him from building the condos.

She admitted to herself that she hoped Lassiter would take her up on her offer to talk. For old time's sake, if nothing else.

Her paws were silent as she crept up the back stairs to Lassiter's sliding glass door. Again, he was with Bud, talking to him as if he were a human being.

His dark hair was ruffled and he looked tired, peering at Bud who sat on top of the cage. There was a sheet of paper sprawled out on the kitchen table and it looked well worn. "Well, pal, we got trouble. I don't know where else to go from here, but I swear to you, we'll find a way." His statement was vehement, said with a conviction she saw written all over his face. It was in his body language, tense and rigid.

Damn it, this was frustrating. A way to what and to whom?

Focusing her mind on the task at hand, Emerson scratched at the back door.

The light came on and Lassiter popped open the slider. His smile was again warm and welcoming. If only he looked at her like that when she was in human form. Her heart shifted when he knelt down at the opening of the door and put his hand out to her tentatively.

Emerson let her muzzle rest in his hand for a brief, lingering moment before pushing past him and into the trailer.

"You're hungry, aren't you?" he stated with a degree of smugness in his tone, picking up the bowl from the floor and bringing it to the refrigerator.

Yeah, bring on the bacon, she thought, admiring his ass from the view she had with his head buried in the fridge.

"I knew you'd be back. So whatcha been up to?"

A little of this, a little of that. You know, dog-like shit. Bone burying. Cat chasing. Cuz I'm a dog. An honest to goodness dog and don't you forget it, vampire.

Who was she convincing here?

"I went looking for you the other night. You sure are a quick one. You just disappeared. But it's okay, I'm glad you came back." Stooping, he ran his fingers over her back, hand over hand.

Even in were form it felt damned good. Shaking her head, her ears snapping, she forced herself to stay on task.

Find the letter.

No sex.

In that order and no variation thereof.

Lassiter tugged at the end of her ear and pulled it upward. "Do your ears bother you? Mites, maybe? I think have something that would help."

She let a low growl out to warn him that wasn't a good idea. Next he'd want to milk her renal glands or something.

"Okay, not today," Lassiter acquiesced. "You gonna eat? I can't figure how you got to be so picky. Strays usually don't demand human food," he teased, holding the bowl up under her nose.

She made a hacking noise, bringing the sound from deep within her throat. Which wasn't hard, considering he was offering her leftover Hamburger Helper. Emerson moved her nose in the other direction, lifting her muzzle to display to him her displeasure at his culinary choices.

"Wow, Princess, you *are* picky. But you know what? It's okay. I went and got you some *canned* food." He went to the lower cabinet and pulled out a can of Decadent Dogs.

How special.

Oh, yay. Spare no expense for the stray, huh? Emerson decided more exploration was in order, so being the dog she was hoping to portray, she sniffed the floor. Beginning in the kitchen, she worked her way out to the small living room.

Someone needed to break out the vacuum. Hector's rabbit could quite possibly mate with the dust bunnies Lassiter had under his couch, thus spawning a litter or two.

Lassiter followed closely behind her. "Are you looking for that sock? Ya wanna play, Princess?"

Oh, hell's bells, spare her from the sock game. She'd be fucked and feathered before she'd put his damned sock in her mouth again.

It had an aftertaste that lingered unpleasantly.

"C'mere, pretty. Come sit next to me and let's talk," Lassiter coaxed with his cajoling tone and beseeching eyes.

Talk? Yeah, let's have a real gab-fest. Hook me up, brotha. Her ears perked and she took her place beside him on the floor where he sprawled out and patted his chest.

This man's best friend thing was going too far.

"C'mon, Princess. Come sit with me." Again, he patted his chest, calling her to him.

Hookay. Emerson harrumphed and blew out a snort, flopping down on his chest and looking him in the eye.

Shoot, he was good looking.

"So, where'd ya run off to the other night? You don't look like you're any worse for the wear because of it. As a matter of fact, your coat is so shiny and clean. What shampoo do you use?" he teased, stroking her back.

Her back foot thumped with a will of its own. Oh, dayuuuuum that was good.

"You like that?"

Yes, please, may I have another?

Her eyelids grew heavy, but as Lassiter prattled on, she fought to stay awake.

"So, have you given any thought to coming and living with me and Bud? Bud's a special case too, just like you."

Special case? A special case of what? Lunacy?

"He needs me."

Huh?

Tilting her head to the left, Emerson hoped he saw the confusion in her eyes, cuz he was lookin' kinda nutty in them.

"I know, you don't understand, but Bud is special to me. His real name isn't even Bud. It's Drake. He's my brother." Lassiter's handsome face looked into her canine one and he winked.

Um, yeah. His brother. This vampire was short a bat wing. He thought a *bird* was his brother.

He was a fucking bird all right -- a loon.

"It's a long story, but I have a letter that says so," he assured her.

From *who*? A letter that said Bud was his brother? Who would write a letter like that? The National Pigeons Society for Reunification of Vampires and Their Winged Counterparts? This was just too much.

It explained everything about this new Lassiter.

He'd gone mad.

As much as she missed him, as much as she wished it could be like it once was, it couldn't. Cuz Lassiter Adams thought his brother was a flippin' bird, and that was on par with the need for a nice comfy couch and a trained psychiatrist.

Maybe even medication.

In large doses.

But he was so freakin' cute, even as a complete nut.

Digging in his pocket, he pulled out a well worn piece of paper. Obviously, he'd fingered it on many occasions. It was the kind you'd use in a spiral notebook, lined and frayed at the ripped edges. "This was from my mother and father. It's why I'm here, Princess."

Oh, oh and oh again. Jackpot!

Bingo and all the other stuff one yelled when they hit the big one.

Come to mama...

Chapter Ten

Emerson had two choices. She could wait until Lassiter told her what the letter said, or she could read it herself.

Seeing as he liked to play sock so much, Emerson decided it was time to play fetch. Snatching the letter deftly from Lassiter's hands, she ran, down the small hallway and into the even smaller bathroom. With a shove of her nose, she snapped the door shut and dropped the letter on the floor. Her muzzle dropped open and her tongue hung off to the side.

Lassiter crashed after her, calling to her to bring it back. His body pushed at the door she now leaned up against and Emerson let out a warning snarl.

Looking down at the letter, her heart skidded to a halt.

How could this be?

Losing her focus, she felt the shift back to human form begin and she had no way to stop it. If she lost her train of thought -- and the letter had certainly taken her focus off of her werewolf form -- she was sunk.

But Emerson didn't care. This was too incredible to believe.

As the fur of her coat melted away and flesh replaced it, tears stung Emerson's eyes, forming at the corners of them and falling to the cheap linoleum.

Oh, my God.

Placing a hand on the worn notepaper, Emerson trembled as she read.

A parakeet you've been these years,
To protect you from our greatest fears,
The loss of your brother too much to bear
We've left you in his gentle care.
To break the spell which we have cast
You must seek out our distant past.
Go back to where it all began,
A place we call Adams land.
Within its earth you will find

A drink to help you join vamp-kind.
The cock that crows at morning's light
Will lead you from the dark of night.
A woman who is strong and true
Will know the secret that is you.
Find her on the Adams land
And carry out our simple plan.
You will awake at break of dawn,
All your feathers and little beak gone.
A family's love will join you there.
They're a strange lot so have a care.

Emerson's mind raced, but was thwarted by Lassiter shoving against the door.

And she was naked.

Lovely.

"Emerson?" he roared, sticking his face through the wedge he'd made in the bathroom door.

Emerson forgot she was naked. Sliding across the floor, she rose on unsteady legs, clutching the letter in her hands. "All this time, Lassiter. All this time you had this secret and you never told me. Why? We were best friends. I told you everything. *Everything!*"

Lassiter glared at her, eyeing her nakedness with anger. "Well, apparently, you didn't tell me *everything*, Emerson."

Oh, yeah. There was that.

Yanking a towel from the rack, she tugged it around her. "This is not the same thing and you know it!"

"You're a dog, Emerson. It *is* the same thing."

"A werewolf, thank you," she corrected, backing up against the bathtub until she felt the fiberglass touch her calves.

"Yeah, I know."

"You know?" How could he know?

"Yeah. Now give me the letter, Emerson." His warning was followed by the tic of his jaw, clenched and angry.

"Explain it."

"Why? So you can call me a meat murderer? An animal killer?"

"That's soooo not fair, Lassiter. I had no idea. None and it wasn't as if you were telling me. So tell me now," she pleaded.

"You're right, but what is fair in this life, Em?" he remarked with dry sarcasm.

Tilting her head, Emerson gave him a narrowed look. "Don't *woe is me*, Lassiter. You didn't have to keep this a secret. You didn't. I would have helped you! I would have helped you figure out whatever the fuck that letter means. Fair? Don't talk to me about fair, Lassiter Adams."

"Give me the letter, Em."

"Nope."

"Em…"

"Nuh-uh."

"Don't make me come get it."

"Don't make me bite you."

"Don't make me bite you back."

Oh, sure, threaten her with his big fangs. Nice. "You wanna have werewolf versus vampire? A little trailer park rumble?"

His eyes opened in surprise.

"Oh, did you forget? You told the *dog* and that dog is me, Dracula."

"Give me the letter, Emerson," he growled at her. His face, handsome even in fury, loomed over hers.

Poking his chest with a finger, she shook her head stubbornly. "Or you'll what? Bite me? Suck me dry? Bring it, vampire. Let's do it because I'm not giving you the letter until you tell me what it means. Tell me about the parakeet."

"No, Emerson," he replied coldly.

And suddenly, she'd had enough. Emerson was tired of denying that she cared about Lassiter. To herself and especially to him. She was tired of pretending he had once been a man capable of great compassion. She was tired of fighting this battle that didn't just wage in her head, but in her heart. She was tired of telling herself he was inconsequential because she had a cause she so vehemently believed in. And she was sick and tired of spending endless nights, like those of the past ten years, pretending that Lassiter had never existed.

He did exist.

She wanted to be a part of that existence, but not without his willingness to let all of his secrets go.

"You know what, Lassiter, this gives you the best excuse ever. You can scurry off to your coffin -- do you sleep in one of those? -- and hide. Pretending like no one cares about you because it's easy, you big, damn pale-assed pansy! I'm standing right here, right now, telling you I care about you. I've *always* cared about you, even when you went off and forgot about me for ten years. I'd help you if you'd just let me. But you have to be all secretive and angst ridden. Everything has to be this big drama. It's such bullshit, Lassiter. Just grow up would you? Grow up and stop making everything so fucking hard." Her voice had risen now, peaking and swelling in the small bathroom. Her eyes flashed a myriad of emotions. Anger, betrayal and most of all, sadness that they could no longer communicate on the level they once had.

His silence spoke volumes to her.

Frustration got the better of her and she shoved his chest hard, knocking him back a step. "Fine. Keep your secrets, Lassiter, and your sad, lonely life, but I'm going to tell the Adams about this. I have to. I don't know if that letter means you really are an Adams from this Adams family, but it means something and I'm going to tell them." Shouldering her way past him, she grabbed the doorknob, but Lassiter's hand, large and strong, drew her back to his chest.

He held her there, pressing her to him. "Wait, Emerson," he said, his voice unrefined, determined, revealing, making her stay.

Emerson didn't know if she wanted her to wait because he was afraid of what she'd tell the Adamses or because he wanted her help. Yet his tone held something so raw, she relaxed a bit against him and took deep breaths of air.

He gripped her bare shoulders, running his hands over them before turning her in his arms and dragging her to him.

Her pulse raced and her anger began to subside.

Lassiter kissed the top of her head, raining kisses along her scalp, moving down to her cheek and, finally, taking her lips in his, sliding his tongue into her mouth with silken skill.

"No, Lassiter. This can't be how we solve this..." was her murmured objection, weak and stilted.

Cupping her jaw, he caressed it with his thumb. "We'll talk, Em. We'll talk, but now -- now, I *have* to have you." Forceful and dynamic, his words slammed into her ears.

"I'm holding you to that," she insisted, putting her hand over his and pressing it to her skin. "Promise me, Lassiter. Say it," Emerson whispered against his hand.

His chest inflated against hers and he looked into her eyes with solemn assurance. "Promise," he repeated.

Emerson wrapped her arms around his neck and firmly planted her lips on his, showing him with her passion that she was ready to take him at his word.

Her hand wove into his hair, clenching the strands with tight fists, and she leaned into him, allowing his body to mold to hers.

Lassiter's hands found her ass, reaching up under the towel and cupping the firm globes of flesh. Massaging them, grasping them and pulling Emerson against him with forceful purpose.

She sighed into his mouth, forgetting their argument. Forgetting that Lassiter hadn't let her into the most confidential part of his life. Forgetting everything but his kiss.

A kiss that left her lungs without air.

A kiss that stopped her heart and prodded her senses.

The length of steel between Lassiter's legs was rigid, pressing between the apex of her thighs with urgency. He lifted her and wrapped her legs around his waist, moving them to the far wall.

Lassiter cushioned her back, keeping her from the cold tile, pulling away the towel with a sharp yank and exposing her heated skin to the cool air.

His breathing was harsh, ragged when he ran his hand along the swell of her hip, gripping it.

Emerson's body trembled with need and her pussy, swollen and hot rubbed with delicious friction against his jeans. Pulling her hands upward, he collared them, imprisoning her wrists to allow him better access to her nipples, now swollen and rigid.

The first swipe of his tongue was hot, like the strike of an iron swiping her flesh, and Emerson's moan resounded in the bathroom, acoustically moving around the small space. Lifting herself, she pushed into Lassiter's warm lips, bowing against the hands that held her until the top of her head pushed against the wall.

Lassiter moved from breast to breast, weaving between them with strokes of his tongue, scintillating and deft.

Emerson's whimper drew him to let go of her hands. She clung to his broad neck, struggling to find her breath before reaching between them and pulling at his jeans. Tearing at the button and zipper, jamming her hands into them and grasping his cock in a firm lock.

Lassiter's hips jutted against her hand and he hissed, letting his head fall back while she stroked him, long pulls designed to tease and taunt him to fuck her.

"Fucking hell, Em. I don't know how much more I can take," Lassiter said between his teeth.

Emerson unwound her legs from his waist and slid down his body, shoving his pants to his ankles with an aggression she didn't know she had in her.

She wanted him naked.

She wanted his cock, hard and hot, driving into her.

He kicked his pants off, shoving them roughly to the side and dragging her forward. With a socked foot, he tipped the lid of the toilet seat closed and sat down.

His eyes locked on her waist, hungry and lit with the fire of passion. He buried his face in her belly, wrapping firm arms around her and splaying his fingers on her ass. Creeping over the smooth globe, he slipped his fingers between her legs from behind, skirting the tender flesh of her cunt.

Lassiter inhaled her scent, moaning with low approval. Emerson's hands, resting at her sides, came up to pull him close to her.

With slow lips that moved in maddeningly deliberate kisses, Lassiter moved over her abdomen until he reached the curls at the top of her pussy. His fingers worked her cunt, slipping in and out of the folds, slippery wet with wanton need. Stroking her outer lips, he moved in time with his mouth, stroking her, licking her skin, until he slithered into her cunt.

The touch of his tongue sizzled her flesh, fraying the frazzled cord of control she held. He parted the flesh of her pussy, laving her clit, suckling it as he slipped into her, his finger thick and seeking.

He stroked her from the inside, hitting her G-spot, dragging his finger over it again and again, sending chills along her arms, making her nipples tighten almost painfully as his tongue lashed her cunt.

Emerson jammed her hips upward, raising her leg to rest on the seat of the cool porcelain toilet, finding the edge of the sink and gripping it to steady her grind against Lassiter's mouth. Orgasm clawed at her, release begging to be made a reality. She fought to savor the feel of his lips against her, his silken head resting against her inner thigh.

When her release hit her, it was with the fury of a bolt of lightning. It dragged her over an edge, yanked her gut, tearing at the speed of light from her feet to the top of her head.

This time, Emerson howled -- a howl of unmatched satisfaction, immeasurable pleasure. Undulating under his tongue, she let it happen. Letting go of her every inhibition with a scream that was wild, unfettered, riddled by lust.

Emerson collapsed against him, letting her leg fall and her hands grab blindly for his shirt.

Lassiter turned her in his arms, seating her with her back to his chest, hauling her backwards until his cock slipped between her thighs and rested between the slick lips of her cunt.

She reached for him, clasping his cock and lubricating it with the juice of her pussy. Stroking it hand over hand, rubbing it against her clit.

She felt his tension beneath her, his muscles hard and coiled tight with control. Emerson wanted him to lose control. Lose the barrier that kept them from connecting on every level.

"Em, now. I need to be in you *now*," he ground out against her ear between harsh breaths.

His hands came to cup her breasts, rolling her nipples between firm fingers. Lifting her hips, Emerson smiled to herself and sank onto his cock. Thick and long. Swallowing first the mushroom shaped head, descending inch by excruciating inch. Holding him firmly at her passage with her hand until she slid down to settle on his lap.

Twitching within her, Lassiter sighed when her ass rubbed against him. The crisp hair on his thighs scraped against her and she luxuriated in his maleness.

He shifted beneath her, but she held him by wrapping her thighs around the tops of his and clenching the muscles of her cunt. On the tips of her toes, bracing herself by gripping his wrists, she rose and drove downward, letting the sleek heat of his cock drive into her.

It jolted him and he reacted by gripping her waist, digging into it to drive deeper. His cock flared, swelling within her. Emerson could literally feel the blood course through it. Her ass hit his thighs with each plunge she took, impaling herself on the rigid fire. Sliding a finger down to her clit, Lassiter stroked it, bringing it to a hard nub.

Leaning back in his embrace, wrapping her arms around his neck, she let the rough stubble of his chin score her neck. Emerson focused only on the complete fulfillment she felt with him inside of her.

Her senses were raw, aware, hypersensitive to every vein that pulsed with the rush of lust. The sweet sound of their flesh slapping together.

His lips suckled her neck, tasting her flesh, rasping his tongue over it, and she caved in that instant.

The throb of his cock, her cunt, slick and aching became more than she could bear. She came with velocity, while Lassiter's hand was buried in her pussy and his lips caressed her neck. With his silken head of hair against her cheek and his puffs of breath in her ear.

She gyrated her hips as she soared upward, letting only the hot seed of his release be her goal.

His arm, tight and sculpted, held her around the waist and he lifted her with his thrusts. He shouted her name when he came, thick spurts of his seed spilling into Emerson while he did.

Quiet overtook the bathroom, an eerie calm with the scent of their lovemaking permeating the air. The harsh breaths they took slowed.

Emerson floated back from where she'd been to the reality that was now between them. If they could only forget everything else but this, Emerson would. But they had so much between them. It was time to bridge that gap.

Now, before anyone else was hurt by this lonely quest Lassiter seemed to think he had to make alone.

"It's time to talk, Lassiter," she reminded him, her voice sounding like that of someone else to her ears, hoarse and scratchy.

"Yeah, baby, it's time to talk."

Chapter Eleven

"The parakeet."

Lassiter rocked back on his heels and gave her a wary glance, taking her with him to the old sofa he had in the living room and plunking down on it. "Yep. He ain't heavy, he's my brother. Drake. His name is Drake."

"And he's always been a bird?"

"For as long as I can remember being in foster care. My parents died when I was seven. I was found with Bud, er, Drake and the letter. I couldn't read the letter for a long time, but I never told anyone I had it and when I could first read, I didn't understand it. I only knew my parents left it with me and told me to always keep it safe, that someday I'd understand. I made such a ruckus about keeping him that I guess the state let me. We were moved a lot until the Fullers found me."

"So you *did* know your parents?"

His face had a faraway look. "Yes. I don't remember them as well as I'd like, though."

"I'm sorry, Lassiter. I'm sorry they're gone." Her remorse was clear when she grabbed his hand to squeeze it.

"Anyway, Drake is cursed. I'm guessing my parents thought the state would split us up. Turning Drake into a parakeet was a good way of ensuring I'd keep him."

"Call me crazy, but I gotta ask. How can you possibly know that Bu -- Drake is really a human? I mean, you don't, right?"

His chuckle was ironic. "Yeah, I do. We can communicate via telepathy. He talks to me all the time. He understands everything. He said to tell you he's glad I stopped being an ass."

Emerson laughed out loud. "Well, tell him, me too. So you had the letter and, if I think I understand this properly, you dug up a lot of Adams land because Adams is a common last name and you were searching for a needle in a haystack, right?"

"Right. As crazy as it sounds, that's what I did and I'll keep doing it until I find what I need, Emerson." His words were sent as almost a threat.

"Hold onto your fangs there, pale boy. I'm not denying you the right to dig stuff up anymore. Now that I understand, of course. See before? Emerson had no clue there was a purpose to Lassiter's mindless destruction, cuz he didn't tell her. Ya feel me?" she teased.

Lassiter rubbed her hand with his. "How do you tell someone, anyone, you're a vampire?"

"Point. Tell me about this vampire stuff. Don't you need blood to survive? How did the state explain that to the Fullers, or any of your foster homes for that matter?"

"They didn't have to. I didn't even know I craved blood until I donated some and eyed up the vials of it like they were a rare steak."

"Huh? If you're immortal and the only way to sustain that immortality is blood, I'd think you'd need O negative in copious quantities."

"No, Em. I'm not entirely a vampire."

Okay, here's where she should tell him his rocker was broken and he was off it, but Emerson had to finish this. She looked directly at him. "Do I look befuddled to you? Cuz this is the face of a woman who thinks you're a whack."

Laughing, he pulled her close and rested his chin on the top of her head. "I'm half werewolf too, Em."

"Are you serious?" she yelped.

"Yep, I shift just like you. I found that out quite by accident on a night with a full moon when I was ten. The only thing I can figure is my vampire werewolf signals are all crossed, and what I need to survive are small parts from each species that make me whole."

"I don't know what to say…"

"What can you say to a guy who wants to suck your blood and mount you from behind, all at the same time?"

Never truer words…

"Why couldn't you smell that I was a werewolf, Lassiter? Why couldn't I smell you?"

"I've got to go with the theory that I don't have all of the perks each species has. My sense of smell is keen, but I couldn't have told that you were a werewolf just by smelling you."

For a moment, Emerson felt the sense of displacement Lassiter must have all of his life and it squeezed her heart. "Why did you stop writing, Lassiter? After you left, I thought we'd still be friends, but you stopped calling and writing."

"No, Em. I didn't. I sent letters. I called and when I did, your mother told me you were out."

Her mother. Never happy about the time she'd spent with Lassiter, she'd obviously decided to interfere. Running her hand down his face, she kissed his cheek. "I'm sorry. I never got the letters and I never heard about the phone calls."

"Are the Adams werewolves like you, Emerson?"

She nodded her head, and then a thought occurred to her. "Do you see what you could have avoided if you'd just told me the truth?"

"Did you tell me the truth about you?"

Sighing with exasperation, she said, "No, but I don't have a brother who has feathers either. I'd say your situation was much more desperate than mine."

"You know what's funny? I didn't know there were others like me, or at least half like me. Do you know what a relief it is to know you're Princess?"

Her face flushed. "Do you know how much it sucks to put your sock in my mouth?"

Lassiter howled with laughter, and it made Emerson smile. This felt like what they'd once shared and it felt so right. "I can't believe you were capable of such deceit."

"Look, I wouldn't cast the first stone there, big boy," she joked, nudging him. "This means you could really be an Adams, Lassiter. Okay, so next we go to the Adams and talk to them," she stated firmly, moving to rise and go to the next step in locating them all.

"No." He remained stubbornly seated.

"Fuck that 'no,' Lassiter. Get up."

His face returned to that glacial expression he wore with such finesse. "I won't be mocked by a bunch of werewolves who won't accept me because I'm half vampire, Em. No way in hell."

Oh, that was rich. She threw her head back and laughed. "Um, Lassiter? Get up off of your ass, and lemme tell ya a story about a family called Adams. Trust me when I say no one will mock you."

She yanked his hand hard. "Get up and move it. We have some phone calls to make."

A reluctant, confused Lassiter tagged behind her as she dragged him out of the house and toward the Adams house.

Emerson waved at Bud in his cage on the way out. "Hang tight there, Big Bird. We're going to figure this out once and for all."

* * *

"Emerson, right?" a woman said from the chair in the Adams kitchen. Her blue eyes twinkled even in the dim light of only the stovetop bulb's glow.

"Oh, my God! You're the infamous Eva, aren't you? Max's grandmother?" Emerson greeted her with a warm smile. "I've seen your picture."

"That's me. Is everyone off in Manhasset with Julia and Xavier?"

"Yep. They were pretty excited."

"I so love babies." She smiled at Emerson and Lassiter. "I must do what needs to be done here and get right off to New York."

"What needs to be done here?" Emerson asked. "I told Max and everyone I'd hold the fort until they got back," she assured Eva.

Eva almost ignored her in favor of seeing Lassiter. Her eyes held him while he hovered at the edge of the kitchen. Rising from her chair, Eva smiled. "Oh, you must be Anna's boy," she cried, moving toward Lassiter and putting a hand on his arm.

Lassiter cocked his head, seeking Emerson's eyes from across the room. "How -- how did you know?"

Eva hugged him and smiled. "I'd know Anna's boy anywhere. Anna and I were raised together. My family adopted her. She was the sister of my heart, though I was a great deal older than her. We had a bond like no other."

"You knew my mother?"

Eva beamed. "I did indeed. Such a beautiful girl. Dark like you. She was an impulsive one, Anna was. Anyway, you're home now, young man. What's your name?"

"Lassiter," he answered woodenly. For the first time in knowing Lassiter, Emerson sensed he was overwhelmed.

"A fine name for a handsome boy. We have work to do, yes?"

"Wait. I have no idea what's going on here. I'm -- I --"

- 307 -

"You're confused, Lassiter," Emerson offered. "Eva? Could we sit down and talk. Lassiter has a lot of questions, I'd think."

"Isn't he here to help his brother? We need to hurry to do that, don't we?"

"Yes, ma'am, I am. How did you know that?"

Eva rolled her eyes at him and put her arm around his tapered waist. "Because I'm the one who created the spell for Anna, silly."

Well, of course she had. Emerson rolled her eyes. Eva was the answer to everything unbelievable and as far out as you could get in the Adams family.

"The spell," Lassiter muttered.

"Yes," Eva said on a sigh. "The spell to keep your brother with you. I didn't know why Anna needed it. You do know she was married to a vampire, yes? Your father?"

Lassiter nodded wordlessly.

"Well, it would seem there were other vampires who didn't like your father, Maddon, mating with Anna. Vampires who have no sense of diversity, if you ask this old woman," she spat. "They didn't want you and your brother to... to... How can I put this delicately? They didn't want you and your brother to, well, *exist*. Not at all. Anna's plan was to hide you, turn you both into parakeets. I'm sorry for the oddity of the chosen animal, but my spells are limited. I personally would have gone lion, like our Xavier, had I known how. It was designed to hide you where necessary. Hide you from your father's family, heathens that they were. Anyway, Anna disappeared shortly after she asked for the spell and then, one day, I woke up and in my heart..." Her voice caught, but she cleared her throat and steadied it. "I felt it. I felt she was gone, and I had no clue where you two were. I searched for you everywhere. It's left a hole in my heart that, now, can finally be filled."

Lassiter's mouth hung open and Eva reached up to close it with a smile. "This morning, when I woke up, I knew in my gut someone needed me here. I'm so glad it was you, Lassiter. What's your twin's name?"

Twin? There were two of them? Ohhhhh, this should be something, Emerson thought. Two over the top, uber pains in the asses.

Lassiter still had that hit by a freight train look on his face. "He's my twin?"

"Yes, dear, and your twin needs saving. That means I have some chicken soup to make."

Holy shit! Eva's infamous chicken soup was the key to this? *A drink to help you join vamp-kind...* Emerson knew the story well of Eva's chicken soup. She'd claimed to read prophecies in it. But wait. Hadn't she told Martine and Derrick that it was all just bunk? "I don't understand," Emerson interrupted. "You told Martine and Derrick that the chicken soup theory was all just made up to devise a way to get them together. The same with Max and JC."

Eva smiled knowingly. "Well, dear, to a degree it *is* made up. I admit to tampering with the chicken soup legacy for my own purposes, a bit of manipulation on my part for the good of my grandsons if you will. But this time the chicken soup is what will turn Lassiter's brother into a fine young man like himself."

Lassiter looked down at Eva, his eyes were dark and unreadable. "Do you know how long I've looked? How many Adams there are in the world?"

Emerson snorted. "Yeah, and do you know how much wildlife he's devastated in his quest?"

"Now, Emerson, I think you'd do the same in Lassiter's position. Let's not cast stones, shall we?" Eva said with reproach.

Lassiter stuck his tongue out at Emerson.

"I do know that this journey has been hard for you, Lassiter, and your brother, but you have lifetimes to make up for it. After all, you're half vampire. Your immortality will grant you some justification. Now, let's make soup!"

"Soup," Lassiter murmured.

"Yeah, pale boy, soup," Emerson chuckled.

Chapter Eleven

Emerson smiled while watching Lassiter and his twin, Drake, plant trees.

What a difference two months could make.

Eva had made the chicken soup that restored Drake to his human form and he was, indeed, Lassiter's double. They were identical in almost every way.

Except the way that made Emerson's loins scream and her knees weak.

Only Lassiter did that to her.

Drake didn't do that for her. He had an easier personality than Lassiter, though, in her estimation, he should be the one who was bitter. He'd adjusted well to life on the Adams' farm and strove to adjust to the conformities legs and arms brought with it.

Lassiter had a much lighter attitude nowadays. He smiled more often and he and Emerson had spent a great deal of time talking again.

Like they'd once done.

Sometimes they laughed. Sometimes they sat quietly, but no matter what they did, they were never far from one another.

Emerson knew she was in love with Lassiter. What once had been an idol-like, schoolgirl crush had turned into love. The kind of love a woman feels when she knows it's the real thing.

She'd learned to temper her impatience and impulsivity with that knowledge. Lassiter was hers and there was no way she'd let him forget it.

Gently, of course…

She could wait until he was ready to admit he felt the same.

And he would.

All in good time.

Drake's transformation, the lift of the spell that had kept him locked in the body of a bird, had happened with little fanfare. Oddly, Emerson thought it would be much bigger than it'd turned out to be. But she would never forget the gratitude on Lassiter's face. She would never forget the wonder of seeing Lassiter finally meet his brother.

She'd left them alone, quietly slipping out to allow them the privacy they needed to get to know one another man to man. Brother to brother.

Lassiter came to find her the next day, and since then the dynamic of their relationship had changed drastically.

Planting trees was all in an effort to not only reimburse the Adams, but to show Emerson that Lassiter's intentions had never been to hurt anyone or anything in his quest.

The Adamses had welcomed him with their usual acceptance, with open arms and questions galore. Lassiter, usually a loner, had opened up in time, eventually allowing himself to come to terms with his unusual heritage and accept the warmth only the Adams family knew how to offer.

He'd signed the land back over to Max one morning over scrambled eggs, and Max had shown his gratitude by giving Lassiter twelve acres to do with as he pleased.

Lassiter planned to build a home there. A home that had a path back to his family right at his doorstep.

The Adams family.

Indeed, the Adamses had come full circle, Emerson thought.

"Hey, Princess," Lassiter called, coming up behind her and scooping her up, rousing her from her thoughts.

Emerson chuckled at the nickname he'd kept from her dog days. "You're all dirty!" she yelped at him. "Cut it out and put me down, vampire."

"Then I think some washing up is required, huh? What say we go do that?" Lassiter teased in her ear.

"You know, you're insatiable. Didn't we just nail each other this morning? Honestly, Lassiter, we have to spend some time out of the bedroom or we'll start producing, like Hector's bunnies."

"Well, I don't think I'd mind a bunny or two if they looked like you," he said against her ear, holding her closer.

Emerson's heart lurched and she knew what Lassiter was saying in as few words as possible. It wouldn't be long before Lassiter made the final leap.

She'd hold the hurdle steady when he finally jumped over it.

"Oh, really. Tell me, what do you suppose we'd procreate? Vampires? Werewolves? Werevamps, Vampwolves?" she teased, wrapping her arms around his neck and allowing him to hurry her off to his trailer.

Looking down at her, his smile was warm, filled with a promise he didn't know how to express. "I dunno, Princess, but I'd like to find out."

Emerson snuggled against his hard body.

Yes, Lassiter was saying exactly what she wanted to hear.

He was telling her it was time.

Emerson mentally held the hurdle steady.

Because Lassiter had just jumped.

Epilogue

And so ends the saga of a family called Adams. Unique in their diversity, strong in their love of one another, created in the mind of a writer who's one can shy of a six-pack.

But there are some things that beg to be sewn up. You didn't think I was the kind of author to leave you out on the ledge without a safety net, did you? That would be cruel... senseless, frustrating as hell, yes?

Ahem.

JC and Max had their baby boy on a fine spring day, crisp and cloudless with Max's mother, Corrina, acting as midwife. JC could be heard thanking deities for the end of the pregnancy that lasted a fricken' millennium throughout the Adams household. "Finally," she'd retorted, "a good hair day is within my realm of possibility." Max and JC named their son Max junior, though JC lovingly teased that Voldermutt might suit him just fine. As yet, Max junior's shifter form, if any at all, has not been determined. Only time will tell what he and little Catalina will grow up to be.

However, you can all rest assured, they will be loved in typical Adams family style.

Xavier and Julia are enjoying parenthood. Catalina is the apple of her daddy's eye and they've decided to make their family official. They plan to marry, as soon as Julia can fit into a size seven wedding dress, that is.

Martine and Derrick are with child again, and Martine has come to terms with her unexplained urge to devour Drake. It wasn't easy and much caviar was needed to help her get over the hump.

Eva and Escobar continue to travel the world together. No one knows for sure when she'll turn up but when she does, you can take solace in the fact that it won't be without mystery and mayhem.

Emerson and Lassiter were married two months after the birth of little Max. They said their vows on Adams land and sealed their life together surrounded by the warmth and blessings of the entire Adams pack.

Hector brought his "date" to the wedding.

His date Pinky.

A surprise to everyone, for sure.

It turned out, Pinky had a secret.

Pinky shifts too.

Pinky shifted into the form of a lovely young woman with eyes only for Hector. Pink eyes, but eyes, googley and filled with devotion, nonetheless. Hector lovingly refers to her as his "Playboy Bunny." Sometimes even the most unlikely of suspects has a match made in heaven, just for him.

Drake, after hearing about the debacle Columbia County made of the Adams taxes, realized he had a passion for the law and justice at its finest. He is attending law school in New York City and plans to begin his own firm, with the aid of his brother, upon graduation.

A were-legal, if you will...

Which brings me to the end of this story, but the beginning of a whole new adventure.

You didn't think I'd leave a hottie like Drake out there without a story, did you? Without someone to teach him the ways of a man and woman. The ways that have nothing to do with feathers and everything to do with passion...

Meet Drake when he takes on the task of the paranormal defending the paranormal, and take the journey of his carnal discoveries right along with him.

A half werewolf, half vampire *virgin*, folks... Does it get any crazier than that?

The End

Dakota Cassidy

Dakota Cassidy found writing quite by accident and it's "been madness ever since." Who knew writing the grocery list would turn into this? Dakota loves anything funny and nothing pleases her more than to hear she's made someone laugh. She loves to write in many genres with a contemporary flair. Dakota lives with her two handsome sons, a dog and a cat. (None of them shape shift--that we know of.) She'd love to hear from you--she always answers her e-mail! Visit her at www.dakotacassidy.com or email her at dakota@dakotacassidy.com

Changeling Press E-Books
Quality Erotic Adventures Designed For Today's Media

More Sci-Fi, Fantasy, Paranormal, and BDSM adventures available in E-Book format for immediate download at www.ChangelingPress.com -- Werewolves, Vampires, Dragons, Shapeshifters and more -- Erotic Tales from the edge of your imagination.

What are E-Books?

E-Books, or Electronic Books, are books designed to be read in digital format -- on your computer or PDA device.

What do I need to read an E-Book?

If you've got a computer and Internet access, you've got it already!

Your web browser, such as Internet Explorer or Netscape, will read any HTML E-Book. You can also read E-Books in Adobe Acrobat format and Microsoft Reader, either on your computer or on most PDAs. Visit our Web site to learn about other options.

What reviewers are saying about Changeling Press E-Books

Kira Stone -- Deadly Sins: Envy

"Every time I read Kira Stone, I fall more and more in love with her writing. Deadly Sins: Envy was delicious. Raphael and Oliver were sexy enough to get any woman or man going."

-- Suni Farrar, Just Erotic Romance Reviews

Lacey Savage -- Deadly Sins: Lust

"5 Hearts! In this story, Lacey Savage has written a lusty, sexy but also sensuously romantic story of temptation and the trials of resistance."

--Valerie, Love Romances

Marie Treanor -- Loving the Wolf

"This was a highly sensual passionate novel. Will set out to get Lara and plays on her obvious desire for him to get her. The two together steamed up the pages in some of the most beautiful scenes written."

-- Elise Lyn, ecataRomance Sensual Reviews

Angela Knight -- All Wrapped Up: Blood Service

"The sex scenes were explosive and should have come with a warning for the reader to have a fire extinguisher handy during reading."

--Tara, Euro Reviews

Elisa Adams -- Immortal Games: Wicked

"I really enjoyed Immortal Games: Wicked. It was fast paced with intense characters. The coming together of Elena and Ian was emotional, intense, erotic and meant to be."

-- Tara, Euro Reviews

Isabella Jordan -- Eyes of the Leopard 5: Captive

"Ms. Jordan once again creates characters, situations and scenery that pull you in and hold on tight. Her love scenes are nothing to sneeze at either; melt you clothes, yes; sneeze at, no."
-- Keely Skillman, eCataRomance Sensual Reviews

Lexxie Couper -- Shifting Lust 3: The Bounty Hunter's Prize

"Just when I thought I knew what was going to happen, the author inserted another healthy dose of twist and turn. A great read, and one I would recommend to anyone who enjoys science fiction with a dash of adventure and steamy sex!"
-- Regina, Coffeetime Romance Reviews

Alecia Monaco -- Ancient Pleasures: Forbidden Fruit

"The sex is steamy and the emotions involved very much apparent. This is not your Sunday school version of Adam and Eve, boys and girls, but I highly recommend it."
-- Jenn, Coffeetime Romance Reviews

Emma Ray Garrett -- Throne of Mercy

"5 Stars! Absolutely satisfying, Throne of Mercy has all the elements of a great story; memorable characters, super hot sex, a great plot, and super hot sex…yes, lots of it. This was a story that will stay in my mind for a long time…"
--Stacey Landers, Just Erotic Romance Reviews

Angelina Evans -- Hard, Fast and Forever

"Ms. Evans' hooks the reader from page one and keeps them hooked until the end. I truly enjoyed how Ms. Evans' has created this romance, and how the heroine gives up everything she knows and loves to get the man of her dreams."
-- Sonya, Fallen Angel Reviews

www.ChangelingPress.com

Printed in the United States
132030LV00002B/80/A

9 781595 963468